HOW TO SURVI'
A HANDBOO

LEVI M

Artwork by Sally Porch
Cover design by Avril Silk and Sam Dean

This book is dedicated to those who have been compelled to embrace sudden change of circumstance, to those who have needed to negotiate difficulty – and to all who remain young in spirit

PART 1 – NEMESIS

1

What the bineo!

He who could hurdle over lofty hedgerows back home without a second thought! It was hard to comprehend how his leg was now refusing to raise itself over such a low rim. He tried once again, leading with the other leg.

It was no good. He flopped down, panting for breath. Perching on the edge of the contraption, and swivelling his body, he toppled in with a loud splash.

Allowing himself to sink until only his chin and nose jutted out above the waterline.

For a while, he was soothed by the warmth. He stretched out one arm, then the other, inspecting his hands. He glowered at his feet poking up through the water.

What was this creature he had become? A gnarled, purple-blotched lizard of a thing held together by stretched papyrus!

Once more, he went over the recent events that had brought him to such depths.

And now for today's weather forecast: Erebus – cloudy; Tartarus – very cloudy; Stygian Marsh – dense fog, with high chance of rain; Acheron Delta – gloomy; Thalassa – warnings of gale force winds, becoming cyclonic later; Phlegethon – very hot, with visitors strongly advised to carry protection at all times; Asphodel Fields – bright intervals alternating with dull spells; Mount Olympus – sunny...

"Do you think some rain would make a nice change? After all, I'm pretty good at making storms happen, only usually, it's down on Earth below."

Hermes considered the question, carefully.

"I think not," he replied, after a while. "It might make some of the residents here a bit jumpy."

That would serve them right," said Zeus, glumly.

They both stared down from Mount Olympus. It was a dizzying height, but as they each had perfect eyesight, they could make out tiny objects far below. Idly, they checked out what was going on down in the area just a little further down the hill, where the demi-gods lived. The aspect at that level was still fabulous, if not quite so wonderful as higher up, the scent of the trees, maybe, just a little less aromatic, the landscaped gardens, pools and fountains a tad smaller.

Not much was going on; the residents there were not known as early risers, and only a single figure seemed to be moving about. He was heading into the woods, carrying a book. Hermes recalled him, instantly, as a rather obscure young fellow, known as Narcie. Zeus did not recognise him at all, only noticing that he was strikingly good-looking, if not cute in quite the same way as his cup-bearer, Ganymede.

His attention wandered, and he scanned far below, towards the realms of mortals, emitting a series of deep sighs as he did. Hermes wondered what he could say to lighten the mood. Being around Zeus was becoming quite trying; no wonder some of the other gods were avoiding him.

"The first millennium of any eon is a bum-hole. We should start each time with the second one."

Zeus did not reply. Perhaps, Hermes was right. All he knew was that he was sick of the wall-to-wall sunshine, each day the same. He was tired, too, of all the petty squabbling, the gossip and intrigue among bored and irritable deities. At this very moment, he could hear a loud argument amongst a group of immortals who must have been about five hundred plethra away, that is to say, around fifteen thousand metres.

Zeus stooped low, picking up an apple and flinging it in the direction of the group. Hermes was peering towards them.

"I think you hit the mouthy one on the head. Good shot! Looks like you've knocked him out."

"He should count himself lucky it was just an apple," growled Zeus.

Perhaps, it would be an idea to chuck things at the other gods more often. He could not put a finger on it, but these days, they seemed vexed by his presence; quite a few did not even seem to laugh anymore at his jokes and

5

pranks. Even when he brayed 'Gelos!', reminding them that it was just a joke, they remained sullen.

He continued to stare down at that other world far below. He imagined happy people there, partying their short lives away. Hermes seemed to read his thoughts.

"Do you remember when we visited them in disguise? That was fun."

They fell silent in private reminiscence.

"Wouldn't it be nice if we could do it again? An ethnographic follow-up study. Only, it's not so simple these days. Nothing's simple anymore."

Zeus yawned. He thought about all the forms that now required filling in. He did not like to admit it, but this was largely his own fault. After all, it was he who had decided to leave these matters to an *ethics committee*. Who were the members? Arete. Pistis. Dike. Horkos...

What a bunch of boring farts!

"Of course," mused Hermes, "if we could think of something informal, a kind of chance occurrence, it might pass by unnoticed. We could avoid all the forms with those endless questions: What risks do you envisage? What have you done to minimise them? Have the subjects of the study given their consent? How will you ensure confidentiality and anonymity? Might any information be recorded that could identify individuals – such as names, addresses, e-mails, IP addresses, social media profiles, visual materials or meta data? Might the study involve children, vulnerable people or discussion of sensitive topics? Does the study include the collection of any biometric data? Might the dissemination of the study have adverse effects, either directly or indirectly, on participants, groups or third parties? What a drag! By the time you have completed the forms, you could have carried out the research."

Zeus had lost interest long before Hermes had completed his list. He was thinking, instead, about what he would like to do to the clowns on the Ethics Committee. He might have to spare Dike, one of the members, on the grounds of family connection. Bumping into her once, he had blurted out that if there were prizes for the least sexy goddess, she would have to be in the running. She had replied that she found his comment inappropriate, still more so, she reminded him, in the context that she happened to be one of his daughters through his relationship with his second wife, Themis. He had stared at her with disbelief. Was she sure?

"Your mother had such a plump, juicy rump. And yours is... well, barely existent."

For a moment, it looked as if Dike was about to slap him.

"Gelos!" he exclaimed. "Just jesting! Where's your sense of humour?"

On another occasion, he had found himself at a festival seated beside Arete. He had joked about her looking less like a goddess than a stick insect, adding that her boobs were tiny even by the standards of that species. For some reason, *she* had not been amused either.

No, whatever happened, he would give the Ethics Committee a miss.

4

From their place on high, the gods maintain vigilant watch. What could be more fascinating than the activities of mortals? Like tiny ants, they toil, re-enacting the same motions day after day. Old mortals fade away, to be replaced by new ones, identical to their predecessors, doing the same old things.

The respectful amongst the Earth-dwellers – not the despicable Sophists, of course – but those worthy of some reward, come to the temples with offerings. Most importantly, they build new temples, new shrines, new sanctuaries. The gods know all of these places of worship. Those who receive less adoration feel as if they are wasting away. Some are beset by a sense of starving. A few become bitter.

Naturally, the Twelve Olympians are the most venerated, but even amongst them, there are rivalries. Poseidon resents the number of places built to honour his brother, Zeus. The two of them are begrudged by their other brother, Hades, who has just the one temple, the Nekromanteion, in Epirus. Which, incidentally, Hades has to share with Persephone!

All the brothers envy Apollo, who seems to have acquired far too many sites of veneration for their liking. They wonder how he has obtained all his positions – god of oracles, knowledge, healing, music, archery, art, protection of the young, sunlight, herds and flocks. Really? How could one deity have the time?

Meanwhile, Hera is indignant about the devotion wallowed in by Athena, a daughter of her husband and one of his concubines. It is not just the number of temples dedicated to her, but their quality. The Parthenon, for instance, in which such ostentatious wealth has been deposited.

Secretly, everyone is fuming about the erection of a spectacular colossus in Rhodes, in honour of the relatively unimportant and obscure Helios, nobody being too upset when, on a woozy morning after a particularly heavy night, Zeus causes an earthquake that topples the ruddy thing. A boisterous cheer can be heard from Olympus when the huge statue cracks at the knees.

5

"It will be a new experience."

"Will it?"

Zeus looked dubious.

"Oh, yes," gushed Hermes. "Completely different from turning into bulls or swans. Inhabiting someone else's body. You've never done that before. It might snap you out of this ennui good and proper. If questions get asked, I'll say it just happened by complete fluke. We can blame Tyche. When dispensing good and bad fortune, at least half the time, she has no idea what the outcome will be."

All Zeus had to do, Hermes assured him, was to inhabit the subject's body a few moments before his death. He could pop in unnoticed, and if any of those silly ethical questions did get asked, subsequently, about harm to participants and all that, they could always reply that it was commensurate with the harm that person was about to experience, anyway.

Zeus thought about this. It was tempting. Hermes had gone through a catalogue of forthcoming accidental deaths, and some of them involved strong, lusty-looking youths. If not for their unfortunate demises, good times had been awaiting them like the lolling tongues of Cerebrus. Well, maybe, not Cerebrus, thought Zeus. That was probably a bit uncomfortable. Rather than a fearsome,

11

three-headed dog, he now tried to picture a coquettish, three-headed Earth-maiden.

And then he thought about Hera. His wife would be furious. She was invariably seething with outrage whenever he went off on such adventures.

"Perhaps," suggested Hermes, who often seemed able to read the thoughts of others from their expressions, "Hera's feelings would be assuaged if you chose to visit the city of Argos. It's what they call a *happening* place, really lively, a proper vibe, lots going on, and most importantly, it's where she is venerated."

This struck Zeus as a sensible suggestion. How excited Hera would be when he came back with information about all the temples dedicated to her, the affection, obeisance, adoration! Her vanity would surely trump her indignation about his very minor infidelities.

There was just one thing they would need to do first, added Hermes: deposit an oath in the Styx.

Zeus seemed perplexed.

"Just in case the Ethics Committee gets wind of it and you are summoned back. It is their right, after all; you, yourself, gave it to them."

Acquiescence did not mean that he could not grumble about the whole thing, Hermes listening, amiably, throughout the tiresome journey. Zeus made the oath, hurriedly, not noticing when Hermes slipped in a few additional words.

6

Something had gone wrong.

He felt feeble. He could barely move. Everything ached. He tried to straighten up. He was sure he could hear clicking sounds and creaks. What was wrong with his body?

He looked about him, blinking. There was some sort of ocular deficiency. Nothing seemed all that clear.

And where was he? Far from seeing the towers and walls of a great city, he seemed to be indoors. He looked around. There were tins and cardboard packets, rows of vegetables protruding, untidily. Beyond them hung cheap clothes.

In front of him there was a small desk. He looked at the sign above it. Although it was not written in a noble alphabet, Phoenician or Euclidean, he had the innate ability to comprehend any language, and was able to read the word: 'Argos'. It was a relief to know that he was in the right city, but this must have been some dismal quarter of it, a giant stall in a backstreet.

Behind the desk there was an opening into a dark space. A shrine? He gulped. Hera would be bat-shit, daughters of Nyx, crazy if she discovered that she was being worshipped in a dump like this. She would run about like that nutter, Lyssa, or the other Maniae, smashing things up: one of those pumpkins in the basket over there, or worse still, people's heads!

Swivelling in confusion, he spotted a shaft of light through an entranceway. In panic, he began to run towards it. Run! It was more of a stumbling shuffle. What was wrong with these bloody legs? He passed a mirror on the way. That was where he passed out.

7

A crowd was standing around him. Mortals with stupid, clay faces. They were mumbling words.

Then with relief, he spotted a face he recognised in the cluster. It was Hermes – in disguise, of course.

"It's all right," he was saying. "I'm his son. He does this sometimes. If we just get him to his feet."

Arms were lifting him. He was still in the same place, in front of that ruddy mirror. Was it enchanted? Some sort of evil sorcerer, perhaps.

He tried to kick it over, without quite managing to make contact and almost toppling backwards in the process. Someone was steadying him. Moments later he found himself outside, gulping in the fresh air. Only it wasn't fresh like the clear air of Olympus. It was filled with odours ranging from nasty to foul, which clogged his head and left a horrid taste in his throat.

He looked around. There were strange little chariots all about, from which people were emerging. Others were being re-entered, bags or infants thrown in, before adult mortals climbed in through openings at the front. Then those chariots disappeared, leaving a fetid trail of smells in their wake.

Zeus coughed again. What *was* this dreadful place?

It took a while to comprehend what Hermes was telling him. There had, indeed, been some kind of error. Rather than being in the great city of Argos, he was in some alternative reality type of place – call it a hamlet, suggested Hermes. By unfortunate coincidence, it also known as Argos, in the village of Sainsbury's, in a town known as Newton Abbot.

It was difficult to take in. So, was this Newton Abbot in Argolis?

Hermes shook his head.

"The Peloponnese?"

Hermes paused, before shaking his head again.

"Attica? Thessaly? Illyria? Thrace? Macedon?"

Hermes' expression suggested not.

"Crete? Rhodes? Corinth?"

Hermes grimaced.

"Father – this place is not part of Hellas at all."

"Bineo me sideways with one of my own thunderbolts!"

For a while, neither of them spoke. They were seated on a bench, watching the arriving and departing chariots. Hermes considered the best way of explaining things, deciding that a laborious step-by-step approach was probably the most prudent.

"There seems to have been a bit of a cock-up."

"You're damned right there has been. Which orrhos-wit is responsible?"

It was probably wise, thought Hermes, not to respond to this particular query.

"Something went wonky with the co-ordinates. But I'm reliably informed that there are some really nice places to visit nearby. On the coast, and also, on a nearby moor. With pubs."

"Pubs?"

"Places to eat and drink. They serve a local, quite palatable, sort of ambrosia, they say. Also a golden or darker brown nectar."

It was difficult to interpret Zeus' response to this. The gurgling sound from his body may have indicated anticipation or anger.

"The thing is you may be..."

Hermes hesitated.

"... well, stuck here for a while, just until we find a new subject in Hellas. Someone with a better physique. Right now, you seem to be in the body of a seventy-four year old."

"Is that a small child? An infant. It sounds very young, and might explain why this body does not seem able to operate properly yet."

"Actually, it's quite elderly. But you should still be able to do plenty of things."

At that moment, an uncommonly attractive, young mortal female happened to walk by. Zeus followed her with his eyes. She headed towards one of the chariots, opening the door and bending across the seat to put down some bags, her skirt rising high to offer a glimpse of her undergarments. Zeus's eyes lit up, before narrowing in a frown.

"The phallos doesn't seem to be working. No movement at all."

He pulled forward the band of the rather odd pants he was wearing, peering down to check it was there.

"What the bineo! It's like a piece of droopy string."

For a while he continued to stare into his pants with consternation. Hermes looked awkward. One or two people had noticed. While it may have been quite acceptable to peer at your phallos on Olympus, it might not be the done thing here.

"It's probably just the shock of transition," he said. "Maybe, I had better get you home. To your temporary accommodation, that is. It turns out that one of the chariots here belongs to you. That'll be fun, won't it?"

It took only a short time for Hermes to work out how to operate the contraption, but by the time they had arrived at the odd, little building in the middle of a terrace, where he was, apparently, staying for a while, Zeus had discovered a bit about himself.

His name was Reginald Montgomery Mudge. Everyone called him 'Monty', which was, apparently, the name of a great warrior. Perhaps, there were epic tales about his exploits, suggested Hermes. He had never married and lived alone, so that meant he was free for any adventures. There was just a niece, who visited occasionally, bringing her two young children. Hermes suggested it might be sensible to be polite to them, and not too haughty, while maintaining a distance. It would only attract attention to himself if he began to behave atypically.

"Always ask yourself what Reginald Montgomery Mudge would say."

"How the bineo would I know?"

Zeus screwed up his face with distaste. He attempted to scan the new data in his brain, the *Mudge Files*, as he would later term this. He seemed to have a jumble of memories in place, minus a few, where there were just blank spaces. As Mudge had been about to suffer a fatal accident at the very moment Zeus had inhabited his body, it was possible that there had been some trauma, with bits of memory lost. It was something of a relief to note that while he could remember many individuals and incidents, he could not recollect the emotions around them.

When he zoned back into the current moment, Hermes was continuing to dole out advice. Perhaps, he should just view it as a brief holiday. Zeus looked dubious.

"I was supposed to be partying: getting blasted and shagging."

"You might still be doing that."

"In *this* decrepit body!"

Hermes gave him a consoling pat on the shoulder.

"It could be the basis of an excellent research paper, after all. You should keep a journal. There have been some really good publications based on field-notes. Academia loves accounts of researchers who go native, though, of course, the neo-positivists will make a fuss about rigour and objectivity and be all sniffy about it. By the way, the term for you here is 'pensioner'."

He stopped short. Zeus' expression did not exactly resemble that of a keen scholar just raring to start a project.

"I've made some notes and instructions, along with a few recommendations for good eating and drinking places. I'll be back soon to check in on you. Don't worry: I'll get you out of this in no time at all."

"You'd better," growled Zeus.

8

All he needed now was to work out how to get out of the bath! It took a while. Getting in had been challenging enough, but this was far worse.

Useless heap of bolbiton!

The body seemed immune to curses. He lay there a while longer, giving himself time to figure it out.

Initially, he had been perplexed by the room adjoining his bedroom, a smaller space, filled with baffling contraptions. The Mudge Files identified them as 'toilet', 'wash-basin', 'shower' and 'bath'. They also revealed that Mudge used the shower fairly regularly, but the bath not at all, which seemed bizarre. Did the fellow have a spotlessly clean head mounted on a filthy body? This would need to be addressed. Zeus had run the bath water till it was invitingly high in the tub.

Never considering how difficult it would prove to clamber into it! The operation had involved many contortions, accompanied by much groaning and ending in an ungainly swivel and fall.

He had lain there, inspecting his hands and feet, soaking into it, allowing the water to rise to the point where it was beginning to lap over the edge, before remembering to swivel the peculiar little gadgets called 'taps'.

It had been the first pleasurable sensation since his arrival. He decided that he would do this every day; perhaps, eight or nine times. He allowed his body to sink low, holding his head beneath the water. Back at home, he could manage this for an age, but almost immediately, he began to splutter, rearing up in a panic, making the water splash over the side onto the floor.

Such pitifully weedy lungs! If this Mudge was really a great warrior, what state must the other mortals be in? When Hermes had spoken of him as a 'pensioner', Zeus had imagined this as an elite and powerful echelon, consisting of great kings and heroes. Might this be a misconception? His situation suddenly seemed still bleaker.

He soaked in the water, thinking of suitable punishments for Hermes for his bungling ineptitude. This was comforting for a brief period before the water began to cool, whereupon he, finally, managed to scramble out, cursing all the while he dried himself and dressed.

He went downstairs to explore the house. There was not much of interest. Furniture, of course, a settee, a rather cramped dining area with table and chairs. A kitchen filled with apparatus which seemed unexciting. Some not very captivating pictures on the walls. A few were of those people Hermes had spoken of, but as he had not been paying all that much attention, he could not recall their names. Two of the more interesting ones were of men in uniform, one dated: 1916, the other, 1944. Both were in black and white. The figure in the first one was in a field, and rather incongruously, carrying both a basket and a rifle. Zeus puzzled over this for a while. He guessed these mortals were more primitive than those on Hellas. The rifle looked far less of a weapon than a sword or a spear. What did they do: poke one another in the ribs? Were they used for mock battles?

The second photograph was more impressive: a man standing on the deck of a large ship. His uniform was smarter, and his face resembled more closely that of a proud warrior.

There were no images of Reginald Montgomery Mudge as a soldier. It felt shameful: all males of Hellas were expected to fight in a war. Had this Mudge had the nerve to adopt a warrior's name then dodged all fighting? Zeus now thought of cowards he had known, not least, his own son, Ares, supposedly, a god of war, with a reputation for extreme ferocity, alongside a tendency to go missing at moments of great peril, before reappearing just in time to take the glory. For a while he ruminated on his son's shortcomings, before returning to the subject of Mudge. It seemed a joke. As there were always wars going on, this man with a hero's name must have been a shirker. This was depressing: as if his own good name was besmirched through association with a limp-willied, lily-livered yellow-belly.

How long would Mudge have survived in Sparta! Zeus had heard that if a warrior returned home there when all his comrades had been killed, he was deemed to be a coward, whatever he had done on the battlefield. He lived in shame and was marked by signs, such as the order to wear a patchwork coat and only half a moustache. Zeus now scrutinised the pictures around the room. Mudge did not appear to have even half a moustache in any of them. Perhaps, he was incapable of growing one.

Feeling a rush of fury, Zeus kicked a door hard. It hurt, and he hopped away cursing.

"Farts of Boreas!"

Once again, he cursed Hermes for allowing this to happen. The ultimate insult! How the others back home on Olympus would laugh! The sky and thunder god trapped in the weedy body of an old dodderer called Mudge, who was, quite possibly, the biggest chicken that had ever lived. Hermes had better not so much as breathe a word about it. Otherwise, he'd be liable to find his staff and helmet rammed right up his orrhos.

He limped off now to check the rest of the house. There was something which Hermes had called a shower, a very poor substitute for a waterfall. There was a toilet with a flush, and Zeus pressed the button about five times before losing interest. There was a kitchen filled with uninteresting devices. The best thing was what Hermes referred to as a 'television', and it was fun to use the control to flick through channels.

Overall, however, this was a dull place to inhabit. Just as well that he would not be staying here for long. The company around him was pretty dismal, too. His house was part of a terrace. In the house to the right there lived three young men. Two were white, one of whom had a long, thin face, creased, though not old, reminding Zeus of a kind of a baubon, in this case, a rather over-used, leathery dildo that needed replacing. The other was black, too dark, thought Zeus, for Numidian or Phoenician. Nor did he quite look like someone from Memnon's tribe in Aethiopia. Zeus vaguely recalled having been so impressed by Memnon's fighting skills that he had granted him immortality. But this fellow did not look like he belonged to the same tribe. He was wiry. If he had been a little shorter, Zeus guessed that he could have been of the Pygmaioi tribe, the ones who were engaged in constant warfare with the cranes. His recollection was a little dim on the cause of this, but it came to mind that it had come about after a queen, Gerana, had boasted that she was more beautiful than Hera, a pretty dumb thing to do, given Hera's widely-known penchant for taking offence. Anyway, Gerana became transformed into a crane for her impertinence – which, come to think of it, was getting off quite lightly by comparison to some others.

For all Zeus knew, this man might have been another from that tribe who had been turned into a crane for offending a god. He certainly had a skinny skull, and long thin legs. Neither he, nor the other men in the house seemed to do all that much. They hung around much of the day, smoking, and were sometimes visited by other mortals. The other men were both scrawny-looking, with a shifty look that made Zeus wonder whether they were related to Autolycus, the thief on Mount Parnassus who appeared to be able to disguise both himself and his stolen possessions whenever anyone came asking questions. All in all, the men living next door did not seem suitable material for companionship.

Nor did the female who, occasionally, visited them, a kind of old crone in a young woman's body. With her straggly hair, she reminded Zeus of a very raddled, far less alluring version of Circe.

In the adjoining house on the left there appeared to live an elderly woman. The postman referred to her as 'Mrs Tucker'. Zeus paid little attention to her. There was nothing about her to inflame desire.

Every few days, there would be a knock on his front door. A fellow who was bent over and looked still frailer than Mudge would shamble in when the door opened. His name appeared to be 'Bill'. He would put down on the table a copy of the *Daily Express* and a *Fudge* bar. He seemed to believe that these were Zeus' preferred offerings. The chocolate was insubstantial and not particularly satisfying, while Zeus found little of interest in the newspaper other than the sports pages. All in all, it was pretty pathetic, and had it occurred in one of his temples, it might even have merited instant death by lightning bolt.

Fortunately for Bill, Zeus seemed to have temporarily lost his ability to fire thunderbolts, not to mention the fact that he had been advised by Hermes to 'keep a low profile'.

There were other annoying things about Bill. He had a habit of *hovering*, even after it should have been clear that he had been dismissed. He had an irritating way of coming out with exclamations, most of which were not in Zeus' language bank. His favourite was 'By Gum!' – a term Zeus felt to be redundant. Yet Bill persisted even when told.

It was dull beyond dull. One day ran into another, indistinguishable. There was little to do beyond watching the television and occasionally taking his chariot out for a run. It took a little time to master the essentials, but before long he was able to pootle around the back roads. Finding something called a horn, it was fun to peep on it, startling people crossing in front of him or other motorists. Once or twice, he looked like he was about to swing onto a pavement, then hooted as if it was the pedestrian's fault. It was also mildly amusing to see how close you could get to cyclists without knocking them off.

Until one day, the car just seemed to stop working. Zeus was forced to abandon it, returning home on foot.

SURVIVING THE 21ST CENTURY: A HANDBOOK FOR PENSIONERS

ENTRY 1

BEING A PENSIONER IS A STEAMING PILE OF BOLBITON.

NO SANE CREATURE SHOULD DREAM OF TRYING IT.

9

A stuffy meeting room on the ground floor of a rather
austere building, high on the slopes of Mount Olympus

The assembled group, one of the innumerable sub-groups
that had been set up on Olympus, included may of the
individuals that Zeus would have objected to. Apart from
those who doubled up on the Ethics Committee, such as
Arete, Pistis, Dike and Horkos, there were other dull,
bureaucratic types, with the perverse penchant of
gathering in stuffy, sparsely decorated rooms, rather than
enjoying the wonderful, warm breezes or crisp, refreshing
air to be found all around Olympus.

There were also representatives from different
groups, including, one of the younger gods, a rather loud
and querulous young deity with a large bruise on his
forehead. Only a few days ago he had been hit hard on the
head by an apple hurled with superhuman velocity from
an enormous distance.

Hera, Zeus' wife, was the last to arrive. Zeus had
always wondered what she saw in attending meetings, but
if it kept her occupied, then it was up to her. There was
the additional benefit of providing more spare time for his
own liaisons.

Themis called the meeting to order. Experienced
as a chair of meetings, she was able to take the minutes

herself while moving things forward down the list on the agenda, ensuring that they did not get stuck for too long on any single issue. It had been cunning of Hera to invite her to fulfil this role, given their past rivalry over Zeus. It provided still greater legitimacy, while distancing Hera from the decisions made by the assembly.

In a stern tone, Themis reminded them now that the matter for discussion in the current meeting was extremely delicate and was not to be discussed outside the room. Everything had to be done following the correct procedures.

Did anyone wish to begin?

There was an awkward silence.

Perhaps, suggested Hera, if the room was in darkness, it might be easier for the members of the committee to speak up. Could Themis still keep minutes in those circumstances?

She hardly needed to ask. Well then, perhaps, it would be best if only comments were recorded in the minutes, without identities being revealed. Might it be appropriate in the circumstances to record it as Committee Member Alpha, Beta, Gamma, Delta and so on?

As soon as they were in darkness the comments began to flow, very slowly at first, as if the pipes were just being turned on after a long time, but soon the suggestions of offences were coming in a rush.

"Dereliction of duty."

"Gross negligence."

"Grossness."

Themis tapped on her desk.

That was not exactly on infringement of anything, and would not hold up in a court of law, even if it was an unappealing trait.

"Libidinous decrepitude. Was that something one might be charged for?"

Themis suggested not.

"Desecration of sacred places through activities of libidinous decrepitude?"

There were murmurs of assent.

Themis now sought the advice of Dyke and Astraea. They both agreed that this would hold up in a courtroom, with the latter particularly firm on the matter. Indeed, it might be able to make a case for 'libidinous decrepitude' as an offence in itself.

"Acts of indecency, maybe, against nymphs – both land and sea nymphs – and also against mortals?"

"Impersonation of creatures during the act of... coitus. Things with lots of legs and wings and horns."

"Procurement of prostitutionalistic participants for the purposes of obscene sexual acts?"

Fortunately, in the darkness it was not possible to decipher the expression on Hera's face during these last suggestions.

"Unrestrained indulgence in sexual activities."

"And not being very good at them!"

There were some titters.

"I think we've had quite enough on this topic," intervened Themis.

"Bullying in the workplace."

"When he's there!"

There were some more titters. Themis tapped on her desk to bring them to order.

"Only the other day he threw an apple at me."

Silence.

"It was a very hard throw."

"Assault?"

"Yes, assault, with intent to knock my head off!"

"Excessive use of profanities."

"In the presence of... minotaurs?"

"Minors."

It was evident that a series of charges could be brought against the king of the gods – or KoG, as he was generally, referred as – more than enough to justify the Ethics Committee to call its own meeting to consider granting retrospective approval to actions already commenced, banishing Zeus, on an initially, temporary basis, to earthly realms. Themis understood that this was being referred to as *Project Z-R* – standing for, *Zeus-Reformation.*

She agreed with the proposal that Zeus' behaviour whilst down in mortal realms should be monitored. The sooner his whereabouts were discovered, the better for all.

It was a satisfactory outcome from Hera's perspective, if just one small, additional step.

Some way further down the hill. A house cum workplace,
with a forge in the grounds, and many smaller outbuildings,
filled with tools and equipment, ideal for a deity keen on
DIY to potter about in.

Once again, he paused by the doorway, returning to the
bowl yet another time to scrub his fingers. It was futile:
there was no way the grime was coming out; it was far too
deeply ingrained.

 Picking up his stick, he sighed, practising his walk
once again in a way that might make his crab-footed
movements less obvious. It was impossible. With a deep
sigh, he hobbled out, making his way up the hill in the
direction of his mother's home.

 Upon reaching the gates, he did not go directly to
the front door, deciding, instead, to wander around the
gardens whilst gathering his thoughts. Everything was
laid out immaculately – tree-lined pathways, flowerbeds,
statues, fountains – a blend of grace, harmony of sound
and colour, geometrical precision. He was overwhelmed
by a sense of unbelonging.

 He wondered again why his mother would have
asked to see him. His visits in the past had been at social
events with hundreds of guests, when it would have
seemed like an omission not to have invited him, and

where he could become lost in the crowd, looking less obviously out of place. He had never been invited there on his own; if she wanted something made, she would send a messenger to place the order, as she had in the case of the waterwheel in front of which he was now standing. As with many of his inventions, he had designed it so that the inner working parts would be visible, with hidden mirrors emphasising the refraction of light. Unlike himself, it was a model of mechanical and aesthetic perfection, everything synchronised with an exactness that would enable it to run smoothly beyond the end of time.

The sight of it reminded him once again of his debt to the Sintians, raiders, plunderers, outcasts, like himself. Wonderfully skilled in crafts, they had taught him so much, and very soon, his talents far outstripped theirs. It had been these rough pirates who had helped the sea nymph, Thetis, to tend him after he had crashed down on the island of Lemnos.

His fall.

He had never discussed it with his mother. Not even after his return, when those on Olympus decided that he was needed. Not that he would have ever agreed, had Dionysus not paid him a visit, deviously, plying him with drink.

Hardly a triumphant return! He had a blurred recollection of a jerky ride on the back of a mule, drunken dancers cavorting around as they made the long climb.

His fall.

Was this an opportunity to discover the reasons?

Hera could not have appeared more delighted to see her son. Why did he never visit? Her other boy, Ares, popped in regularly.

She pretended not to notice his frown. Ares, the ideal son, immaculate from the highest curl on his head to his little toe; good-looking; heroic; **not** a cripple! And also, the one who had robbed him of the wife they had been forced to give him in payment for his return, the slut, Aphrodite. Of course, the great colossus, Ares, could have slept with any goddess, but he just had to screw his brother's wife, too. Why stop with everyone else's?

"You must be thirsty, dear, after such a long walk."

His mother was pouring him a drink.

"I wanted so much to see you, to find out what you are up to these days."

She had invited him after all these centuries to ask how he was doing!

"Oh, and while you're here, a small favour."

Sliding down on an elegant-looking couch, she patted the space next to her. Rather awkwardly, he slumped alongside her, keeping his arms pointing inwards

37

and tight against his side so that she should not see the state of his fingernails. Leaning towards him, she smoothed back a lock of hair that had fallen across his brow.

"You know, when you glower like that, it gives you a sultry look; almost handsome."

She smiled.

"I suppose you must, occasionally, wonder why we ever gave you up."

She took a sip from her cup.

"I have so wanted to explain it, but I did not want to place your father in a poor light. But now he's vanished again, I suppose..."

Was she keeping him in suspense or was it genuinely difficult for her?

"But, Hephaestus, dear, if you would prefer not to know..."

"I *would* like to know."

She sighed.

"Well, dear, when you were born, and we discovered... you know... the funny thing with your feet curling inwards, your father... you really mustn't think too badly of him, well..."

She gulped, letting out a small squeak that may have been a whimper. Hephaestus could not be certain, but so sorrowful was her expression that, very awkwardly, he put an arm around her shoulder.

"He said... no son of his could have been born so...
so deformed, and the only explanation could be that I
must have had a... you know, some sort of liaison... with
an ogre or something. Such a horrid thing to say! He
picked you up in a rage, marched to the edge of mountain,
and flung you off. It was such a shock. All so fast and
sudden."

She put her head in her hands.

"So he threw me off the mountaintop because of
my... funny feet, breaking my legs and spine in the
process?"

"Well, it was very unusual, dear, unheard of on
Olympus, and you know your father: such a terrible
temper!"

Hephaestus was silent, staring at the pictures on
the walls, Arcadian landscapes filled with gods, each more
perfect of form than the last.

"If you never want to see me again, I understand."

It was a lot to take in. He had heard so many
different accounts. The memories were so confused. Cast
down from Mount Olympus, he had crawled away into
the shadows, deep in the earth. Barely able to move, lost
and solitary, unable to die.

He had always assumed that the fall had caused
his bent back and lameness. One story he had heard was
that he had been trying to protect his mother. His father
had been drunk, as usual, and his mother had been

taunting him about one of his sexual adventures – Zeus'
uncontrolled libido being something of a joke among
those who liked to gossip around Mount Olympus. And
almost everyone liked to gossip.

Anyway, the events on the night in question
remained a blur, but the story had gone that, in his typical
way, his father had joked, blustered, and then become
inflamed by the taunts. Hera was only jealous because she
was not getting enough *action*. Well, no problem: there
was plenty to go round!

Zeus had grabbed Hera, and ripped her blouse.
Hephaestus had jumped between them to protect her. In
a rage, Zeus had picked up the infant by the throat,
marched him to the edge of the precipice, and cast him
down. His legs had broken on the impact of the fall.

But that did not tally with this version of his story.
He would not have been old enough to protect his
mother, even if he had been able to comprehend what was
going on. His father had crippled him – on account of two
tiny feet turned inwards.

11

Mudge had a niece. Zeus was not sure of her age. Clearly, she was younger than him, but that could make her anything between the age of one and seventy-three. Her name was Ember, which seemed appropriate given the spark in her eye. Her hair was dyed purple and she wore multiple rings, through her lips, nose and ears. Ember's strikingly fierce look brought to mind his daughter, Artemis.

She had two children, Frida and Antonio, named in honour of Kahlo and Gramsci, two of Ember's heroes. Approaching her tenth birthday, Frida was a serious-looking girl, unsmiling and blunt.

"You look... sensible," said Zeus, trying to be formal and polite, as Hermes had advised.

"You look ridiculous," replied Frida, eyeing up his clothing.

The girl seemed extremely protective of her brother, who was three years younger. Despite a face that looked as if it would like to be cheeky, Antonio was chronically shy, looking at Frida to answer for him if he got asked a question.

The two of them went off and sat on a settee, ignoring the adults. Frida took out a book to read and Antonio started to play some game on his phone.

There was no husband or boyfriend in Ember's life, or if there was, she did not speak of him. Between looking after her children and working as a waitress, she was studying for an Open University degree on Gender and Social Policy.

It appeared that she was intensely family-minded, bringing the children to visit their great-uncle each week, even though the expression on her face did not imply that she held him in the highest regard. She seemed most surprised that he was now inquiring about her studies.

She was a fourth-wave feminist, she told Zeus, but that did not mean a rejection of the achievements of those who came before. Naturally, she was still interested in issues regarding gendered norms and relative empowerment, but there was also an attention to issues of intersectionality, she explained, adding that she was engaging with queer theory and things like that.

She fixed him with a rather dismissive stare.

"I don't suppose all that is of much interest to an unreconstructed chauvinist, an advocate of male hegemony who once advised me that the most sensible aspiration for a girl was to marry well."

"Did I?"

Zeus considered the matter. He suspected that he liked girls who were obedient, but his preference was for them to be feisty before they were obedient.

He was still thinking about this while she was telling him about her particular interest in feminism from anthropological and mythological perspectives.

"Really, it all goes back to people like Eve and Pandora."

Zeus sat up in his chair with interest.

"Tell me more. I didn't know about that."

It seemed as if Ember did not get much of a chance to talk about her studies at home or work, and though she doubted that her uncle understood or cared about the topic, he was, at least, a temporary audience, a soundboard for her to listen to her own ideas.

"Well, Pandora's offence being one of curiosity..."

"No, the other one you mentioned. Everyone knows about Pandora."

She gave him a strange look.

"Well, you know, Eve, biting into the apple of forbidden knowledge and all that; mankind expelled from Eden. Same thing as Pandora opening a wedding gift, isn't it: the offence of female curiosity bringing down the wrath of the heavens?"

"Fascinating," mused Zeus.

"Are you taking the piss?"

She eyed him with suspicion.

"No, I'd never really thought of it that way."

"Well, Eve was put up to it by the serpent, who is, of course, a classic mythological trickster figure. While

43

all Pandora did was open a wedding gift to find out what it was. Why wouldn't you? And who's the trickster there: Hermes who handed her the box or that sneak, Zeus, who ordered him to do it?"

"How dare you call Zeus a sneak!"

Ember had never seen her uncle look so furious. She wondered if he had gone mad.

Zeus took some deep breaths.

"The point is," he managed to blurt out, finally, "Zeus was angry about being deceived by Prometheus, the real trickster. So it was revenge against him for stealing fire to give to the mortals. It was never really about Pandora."

"And yet Pandora got the blame. In human terms, she is the guilty one."

Zeus looked thoughtful.

"I'd never considered it from that perspective."

For a while, they sat sipping tea, while the children played games on their phones.

"You seem very different, Uncle Monty. Like you've had an epiphany. And as Frida mentioned, if rather rudely, you've bought new clothes."

"Do you like them?"

"Well, definitely, makes you more interesting – all those daring colours, and styles aimed at teens."

"Well, Hermes chose them, really."

"Hermes? You mean you chat to the driver who delivers stuff."

"Something like that."

They continued drinking tea, weighing up one another. Ember leant, forward, lowering her voice to a murmur.

"Do you think you may be going through a belated mid-life crisis?"

PART 2 – HAMARTIA

SURVIVING THE 21ST CENTURY: A HANDBOOK FOR PENSIONERS

ENTRY 2

WHEN HERMES TOLD ME TO KEEP A JOURNAL, I ASSUMED AT FIRST IT MEANT KEEPING A LIST OF THE HABITS AND BEHAVIOUR OF MORTALS. AS I WAS GOING TO BE INHABITING THE BODY OF ONE, HOWEVER, HE SUGGESTED THAT THIS COULD BE A KIND OF 'AUTO-ETHNOGRAPHY'.

AUTO-ETHNOGRAPHY! WHAT THE BINEO IS THAT? I LOOKED UP THE TERM, RECENTLY, IN A BOOK ON MUDGE'S BOOKSHELF – HE DOESN'T HAVE MANY, BY THE WAY. THE BOOK GIVES THE MEANINGS OF WORDS YOU MAY NOT KNOW. ALL I FOUND WAS:

AUTO-EROTIC – THE PRACTICE OF BEING STIMULATED THROUGH INTERNAL STIMULI.

THIS SOUNDS A BIT CONFUSING, BUT COULD MAKE THE RESEARCH MORE INTERESTING WHEN I WORK IT OUT.

IN THE MEANTIME, I HAD AN IDEA: WHAT IF I WRITE THIS NOT SO MUCH FOR ACADEMIA BUT FOR THE MORTALS THEMSELVES, A KIND OF SELF-HELP GUIDE, GIVING THEM TIPS?

AS YET, I HAVE NOT PUT THIS TO HERMES. HE MAY MAKE SOME COMMENTS ABOUT LACK OF

RIGOUR OR IMPACT IN JOURNALS. I HAVE DECIDED
TO START IT WITHOUT HIS APPROVAL.

SO, LET'S BEGIN. IN THE FIRST PLACE, IT WAS A
TERRIBLE DESIGN CHOICE, A BODY THAT ROTS. THIS
MEANS THAT YOU WILL NEED TO BE REPLACED VERY
SOON AFTER YOUR MANUFACTURE. THERE MAY BE
A FEW SPARE PARTS TO SLIGHTLY PROLONG YOUR
ROAD-LIFE, BUT THE INBUILT OBSOLESCENCE MEANS
THAT, BASICALLY, IT WON'T MAKE MUCH
DIFFERENCE. IT IS A LITTLE DEPRESSING THAT YOU
HAVE TO GO THROUGH LIFE WITH DECAYING TEETH,
CRUMBLING HIPS AND KNEES, NOT TO MENTION
MOULDERING ORGANS ON THE INSIDE, BUT
SOMETHING OF A MERCY THAT, AT LEAST, YOU DO
NOT HAVE TO SUFFER THE EMBARRASSMENT OF
THEM FOR VERY LONG.

BEING A PENSIONER LEAVES YOU WITH PLENTY
OF SPARE TIME. YOU CAN SPEND THAT IN VARIOUS
WAYS, SUCH AS FLICKING THROUGH THE TV
CHANNELS, OR JUST STARING AT THE WALLS IN YOUR
HOUSE, WONDERING WHEN SOMEONE IS GOING TO
COME AND GET YOU OUT OF THIS BOREDOM.

IT IS ALSO AN OPPORTUNITY, HOWEVER, TO
REFLECT, TO RE-EVALUATE ALL THE THINGS YOU
THOUGHT YOU BELIEVED. THIS CAN KEEP YOUR MIND
OCCUPIED FOR QUITE A WHILE, WHICH IS VERY
IMPORTANT GIVEN THE TEDIUM IMPOSED ON A
PENSIONER – PRESUMABLY, A PUNISHMENT FOR
CRIMES COMMITTED IN YOUTH.

THESE CRIMES COME WITH A LONG LIST OF OTHER PENALTIES. A PENSIONER IS SEPARATED FROM FELLOW BEINGS, CONDEMNED TO WEAR CLOTHES OF A DULL HUE. AIR SUPPLY IS RESTRICTED. A CURSE HAS BEEN PLACED ON YOU, MEANING THAT YOU CAN ONLY MOVE LIKE A TORTOISE. HYPNOS SLINKS IN WHEN HE IS UNWANTED TO PUT YOU TO SLEEP.

WHEN YOU ACTUALLY WANT TO SLEEP, THE CURSE IS REVERSED, AND YOU WAKE WITH A SUDDEN DESIRE TO EMPTY YOUR BLADDER. YOU STAGGER TO A BOWL THAT HAS BEEN PROVIDED FOR THIS PURPOSE, AND THEN FIND THAT ONLY A DRIBBLE COMES OUT.

YOU RETURN TO YOUR CHAIR OR BED, WAKING UP ALMOST IMMEDIATELY AFTER DRIFTING OFF TO SLEEP, TO FIND THAT YOU NEED TO GO AGAIN!

NOTE TO SELF: TAKE UP THIS MATTER WITH THAT WANKER, HYPNOS - HYPNOS THE MALAKA! - AS SOON AS POSSIBLE.

ONE SOLUTION WOULD BE TO KEEP A SMALLER VESSEL CLOSER TO YOUR BED TO PEE INTO. MORTALS SHOULD GIVE CAREFUL CONSIDERATION TO THE INVENTION OF SUCH A DEVICE.

ANOTHER TIP: PENSIONERS SHOULD AVOID CHILDREN AT ALL COST. THEY ARE EITHER RUDE OR SILENT.

A FINAL POINT: ONE OF THE RISKS FACING
PENSIONERS IS GOING THROUGH WHAT IS KNOWN AS
A MID-LIFE CRISIS. THIS CAN HAPPEN UNEXPECTEDLY.
IT IS NOT SOMETHING TO PANIC ABOUT.

12

His chariot had been returned. There had been a knock on his door, and two very polite mortals were standing there in funny uniforms. Having watched programmes on television, he recognised that the taller, quieter one was a policeman. The smaller, friendly one must be – using the suffix that mortals have chosen to use for female in roles – a policemaness. It took him a while to realise that they were asking whether his chariot had been stolen, as they used another term to describe it.

Deciding that it was probably sensible to concur, he agreed that it had been stolen. Could he explain, in that case, why he had not reported the theft? Zeus stared at them, uncertainly. Was it because he only drove it, occasionally, and had not parked outside his house? Perhaps, another vehicle had been outside his property, so he had had to park it further up the road or round the corner. Zeus agreed that this was almost certainly what had happened.

Well, fortunately for him, his chariot could not have been filled up with petrol recently, as it had run out only a few miles away. Zeus agreed that this was, indeed, fortunate.

"We suggest that you keep your car with sufficient petrol in it for your journeys, Mr Mudge," said the policemaness, with quite a friendly expression.

'Mudge' thought Zeus after they had left. He did not want to take on the mortal's name. This was just a temporary aberration. He would be out of here in no time. Zeus thought of this being with utter distaste. Why had he never married? Who would choose to live alone? What was this Mudge thinking?

Maybe his nous and phronesis were as droopy as his phallos.

He felt a sudden rush of fondness for Hera. If only she could be there with him. Yes, she got angry with him sometimes, but she loved him, passionately. It was that passion which led to jealousy. In the end she was his rock – she would do anything for him.

13

Although deep in a cavern hidden on a hillside, a preternatural light poured in, perhaps, emanating from the figures seated around the large boardroom table. Great care had been taken by each of them to ensure that they had not been spotted. The meeting had been deliberately scheduled for dawn when most of the denizens of Olympus were sleeping off their hangovers from the revelries of the preceding night. Nevertheless, they all glanced around nervously, as they arrived at the remote destination.

Hermes cleared his throat.

"His friends, the Hecatoncheires, are beginning to ask questions. They want to know where he is. I mean, he's been away before, but never for so long."

Aphrodite smiled, rather mirthlessly.

"Tell them he's down with the mortals. He often went there for his rumpy-pumpy."

Hera pulled a face.

"Do you have to use that term?"

Aphrodite's smile broadened.

"It was *his* word – I think he made it up – and really, Hera, after all these years, all the infidelities, one might be expected to lighten up."

Hera ignored the remark.

"The Hecatoncheires will need to be cuffed after one of their parties, then locked away."

"Cuffed! You do know they each have one hundred hands."

"I'm sure Hephaestus can arrange something."

Hephaestus inclined his head ever so slightly in what may or may not have been a nod. He had begun to feel awkward the moment he had spotted the stranger sitting in the far, shadowed corner. Even if the others had not seen though the disguise, he had recognised his uncle, Hades, instantly.

"And then there are the Cyclopes."

"We could send them on a long holiday," grinned Hermes. "Other than producing thunderbolts for Zeus, they're not over-bright. We could tell them they won a competition. First prize – an all-in luxury trip."

"They say that Tartarus is nice at this time of the year."

They all twisted their heads to survey the stranger. He spoke in a soft voice, which one or two felt was familiar. It was just a little difficult to place him, exactly, especially as he seemed enveloped in thick murk.

Eulabeia looked troubled. She was a slender, pale figure, by nature timorous, who, habitually, looked like she was biting her lower lip. She was not so much biting as chewing on it right now.

"He's going to be ever so annoyed if he gets back."

"In which eventuality, we have arranged for... a form of insurance."

Heads turned once more to glance into the recesses of the cave.

The figure sitting there did not move. They all stared again at the stranger, who paused, before speaking in a voice so low that they had to strain to catch his words.

He had paid a visit to Atlas, he now informed them, which resulted in a sharp intake of breath and an exchange of nervous glances.

"How was he?" came a rather uneasy question.

"Well, you know, bearing up. Says he gets a few twinges in his back but that's only to be expected, what with holding up the sky all these years. We have come to an understanding. If we give an oath to free him, he will let bygones be bygones. He is even willing to support our endeavour."

"But what about the sky? If he just walks off, won't it come crashing down?"

The stranger stared, pityingly, at Eulabeia.

"Some folk are just so pre-Kronos! As if Atlas is there for the sake of the sky! Really! He's there because Zeus is a spiteful sod who suckles on old grudges like a ravenous baby. Do you think it would not be easy to put up a few acrow props instead? Is that not so, Hephaestus?"

55

"I suppose so."

It was more of a grunt than anything. Hephaestus was scowling at the intruder. Hades was trouble, never to be trusted. It seemed crazy for his mother, Hera, or anyone else for that matter, to wish to involve him in any plot, let alone a coup requiring secrecy, stealth, and above all, trust in your fellow conspirators.

Of course, even in his hermit world, he had heard the gossip about his mother having a *thing* about Hades. He preferred not to believe this. There was something beyond creepy about Hades. He was known for gluttony at expansive banquets, gorging himself as if he had been starved for months, without ever putting on an ounce of fat. He rouged his cheeks and dyed his hair in vivid shades while still managing to look colourless. His smile could be gleeful and mirthless at the same time. He was a lifeless, saturnine creature who gave Hephaestus the shudders.

It should be said that Hephaestus did not scare easily. And while he had good reason to loathe his father, it was possible that Hephaestus detested his uncle still more. It left him grappling with conflicting emotions, and on such occasions, all he wanted was to be back in his forge, making new things or just repairing objects that were broken.

His reverie was broken by the voice of Eris. Hephaestus was not over- keen on her either, and was always wary. She always had such a sneaky look on her face, and it was commonly known how she loved to cause trouble.

"Eulabeia has a point," she was saying. "Zeus is going to be proper pissed off when he finds out about this. If it's true that, as Hermes says, he is in such a weak form right now, then this is kairos, the moment to strike. Should we not be giving Atlas his whereabouts already? Come to think of it, has Hermes shared with us where that is?"

Hermes did his best to appear unruffled by the question. There had been a loss of connection during the operation, but he was working on the co-ordinates. However, he could concur that Eris was quite correct in the assumption that Zeus was in a frail body, one that could perish at any moment. Who knew what might happen? Would it not be rash to make a move before matters were clarified? Besides, Hephaestus would need time to set up a construction to stabilise the sky.

It was a relief that, before Eris could push him on the matter, someone else raised a new question: whether they should avoid risking including Atlas in the plot if his services were not likely to be required. Another hour was spent in consideration of all the options before they began dispersing, one by one.

Hermes felt a hand on his shoulder just as he was about to slink away. Hera was giving him one of her taut smiles.

"I don't suppose, dear, that you know where Zeus left his crown. I've been searching everywhere. For some reason, they are viewed as a symbol of legitimacy."

Hades was standing just behind him on the other side. Hermes had not heard him creep up.

Hermes shrugged. He had not seen it. All he knew was that Zeus had not been wearing it when he left. He would have noticed.

Hades' expression was inscrutable.

"I suppose you'll just have to widen your search. Up here on Olympus, down on Earth, the Underworld... even Tartarus. Things have a habit of finding their way there."

So true, thought Hermes. Things like Sisyphus, the giants, Otus and Ephialtes, and the Danaids. However oblique, it was a threat. Hermes promised to hunt for the missing crown. He wished them well before departing, feeling their eyes on his back till he was out of sight.

"I don't trust him," muttered Hera. "Despite the oath he made."

It had been witnessed. An oath made by Hermes, duly deposited in the Styx and entered into the records by Horkos. It could not be undone.

"Nevertheless," continued Hera, "did you notice the way the sneak was playing for time when Eris made that suggestion? Maybe, he's still chummy with his dear daddy. It strikes me that, sometimes, he has the look of his mummy, the slut-nymph, Maia, lying in wait in her cave for anyone passing, with her legs spread wide apart. I want him followed."

"His chariot's too fast."

"I'm sure something can be arranged."

Scanning those remaining, she spotted Hephaestus and beckoned him over. With some reluctance, he complied.

"That thing, dear, you know, the one that Hermes bimbles around in, do you think you could build something as fast?"

"I suppose I can make another chariot and get it souped up."

"There's my clever boy."

Hera patted his head. Hephaestus limped away, cheered by the thought of his workroom. And yet, he was also uneasy, and not only about his mother's closeness to his uncle.

There had been another story about his accident, told to him long ago by one of the nymphs, which he had done his utmost to forget. His injury had been caused not by his father but his mother. She had loathed him from birth, calling him hideously ugly. It had been *she* who had cast him from his birthplace.

Subsequently, when his gifts were discovered, she had persuaded Hypnos to visit him in his sleep. Hypnos had poured some drops of water taken from the River Lethe onto his forehead, before insinuating a dream in his mind, the image of his father attempting to rape his mother, before flinging his young son from Olympus when he had tried to intervene.

Hephaestus preferred not to believe the nymph's version of the story. It was too much of a curse to bear. Besides, it was well known that nymphs were not to be trusted.

And yet, the nasty notion continued to lurk in the back of his mind.

14

He parked his chariot as close as possible to the school gates. It was a little irksome. An interruption in his day when he had been planning to...

Well, he did not quite know what he had been planning to do, but it had not been driving through busy traffic to park outside a school and wait with gossipy mothers to collect young children. There were very few other males, and certainly, none in his age group.

He had not quite followed the garbled reason why the usual childminder at such times was no longer available, but he hoped that Ember was not going to be on many other last-minute work shifts that ran into mid-afternoon. It was only mildly assuaging to plan all the ways in which she might be taught a lesson at some future date for her impertinence. The nerve! Asking *him* to do chores!

There were a few odd glances in his direction as he stood by the gate. He was wearing fluorescent lime tracksuit bottoms, a t-shirt with a picture of Bart Simpson on a skateboard, and a hoodie bearing the logo: ZOMBIES EAT BRAINS: DON'T WORRY YOU'RE SAFE.

He watched some of the children as they disgorged from the building. A few of the youngest ones rushed straight to their mothers to be led away. Others, just a little bigger, ambled towards their mothers, not wishing to appear quite so happy to see them. The older ones came out with less haste. Some were shouting jokey insults to one another across the yard. Quite a few were in groups, laughing. Frida and Antonio were among the last to appear. Frida looked far from pleased when she spotted her great-uncle; Antonio just looked bewildered.

"As if we weren't already viewed as freaks," he overheard Frida whisper as they climbed into the rear seat.

He took them back to their house. Ember had said they would be happier there and could get on with their own things. He should make himself a hot drink, she said. She would not be long.

Frida gave him directions, tutting whenever he got into the wrong lane. She went silent as they approached the house.

"Have you forgotten which one is yours?" asked Zeus.

They all looked pretty much the same to him, so it would have been understandable.

Frida did not reply. She was watching two children from down the road. Only when they had vanished into their own home did she allow them to get out of the car.

Antonio muttered something to Frida, who nodded. He vanished up a staircase.

"I'll show you where everything is before I go up to do my homework," she said, stiffly.

The house was quite a bit bigger than the one Mudge lived in, with lighter and more interesting furnishings. Zeus' attention was caught by small bits of bric-a-brac, such as an ornate soap dish in the bathroom, decorated on each side with sirens.

The lounge was cluttered with all sorts of things on shelves or side tables, and a surfeit of cushions strewn across the settee. The walls were covered in pictures, some done by the children, and others which were posters. There was a large one with the name Che Guevarra on it. There was another of a young man in profile, wearing a huge hat, holding a gun. There was also a name – Emiliano Zapata, along with the words: VIVA LA REVOLUCION! Another showed a woman in silhouette, with a huge moon in the background, and a cat at her side. It bore the words: WE ARE THE GRANDDAUGHTERS OF THE WITCHES YOU COULDN'T BURN. There was one with women with fists in the air, with the slogan: FUCK THE PATRIARCHY. There were one or two with only words: FEMINISM ENCOURAGES WOMEN TO LEAVE THEIR HUSBANDS, KILL THEIR CHILDREN, PRACTISE WITCHCRAFT, DESTROY CAPITALISM AND BECOME LESBIANS.

Frida surveyed him as he read the words. There was something that she could not quite determine about this incarnation of her great-uncle, though she still did not like him.

"Do you want a mug of hot chocolate?" she asked, a little reluctantly. "We usually have one when we get back from school."

Zeus nodded without thinking about it.

While she was in the kitchen, Zeus' attention turned to the other images on the walls. One was an art poster by Frida Kahlo, with a woman's face covered in flowers. There was another of an original book cover. FRANKENSTEIN; OR, THE MODERN PROMETHEUS by Mary Shelley.

Zeus was still staring at this when Frida returned with a tray. There were three mugs on saucers, Zeus taking one of the two with marshmallows on it. He did not appear to notice the look Frida gave him, as she went back into the kitchen to get marshmallows for the third mug. Nor did he notice when she got back, so intent was his attention on the Frankenstein poster.

"Is there something particularly interesting about that one?"

He frowned as he turned to her.

"I just wondered. Who is Frankenstein?"

It flitted across Frida's mind that he was putting on an act of being dumb. Or, maybe, this was part of dementia. Her face softened.

"The monster. Well, actually, and most people get this wrong, he was not the monster but the scientist who created and brought it to life. The creature was made up of the parts of dead humans collected from graveyards."

Zeus' eyes widened.

"Can you do that?"

Frida was about to pull a face, and say something along the lines of 'well, dur', when she noticed that his expression was earnest.

"No," she said, quietly.

She took the hot chocolate upstairs for her brother, and after considering the matter on the landing, decided to come down again with her own mug.

"Are you... OK, Uncle Monty? You seem..."

"You don't like school, do you?"

She was caught unawares by the question.

"What makes you say that?"

"I could tell by the way you were walking on the way out. You both... sort of slouched. You looked unhappy. And that was even before you saw me."

He smiled. It was the first time he had done so since arriving there. The movement of the muscles on his face to achieve it felt odd.

"We... Ant and I get picked on. For... you know, being different. Our names don't help. People think there is something wrong with Ant because he doesn't like talking. And probably, it doesn't impress people that I love reading. But I won't stop because of what other people say."

"Good for you!"

She glanced up, quickly. He *meant* it. He was not faking it. Perhaps, there had always been something nice about him but she had never really searched for it. She looked away.

"I like marshmallows," he murmured.

15

Something behind him, a flash of light, the briefest of glimmers. He had caught sight of it in the rear mirror that he had fixed to his chariot, inspired by what he had seen on the sides of the vehicles outside that other Argos.

Whatever was behind seemed to be keeping up. When he swung right, it did the same thing; when he went left, it turned left, maintaining the same distance. Hermes accelerated. Nothing could keep up with his chariot when it went at full speed.

The vehicle behind did not fall back. This was worrying. Hermes slowed right down, as did his pursuer. Then, suddenly, in a thick cloud, he accelerated, veering off course slightly and landing in a new location.

There were far brighter lights here, and quite heavy traffic even though it was dark. There was some monument in the road ahead, with several lanes of traffic whizzing around it. From the corner of his eye, Hermes spotted his pursuer landing, around five or six vehicles behind him.

I'll lose this slimeball bdelyros in this chaos, thought Hermes. Picking up speed, he now shot across the roundabout, weaving in and out of the traffic. Round and round he swerved, and to make things more confusing, Hermes swung his chariot in number shapes based on the Stomachion, the great puzzle invented by

Archimedes. The vehicle behind was losing ground, and was lost in the crowd, when Hermes suddenly cut across lanes onto an exit.

"Don't play chezo with the king of chezo!" he shouted in exhilaration. Entering Argos, Newton Abbot on his destination screen, he now relaxed.

Some time later, he pulled in at the market car park, remembering to cloak his chariot in an invisibility cover, just in case. For good measure, he purchased an overnight parking ticket, leaving it in view in case a ticket inspector who could see through invisibility covers came by. It seemed unlikely, but you couldn't be too careful.

Zeus seemed a little less pleased by the visit than Hermes had hoped. Why had he been gone for so long?

So long?

It took a while for Hermes to remember that while there was little sense of time on Olympus, here it was very different. Time sped by, yet also dragged. He wondered whether he should warn Zeus that dangerous creatures might come in search of him, deciding that this was, perhaps, not the best time.

"You never told me that chariots here run out of something called petrol."

Zeus was glaring at Hermes as if the information had been, deliberately, withheld.

"I assumed you would be aware of that. You know... from the Mudge Files."

"There are gaps. Lost data."

Once again, the expression implied that this had also been due to some act of sabotage on the part of his son.

"So what's the gossip? There must be some news."

The question was asked in a thin, peevish voice, so unlike that of Zeus that Hermes struggled to recognise him. Somehow, it was still more disconcerting than the body. Nevertheless, he did his best to pick up this old fellow's spirits.

"Well, I think something is going on with Eros and Anteros. Both chasing the same mountain nymph. Oh, and you'll never guess: Dysnomia slipped something into Dike's drink, and the next thing, she was in the bushes, making out with Pan!"

"Dike! Are you sure? Pan must have been off his head, too. Who else?"

"Iasion had a brief thing with Calypso, and Hermaphroditos is still shagging himself."

"What else?"

Zeus seemed suddenly ravenous for news. Hermes went through a list of those involved in affairs, mentioning almost all the sexual liaisons except the one almost everyone on Olympus was talking about – that involving Hera and Hades. It was evident that the thought of all the action everyone else was getting had left Zeus in a paroxysm of frustration.

"It's unbearable."

"It won't be for long."

"It better not be. I think this akos-peos, walking carcass is running out of air."

While Zeus continued to moan about being stuck in a useless body, devoid of an ithyphallos, Hermes settled at his dining table, busily setting up a new bank account with a payment card, and an online social media account for R. Montgomery Mudge. He also managed to sort all the bills in advance for things like council tax and heating.

He did not expect any thanks. Nor did he get any.

Zeus continued with his grumbling.

"What's the point of this *bank account* if I can't get any choiros?"

Hermes ignored the comment. Having sorted out the essentials, he turned to other matters. He tried to explain to Zeus the basics for using this machine that he had brought, which he called a 'laptop'. Zeus did not seem to be concentrating.

"It's quite ingenious. Hephaestus explained how it works. He's very clever, you know."

He's a disappointment to me," growled Zeus. "All my children are disappointments. Perhaps, I should have eaten them all at birth."

Hermes looked horrified.

"Gelos!" added Zeus. His words subsided into an angry mutter as he pottered off to the kitchen. "Just no sense of humour. None of my kids have it."

"I'm still here, you know," called Hermes, as he typed in something else on the laptop.

Some pictures came up on screen from clothing and shoes from catalogues. Hermes waited for Zeus to return with a cup of hot chocolate. He sat down, heavily, noticing Hermes' expression.

"Did *you* want one?" he asked.

There was no sign of a movement to get back to his feet to make a second cup. Hermes gestured to the laptop screen. Rather sulkily, Zeus pointed to items.

"Anything else?"

Hermes was enjoying the device. Zeus watched his son from the corner of his eye. Hermes had been adroit from the moment of his birth, a quick learner. He had always looked forward to visiting the mortal realm, if only to check out the latest inventions. Many times he had praised the ingenuity of humankind, saying that with a few exceptions, most notably, Hephaestus, the gods were indolent, complacent because they had too few problems to solve.

It had not been part of Hermes' plan, but, before closing down the laptop, he added one more online order, that promised 'discreet online delivery' within one day.

SURVIVING THE 21ST CENTURY: A HANDBOOK FOR
PENSIONERS

ENTRY 3

YOU MAY HAVE BEEN SENTENCED TO BEING A
PENSIONER, BUT THERE ARE WAYS OF MAKING THE
CURSE A LITTLE MORE BEARABLE.

IN THE FIRST PLACE, YOU SHOULD KEEP YOUR
MIND ACTIVE. FOR INSTANCE, ONLY TODAY I WAS
THINKING ABOUT A PICTURE OF SOMEONE CALLED
FRANKENSTEIN. HE HAD CREATED A MONSTER, A BIT
LIKE PROMETHEUS. I SPENT A LONG TIME THINKING
ABOUT THIS. DON'T GET ME WRONG – PROMETHEUS
WAS – IS, A MONSTER, A TOTAL MALAKA, WHO
DESERVED EVERYTHING THAT HAPPENED TO HIM.
BUT, HE IS ALSO A VICTIM.

SHOPPING IS A GOOD WAY OF KEEPING YOUR
MIND AND BODY ACTIVE. LAST WEEK, I DISCOVERED A
NEW SHOP. IT IS CALLED 'LIDL'. VISITING *LIDL* IS NOW
PART OF MY DAILY ROUTINE. THE MAIN PURPOSE OF
THIS SHOP APPEARS TO BE TO TRAIN THOSE WHO GO
THERE IN KAIROS, IDENTIFYING AND EXPLOITING THE
CRITICAL MOMENT. THEY CHANGE THINGS ALONG
THE AISLES, KEEPING YOU ON YOUR TOES, MOVING
THINGS FOR NO REASON, AND THROWING IN
RANDOM ITEMS FOR YOUR HOME AND GARDEN,
MANY OF WHICH HAVE NO OBVIOUS PURPOSE.

PERHAPS, YOU SPEND THE EVENING, CONSIDERING WHETHER THESE ITEMS MIGHT BE OF USE TO YOU, COMING TO A DECISION IN THE MIDDLE OF THE NIGHT, THAT, YES, YOU WILL TAKE THE PLUNGE. ONLY THE VERY NEXT DAY, WHEN YOU RETURN, THE CHOSEN ITEM HAS DISAPPEARED, MYSTERIOUSLY.

IMAGINE THAT HERACLES HAD DALLIED ON HIS WAY TO GET THE GOLDEN APPLES – *MY* GOLDEN APPLES, WHILE WE'RE ON THE SUBJECT. IMAGINE HIM GETTING THERE, SEARCHING AROUND, AND THEN HAVING TO ASK AT THE CHECKOUT. AND SOME SPOTTY YOUTH THERE SAYS: 'SORRY, FELLA. SOME OTHER GRASON CAME IN AND GRABBED THE LAST ONES ONLY A FEW MINUTES AGO'.

HERACLES WOULD HAVE BEEN RIGHT PISSED OFF, WOULDN'T HE, AND IT WOULD PROBABLY HAVE GIVEN EURYSTHEUS A GOOD LAUGH, TOO. NO ONE LOVED A COCK-UP MORE THAN EURYSTHEUS! WHILE WE MENTION IT, *HE* WAS A RIGHT MALAKA AS WELL.

ON THE SUBJECT OF A GOOD LAUGH, YOU CAN COME ACROSS SOME REALLY INTERESTING VISITORS TO SUPERMARKETS LIKE LIDL. ONLY YESTERDAY I SPOTTED A WOMAN WHO COULD NOT SEE. LITERALLY! IT WAS BY THE FRUIT AREA, AND AN IDEA CAME TO ME OUT OF THE BLUE: I PICKED UP A BANANA, PEELED IT, THEN DROPPED THE SKIN INTO HER BAG. IMAGINE HOW SURPRISED SHE WOULD BE TO DISCOVER IT THERE ON GETTING HOME! GELOS!!

FINALLY – AND THIS IS VERY IMPORTANT, YOU
NEED TO WORK HARD AT SMILING. AT LEAST ONCE
EACH HOUR OR TWO THIS CAN BE PRACTISED IN
FRONT OF A MIRROR.

YOU SHOULD ALSO EAT MARSHMALLOWS.
LOTS OF THEM. DUNKED INTO MUGS OF HOT
CHOCOLATE.

16

Hermes avoided direct eye contact, which was unusual for him, not fitting in at all well with his role as a messenger. He had felt increasingly uncomfortable in Hera's company for some time. And now, after everything, she was demanding that he should deliver a message to Boreas, of all gods. And at this time of year!

"It's a get-well card," she explained. "Apparently, he's had a persistent cough. It's not a healthy lifestyle he follows. All that gallivanting across the northern skies.

"Boreas! You've never sent him a message before."

"As I said he's not been well. Were you not paying attention, dear? After all, he's a relative. A distant cousin, I don't know how many times removed. I seem to recall he's also related through marriage. Family is very important, you know."

Hermes half turned to conceal his scowl. A subtle reminder that he was not quite 'family', given his mother, Maia's genealogy, which included his own dodgy grandfather, Atlas. Or was she just trying to get him out of the way for a time, while facilitating her schemes? Or was this a punishment for not, as yet, giving the precise location of her missing husband?

"You promised that I would not have to do all this malarkey anymore. Just as soon as I had persuaded him to go off and visit the mortals. Birthday greetings, Mothers' and Fathers' Day cards, *Wish You Were Here* postcards. All the stuff Zeus had insisted on, even though there are so many easier ways to communicate these days."

Hera smiled, primly.

"Letters and cards are more personal."

"But our deal was..."

"Our deal *is* that you get laid off as soon as we know that Zeus is out of the equation."

She gave him a rather patronising smile, that of a patient parent dealing with a somewhat obstreperous child. Hermes was never sure quite how Hera did it, but somehow she left him – one of the slickest communicators in existence – almost tongue-tied in her presence.

"You never told me that the plan was to have him murdered. Your words were 'bloodless coup'."

"Which is the very point. If Zeus is eliminated, he will not be around to rally support. There will be no terrible battles and slaughter like the last time. Nobody gets hurt and the oppression is over. Did you really believe that the plan was to just leave him in a weak body, waiting for him to come back? Really Hermes! Are you just naïve, or did you prefer not to think it through? But it's up to you; we can end this right now."

She fixed him with a piercing look.

"Where exactly is he, Hermes?"

Hermes gazed into the distance, as if scanning for Zeus at that very moment.

"I'm not quite sure. In the way it was handled – you know, so as to make it look like he was, temporarily, entering the body of a hero, someone who might one day be elevated to semi-divinity, well, it all became a bit random. We were zooming about, these elderly mortals flashing in front of us ever so quickly, and... well, I sort of... lost contact during the transition."

The expression on Hera's face remained unchanged throughout this halting explanation: a rather inscrutable, tight-lipped smile.

"Well, let us know if it comes back to you. In the meantime, I seem to recall you have a card to deliver. Remember to pack the right kind of clothes. I understand the climate there can be thoroughly nasty at this time of year, and we wouldn't want you catching a chill."

17

They studied the catalogue on the screen. It struck Hermes as slightly excessive, given the previous order, but if Zeus had decided that some of his previous selections had been inappropriate, it seemed only fair to humour him.

"I did not take into account how inadequate the mortal body was. You really feel the cold. What about that one?"

He was pointing to a thick, woollen skirt.

"You're looking at the women's section."

Zeus looked surprised.

"Well, does it matter?"

"I don't think we should attract attention to ourselves. Do you?"

Zeus gave a half shrug. He now asked Hermes for the umpteenth time when he was going to get him out of this awful place. And for the umpteenth time, Hermes assured him that they were working on it, and it would be as soon as possible.

Zeus muttered something about even the fruit rotting here, but Hermes was not listening. He was opening a box containing a new device he had ordered. He had to explain three times how it operated, as Zeus did not seem to be paying attention.

"I've put in the numbers of your niece, Ember, and your friend, Bill."

"He's not my friend."

A plate rattled as Zeus brought down his fist on the table.

"OK – the number of your... Bill. Now more importantly, there's another number. I have not put in a name as it's the number to contact me, in case you really need me."

"Why don't you just write 'Hermes' there to make it easy to remember?"

"Because..."

Hermes went ever so slightly pink in the face.

"Because... the name is very unusual here. It may look odd if anyone saw your phone."

The sceptical look on Zeus' face was a bit unnerving.

"What I'll do is to type in the first letter to remind you."

There was an uncomfortable silence.

"I may be away for a while. Got a ruddy card from Hera to deliver to Boreas. Apparently, he's got a cough."

Zeus' face softened.

"That's so sweet of her. She can be very caring, you know."

"Oh, ever so caring!"

Zeus gave Hermes another long look, part quizzical, part disapproving.

"I know she's not your biological mother but you could learn a lot from Hera if you would just be a little more open to it."

Hermes decided it might be best to change the conversation.

"This messenger thing, the glorified postman role, it can get just a wee bit of a drag. I'm not complaining, but, maybe, we might consider one of the lesser gods..."

Zeus grimaced.

"We've discussed this a million times, Hermes. The job is a huge honour. It's not for negotiation."

Hermes sighed. He had not really expected any other response. Once Zeus had made up his mind, he was intractable, as stubborn and stupid as Koalemos' mule.

"Well, I'd better be on my way. This *Get Well Soon* card is not going to deliver itself. I may be gone for a while. As I say, it might be sensible not to draw attention to yourself in the meantime. You might want to keep those curtains closed, the ones overlooking the main road, especially, after late afternoon. And keep a low profile."

"Don't you worry your pretty head about me. I'll be just fine," said Zeus, crabbily.

18

For a while, Zeus ignored the rat-tat on his door. He had been feeling a bit sorry for himself the moment Hermes had left and was not in the mood for seeing Bill. In fact, the very thought of the egregious, little twerp with his newspaper and piddling bar of chocolate made Zeus' stomach churn. His friend! Was Hermes off his head?

Only the banging continued. Marching to the door, Zeus swung it open, managing to knock over an umbrella stand that had been put there by that akos-peos, Mudge. Its contents spilled out: two crappy, tattered umbrellas and an old walking-stick.

It was not Bill, but the woman from the house next door, the one of absolutely no allure or interest.

"Cecil," she said.

"Nobody here of that name," snapped Zeus.

He tried to close the door, but her foot was against it, and she was stronger than she looked. Or he was weaker.

"My cat."

Zeus blinked at her, uncomprehendingly.

"He's gone missing."

Was this supposed to be *his* problem? She looked distraught, in utter panic. Perhaps, the woman was a moron.

"Have you seen him?"

Zeus shook his head.

"Will you keep an eye open? He has, occasionally, come round to your house in the past."

Had he, indeed? All Zeus needed!

The woman looked tearful.

"You'll let me know if he does come here, won't you?"

Zeus nodded, before managing to force shut the door.

19

Even for a nymph, Psecas had done rather well for herself. Of course, it had helped that the great goddess, Artemis, had selected her to comb her hair. It had been worth all the jealousy, and her first salon on Olympus had attracted busy custom. After all, if you were good enough for Artemis, you were pretty well good enough for anyone.

And now she had a chain of salons, not just around Olympus, but dotted all across Thalassa, which were profitable despite the fact that Poseidon charged outrageously high rentals for some of them. Hades had been more generous, allowing Psecas to open up branches across his kingdom, firstly, the one close to his palace, then others in the Elysian Fields, the Asphodel Fields, the Vale of Mourning, the Rock of Unburied Souls, and even, Tartarus.

Right now, she was working in one of her favourites in the Vale of Persephone. The place was busy, as it was whenever she made a personal appearance, and the air filled with chatter. She listened in to some of the conversations around her.

"Nobody's seen him for ages."

"They say Hera's had him drugged and removed."

"He was spotted a few days ago, not all that far from here. Crossing the river Acheron. He was with that creepy boatman guy."

Psecas' attention was distracted by a question from the customer whose hair she was doing.

"You really think I can carry off the Medusa style?"

"Of course, Sweetie. It will be perfect on you, a look to die for."

She tuned in again on the conversation close by.

"Well, they brought him across the marsh, took him to the edge of the Lethe, opened his mouth, and poured in some drops of forgetfulness. Quite a lot, I'm told. Way beyond the prescribed safety limits. And he doesn't remember a thing. Walks around with an empty gaze and open mouth. When someone mentioned the name 'Zeus', he asked: 'Who's that?'"

"No! It's not possible. Someone's having you on."

"If you don't believe me, tell me this. A few days after Charon drops him off here, guess who disappears? Hades! And can anyone remember when they last saw *him*?"

"It's well known that he always had a bit of a thing for Hera."

"Exactly, only he has that problem."

"What problem?"

"You must have heard. He's not really a one on one guy. Needs to be in a group situation. It's a sexual kink."

"A what?"

"He can't get it up if it's just the two of them. And you know Hera: a bit conservative about that sort of thing. It's why Zeus was always looking elsewhere."

"I did hear she was a bit of a prude."

"And with Hades gone – and you didn't hear this from me – they say that Erebus is stirring. And *he's* proper scary. Without shape or features. You wouldn't know he was there till the darkness engulfed you."

20

Hades was now thrusting, furiously, his eyes, as ever, fixed beyond her. As she was facing upwards, Hera could not see the images behind her across the pillow and bedsheet: priapic satyrs and huge-bosomed nymphs, creatures made up of all sorts of different animal parts, faces contorted in ecstasy.

He groaned with pleasure. Before she shifted, the images had dissolved.

"Wonderful!"

She was not quite ready to sleep.

"It's all so slow."

"You need me to go faster. Does your ex thrust with greater vigour and velocity?"

"I didn't mean *that*. I meant our project. Getting rid of him, permanently. Us being together without worrying that *he's* going to walk back in and you're going to get one of his thunderbolts up your neat, little orrhos."

Hades imagined this for a moment, deciding on balance that the experience might not be pleasant.

"We need Atlas *now*. What's happening with that acrow prop thing that Hephaestus was inventing?"

"He says it's more problematic than he had anticipated. Not just simple engineering. Calculating weights is difficult, apparently. He went on about boring stuff that I didn't really follow: reinforced beams, canopies, brace formwork, timber needles, strongboy brackets, forkheads, prop bracing couplers... Can you imagine going on a date with him? Must be a barrel of laughs."

Hera frowned.

"Sounds as if he's stalling; playing for time. He can usually invent something within hours. You don't think he's having second thoughts about the project?"

Hades hesitated. He really did want to go sleep.

"Well, I have heard – you know, where I am, we pick up all kinds of information – that he may be beginning to remember things."

"Things?"

"Odd little fragments. Such as when he was an infant. What actually happened."

Hera pulled a face.

"He was such an ugly little bleeder. And that horrid, deformed leg! What did you expect me to do? It reflected on me. All of us! Imagine what everyone would have been saying. And I had no idea that he was going to turn out so damned clever."

Hades squeezed her hand. Sometimes, Hera had this winsome, helpless look. It was quite a turn-on this thing with her moods. Maybe, they could do it again. He edged closer, moving his hand across her shoulder, down her side, to her thigh...

"Hades! Concentrate! Does he need another visit from Hypnos? We could remove me from his memory on the night it happened, and make Zeus still more violent."

"You do know the risk to Hephaestus. It could wipe his mind, completely."

"Do I care if he is a slobbering, brain-dead defective? We need this thing done."

"OK. If he doesn't comply soon. Of course, we'll need to get hold of his acrow prop design plans first."

Hades sighed. The desire to make love again had waned. At least, he could now give himself up to sleep. But Hera had not finished.

"And then there's the matter of locating Zeus. We need to get the whole thing done and dusted while he is there. Having Hermes followed has not exactly provided leads. He is a crafty creature, Hermes. And what's more, mortals could be protecting Zeus. Perhaps, descendants of his offspring. He had enough!"

Hades yawned, widely. Surely, this discussion could wait till the morning.

"I suppose I could send an empusa among the mortals. They're awfully good at tracking – and also shape-shifting. So they are never recognised until it is too late. They can become animals, beautiful women... or just an object!"

"Excellent!"

Hera reached down in the bed and groped between his legs. Now *she* was ready for sex again.

21

There was a sound from the outside of the windowsill, a sort of scratching. It was early evening, so he pulled back the curtain, cautiously, from a corner, peering out. Two amber eyes were gazing back at him.

His first instinct was to draw the curtain again. His own favourite animals, eagles and bulls, would not have had much time for this creature, possibly, either pouncing on it or trampling on it. His daughter, Artemis, seemed to have a thing about these pets, and, of course, his sister, Hestia was very fond of them, but he could take them or leave them. All in all, they were more of an Egyptian than a Hellenic fetish. What's more, he could not be sure that this was not an enemy that had taken on the form of a cat to trick him.

Despite all this, he opened the curtain wide, sliding up the sash window enough to reach out. The cat lowered its head and rubbed it against his hand. A little gingerly, Zeus moved his hand, listening to the contented sound coming out of its body. He picked it up, sitting down in an armchair, continuing to stroke it. It was surprisingly soothing.

Both he and the cat awoke with a start at the sound of banging on the window. Neither had thought to draw the curtain again as they had drifted off to sleep, and neither seemed over-pleased by the interruption.

"You've found my Cecil," a voice called through.

Zeus yawned and nodded. Rising to his feet, he passed the animal to her through the window.

"Where have you been, you naughty boy?" she crooned. "Oh, thank you, Monty."

They were on first name terms? He scowled. He did not know or wish to know Mrs Tucker's first name.

"Good night," he mumbled, closing the window, before pulling back the curtain.

22

"I see you've acquired a new soap dish."

Zeus made no comment.

"It looks rather like one I used to have, with mermaids on it."

This, also, did not seem to require a response.

"And, while we're talking of recent acquisitions, are those more new clothes?"

Zeus suspected that Ember was mocking him, a new experience and one that he was having to get used to.

"A few small items Hermes ordered."

"You mean delivered?"

Zeus nodded.

"Well, they still look a bit young for you, but why not? It's just a bit surprising, given your image in the past and the way you used to behave."

She grinned again.

"What did Mudge... what did I... used to be like?"

"A miserable old git!"

Zeus thought about this.

"Then why did you visit... me?"

Ember sighed.

"You want the truth? Because I told my mother I would. When she was very ill, close to the end, she made me promise. For some reason, she had a soft spot for you."

They both fell silent.

"She was the nice one in the family," continued Ember, "always looking for the good in people. The rest of you were tossers, holding grudges, believing that everyone else was doing better. Everyone else was on easy street, looking down on you. Some kind deity was keeping an eye out for them. But not you."

"Well, it does happen," mused Zeus.

"Seriously! You believe that?"

"Yes, the gods have their favourites. It's a way of competing with one another. Perhaps, the Mudges had displeased some god. They can be vindictive."

Ember giggled.

"You really managed to sound like you believe that."

She laughed again. It was a nice laugh, thought Zeus. Idly, he speculated whether it was a done thing here to have carnal relations with a family member. He suspected not, though he was unclear why this should be so. And strictly speaking, he was not exactly Ember's relative, just a passing visitor in the fellow's body. He was, all said and done, Zeus, King of the Gods, and as such, quite a catch.

And then the reality of his current form came back to him, not such a catch, perhaps. Like fishing for a leaping salmon and finding a shrivelled turd in your net!

As she was on the way out, rather idly, she inquired why he had taken her soap dish.

"I wanted it."

"Do you always just take something you like?"

He wondered whether this was a trick question. Why wouldn't you take something you wanted?

"You can have my old one. It does the same thing."

"I don't want your old one. I liked mine with the mermaid handles on the sides."

She looked more amused than angry.

"They're sirens," she was corrected.

The thought of Ember's vivacity, that mischievously ironic smile flitting across her lips, had aroused something in him. He remembered the tablets that Hermes had ordered for him.

23

Something rotten snapped beneath his foot, making him
catch his breath. The air was filled with a pungent smell,
so sweet that it enticed you to sniff it, which then turned
putrid as soon as it had entered your nostrils. Similarly,
beautiful notes tinkled all around, compelling you to
listen, and then turning into groans and howls that
reverberated more and more piercingly in your ears. Dark
shadows, indiscernible shapes flitted all around,
appearing to change form as you watched them, emitting
blasts of warmth before draping you in cold, dampness. It
was a place to give someone the creeps, and Hades did not
scare easily. He shivered.

The empusa was waiting for him. Judging by her
gossamer clothing, she seemed not to feel the coldness.
She was reclined across two branches, her skirt rising high
on one side, revealing her human leg. She shifted slightly,
letting it rise higher up her thigh. Was she trying to
seduce him?

He looked away.

"You know the terms; you have just the one shot
at it. We can't be drawing attention to ourselves like we
did in the old days. The world now is teeming with
mortals. We can't have them alerted to our presence,
searching for us and stealing our secrets. Some oaf, like
Prometheus, might just give them away. When you find

him, and are sure as to his identity, you know what to do."

She smiled, her lips parting to reveal her sharp little fangs. Very slowly, she moved her tongue around the full circle of her mouth. Hades turned away, so as to avoid falling into temptation. The act of lagneia with such beings might be enjoyable enough; it was what they did after mating that put him off.

24

Unfortunately, there was not a group of females like he had seen a few days earlier upstairs on a bus, raucous, on their way to pre-drinks at a hen party. Today he could only hear a group of rowdy schoolkids upstairs, so he went to the back downstairs. There were two hefty-looking women sitting with their shopping in the seats there, a little past their prime, he suspected, but then who was Mudge to be fussy?

He had done as Hermes had told him, taking the tablet one hour before he was anticipating an outcome. For good measure he had taken two additional tablets.

He smiled at the women. They ignored him. And then they noticed the large bulge in his tracksuit bottoms. One of the women seemed to be staring at it with fascination. Perhaps, she thought he must have stuffed something down there, such as a large courgette, or even a leek. She had a fulsome figure and wide, sturdy hips.

He winked at her.

Neither she nor her friend winked back. With a lot of rustling of bags, they moved to some empty seats further forward. This was disappointing.

Or maybe, it wasn't. Only a couple of nights ago he had watched a nature programme on his television set. It had struck him that females of species living down here on Earth often acted coy, forcing the male to perform elaborate acts of display before mating. Perhaps, this was what was going on here. After all, mortals were closer to animals than they were to gods. All Mudge had to do was to demonstrate that he was still a fit specimen, one who was worth mating with.

Zeus now moved along the bus, standing in the aisle parallel to the women. Somehow he managed not to tumble over when the bus braked. Holding a rail with one hand, he swayed forwards and backwards, then sideways in both directions, so as to best show off his protuberance. He attempted a small hop off the ground to demonstrate his agility.

One of the women now got to her feet, clearly impressed by his performance. She was the one with the wide hips. Now this was promising.

And then he felt it, a knee jabbed hard into his groin, and this time, he did topple to the floor.

25

While it may not have been quite as impressive as in its
heyday, the glory years of the Titanomachy, the war
between Zeus and his allies and the forces of Kronos, the
factory complex in Thrinacia remained mightily
impressive. If required, the production line could still
churn out fifty thunderbolts per hour, more than enough
for Zeus' needs in the event of another war. Such a
conflict would be excellent for business, countering the
demands made for spending cuts by some of those in
Zeus' circle.

A huge gateway at the entrance to the complex
was emblazoned with the names of its founders: Cyclopes
Brothers. Of course, the three original founders, Brontes,
Steropes and Arges, were not spotted around as often as
they had been during the golden era, but the complex still
stretched over many miles, producing a store of
thunderbolts that would be available to Zeus should he
ever need them.

Famously secretive, the factory enclosure was
almost impossible to penetrate. Wherever you looked,
orb-eyed giants strode, purposefully, between the
buildings. They were a tight-knot group, and it had taken
a long time for Hera to find one who could help infiltrate
the legendary security system put in place there. Such
were the perks, the flexible hours, allowance for

maternity and paternity leave, an excellent working environment with social areas and a gym – not to mention a very generous pension scheme, that it was almost impossible to alight upon an employee who was even slightly disgruntled.

Nonetheless, there was one. A descendant of Polyphemus, the black sheep of the family, Sid had felt dissatisfied for a while. His engineering qualification should have led to an office-based, white-collar role in the establishment, but for some reason, he was still pushing around heavy materials in carts. Convinced that it had nothing to do with the shifty, squinty look in his one eye, he decided, instead, that it was an outcome of discrimination that was based on the cavalier, and sometimes, anti-social behaviour of his great-grandfather, as recorded by that liar, Odysseus. Sid's resentment had been building for some years, and Hera's suggestion that it was a blatant breach of equal opportunities chimed precisely with his own suspicions.

The explosion that rocked the factory, triggered by the exposure of nuclear-tipped thunderbolts to highly flammable materials, halted production, entirely. Rumours were quickly disseminated that, given the legendary security systems, it had to have been an inside job for insurance purposes.

Only so confident in those systems were the owners and directors of Cyclopes Brothers, no one had ever bothered to take out insurance.

It would take decades to rebuild the factory, restoring it to its previous condition. Despite an inquest, no culprit could be uncovered and held accountable for the crime.

26

The two police officers at his front door were not smiling. It appeared that his antics in a public place had been reported, and cameras had recorded him boarding the bus.

"You do realise, sir, that indecent exposure is an offence, and one that can carry a stiff penalty."

Zeus weighed up the possibilities. Would Hermes have advised him to be polite at this juncture? Perhaps, he should offer them a glass of Ribena, or even, hot chocolate. Not with marshmallows, though. Or, perhaps, he should be firm.

"I don't think I actually exposed anything? As I understand things, that would mean making something visible by uncovering it."

He felt pleased with himself. Themis, herself, would have been impressed. He sounded almost like that guy – what was his name? – Solon of Athens.

The police officers seemed less practised in the art of disputation. They exchanged glances. It seemed a prescient moment to ram home his point.

"Of course, had I taken out my ithyphallos, the situation would be different."

They seemed lost for words.

"Indeed, in the circumstances, should you not be paying a visit to the female with the large hips, the fat orrhos who kneed me in my orjiks? Or does that not constitute assault?"

The officers hesitated.

"We're going to leave it with a warning on this occasion, Mr Mudge. But we'll come down hard on any inappropriate behaviour of this nature in the future."

It sounded limp. They knew it, and so did Zeus. He smiled, glad that he had not wasted good Ribena on them, let alone hot chocolate.

He felt emboldened. Going to the table as soon as they had left, he switched on the laptop that Hermes had brought him, feeling pleased with himself for remembering his password: Thunderbolt33.

Going straight to his *ok-Eros* account, he typed in an advert:

Local mortal; Newton Abbot area; possesses chariot; willing to travel – seeking partner(s) for a good time.

SURVIVING THE 21ST CENTURY: A HANDBOOK FOR PENSIONERS

ENTRY 4

IN GENERAL, MORTALS DO NOT APPEAR TO BE AWARE OF THE INTEREST TAKEN BY GODS IN THEIR LIVES. THEY SEEM TO PUT EVERYTHING THAT HAPPENS DOWN TO THEIR OWN CHOICES, OR MAYBE, TO LUCK OR ILL-LUCK, WHICH IS RATHER QUAINT AND MAKES THEM ALMOST ENDEARING.

SOME GENERAL ADVICE.

DO:

TRY TO SEE THE BEST IN OTHERS, EVEN THOUGH THIS CAN BE DIFFICULT;
GET A NIECE. ONE WITH A GOOD SMILE! THEY CAN BE GREAT FUN.
GET A CAT. THEY MAKE GOOD COMPANIONS.

DO NOT:

TAKE THE PHALLOS STIFFENING TABLETS BEFORE GOING OUT ON PUBLIC TRANSPORT.

27

Hera had anticipated an uncomfortable meeting. It was not easy to maintain an air of absolute confidence in front of the inner circle, those who had been involved in the plot from the outset. It was a much smaller group than the one that had gathered in the hidden cave, and included some of Hades' associates who had stayed away from that larger meeting, in case their presence put off some of their allies.

Hera and Hades sat alongside one another at the centre of the table. There was no need to conceal their closeness in this company. On Hera's other side, her son, Ares, gnawed on his nails. Next to him sat Porus, son of Metis and brother of Athena. Hecate, Thanatos and Hypnos huddled close at the other end of the table, each trying to inhabit the gloomiest slice of shadow. Nix was not present. She did not *do* meetings, she had told them. At the edge of room, barely noticeable and remaining absolutely still, sat the ferryman, Charon, a gaunt and silent figure. His demeanour suggested that he could slip away at any moment.

Impetuous one moment, cautious the next, Ares was today full of bluster. When would they move against Zeus? What difference did it make whether orjiks for brains was in a mortal form or in his true likeness? Either way, Ares would inflict on Zeus what Zeus had done to his own father, Kronos, and what, in turn, Kronos had done to *his* father, Uranus. He would castrate him, before cutting him up into tiny pieces, casting down the bits deep into the pit of the Earth.

Hera smiled. She was confident that this would happen as predicted. She glanced, quickly, at Hecate for confirmation. Hecate gave a nod, but not one that appeared to carry huge conviction.

As insurance, Hera continued, it was crucial to make sure that the mighty Titan, Atlas, was beside them. Of course, he would want to batter Zeus to the point of death before anyone else got to work on him.

"But, mother," Ares reminded her. "It must be me who is seen to dispatch the old goat. Otherwise, the authority of my rule could be disputed."

He could not have looked more peeved by the possibility that somebody else might usurp his destiny.

"Of course, dear," soothed Hera.

If Hades smirked, it was lost in the shadows that constantly surrounded him.

"Why was it taking so long for Atlas to join them?" inquired Porus.

Son of the Oceanid nymph, Metis, Porus had waited many centuries for revenge on the KoG, or as he called him, the *Lord of Lechers*, that *Tiny Wiggler at the end of his own phallos*. Porus' mother had helped Zeus to free his siblings from the belly of Kronos. It had been

Metis who had given him the potion that made Kronos vomit them up. As reward for her services, she had been forced into marriage with the debauched Zeus.

Subsequently, upon receiving a prophecy that she would bear a son still mightier than Zeus himself, he had devoured Metis whole during her first pregnancy. Somehow, she had survived inside him, giving birth to Porus' half-sister, Athena, inside his head. Athena had emerged fully formed and wearing armour, banging on the inside of the Wiggler's skull with her shield, until he had been forced to seek help, and have his head opened up to let her out.

For whatever perverse reason – Porus could only imagine that a spell had been cast on her - Athena seemed to have grown up fond of Zeus. It was left to him to exact revenge.

Hera considered the question. It was very frustrating, she now told Porus, but constructing acrow props seemed to be an extremely complex and difficult task, even for someone as smart as Hephaestus.

"You wouldn't believe all the stuff that is needed... reinforced beams, canopies, brace formwork, timber needles, strongboy brackets, forkheads..."

"Not to mention prop bracing couplers," added Hades, drily.

Porus clicked his tongue, impatiently, against the roof of his mouth. Was Hephaestus having second thoughts about the project, he wondered?

"Oh no!" exclaimed Hera. "He's one hundred per cent committed."

She could not afford the risk of doubts arising within the inner circle.

The meeting petered towards a rather inconclusive end. There was much whispering. Zeus may no longer be around, but was it not just a little premature to be going around referring to him as *orjiks for brains*? Until there was actual confirmation of his disposal, one had to be wary of consequences. Attendance at such meetings might be explained away in some kind of neutral light, but openly sneering at the KoG seemed needlessly reckless.

While they were dispersing, Porus skulked in the background. Only when everyone had gone, did he approach Hera. If Zeus really was hiding out among the mortals, he wanted to be the one to seek him out and kill him. Did he have her blessing to do so?

Hera avoided eye contact. What Porus did was up to him, though perhaps, it would be advisable not to mention the matter to Ares.

28

It was the first real bit of fun he had had in all the weeks since finding himself in this bolbiton body in a bolbiton town, where the closest thing to entertainment was going down to the market to watch cows plopping their bolbiton onto the ground and people stepping in it.

Why, he now demanded, had Bill never mentioned it before?

Bill shrugged. They had not been to the course for ages.

"Don't you remember?" Bill whined in his thin, raspy voice. "You said it had all got too noisy, Monty. Too many nasty people with fag breath, stubble and flat caps. Those were your words."

"Well, you should have dragged me here, anyway."

He sucked in the air, as if it might enable him to imbibe the atmosphere deep enough for it to linger in his lungs later back home. He wanted it held deep within: the big horses thundering down the straight, the noise from the crowd: gasps, sighs, exhortations.

"Shall we have – what did you say the word was? – a *flutter* on the next race?"

Zeus was still flushed with excitement. Much to Bill's distress, he had lost over two hundred pounds, but felt that it had been well worth it. Besides, he assured Bill, next time they would win. He had a system.

This was news to Bill. Monty had always been a very cautious gambler, quitting if he was just a few pounds ahead. Whatever had come over him? He would need to be on his guard to protect Monty from himself next time.

29

It was the second time in a fortnight that Ember had been stuck for someone to collect the children and take them home. Would he be an absolute pet?

The two children looked even glummer than the last time. Antonio sat cowering in the back, while Frida just glowered. Neither of them said a word during the journey home. When they got there, Antonio shot upstairs to his room, while Frida stood around, uncertainly.

"I should check on Ant," she said. "He's had a really bad day. I always know."

Zeus thought about the correct response. Should he just nod? For some reason, Frida's emotional switches left him feeling helplessly out of step.

"What will have happened at school?"

"The usual. People bullying him. Hiding his stuff. Pushing him over in the playground when no one is looking."

"Is there not a council at the school that resolves such matters? No apagoge or endeixis, the offenders denounced and dragged off for trial and punishment?"

If it had not been for the earnest look on his face, Frida would have been certain that her great-uncle was making light of her brother's misery with these made-up terms.

Teachers do not want the bother. They don't want anything in the open if it puts them in a bad light. When I mentioned it to Ant's teacher, she told me that it takes two to make an argument. As if *he*'s ever started up anything!"

"Does your mother not do anything about it?"

He shrunk under Frida's withering look.

"She doesn't know the half of it. Happy to accept it when they say nice things on his report. *Making good academic progress; improving in terms of social integration; making friends.* Friends! He's got one friend, Daniel, who's got cerebral palsy, and gets bullied even more than Ant! It's so funny, isn't it, to write *Spaz*, *Mong* and *Retard* on all his books? But of course, there's no problem, because there is all that paperwork to prove that the management of the school has put in place anti-bullying and anti-discrimination policies!"

Frida looked so ferocious that Zeus was lost for words. Then her face seemed to crumple a bit. She turned away, gathering herself.

"Mum has two modes. If she knew what was going on, she would either go in and batter Ant's teacher, along with the parents of all the children who are so horrid, or she would tell Ant not to worry; after all, Gramsci also suffered years of abuse in Mussolini's prisons and it led to so much *seminal, radical* thinking. Those are her words, not mine, and she forgets that

Gramsci died within a week of his release. Either way, Mum would only make things worse."

Zeus was thinking that there was something rather wonderfully fierce about girl children, and once again, he was reminded of his own daughters, Athena and Artemis.

"Shall I make the hot chocolate," he suggested, "while you go upstairs to check on your brother?"

It was so out of character, this sudden mellowness. Just as well no other deity had been there to overhear it! They might think he was going soft.

Another first! Frida roaring with laughter, so much that some of the hot chocolate was snorted out of her nose. Even Antonio was grinning.

"You like it?"

"It's terrible."

Zeus looked hurt.

"I thought you enjoyed hot chocolate."

"How many spoons did you put in?"

Zeus shrugged.

"And all those marshmallows! Wherever did you find them all?"

She rolled onto the floor, spluttering with mirth. Such childishness was totally out of character. Her brother imitated her. Zeus tried to put on a stern face.

"I did my best."

"Your *best*!"

They were both convulsed and rolling around again.

"Well, I'm drinking mine and then I'll drink both your mugs if you don't want them."

He waited for them to pull themselves together. They all took a few sips, Frida and Antonio's faces creasing into all kinds of hobgoblin beams and grimaces. Antonio whispered something to his sister.

"He would like to show you his room," announced Frida. "He wants you to see his toys and games. And by the way, from now on, he wants you to call him Ant, like I do."

Zeus followed them upstairs, peering at all the knick-knacks. He pushed the toy cars along the carpet, imitating the motions of the boy. He inspected the model figures, like a general at a military parade, showing particular interest in the superheroes.

Frida's room was a little disappointing by comparison. It was filled with shelves with books on. Book after book, since she had been a small child. She kept them all.

"I didn't know there were so many books in the world," marvelled Zeus.

"Did you not have books at home when you were growing up?"

Zeus shook his head.

"Not a single one. There was Cadmus, I suppose. He was a good storyteller, but he lived a long way away. When he started with his stories, everyone thought he'd turned from being heroic into a bit of a... I guess you'd say, wuss."

Frida could not have looked more horrified.

"Did your parents not read stories to you when you were little?"

"My parents! My mother was too busy hiding from my father. As for my father, he was not exactly a reader himself. Too busy digesting... other things. Why don't you read us something? That would be nice."

He went and picked out a picture book from her shelf. If her brother had not already settled down on one of the beanbags, thumb in mouth, she would have certainly refused. Rather creakily, Zeus sat down on the adjoining beanbag.

Blushing, Frida settled down on the bed and began reading, holding up the pictures before each page.

NOT NOW, BERNARD

"Hello, Dad," said Bernard,

"Not now, Bernard," said his father.

"Hello, Mum," said Bernard,

"Not now, Bernard," said his mother.

"There's a monster in the garden, and it's going to eat me," said Bernard.

"Not now, Bernard," said his mother...

Zeus was enthralled by the story. When she had finished it, he asked for the book, studying the pictures. He demanded to know how Bernard's parents never noticed anything, not even Bernard getting eaten by the monster. He was most indignant that the monster had come into the house, causing havoc, without Bernard's parents even looking at it once. It appalled him that it got fed and sent to bed, becoming 'Bernard', despite its protests that it was a monster.

While Frida assured him that it was just a *story*, Zeus was reflecting on his relationship with his own parents, then with his children, and finally, he thought about his situation now.

"Another story," demanded Ant.

"Just one more, then, but I choose this time."

Frida took down another book, *The Little Prince* by Antoine de Saint-Exupéry. Once again, Zeus was enthralled by the Little Prince, alone in a desert, searching for friendship. He thought a lot about the characters: the snake who offered to take him home; the little flower he had abandoned, convinced its thorns would protect it from the tigers. Above all, he turned over and over in his mind the words of the fox, instructing the Little Prince that he could not just be tamed and become a friend, instantly; the child would need to sit a little closer to him day by day. Zeus closed his eyes, considering the matter.

When Ember returned, Frida was downstairs cooking. She went upstairs to find Antonio resting on a beanbag, his head against Zeus' shoulder. They were both asleep. She took a picture on her phone, before awakening them.

31

Everyone seemed to be talking about the explosion in the factory owned by the Cyclopes Brothers, the same chatter in all her salons. This was interesting, though also perturbing. Here in the salon at the Rock of Unburied Souls, it usually took time for things to filter down, often leaving customers a bit out of touch with the current news. Psecas always found it rather sweet that they would get excited about the very *latest* hairstyle, not realising that, actually, it had already been around for a century or so.

The conversations now were exactly as in her other branches.

"They say that Cyclopes Bros and Co. caused it themselves. Quite funny when you think that they had failed to send in the insurance paperwork first."

"I heard sabotage, but don't let on you heard it from me. All part of Project Z-R."

"Project Z-R?"

"Zeus Removal. I happen to be friendly with a nymph who is in a relationship with a certain someone who goes to their meetings. I can't name names, you understand."

"I heard that Hera was involved."

"You don't say!"

"Yes, along with You Know Who... Hades. Of course, he got the short end of the stick when it came to all the transactions after the Titanomachy. Then having to climb down and compromise after Zeus had all but promised him Persephone. Having to settle for part ownership and all that. Well, it's payback day, isn't it?"

Psecas considered the implications for her business? If Zeus' days were, indeed, numbered, was it not likely that there would be a boom, new styles to fit in with a brand new epoch? What if he came back and defeated the conspirators? In that case, she guessed – and usually, Psecas' guesses were pretty on the mark – it was likely that the styles of Zeus' golden era would come back in. Definitely not the Hera look. That would be out for millennia.

But what about during a war? Did people go to their hairdresser more often, a form of reassurance, a semblance of normality in a brutal, unstable universe, or did they avoid the risk of being hit by a stray thunderbolt – or just emerging with a hairstyle preferred by supporters of the losing side?

It was a conundrum.

32

Frida seemed to be returning home from school with increasing amounts of homework, and she would set out her books on the table almost as soon as they got back, despite her great uncle's advice.

"I really don't know why you are bothering about it, Frida. If they can't teach you all they want to during your lessons, it's hardly your fault."

She persisted, nevertheless, and while she was doing it, Zeus would follow her younger brother upstairs to play video games. At one point, while they were in the middle of a particularly enthralling game based on Greek legends, he could not desist from making an observation:

"You do know, Ant, the game only tells you part of the story."

The boy paused, waiting for Zeus to explain more. By the time Frida came up with hot chocolate, they were sprawled on the beanbags, her brother listening, intently, to an account of the five races of man.

"The first was the golden race, created by the Titans in the days of Kronos. They never experienced hard toil, sickness or death. When they got very old, they just fell into a peaceful sleep, reawakening as benevolent daimones, spirits helping all living things around them, warding off all evil.

Next came the silver race, made by the Olympian gods. They had to be removed on account of their pride, which was so overweening that they refused to honour their creators. They were transformed into underworld spirits, known as the Blessed Ones.

The final three races were fashioned by Zeus, himself. The third was the bronze race. They were brave and fierce, like myself, perpetually, seeking war to embellish their honour. Sadly, they could never stop, consuming themselves in their violence. They sank in broken glory, deep into the ground. Still, they wander, trapped within the confines of the vast House of Decay, the dark realm ruled by Hades.

The fourth age, in many ways my favourites, was that of heroes and demi-gods who fought and perished at Troy and Thebes. Of course, you are wondering where they ended up. Mainly, you will find them at the end of the Earth, on the Isles of the Blessed.

The present men of Earth are the fifth, an iron race born to hard work and suffering, destined to pass away as its predecessors did. You belong to them."

"You mean, we," chirped Frida.

"Yes... we," said Zeus, faltering only slightly. "We were too engrossed to hear you come up the stairs."

It became a pattern each time they got home: Frida completing her homework, while Zeus went upstairs with her brother, telling him stories, largely about his own exploits, but also a few about those of other gods. Sometimes, Frida would pop up, finding herself having to admonish her great-uncle for recounting things in inappropriate ways.

"You see the gods have always had their favourites. Aphrodite was really partial to the Trojan prince, Paris, mainly, because he had once declared her in a contest to be even prettier than Hera or Athena, and, trust me, they are all what you might call *hot chicks!* Well, the other two were hardly likely to back Troy after that, and war with Greece broke out pretty fast, as soon as Aphrodite gave Helen to Paris as a gift, causing her to feel such passion for him that she couldn't wait to shag him..."

"Uncle Monty!"

"What?"

Zeus looked surprised by the interruption. Nor could he interpret the piercing look that Frida was giving him.

"What?"

"Nothing. Just drink your hot chocolate before it goes cold."

33

Can you get back soon? I need you here for something desperately important.

It had taken a little time to work out how to send a text message when Hermes was not answering his calls, but Zeus was nothing if not resourceful. After a while, a message was pinged back:

Quite busy at the moment. If you recall, I got sent to the middle of nowhere to deliver a Get Well card 😔
And it's bloody brass monkeys! 😨
BTW - it may come as a total surprise to you, but I am frequently out of range. The coverage here is terrible, so it takes a while to pick up calls.
Nice of you to ask how I am!
LOL

This message took a bit of working out. Finally, Zeus composed a second text message:

Dear Lol,
I thought this was Hermes' number. If you see him, can you pass on my message. Tell him it's urgent. Zeus

It was very frustrating, hanging around, just waiting for Hermes to show up. Zeus had to busy himself as best he could. He offered to do school collections on a daily basis, even when he was not needed. And although there was another week to go before another event at the racecourse, he went out with Bill to play Bingo. This was less exciting than the racecourse, but at least, it was a diversion.

When Hermes did appear, he looked tired and gaunt.

"Is everything OK? Have you seen something? An empusa? I heard... only a rumour..."

His voice dropped to a whisper.

"Only a rumour..."

He was shivering. Zeus worried that he might not be able to keep steady.

"Shall I make a hot chocolate?"

"For you?"

"For both of us. I'll even put in some... a marshmallow for you."

Zeus returned a few minutes later. There were about ten marshmallows in his mug, but just the one in Hermes'.

"You may not like them. It would be a waste."

When Hermes looked as if he had warmed up, Zeus spoke again.

"I need you to order me something on the laptop machine."

Hermes spluttered out some of his drink back into the mug.

"You said it was of desperate importance!"

"And so it is. Antonio – Ant, my great-nephew – has this marvellous thing, called an Xbox. You can play games on it. There is a particularly wonderful game, called *Immortals Fenyx Rising*. Apparently, it used to be called *Gods and Monsters*. You unlock the Hall of Gods, then you travel anywhere. You can ride on a stag or fly on the wings of Daedalus, if you like. You have to be careful not to fall into the Vaults of Tartarus, of course. You even get to use Aphrodite's Beauty Chair. You fight minotaurs and cyclopes. I'm in the game, of course, as are lots of other gods. Even you are in it, Hermes. You're disguised as a youthful and mysterious stranger. At the end, we have to kill Typhon. It's such fun. Kick-ass!"

"You dragged me back for this. I raced through hail and howling winds for you to get me to order a... game?"

"And did I say, there are these great sound effects? And funniest of all – this is going to kill you, Hermes – Ares has been transformed into a rooster. A rooster! The smug, little malaka would just love that!"

Zeus was smiling, eagerly. Could Hermes order his Xbox now, making sure he also included that game in the package. It would be utterly catastrophic if they had sold out.

"Utterly," agreed Hermes.

34

Was it really such a big deal? So, he had missed Frida's birthday. It was difficult to understand why Ember was so indignant. She was now fumbling in her bag, pulling out a card.

"Just sign it."

She pushed it over the table, along with a pen. He began to scribble his name on the card, just remembering in time to change it.

"Reginald Montgomery Mudge! Just that? Your full name! Is that meant to be funny? And why is there a Z crossed out in front of it?"

He looked perplexed. What exactly did she want of him?

"For some reason – I have no idea what that could be – Frida has decided that she likes you. And all you can do is write out your name as if for some legal document, with no message."

Still he looked blank.

"No *To Frida, with love* – or something like that?"

He picked up the pen, and added *To Frida, with love*.

For some reason, his niece still did not look satisfied. It might have been a small courtesy, she suggested, if he had offered to pay for the card. A token gift would have been nicer still.

Zeus looked around the room. Rising to his feet, he pottered over to a sideboard, returning with a small object, and holding it out, obligingly.

"A pepper cellar! Really?"

"It's OK; I don't need it. I only use the salt one."

Now she was rolling her eyes at him. Whatever was wrong with the female mortal?

"I suppose you think you are a real comedian."

She got up to leave, pausing at the door.

"There's something else."

She hesitated.

"I've met someone."

Her expression had changed, abruptly. Ember's face was suffused in a glow that he found rather fetching. Zeus wondered how she expected him to respond to this. He met people every day; had she been expecting him to report it to her?

"We're in a... well... you know... relationship... taking it step by step... seeing how things go."

"Agh. You mean you're shagging someone? Good idea."

She looked as if she had just been slapped in the face.

"Uncle Monty – I'm confiding in you. I expected... well, something more sensitive. And maybe, a little less crude."

"Point taken," said Zeus. "Does he have a big phallos?"

"Uncle Monty! Do you mind? Anyway, it's a she. Her name is Mo. It's my first relationship – you know... intimate relationship with another woman."

Zeus grinned.

"Nothing wrong with it. Aphrodite has always found women attractive. Mind you, she'll go for anyone or anything. It can have testicles or tentacles, for all she cares."

"Afro who?"

"Oh, just someone I used to know."

"Well, the thing is, we don't know how long we have together as Mo has recently been diagnosed with cancer. She had to have her left leg amputated."

"That's terrible. Couldn't you find a healthy woman?"

Ember gaped at him.

"Just when everyone was beginning to think that you were turning into a nice person."

"Apologies. I am learning each day."

Was that really *him* speaking? It was the most humble thing he had ever said, a shock to hear those words come out.

And he looked genuinely remorseful. She remained in the doorway, frozen in the act of leaving, studying his face. He was staring at the carpet, seemingly, deep in thought.

"I think Frida's all right about it, but Antonio seems to have taken a strong dislike to Mo. I have no idea why."

Zeus frowned. That *was* a problem, he agreed. Ant needed to be surrounded by people he trusted.

"He's very good in the role of Fenyx?"

Ember looked blank.

"In *Immortals Fenyx Rising.*"

What did that have to do with anything? Ember wondered whether Uncle Monty was actually taking things in. Perhaps, it had been a mistake to mention anything to him.

"The fact is, he appears to have taken a real shine to you. Perhaps, if you had a word with him. Or maybe, it would be best if you met Mo yourself. Then you could reassure him. I'm a bit tied up this coming weekend. Are you free the following weekend? Saturday night, maybe?"

He did not like to admit that he had been planning to spend his weekends playing on his Xbox. He would check in his diary, he told her. It was an expression he had heard someone use in a TV programme he had watched.

"Would around seven-ish suit you? That's assuming it fits in with your busy schedule, of course. I'll call to remind you at the end of next week."

For a while he just continued to stare at the doorway. A woman with only one leg! Sick with an incurable disease! So much misery in this world, he thought, with just a pang of guilt. After all, what had he done exactly to stop Pandora from opening that box? Had he not even commissioned Hephaestus to create Pandora, an act of revenge against Prometheus? He had hardly thought about it since, but right now, it struck him as more like the act of a petty tyrant than a great god.

35

He was in the midst of fighting the Chimera when there was a knock on the door.

"What the bineo!" he cursed.

He ignored it, waiting for the unwanted visitor to go away. The letter box was pushed open.

"Yoo-hoo! Monty!"

It was his neighbour, the old lady, Tucker. She was stooped low, attempting to peer in.

"Monty! I know you're there. I can see your slippers."

He stayed silent.

"And your ankles just above the slippers."

He sighed.

She was standing straight by the time he answered, holding out a plate.

"I made some jam tarts. A little thank you for finding Sir Cecil."

"*Sir* Cecil?"

"I started to call him that because of all the supercilious looks he was giving me."

He took the plate from her hand, and then remembered his manners.

"Thank you."

"I thought we might..."

She looked hurt.

"Don't worry. I'll return your plate."

He swung the front door closed, returning to the table. He tried to concentrate on the Chimera, but it was not easy. She was still standing there outside the door. He could see her silhouette through the frosted glass. Cursing, he got to his feet again.

"I thought we might share them and have a cup of tea together. A little chat."

He pulled a face.

"I don't drink tea. I drink hot chocolate."

"Hot chocolate would be nice."

Farts of Boreas! Unless he could get rid of her quickly – and by the way that she had been hanging around outside, this seemed unlikely, it would mean another night off the Xbox. Somewhat gracelessly, he allowed his neighbour to step inside. Just his luck to be stuck with this old grason for an evening!

He could not deny that the jam tarts were good, though. He ate five in quick succession.

"Monty Mudge," she said, sternly. "Something gives me the impression that you are not eating, properly. I'll tell you what. Saturday night, I'll cook you a proper meal. Then we can watch something. Do you like *I'm a Celebrity?*"

The impression she got from Zeus' face was that he did not.

"Never mind. We can always choose something off BBC i-player. Sir Cecil will be delighted to see you again."

36

The sound of hammering was relentless. Heat, smoke, noise! Each time he visited – which was not all that often, in truth – Hermes found himself wondering what sort of being would choose to work in such an environment. And not just work there! Inhabit the place at all hours.

On a crate beside him, there was some food – large amounts crammed, clumsily, in pitta bread, so that a lunch-break did not need to interrupt the working day.

Hermes was pretty sure that Hephaestus was aware of his presence, and was deliberately taking his time over a welding job. It could not be denied that Hephaestus was highly skilled. It occurred to Hermes that he simply could not resist the temptation to show off these skills once again to an audience.

When, finally, Hephaestus lumbered over, he ignored the friendly grin on the face of his visitor.

"You know, sometimes, I think we have a lot in common."

"Do we?"

Hermes considered the matter. Perhaps, it had not been the most strategic opening line. In actuality, he suspected that, other than names that began with the same letter, as well as a shared parent, they had very little in common. Perhaps, they were more like opposites. He was bright, chatty, easy in company, whereas Hephaestus was... well, some folk might have called him unsociable, not to say, dour – and that was, probably, in his more affable moments.

Hermes decided to change tack.

"We're brothers."

"Half-brothers," came the reminder.

Perhaps, there was no point in exchanging pleasantries.

"I've come about a job."

Hephaestus looked sceptical.

"My chariot. It could do with some modification to augment its speed."

A snorting sound popped out of Hephaestus' mouth. It seemed to Hermes that it came from somewhere much deeper, a sneer, a deep aversion, maybe, towards himself. Perhaps, he had not shown sufficient gratitude for the winged helmet and sandals that his half-brother had made him all those millennia ago. As he recalled, the sandals had chafed for quite a while. Perhaps, that had been deliberate.

"I thought you already drove the fastest chariot in the Universe."

Was Hephaestus mocking him?

"Things can always benefit from a boost, some new accessory, perhaps."

"Such as go-faster stripes?"

Hermes wondered when his brother had developed such a sense of humour. He began to think he preferred him in his surly, silent incarnation.

"Funny thing, but only recently, something seemed to be keeping up with me."

Hephaestus hid a look of satisfaction.

"I'm not sure our father would approve of some other vehicle being out there as fast as my own."

Hephaestus appeared to chew on the thought, then, without a word, rose to his feet and resumed his work. He seemed to be flattening out a piece of metal. Perhaps, he was picturing it as the visitor he was now doing his best to ignore. Whatever, it was difficult not to admire the smooth, if brutal, precision of his blows. Again and again, his muscles flexed in time with the fall of his arm. And then something altogether gentler, almost a caress, as the object was shaped – and was that a low croon, audible only to someone with preternatural hearing?

Hermes cleared his throat.

"As I was saying..."

"If I were you, I might be hoping that your father doesn't come back too soon."

The comment caught Hermes off-guard.

"Why's that?"

Hephaestus made Hermes wait for an answer. He wandered away to fetch another tool, before continuing in a casual voice.

"Because Hera arranged for your voice to be recorded."

"Really?"

This was news.

From the corner of his eye, Hephaestus took great satisfaction in watching his half-brother gulp with alarm before attempting to conceal his surprise.

"Yes, I thought you had not noticed that sneak Echo's presence in the shadows. I watch, you see, while others blather on. Apparently, she's been testing some apparatus she hopes to market. Says it will make her a fortune; every home will want one. It will put her up there with Midas, Croesus, even Tyche, though what she will do with it I haven't a clue. Well, her device just so happened to capture you swearing allegiance to Hera."

Not too bad, then. Zeus would approve of his sense of filial duty, and was sure to believe, in any event, that Hermes had been forced into the conspiracy.

"And Hades."

Hermes took a few moments to digest this information.

"Well, maybe, we've both betrayed others, and been betrayed."

"Have we?"

This tendency to bounce back questions was beginning to be irritating.

"I suppose you'll be well looked after," Hermes remarked, sourly, "if the project goes to plan, and the conspirators comes out on top. I mean all those acrow props, the speeded-up vehicle..."

Hephaestus did not bat an eyelid.

"And there was me thinking you detested Hades."

Hephaestus shrugged.

"What difference does it make to me who wins? Hades? Zeus? I've no reason to like either of them."

"But you'll get your reward, won't you? Maybe the keys to the rebuilt Cyclopes Brothers factory in Thrinacia."

"I'm quite content just here with my forge and workshop."

Not even out of entrepreneurship! It was almost impossible to spot a motive in the collusion.

"Don't you care about anyone else? Anything?"

"I look after myself. It's what I've always done."

After he had departed, Hermes reflected on how different they were. While he craved fellowship, witty interaction, bonhomie, it struck him that his half-brother did not like any company other than his own. Perhaps, he did not even enjoy that.

37

Soporific farts of Hypnos! Had there ever been a duller female?

It had begun, not unpromisingly, with some food, plenty of treats for a sweet tooth. He should have left directly after that.

Afterwards, Sir Cecil had jumped up into his lap, snuggling down to be stroked. Lily Tucker had watched, pensively.

"Funny, really. He doesn't usually like men. And until the other day, when he was in your house, he'd always avoided you. Had you not noticed him scuttling away whenever you came out?"

Zeus said that he had not.

He continued rubbing Sir Cecil's thin skull, scratching him under the chin. Perhaps, Sir Cecil sensed that he was not the old Monty Mudge.

"Do you recognise me?" he whispered.

Sir Cecil neither answered in the affirmative nor denied the suggestion.

The alarming thought came to mind that this was not a cat, but something much more dangerous, an empusa.

"Are you here to kill me?" he now whispered.

The cat just purred, loudly.

A much more pleasant thought occurred to him. Perhaps, this might be someone familiar. One of his daughters? Athena had always liked cats, and Artemis, had been seen accompanied by large cats while hunting. It was even said that she was able to transform herself into one, which would not have surprised him in the least. He, himself, had often metamorphosed into animals, usually, as a prelude to some act of seduction.

He tried whispering the names of his daughters, but if one of them was posing as the animal, she did not let on.

Surely, if this were really one of his daughters, he would be able to recognise her. But then, why would he? It's not as if he had ever had much to do with them.

He had noticed how much the mortals seemed to worry about their children. It had struck him as rather weird the way they peered after them when dropping them off at school, right till the moment they entered the school building, even though the children did not glance back once. Then the anxious faces at collection time when other children appeared before their own child emerged. After all, someone had to be the first out, and someone else the last. And then there was the constant apprehension of mishaps or ailments.

Did every living creature down here worry so much about its offspring? Did flowers bend to try to check how their seeds were doing in the adjoining field or garden? Was it because mortal things were so fragile? An existence spent on constant tenterhooks!

Up there on Olympus you just had children. Then that was sort of it. They looked after themselves. After a while, it was easy to forget they even were your children. Many times he had been in the company of young gods and goddesses and wondered which were his!

Of course, maybe, it was different for Hera. He thought of her, fondly, wishing he could go and pick some flowers for her right now. Like those nice purple and white ones he had spotted this morning. He would make them into a daisy chain, placing them round her neck, and they would lie together in a meadow. How he missed her! How she must be worrying about him!

His reverie was interrupted by the blaring of the television set. Sir Cecil stirred, too. After staring at it, disdainfully, for a moment, the animal jumped off his knee, wandering away with a rather baleful expression towards the cat-flap. Clearly, he had higher standards than his owner.

Mrs Tucker did not watch the programmes he liked. But worse was to follow! She spent an age fishing out old photograph albums, showing him pictures of, it seemed, every person she had ever met. Who gave a flying bineo about a single one of them? Most of them were deceased, which really did seem to be a favourite pastime among mortals. Probably, thought Zeus, most of them had bored themselves to such an extent that they just expired.

"It was nice spending some time together," said Lily as he got up to leave.

He glowered.

"Nicer for you than for me."

Lily Tucker was beyond dull, a stadium of stodge on a mountain of monotony in a galaxy of goo. She would need to be avoided, at all cost in the future.

38

Two visits in a single day! He could go months without seeing anyone – which, incidentally, suited him just fine. How could he be expected to keep up with his assignments with all these interruptions?

The figure standing in the doorway was huge, and Hephaestus himself was an imposing figure – or would have been had he been able to stand up straight. This fellow towered over him, and despite the poor light, he shimmered, covered, as he was, in gold and silver. Rings, necklaces, bangles – almost every part of his head and body boasted some adornment.

"Uncle Poseidon."

It was not said with any enthusiasm, or even in greeting. He might have been making a mental note of just another item from his toolbox.

His uncle beamed at him.

"Long time no see. How's it hanging, bro?"

There was not a flicker from Hephaestus. How cringey when older family members thought it was cool to address younger relatives in what they thought was the *lingo* amongst those more youthful.

"Nothing's hanging, *unc*, and I'm your *neph*, not your *bro*."

His uncle just grinned more.

As the small talk seemed to be over, Hephaestus nodded, wandering back to his workbench. His uncle followed him.

"I wondered if you could sort this out first."

He was holding out his trident. Hephaestus gasped, reaching out with diffidence to touch it, inspecting the damage, closely. Forged by the Cyclopes Brothers, it was supposed to be unbendable. How many rocks had Poseidon struck with this flawless weapon without the slightest dent? How many giants had he struck down? Was this not the very instrument he had used to affix the island of Delos to the sea floor? However had he managed to get it bent like this?

"It's the malaka ships they build these days," his uncle was explaining. "In the old days a couple of big waves would suffice to sink them, but they seem to be building them of ever stronger stuff. As if they're getting assistance."

He cast a suspicious glance at his nephew, but could not detect any awkwardness.

"Nothing's how it used to be. The murky waters. The lack of fish – which is a problem, by the way, in a kingdom of pescatarians. Not to mention, my beautiful gardens, my coral reefs: you should see the state of them! And now this thing with my trident. I was just banging on the hull of a boat when I felt something give."

Hephaestus ran a finger along it, wonderingly. It really was a beautiful piece of craftsmanship; heart-breaking that it could have been blemished. Before Poseidon could complain, he strolled to his furnace, placing the end with the slight kink close to the heat, as delicately as a mother might place a baby in its crib. Gentle sounds were emitted from the back of his throat, as if in reassurance to the object.

Withdrawing it a few times, and testing it gently, he was finally, satisfied. Placing it on a large anvil, he moved a torch backwards and forwards across it, crooning and mumbling encouragement. If his visitor commented on the operation, Hephaestus did not notice; his entire attention was fixed on the trident.

Selecting a smooth face hammer from several on a shelf, he began to tap it gently. He placed his ear close to it, as if listening to a being that spoke only to him. He nodded, aiming his blows a fraction further along the trident, tapping a little more firmly. Then a sigh that only he heard.

He nodded with satisfaction, signalling to his uncle that he should allow it to cool before picking it up.

"I wondered whether my brother had found some way of cursing it."

"Hades?"

"Why would *he* be interested? The other one. Your father. He's always had his eye on it. Full of envy."

Hephaestus looked doubtful. Had Zeus not had enough possessions of his own? They had shared things out, after all.

"Well," he said, finally, "as he is off the scene, there is a position going."

"KoG! Why ever would I want that?"

The expression on his uncle's face suggested that the disdain was genuine. Nevertheless, he seemed to mull over the idea.

"A piece of the action, maybe. Obviously, I had been thinking of diversifying, what with all the difficulties in my own kingdom, but really, who'd want to be in charge of that mob? Not that there aren't opportunities. I mean, the little bro could have been in on a slice of everything. He may have inherited a massive pair of orjiks, but I got the acumen."

Hephaestus watched him depart. It struck him that his uncle was not quite so ebullient as he had remembered him. Maybe, his infuriating jauntiness was just an act. All in all, he had a sense of things being out-of-joint. Wherever you looked, there were plots being brewed, petty jealousies, disaffection, perhaps, just boredom. And unlike Poseidon's trident, he could not repair it.

Not that he would have wanted to.

39

It was still dark when he sat up in bed, a throbbing pain in his mouth that made him moan with pain. Of course, he realised, immediately, what was happening. There was only one rational explanation: myrmidons!

The seduction of Eurymedousa had been a huge mistake for several reasons. A princess, the wife of – well, who could even recall the name of the fellow? – she was an absolute stunner, and, as such, fair game for the KoG. But whatever had he been thinking when choosing such a form for the act of seduction? An ant! Such a transformation had seemed unusual and witty at the time, but for the life of him, he could never remember, afterwards, what exactly had been so amusing. Not to mention the fact that it had been a most impractical form to select when embarking on coitus.

The second mistake had been to tell Hera about it later, thinking she would find it hilarious. Far from it. She had flown into the most spectacular rage, which lasted for days, inflamed still further when she heard about an announcement by the inhabitants of Aegina. Their island was to be renamed in honour of Eurymedousa, the princess who had enticed such a distinguished suitor.

The rest was a bit fuzzy, but Zeus recalled that it had all ended rather convivially, with a pleasant holiday rapprochement between himself and Hera on the island of Samos, a particular favourite for her as the place of her birth. As for the inhabitants of Aegina, they had all been transmuted into ants. Particularly fierce ones, as he remembered. The ancestors of myrmidons!

Which was clearly the explanation for what was going on right now. The culprit must be someone still bearing a grudge about the matter, perhaps one of Hera's retinue, for surely, his wife, herself, would never wish to harm him. Having discovered his whereabouts, he or she had sent some agent to deposit a bunch of fire ants into his mouth while he was sleeping. When he discovered who it was, he would...

But this was unbearable. Clutching his jaw, he staggered out of bed towards the sink, filling it with cold water and plunging his head into it. Soaking a towel, he tried to wrap it tightly round his mouth.

Which was how Bill found him later that morning, sprawled across his settee, face down, groaning. Seizing the fudge bar, in the hope it would alleviate the pain, Zeus tore of the wrapper and rammed it into his mouth.

It did not help. Quite the reverse.

The matter was not resolved until Bill bundled him out of the house for an emergency visit to a local dentist. The afflicted patient was still screaming abuse when the dentist decided that a local anaesthetic would not suffice.

He did not show any gratitude when he came round, the pain having subsided. Nor did he thank Bill for taking him there and footing the bill for the emergency work.

40

"What shall we do?"

"We could slide down the waterfalls."

"We did that yesterday."

"Do you remember the time when Dionysus followed us and banged his head at the bottom?"

"OMG – it was the end! Hilarious. We all pissed ourselves."

"Served him right. He's too old to hang out with us, even if he is a laugh."

"Two-faced or what! You used to call him a DILF."

"More like a great-grand-DILF these days, and no way am I going there."

There was a whole bunch of them – a group who enjoyed having fun: Calypso, Pan, Hedone, Hermaphroditos, Iasion, Dysnomia, Eros, Anteros and the gang. The Kharites were there, too, of course, and had already divested themselves of almost all their clothing. Although not renowned for lively conversation, their incessant giggling provided still more of a feelgood factor.

"What about the beach?"

It seemed as good a suggestion as anything else.

They swam, played a few games, lay around, trying desperately to keep thinking of the next thing they might do.

"Shall we go for a ride on the winged donkeys?"

They were tethered nearby. Calypso was staring at a particularly grumpy one.

"I'm not sure I like the look of the one at the back. You see? With the grey tuft on his head."

Dysnomia, who was always great fun, still wilder than her mother, Eris, and loving nothing more than something riotous, now had an idea.

"Eros – if you fire your arrow up the orrhos of that winged donkey with the tuft, let's see what happens."

They all laughed.

For a while, they were in hysterics, watching the animal run around, casting moon eyes at anything before it. Then it wore off.

"The thing is we need something to happen. Something new."

"It *is* happening."

Calypso sounded quite definite on the matter.

"Any moment it's all going to start. Absolute pandemonium."

"Who are you backing?"

"Whichever side Ares is on. He's got a great body. Really hench."

There was a good deal of swooning, heavy sighs.

"Mmmm, super buff from head to toe!"

"Hot, hot, hot!"

"Strictly-speaking, Hephaestus is hotter."

Laughter.

"Ugh! You'd have to be so...ooo wasted to go there!"

41

By coincidence, Ares was working on his physique at that
very moment. For the coming war, he needed to be in
peak condition. The gym, run by Iapetus and Sons, was
the oldest and most prestigious of its kind on Olympus. It
was both amusing and salutary for Ares to check out the
original equipment. How basic could you get! No wonder
the primordial deities had been chucked out!

The gym had flourished, for a while, when Iapetus
was around. His son, Atlas, was steady while he was in
the zone, but seemed to be a dreamer with his head in the
skies much of the time. Prometheus, his brightest son, the
only one with ideas, seemed disinterested. Under his
other sons, Epimetheus and Menoetius, the business had
gone downhill after that.

However, taken over by an obscure investment
company, there had been a revival. The investors had
been canny to retain the original brand, purchasing post-
Titanomachy, state-of-the-art, equipment, which included
wall-to-wall mirrors, manufactured by the Narkissos
Daffodil Group, enabling clients to watch their every
movement.

Right now, Ares was admiring his bulging quads.
But was his gluteus maximus getting too... maximus? Did
that detract from the look of his thighs? He should do

some butt work, maybe: high-intensity interval training, squats, step-ups, dumbbell lifting and the like.

While he worked out, his mind was racing. Hades and his mother, Hera, could do all the dirty work. He would fight alongside them, not taking any huge risks, of course. It was the right moment. He could sense it from his buff head all the way down to his buff toes.

Even if he returned, his father, Zeus had become effete. He had let himself go to pot. When had anyone last seen *him* in a gym? His six-pack was a twelve-pack, and even that was being generous! As he paid no attention to his diet, he did not have a clue about cutting or bulking, and as a result, his macros were all over the place. He would need one of Hephaestus' acrow props to plank!

The guy may as well have had LOSER tattooed right across his forehead. Maybe, Ares should do that before chopping him up.

Once Zeus had been great, as had Ares' grandfather Kronos. Each had slaughtered his own father. Ares would be greater still; he would kill both parents. If his mother could not commit to his cause ahead of that of Hades, she deserved no less. Naturally, he would kill his Uncle Hades, too. He could throw in Uncle Poseidon, for good measure. If they wanted greatness, they would get great flesh-lumps of it.

Nevertheless, there would be insurance. He had already reached out to Erebus, primordial, formless, and,

unlike Hades, not motivated by malice. Erebus was...
indifferent. Yet, Ares had sensed that something within
him wanted to *be* again, wanted to *feel*. Erebus would be
quite happy to destroy Hades. He could have the entire
Underworld. What did Ares want with the gloomy place?

Just think of the panic in the salons of Psecas. He
thought of the nymph with distaste. Long ago, he had
taken a passing fancy to her when he had spotted her
tending Artemis. Who was *she* to reject the advances of a
god? Did she think she was too good for him?

Ares allowed himself to luxuriate in the image of
the forthcoming destruction of her premises. Why did
hair salons even need chandeliers? Why did they need
grand staircases, winding upwards? How pretentious! The
pointless vanity of hair stylists appearing at the same
moment at the top of each of them, timing it so as to
appear in view of the clients at exactly the same moment!
He pictured the stylists now, with their identical, pearly
smiles and choreographed movements, with everything
crashing down around them.

How Psecas would regret spurning him! He could
see her – along with all her feather-brained customers,
running hither and thither in panic as the building around
them sank into oblivion!

For that sight alone, it would be worth sealing a
pact with Erebus. And if more was needed for a deal to be

struck, let Erebus have part of Poseidon's kingdom, too. Poseidon could like it or lump it.

Ares now imagined Erebus rising from his void to inhabit the great oceans, terrible waves swelling higher and higher, devouring the land below. He pictured the terror on the faces of the mortals – those insects who made sacrifices to him, offerings, he could sense, without real warmth or affection. He imagined their flailing limbs as dark seas engulfed them. It was all they deserved.

And when Erebus' hunger for carnage was sated, he would return to the shadows, where he belonged.

Ares' mind turned to all the wondrous things that would then be his. He would not be like his puny father, having to cede portions out to his brothers. How pathetic! He would be omnipotent, the sole ruler of all. No snooty brat of a hairdresser would ever have the nerve to turn him down again.

42

In actual fact, Ares could have had no conception of the state Zeus was in at that moment. By one of those odd coincidences occasionally thrown up by the Cosmos, the great ruler of the gods was staring upwards, his head tilted at a south-easterly angle, in the very direction of Mount Olympus. Why – he might even have been squinting, directly, towards the Iapetus and Sons gym in the dazzling distance!

The sequence of events that had brought him there had begun with a shimmering dawn, during which Helios, having awakened in a state of seeming disarray, had driven his chariot across the sky in such a haphazard fashion as to cause the rays to fall with their greatest radiance across a small street in the undistinguished town of Newton Abbot. Zeus had been luxuriating in the warmth for a good hour after waking up. Finally, dragging himself out of bed and tottering towards his bedroom window, he had glanced through the curtains to spy a rather enticing, young neighbour, who lived on the other side of the road. He had asked Mrs Tucker about her, previously, and the old lady thought the woman's name might be Siena, but was not sure. Zeus had noticed 'Siena' on several occasions, and been captivated by the impression that she seemed to possess only very low-cut tops. And here she was, chatting with a friend, only

slightly less alluring and clad in similarly revealing attire.
The two nymphs had only paused from conversation to
stare at a young man, walking down the street. The fellow
was nothing special, thought Zeus, although he could not
help but register that he did possess what was referred to
down here as a *six-pack*. As the man was not wearing a
shirt, it was annoyingly easy to spot.

He felt a sudden pang of jealousy. What right did
this upstart have to youth when *he*, Zeus, was stuck in
such ramshackle form? If only Hermes had been here
right now, there might have been some means of worming
his way into the chassis of this passing rival. How
satisfying it would be to see the cocky youth's expression
on finding himself inside Mudge's body! Zeus pictured
him peering down into his pyjama bottoms at that useless
piece of dangly string. The thought made him cackle
aloud.

Only Hermes was not here. He would need to
improvise in the meantime. Withdrawing into his
bathroom, Zeus removed his pyjama top and studied
himself in the mirror. It was difficult to deny that, by
comparison, Mudge's torso left much to be desired. But if
he leaned back far enough, his saggy moobs were less
obvious, and if he threw his head back at the same time,
the wrinkles in his neck were pulled taut.

He might not quite look like the young man the
two ravishing nymphs had been ogling, but he was getting

closer. Besides, surely even in his Mudge form, something of his inner magnificence must shine through. Was he not Zeus? Had he not seduced young females while in the guise of bulls, swans, and all manner of things?

At this point, dropping his pyjama bottoms, he had craned round to consider his rear, discovering that if he squeezed his glutes hard enough, he looked neater around the buns.

This was do-able!

Before there was time for doubt to creep in, he had reached for a bottle in his cabinet, swallowing two of the tablets that Hermes had ordered. How much quicker it was to dress when you were not considering what to wear above the waist!

And then he had strolled downstairs, out through the front door, out into the sunshine, remembering to breathe in, lean backwards, tilt back his head, clench tight his buttocks. Perhaps, disaster struck because he was not looking where he was going as he crossed the street. Or because he had forgotten to breathe. Or because the ferocious contractions via his glutes had impeded his capacity to walk. Or some combination. Maybe, it did not help that he had paused in the garden adjoining that of the nubile nymph to pick some colourful flowers that grew there. The white ones were nice, and didn't they look good alongside the purple ones? Zeus was not all that clear about the names of flowers.

While he had been stooping for those very purple ones, there had been a kind of *ping* in his lower back, whereupon he had found himself lying in the flowerbed.

For some time, it appeared that nobody had noticed him. The nymphs had disappeared. He wondered whether to call out, but decided to wait for the pain to subside. After what felt like an age, someone came out of the house. More neighbours appeared. There was a phone call. People were telling him not to move. An ambulance was on its way. The neighbour, the catalyst of all this, was among the group around him, bending low over him with a concerned look on her face.

There was a feeling of rising panic. His flowers may have been crushed during the fall, but something else was swelling. Something low down and entirely inappropriate. He tried to shift to conceal it, groaning as he moved.

By some good fortune, and quite possibly, it struck Zeus, sent by Tyche, the goddess of chance, Hermes appeared at the back of the group. He was ordering people to move aside.

"Please, stand back. I was trained by St John."

Such was the confidence of tone that the assembled crowd ignored the oddness of the wording, complying with the subsequent order to fetch something that would serve as a stretcher. Somehow or other, in great discomfort, Zeus managed to get back to the safety of his own home.

"Lie still on your back. Knees in the air and rotate your lower body. Keep the top part of your body still."

There was a popping sound. The pain subsided as suddenly as it had struck him down.

"Whatever were you doing out there with only half your clothes on?"

Zeus pretended he had not heard the question. Getting to his feet, he shuffled off to the kitchen, muttering.

"There must be something wrong with those pills you ordered. They did something to my back."

Hermes ignored the comment. It really was pointless to expect gratitude.

Nevertheless, Zeus did offer to get an all-day breakfast at a transport café which he had discovered.

"It's on me. Not that this was *my* fault."

He glared, accusingly, at Hermes, who merely sighed.

"You plan to go out with that?"

Glancing down at the bulge in his trousers, Zeus grinned.

"Impressive, isn't it. Like the Pelian Spear that only Achilles could wield! Do you think I should tape it to my thigh?"

The idea caused him to keep bursting into giggles all the way to the café. He was in high spirits by the time they got there, not to mention, ravenously hungry. He ordered extra eggs, which led Hermes to speculate on the mystery of the Orphic egg, from which Phanes, the very first god was hatched, both male and female, with a serpent coiled around the body.

"The point is," mused Hermes. "How did the egg get there? Tell me that. Or is there something or someone still further back?"

"You mean like the great *Hencales*, who laid it? Seriously, Hermes, do you believe that stuff?" replied Zeus in mid-mouthful. "Don't you think it sounds far-fetched?"

Hermes' cheeks had reddened.

"Well, what do *you* believe?"

"Rational things," said Zeus, "starting with my grandparents, Gaia and Uranus. Then their offspring, the Titans. And of course, Gaia's other children, and then our cousins – Cerberus, the Hydra, Chimera, Sphinx, Caucasian Eagle and Nemean Lion. Oh, and the sea gods, of course. I never really took you for one of those way-out, *Hey guys, let's hug some primordials* brigade."

He continued tucking into his food, hungrily.

"Sausages are good, too, aren't they? Especially, with lots of brown sauce. Which do you prefer: HP or

163

Daddies? And have you ever tried baked beans? All with a good mug of tea with plenty of sugar."

It struck Hermes as more than a little incongruous that Zeus was grappling with the relative merits of two brown sauces at a time when havoc was about to be unleashed in the form of Atlas. Probably best, he decided, not to mention that!

"I'm not sure Hebe would approve of frying eggs. I think she might prefer some healthier means of cooking them."

Zeus thought about the obvious rejoinder – *well, she's not here, is she?* – but suddenly felt overcome by a surge of warmth for his daughter. Although he had never spent much time with her, and had at their last meeting, patronisingly, referred to her as a 'pretty, little bubble-head', he suddenly wished she were there right now, having all-day breakfast with him, instead of this increasingly stolid and boring version of Hermes. Seriously, he needed to lighten up.

"This is the life, ey? All a bit more interesting than ambrosia with nectar every day. Don't get me wrong. I can't wait to get back home. So much to tell Hera. She'll be fascinated to hear that there's such a thing as 'backache'. On which note, it was nice of Tyche to send you."

It was as close as Hermes was going to receive to a thank you.

PART 3 — HUBRIS

JOINING THE PANTHEON OF GODS: A BEGINNER'S GUIDE

1. It may be considered presumptuous to expect the erection of a temple in your honour prior to the attainment of divinity, but it is advisable to have a couple of shrines in your honour.

2. The regulations state, explicitly, that you cannot commission the construction of such places of veneration, but that does not mean that there is any proscription with regard to intimations.

3. As mortals are notorious for being not the brightest of creatures, these may need to come in the form of strong hints.

4. Leaving messages on walls or issuing threats on the matter might not be viewed in a positive light when it comes to your application. For instance, in the case of one unnamed aspirant, his solicitation was rejected as soon as a note was discovered with the following message:

   If you do not build a shrine in my honour before my next birthday, I will break your legs. I will also break the legs of your donkey, your hens, and anything else you own. With gratitude for your co-operation.

   You will need to be more subtle than that.

166

5. The regulations make no reference to future plans, which means that you are permitted to commission designs for your larger-scale temples. Indeed, it is advisable to get these sort of things prepared as soon as possible, given all the bureaucracy and lengthy delays in temple applications. It is important to bear in mind that your forms will need approval by numerous committees before a single stone can be laid. A new god or goddess can look rather silly if they are left hanging around for too long without their first temple.

43

The immodesty of the advertising blurb did not give the slightest discomfort to Tyche, goddess of fortune and prosperity. The most spectacular phenomenon in the Universe: it was hardly an exaggeration. What was there to compare? The great acropolis on Mount Olympus? The bronze, gold and marble palaces dedicated to each of the gods? You had to be kidding! Fabulous of course, but here fabulous was mundane.

If you imagine the most famous hotels and casinos in Las Vegas – the Bellagio, the Venetian, the Palazzo, Caesars Palace, the Luxor, the Excalibur – the entire Strip; then throw in the Casino de Monte Carlo, the Marina Bay Sands of Singapore, the Wynn Macau and the Venetian Macao... - multiply it all by a thousand, and, still, you would not be getting anywhere close to the glitter and opulence of Tyche's Palace.

Here you could play all the games you found at those other places – roulette, poker, baccarat, blackjack, Big Six Wheel... not to mention hundreds more you have never heard of. Alternatively, you could idle away your time watching one of the spectacular shows, miraculous combinations of music and light.

You could visit grand halls, wander along a labyrinth of twining corridors, passing centaurs or unicorns, and if you were lucky, an Ethiopian crocotta or two, part stag, badger, hyena and lion, with the ability to mimic the sound of any voice they heard. If you were sufficiently daring to wander further, you might encounter sirens, Stymphalian birds, or even a chimera, gorgon or sphinx.

All the pleasures to be found on Earth amounted to a tiny bauble in this place. And at the heart of it all presided Tyche, bathing everything in a still greater vibe of glamour.

It was to this place that Hera had sent the demigods, the heroes, Heracles and Perseus, lest they should discover news of Project Z-R and rush back to join the fray on the side of Zeus. They had been in this gilded palace of delights for a great many years, not that years were counted here, but from around the time that Hera and Hades had begun their scheming. The two superheroes had been accompanied by Hera's trusted staff, and kept in a spa area far away from the room of wagers, where, at this very moment, huge amounts were being put down as bets about the outcome.

Currently, the odds were as follows:

Victory of Conspirators – 2 to one on
Victory of Zeus – Evens
Assassination of Zeus - Evens
Hades to become ruler of Olympus – 3 to one
Ares to become ruler – 5 to one

Hades and Hera to become joint rulers – 6 to one

Poseidon to take over – 9 to one

Apollo to take over – 11 to one

Atlas to take over – 14 to one

Return of Kronos – 33 to one

Tyche's house was making a nice little stash on the Apollo bets. Those in the know at the casino had managed to keep it quiet that the god, commonly considered to be Zeus' favourite son, was safely out of the way, a mysterious benefactor with close links to Project Z-R having approached him with an irresistible offer: a fully-funded project enabling him to take a long sabbatical. During that time Apollo could travel across mortal realms, conducting an interdisciplinary study examining the potential uses of music in health and penal systems. The funder left leeway for Apollo's restless mind to head in whichever direction he liked, and had the added bonus of requiring no formal permission from the Ethics Committee.

The possibility of a Kronos comeback was the cause of particular excitement, leading to some impetuous, optimistic wagers being put down on him. The reasoning among those taking a punt on that particular outcome was along the lines that form was temporary, but class permanent. The clever money tended to go elsewhere. Ares had moved, stealthily, up from being a long shot.

Neither Heracles nor Perseus was aware of such gambling. They were two of the very few immortals not yet to have heard of the disappearance of Zeus. Instead, they were being pampered, fed with the greatest delicacies, encouraged to wallow in sybaritic springs, whirlpools and saunas.

Of course, it was easy for anyone to tell from their faces – not to mention, from the tales they recounted – that both were great heroes. The corporeal impression was somewhat more equivocal; the fact was that neither was in prime fighting condition. Truth be told, they had each built up a layer of flab, then a second layer of flab on flab. Their once mighty thighs wobbled with each step. Indeed, you might be forgiven if you mistook them for two lumbering walruses, ageing superheroes waddling around their luxury suites and spa rooms.

If push came to shove and they did choose to fight for Zeus, the action would be done and dusted long before they were fit for combat. They would be fighting under the banner of the chopped-up bits of the KoG. Even finding those bits would be a labour fit for... well, Heracles.

44

Did he do it on purpose? To make you jump?

Charon had this way of creeping up on you. Still more unnerving was his habitual inspection of you from the side, a snakelike undertaker measuring you up. On his rare visits to Mount Olympus, despite the sunshine, he always ensured that he was fully covered from head to toe, not an inch of his pallid skin on display. Unaccustomed to light, he blinked repeatedly, even in his thick sunglasses.

The fact was that, having been persuaded by his master, Hades, that unionisation was a terrible idea, resulting only in exploitation by those who claimed to speak for you, he was given very few days of centenary leave. As a result, he barely left the Underworld, and light was, truly, oppressive.

His facial expressions seemed best suited for darkness. The thin widening of his mouth in a mirthless grin was chilling to the depths. His voice was soft, with a slimy kind of tone about it, if sounds could be slimy.

Sometimes he seemed to omit words, or maybe they just slid into the shadows.

"You and I, a lot in common."

"Do we?"

Hermes certainly hoped he shared no attributes with such a specimen.

"Oh yes – you stuck in your job, me in mine. But an uprising soon of the oppressed."

Was he practising to be a ventriloquist? His lips barely parted when he spoke. Maybe, that was why the occasional word got left out. It became too difficult to squeeze through.

For a while neither of them spoke. Conversations with Charon were always like this – not that Hermes could recall more than – maybe three or four interchanges with the creature throughout all the passing millennia.

"Atlas. We spoke, he and I. He is rising. Kronos, too, perhaps. Atlas is searching."

If it were possible, he lowered his voice still further.

"For all the scattered pieces."

Another long silence.

"And the upstarts overthrown. The old regime. No more endless jobs. All slaughtered. With no one to collect their rotten souls."

Was that rasping sound a laugh?

"Friend Charon knows something."

Hermes recalled now that Charon often spoke of himself in the third person. And, for some obscure reason, liked to call himself 'friend'.

"Secret for secret?"

The offer caught Hermes by surprise.

173

When the immortals made such a pact, a mutual nod of agreement sufficed for a set of scales to materialise. By the end of the exchange, the information on each side had to be of equal interest and usefulness.

Hermes hesitated, trying to think of information he might give away that might be of interest to Charon, weighed against the importance of what Charon may know. With a little reticence, he finally nodded, reluctantly, accepting the additional offer of a handshake.

"Friend Charon went first."

This seemed confusing, until Hermes recalled that, in addition to the third-person stuff and the ellipses, Charon also had a tendency to skid between tenses. Given the fixity of their existence, time could become an elusive notion for all immortals. It was not uncommon, especially in the Underworld, to forget whether something had happened or was going to happen.

"Hades' plans. Use Atlas. Kill off allies of Zeus."

The scales did not move. They never did if the listener already knew the information.

"Afterwards, Hades disposes of Atlas. Already making plans with Hephaestus who is building great weapon."

The scales lurched.

"Something else. Atlas already free. Sky holding up firm. Very few people noticing. Atlas has no ambition to rule. All he wanted one thing: Kronos back; and Atlas is searching. Looking everywhere for pieces of Kronos. Already finding this bit here, that bit there."

The scales lurched further.

"Hades keeps secrets from Hera. Between sheets all not so good. But Hades needs her as his consort – at least, at first. For legitimacy."

The scales fluttered a little. None of this was a great surprise to Hermes.

"And you. Hades does not trust Hermes. No affection. But no great animosity either. After all is over, if Hermes remains neutral, he can keep his old job. Or give it up. Though in longer term, if you displease Hades, things may change. Things clearer with Atlas. As go-between, Friend Charon has already spoken to him. Atlas wants no more messengers. No more ferrymen. You and me get nice, fat redundancy package. Now, your turn."

Charon's thin belly was swelling and deflating, gasping like a fish on deck. He must have gone through his annual conversation quota in the last couple of minutes. Glancing at the scales, Hermes gulped. They had tipped some way.

He began to gabble out information. The scales moved a little but nowhere near enough. Soon he had all but exhausted the things he had thought of. As he was entitled in such circumstances, Charon asked him a question. Where was Zeus?

Why would he want to know?

"On an island."

The scales moved slightly.

"I think it could be... Albion."

The scales tipped again, but not enough.

"Where in Albion?"

"I'm not exactly certain. As you know, we lost contact during the transition. A town, I think."

"Big town? Small?"

"Quite small."

If the scales shifted, it was barely perceptible.

"Tell Friend more about small town."

"It has some kind of bazaar where people come to buy things. And pubs. Where they drink. And a marketplace, where they bring animals sometimes..."

Still the scales were not balanced.

"And...and a racecourse for horses."

For some reason this nugget of information appeared to be more significant. He could tell that Charon had noted this, too.

"Of course, it's not all that relevant anymore," added Hermes. "After all, without his allies, without his thunderbolts, with production at the Cyclopes Brothers factory halted, it's not as if he can do anything."

Charon did not reply. Right now, it looked as if he might have wanted to smile but couldn't quite remember in which sequence the facial muscles were supposed to move in order to make that happen.

45

Zeus was in the town centre, it having occurred to him around mid-afternoon that, maybe, he should take an offering for supper. Lavish gift-giving was a norm if you were invited to someone's house for a feast back home, generally, entailing several items, although, usually, his company was viewed as a gift that sufficed in itself.

Not always, though. His mind slipped back to the time that he and Hermes had gone to Phrygia, disguised as poor travellers, seeking out hospitality. To find barred doors and rudeness! Only at a single household did they receive an invitation to step inside. It was a scruffy, tumbledown cottage belonging to an elderly couple, whose names he could not recall. He could only hope that the food and wine that Ember provided would be of higher quality.

He managed to find a new game for Ant's X-box, and then went into a bookshop for something for Frida. This was difficult. There were so many books. How should he know which she would like, or had not read? He chose four in the end, two with pictures on the cover, so one way or another, she should be happy.

Ember and Mo were more difficult. Having no idea what Mo looked like, clothes seemed a bit risky. He mooched around a few shops, eventually, settling for a set of *His and Hers* pinafores. Wondering whether this was appropriate, he bought two pairs, allowing for different permutations. He could ask Frida for advice when he got there.

Some sandals in a shop window caught his attention. He nipped inside. Quite quickly, it became a bore, with the two women on duty busy with other customers. After waiting a while, he departed, rather pleased with himself for managing to look so casual with two boxes under his arm.

Finally, he remembered to pick up a box of chocolates, in case he still felt hungry at the end of the meal. Perhaps, he could escape early on some pretext, bringing them home with him. It would be nice to pig out while playing a few games.

Only later did he remember what Ember had said about her partner. Thoughtfully, he removed the left sandal from one of the boxes, depositing it in a bin.

SURVIVING THE 21ST CENTURY: A HANDBOOK FOR PENSIONERS

ENTRY 5

THERE ARE WAYS FOR A PENSIONER TO FORGET ABOUT SOME OF THE ACHES AND PAINS OF LIFE, ALL THE LIMITATIONS.

DO:

1. GET AN XBOX.

2. VISIT THE RACETRACK WHENEVER POSSIBLE.

3. GO TO A TRANSPORT CAFÉ FOR LUNCH EVERY DAY. YOU DON'T HAVE TO BE A DRIVER!

4. ASK FOR EXTRA EGGS.

5. EAT CHOCOLATE – LOTS OF IT.

6. ON WHICH NOTE, MAKE LAVISH OFFERINGS TO THE GODS, PRAYING FOR YOUR TEETH TO FALL OUT AS SOON AS POSSIBLE, IN ORDER THAT THEY CAN BE REPLACED BY FALSE ONES.

7. TAKE STUFF FROM SHOPS WITHOUT PAYING. ONE OF THE FEW ADVANTAGES OF BEING A PENSIONER IS THAT, IF CAUGHT, YOU CAN MAKE PEOPLE BELIEVE THAT YOU THOUGHT IT WAS YOURS OR YOU WERE ONLY BORROWING IT.

DO NOT:

8. KEEP OLD PICTURES IN A PHOTOGRAPH
   ALBUM. IN CASE YOU CANNOT RESIST, PUT
   YOUR ALBUM SOMEWHERE INACCESSIBLE.
   BURYING IT UNDER THE FLOORBOARDS
   WOULD BE A GOOD IDEA!

9. TAKE MORE THAN ONE PHALLOS TABLET AT A
   TIME. THERE COULD BE SIDE EFFECTS, SUCH AS
   SUDDEN BACK PAIN.

46

Part way down the hill on Olympus, in the area known by those who lived there as 'The Favela', one of its more colourful personalities had arisen early. The residents of the Favela loved Narcie because, despite all the grime they perceived around them, he was more perfect in himself than any of those swanning around above. Even the goats on the hillside would stop and stare when he strolled past.

Sadly, the adoration felt for Narcie was not reciprocated. Narcie did not love the Favela. Such ugliness all around him! He belonged somewhere far better, above the slum-realms of demigods. He wanted out, spending most of his existence dreaming about what he would do when he was finally embraced as a full deity. He imagined shrines and temples grander than anything yet in existence. Far below, in the world of mortals, they would come in droves, bearing their gifts, and he, the god, Narcie, would cast his eye across them, choosing a select few who had pleased him most. He would dispense favours, accordingly.

More cherished than other gods because, in a way, he was one of their own, the kid who had made good. They would not get that, the other deities, the privileged, those who took everything as a silver-platter birthright. He, on the other hand, was humbly born, the son of a very ordinary river god and an obscure naiad nymph.

All he needed was one big break, which was why he hung around up here, where the air was clearer, where everything had so much more class, where he belonged. Pretending not to notice the heads turned in his direction, he acted like a visiting sightseer on a standard tour. It struck him outside a hairdressing salon that there were places where he received still more attention. This gave him an idea.

Soon he knew all about different hairstyles. He read up about the slightly different techniques used in Egypt, Persia and Greece to plait hair and beards. He quite liked braids, though he was not over-keen on the Egyptian shaved head and wig look.

Close to his home there was a wood, filled with subtle perfumes from the oaks, cedars, maples, elms and pines. Of course, in comparison with the woods higher up the slope, it wasn't much, but it was, nevertheless, somewhere Narcie liked to be, somewhere you could, temporarily, forget life's injustices.

Sometimes he would read his favourite book: *Joining the Pantheon of Gods: A Beginner's Guide.* He was surprised by the number of misconceptions in the area: how could anyone have thought that the only thing entailed in apotheosis was the imbibing of ambrosia and nectar?

Past a cluster of sweet chestnuts, there was a pool, clear enough to offer a decent reflection, and there he now went to experiment, trying out both male and female styles on himself. Naturally, he was drop-dead gorgeous in any style. In general, he preferred Greek fashions, with the exception of the harsher, Spartan look – though, of course, Narcie would still have looked stunning with a bucket on his head!

47

Such strikingly red hair! It was all he noticed at first.

Ember's girlfriend, Mo, was not what he had expected. She was pretty in her way, if not his type, slender, with a pointy little chin that jutted out, defiantly. Her green eyes went well with the red hair, which appeared from the roots to be natural. Just like Ember to go for someone who stood out! When she walked, he noticed she had a limp. Of course, thought Zeus, this would also attract Ember. So typical of her to think that she was protecting the weak, somehow or other, fighting social injustice by adopting someone who looked in need of help.

Mo barely glanced at him as he arrived, which was positive; it meant it would not look rude if he left early. Ember seemed amused by his gifts, Mo bemused, and a bit indignant that the sandals were not just the wrong size, but missing one. Frida was a little surprised by the picture books.

"Did you get them for me to read to you and Ant?"

Zeus nodded.

"But you can read, yourself, of course."

"It's nice to be read to. I like listening to your voice, and it sounds better in my head than when I read it to myself."

His great-nephew, at least, seemed delighted by his gift, managing not to let on that it was a game he already had. Ember looked thoughtful. That pretence would not have been possible even a few months ago. He was coming on.

The table had been set as if for a special occasion. There was a cloth and serviettes, and Zeus was reminded of the formal dinner parties that Hera took so seriously. Sometimes, as she was preparing for them, Zeus would, deliberately, get in the way, pretending it was accidental. Usually, she would push him aside, but on occasion, she would tousle his hair, as if humouring a cheeky boy. The thought made him pine for home, and almost more, for the warm touch of a female.

Ember was probably off-limits. He took a second glance at Mo as she took the seat beside him. Without really thinking about it, he slid his hand under her bottom as she sat down.

The sound of the ensuing slap was ensued by an awkward silence. Zeus rubbed his cheek, while Mo shuffled across to the other side of the table. He began to mumble something about having been resting his hand on her chair. Ignoring this, Mo insisted on switching seats with Antonio.

She was now opposite Zeus, averting her gaze. With a glare, Ember banged down the bowl she was carrying.

For a while, they ate in silence.

There was something brushing against his leg. He took a quick peek under the table. Mo's good leg under the table, touching his shins. Perhaps, that was damaged, too, and she had no feeling in it. She was not even looking at him.

It moved to his knee. And onwards to rub the inside of his thigh. Once. Twice. All the while continuing a conversation with the others. He gulped. Thank goodness he had not taken one of those tablets!

The children excused themselves after the meal. Soon after that, Zeus muttered something about a tiring couple of days, what – with shopping and everything, and a meal with his neighbour.

As he was leaving, Mo gave him a sidelong glance, before giving Ember a fierce, lingering kiss on the lips. There was something provocative about it, coquettish, as if intended to inflame his desire. He was confused, but aroused sufficiently to wonder whether she might be borrowed, at some stage, like a soap dish.

After all, Ember had not seemed to mind so much about that.

48

While the palaces of others were often grand, opulent, magnificent, Hera's retained a feel of intimacy. Wherever you looked, there were homely touches. Seismic cataclysms could be going on outside: lava might be spewing, fires raging, fissures cracking open. Yet, within the walls of Hera's palace, all would remain serene, safe, reassuringly mundane.

With no recent visits from Zeus, everything seemed still more orderly. When he was there, things got strewn around. He moved things about, put other stuff down, forgetting where he had left it. A slob from head to toe, his very presence added to the mess.

"If you must lollop," Hera often sighed, "can't you go outside and do it on one of the balconies or patios?"

It was the same as the way he ran Olympus, she felt: no system beyond divvying out realms he didn't want to his brothers. He thought nothing of allowing rowdy factions to build into dangerous groups. And when dissenters got too noisy, he would crush them with one of his thunderbolts, courtesy of the Cyclopes Brothers.

He had always been impulsive. Never any deliberation for Zeus. If he wanted something, he would snatch it. Herself, for instance.

It had seemed entirely natural that she should marry her brother. It had not been seen as at all weird in those days, no talk of monster children or anything like that resulting from such unions. It was simply viewed as a sensible way of ensuring stability, siblings being partners. And Hera liked stability. There were just the three brothers, and with Zeus having just been elected as KoG, she could recall telling herself that it was – as her son, Ares, would term it – a *no-brainer*. Of course, had she known that something so deformed as Hephaestus would emerge, she might have thought twice.

Nevertheless, she was not so foolish as to have succumbed to his first offer. What authority would that have given her? She would make him wait, just long enough for him not to take it for granted.

It was a lousy trick, the cuckoo act with the injured wing. She had brought it inside, warming it against her breast. And then the tiny bird had transformed back into Zeus, forcing himself on her. How he had chortled about his own trickery after ejaculating into her! Not even noticing her shame. There was no putting off the marriage after that.

Hera was musing on all this as she set the table, laying out each item in its place with meticulous care. While it often went unappreciated, it was a habit thing, the mark of both a good mother and a good hostess, even though, in truth, a visit from her daughters, Hebe and Eileithyia, was not really convenient with so much going on right now. Whatever was so urgent?

Although not quite so dull as their aunt, Hestia, who had cornered Hera at a recent family event and droned on all evening about tea towels, neither of the pair was the most stimulating of company. Hebe would babble on about food recipes and healthy eating, while Eileithyia would try and bring the subject round to babies.

It was a surprise, therefore, when they brought up a different topic, entirely, one that did not really concern them. It seemed that they had been discussing it at great length in private.

"We thought the plan was to just teach him a lesson. For all the... you know, philandering."

"And so it is," said Hera.

"But this looks like he won't be coming back. Not ever!"

Eileithyia's chin wobbled. Oh dear, thought her mother, here come the waterworks. Hera sighed.

"You do realise, don't you, that whatever I have done has always been for the sake of family. Whereas, in the case of your father, it's always about self-gratification."

"But the point is," said Hebe, firmly, "he *is* our father. Our male role model."

Of course, she would think that, thought Hera, married to that big doofus, Heracles.

It was most irksome. Would they have made such a fuss if *she* had been the one to go missing? What had

Zeus ever done for his legitimate children? How much time had he spent with them? What was so wonderful about him? Sure, he was great at never thinking about anyone else.

"And mother, this thing with Hades..."

Hebe was interrupted before she could go any further by one imperious snap of fingers.

"Whatever else he is – and I know people use words like *scheming, devious* and *evil* – Hades does happen to be reliable. You know where you stand with him. Whereas your father is unpredictable. He can go off on a whim at any tangent. He puts us all in danger. Why even now, he's pootled off to the mortals, where he might be giving our secrets away. He's more of a threat to our wellbeing than Prometheus was, and we're being a good deal kinder to your father than he was to Prometheus."

Her daughters looked less than convinced by the argument.

"Besides," continued Hera, with a sweet smile, "if Hades becomes a problem, we can dispense with him, afterwards."

She was all hugs and smiles as they departed.

"I am told the sanctuary in your honour, Eileithyia – you know, the new one in Arcadia – is just adorable. Perhaps, we could pay it a visit soon? A mummy and daughter jaunt. And Hebe, darling, I don't suppose there's any news about your missing hubby? Wherever could he have got to? Going off so suddenly, without even sending a postcard! I do hope he doesn't turn out like your father... unreliable."

Hera continued waving as her daughters made their way through the gardens towards the huge bronze gates, her cheeriness receding with each step they took. The visit had left her unusually flustered. She soothed herself by fishing out some old pictures of the children and hanging them round the fireplace in the dining room. Pictures of all her four children, except Hephaestus, that was. It had pained her, horribly, but disposing of him had been the only option. The presence of something so hideously imperfect would have reflected badly on all of them, undermining their status. It had been a means of protecting the family.

And similarly, Ares, the child she had cherished most. She would kill for his sake, but right now, he would tear them all apart. His reign would only be overthrown by the next generation, which, she felt, was a poor way to build dynasties. Right now, Ares needed to be protected from himself.

49

"A bit like the discus throw, only with a heavy, lead ball. Well, not lead. I think it's made of something else that's hard. I did ask. It was once a hardwood, Lignum Vitae? Is that a wood? And now... oh, how did they describe it? Phenolic composites? Ask Hephaestus; he's sure to know."

For some reason, thought Zeus, Hermes was being particularly dim this morning. Or perhaps, he was just hung over from travel.

"What if these balls land on someone's head?"

"You don't throw them in the air," exclaimed Zeus, with just a little impatience. "You roll them across the grass."

"It sounds a bit tame."

"On the contrary, it's very exciting."

Zeus rather wished he had never mentioned his new hobby to Hermes. He changed the subject. How were things progressing in the plan to get him back home?

It was the turn of Hermes to look impatient. Had he not explained this already, a hundred times, the obstacles to executing the plan? Finding the far superior body of someone who was about to die was only one issue. Of greater salience, was the beady eye being kept on everyone with regard to mortal affairs. In particular, Hermes' every movement was under scrutiny by members of the Ethics Committee. Not only was there indignation about Zeus' latest trip, undertaken without approval, but there was a tort case pending, injuries by a young deity sustained after some kind of apple-related assault. Why would Zeus even want to return while things were so volatile?

Once again, Hermes was careful not to make any reference to Hera's treachery. Who knows how Zeus would have reacted to that? Probably, he'd have insisted on returning immediately to punish her. Or maybe, he would have accused Hermes of lying and tried to strangle him, an act that would have been of extreme peril to Zeus, given the almost comically weak heart he currently possessed.

Naturally, Hermes did not mention his own duplicity. He simply repeated the original story. There was a mini insurrection. Some lunatic had the idea that Atlas could be liberated. It was being dealt with.

For the present time, it made more sense for Zeus to continue where he was. How was the journal coming on? He very much looked forward to reading it. He hoped Mudge's family was not being too demanding. But there were always things to do, weren't there? Had not Zeus told him that he enjoyed shopping? And now there were these bowls to hurl... to roll across the grass.

"They say I'm a natural. We go for drinks in the clubhouse, afterwards," remembered Zeus. "I like that, too."

"You see, it's not too bad," beamed Hermes. "And there are regular horse races as well."

"Which reminds me," said Zeus. "There's something I need you to organise about that. I'll phone you next time I'm at the course."

"You do that."

Hermes rather regretted ever giving Zeus his number. It had been supposed to be for emergencies only.

50

Ember acknowledged that it was an imposition, but as she and Mo were planning a romantic weekend, would he very much mind staying with Frida and Antonio? It was a long weekend, and as they might be returning home on the Monday, would he mind dropping them off at school as well as collecting them?

It was an imposition, actually? Did Ember not realise that he had lots of things to do at weekends – the bowling club he had joined, his X-box, weekend shopping... and probably, lots of other things. Then he remembered that his great nephew had many more games than he did, and Frida really was a lovely reader, and she also baked nice cakes.

It was not quite as much fun as he had anticipated. Antonio seemed on edge all weekend. He had a SATs test on the Monday, and Ant hated tests, whispered Frida.

"It's not that he's stupid. He just gets very anxious."

By Monday morning, his face was drained of colour. Zeus noticed that he was shaking as he came out of the house. He could have been on the way to his execution. His head drooped. He was staring at the car floor as if there was something mesmerising there.

"We could have a treat," soothed Frida. "Something to look forward to. Maybe, next weekend. Where would you like to go?"

"Waterslides," muttered her brother, in such a tiny voice that it was barely audible.

"It's a theme park," explained Frida. "We went there for his birthday last year. Lots of rides, including water-slides."

Zeus had no idea what she meant, but came to a decision.

"Why wait till next weekend? We could go now. That way nobody has to take a test."

He was adamant on the matter, feeling quite like his old self. The ten-year war against the Titans for the cosmos had hardly been won by considering trivial, prior appointments in the diary!

They went on all kinds of rides, a pirate ship, a death slide, bumper boats – but Antonio was right: the water slides were the best. They were laughing so much that they did not notice the people in uniforms waiting at the bottom of the run as they came down for the umpteenth time.

"Mr Mudge? Can we have a few words?"

It probably did not help their cause that Zeus just burst out laughing.

"Is something amusing?" asked the male officer.

"Your hat!" giggled Zeus. "It looks ridiculous."

196

Ember and Mo were both at home when they arrived. Ember looked as if she wanted to strangle Zeus, and Mo gave the impression that she would be delighted to assist.

"Did it not even occur to you that you need to inform the school when children aren't coming in? What do you expect them to do when they don't arrive?"

"We had fun."

"FUN!" snapped Ember.

She swivelled round to face her daughter.

"And as for you, you should know better."

Zeus was not offered supper. On his way out, he whispered something to Antonio, who was heading upstairs to his room.

"It was worth it though, wasn't it."

The boy continued up the stairs, without turning. Sticking his arms behind his back, keeping them very low, he gave Zeus a surreptitious thumbs-up with each hand.

51

It was a something of a relief that he had managed to keep
Lily Tucker at arm's length. No, it was nothing to do with
her, he had assured her. It was simply that – what with
the shopping, the bowling club, the collection of his great-
niece and nephew from school, well, it was a wonder
where the time went, and by the evenings he usually just
flaked out.

No sooner had he seemed to have escaped her
clutches, when the neighbours on the other side began to
make unwelcome demands. Instinctively, he had disliked
from the outset the two scrawny, white men who
inhabited the house. On the rare occasions he saw them
outside, Zeus avoided them. Nor did he have much to do
with the other lodger, the one Zeus had taken as being too
dark for either a Numidian or Phoenician. The fellow
had, for some reason, appeared to take offence one
morning when they had bumped into one another.

"Good morning, Pygmie," Zeus had said, politely.

The man had replied rather stiffly.

"My name is Ermias."

One of the housemates had spotted the two of
them in conversation, banging on the window and
mouthing to Zeus that he should 'piss off'.

After that, there had been a few brief exchanges
when they met, about things like the weather, with Zeus

sometimes remembering to call him by his proper name. However, one morning, Ermias had approached him rather awkwardly.

"The two guys I live with asked me to put something to you. They want to know whether, occasionally, you would mind storing some packages for them."

"Isn't there room in your own house?"

"Well, it's not really my stuff. There have been a few visits from the police, and I think the guys have got in a bit above their heads. It would not be for long; just till the heat is off."

It was difficult to work out what he was talking about. How big were these packages? Ermias assured him that they were small, and would take up very little space. They could easily be stored on a shelf at the back of a wardrobe. Or even under a rug. Somewhere dry, that was all that mattered.

"There may even be something in it for you."

Zeus could not think of anything that Ermias and his housemates could possibly do for him.

"For instance," said Ermias, "I noticed there were problems with your car, recently. If you needed to go anywhere, you could borrow my bicycle."

52

Gyges had been partying the previous evening. Having received an invitation to a gathering to celebrate his birthday, it was only polite to attend, particularly as the mysterious 'admirer' who had organised the surprise event had put on so much food and drink.

The address he had been given turned out to be in quite a remote place, at the foot of a cliff, with the crashing of waves and the shrieking of giant birds cutting out all other sounds. The identities of the other guests became a blur. His family and close friends would be arriving any minute, he was assured. Why not tuck in while he was waiting?

The drink was particularly more-ish, with no obvious sense that it had been spiked.

No research project has ever reported the details of the types of hallucinations that Hecatoncheires might experience when spaced out. All that was evident was that some kind stranger, looked after him, and took him to a nearby annex with a comfortable bed, where he could sleep it off.

Which was where he was, snoring like some huge baby, when the roof was smashed in by a gigantic, iron mallet. It all felt like part of the psychedelic dream he was in, even when the hammer began to pummel his thick skull.

The chalk cliffs around were splattered with bits of house mixed with blood and blobs of flesh.

Not my problem, thought Atlas, as he stomped away. Someone else can clear up the mess.

From a vantage point, far above on Mount Olympus, Hera and Hades had been watching the carnage. When on the rampage, Atlas certainly looked the part.

"What if we can't control him?" said Hades. "He's not exactly the temperate type."

Hera treated him to her most serene smile.

"Everyone and everything has a weakness. In the case of Atlas, it happens to be lightning. Peculiar thing about Titans but they do seem to conduct electricity remarkably well. That's how Zeus struck him down last time. There is something else about them that not many people know. Their fontanelles never close entirely. If you hit them directly on the weak spot, they go down like ninepins."

"Is that so?"

Hades wondered how he had never heard this before. Hera really did have a way of unearthing information that no one else knew.

"Absolutely! You don't even need a humongous iron mallet for the job. But as it happens, I have something still better. Zeus just happened to give me one of his thunderbolts. An anniversary gift, a kind of peace offering, as I recollect, after one of his dalliances. I'd have been quite happy with flowers, though he's clueless about choosing them. Always goes for purple or white ones, my least favourite colours!"

Hera poured them both another drink from the jar they had brought along on their picnic. She settled down on the rug. It really was a perfect evening for an al fresco meal. Perhaps, they might even sleep out, and stare at the sky, still perfectly in its place, supported by the new acrow props.

"So you see, we can just sit pretty up here, let Atlas do his job, finish off all of Zeus' former allies, and then we can dispatch him."

Far below, the sound of bashing continued through the early hours.

53

For a while, he ignored the hammering. It was far too late for visitors.

The banging went on. There was nothing to do but to face up to it. Putting on a dressing gown, Zeus shuffled down the stairs to open the front door.

His neighbours were there, the two scraggy white guys, as well as an ill-at-ease Ermias. Behind them, there stood three other men.

Now the door on the other side opened. Lily was peering out. She was wearing a coat over her nightie, and brandishing an umbrella.

"Off with you! Hop it!"

She was flapping at the men. One of them grabbed the umbrella, snapping it in two and slinging it across the garden. In the melee, Sir Cecil slunk out.

"Is everything all right?" Lily inquired, her voice quavering. She addressed her words to Zeus, barely looking at the other men. "Do you want me to call the police?"

Now she turned to glare at the men.

"I've got an eye for faces. I don't forget them. You'd better take care."

Zeus intervened.

"It's all right, Mrs Tuck... Lily. There's no need to worry. You go back inside now."

Without any invitation, the group of men bundled into Zeus' house.

Two of the three other mortals were large and swarthy. They seemed to fill his room. The other one was a well-dressed man, who looked as if he might have been an accountant. He was rake thin, with a shaved, bald head and chocolate brown eyes that suggested a rather sleepy dog one moment, but which suddenly switched into something far more penetrating. Despite his doggy eyes, the tone of his voice was altogether more feline.

"Mr Mudge," he purred, so quietly that Zeus had to strain to hear his words. "I'm informed that you're in charge of this operation."

Zeus wondered what he was talking about. He turned to Ermias for some explanation, but Ermias avoided his gaze.

"In the first place, we'd like our merchandise back?"

It took a few more seconds for this to click with Zeus.

"Yours? I thought they were..."

"Mr Mudge. Monty. Shall I call you Monty? Do you see Mr Marku here?"

Zeus followed the direction of the man's glance to one of the swarthy men.

"It may strike you as a bit unusual to come upon a man who often forgets to shave, yet who always carries a razor. Is that not correct Mr Marku?"

The man – Mr Marku – seemed to smile without moving his lips.

"Do you think you should go and fetch our merchandise, Monty?"

Zeus looked over at Ermias, who gave the slightest of nods. He went upstairs, returning with the packages he had been handed.

The man smiled at him.

"I see eight. Where is the ninth?"

Zeus blinked. It struck him now that the man looked like one of the keres, the skeletal death spirits who hung around on battlefields to feast on the remains.

"I'm not scared of you," said Zeus, almost managing to contain the tremor in his voice.

The keres, as Zeus thought of him, just smiled.

"Listen, Monty. Listen to me, carefully. I know everything about you. It is my business to know all about my associates. I've had you followed for the last few days. I know your routine. The shopping trips to the supermarket; the bowling club; the people you meet; the two children you collect from school, the little boy and the little girl. Mr Marku has a soft spot for little girls, don't you, Mr Marku?"

The man gave his smile without a smile performance again.

"They are, maybe, your grandchildren. You take them back to their home. Shall I remind you of the address? They seem very dear to you."

"No," croaked Zeus. "Just two children."

He squeezed his bony old fists into a ball. If only he could resume his true form at this very moment?

"I have friends," he said, weakly.

"In the bowling club?"

The keres smiled.

"We all have friends, Monty."

He beckoned forward the burly henchman standing next to Mr Marku. The next bit was something of a blur. Zeus had a recollection of a small axe being swung. Wherever had it come from? Then a yelp, and then two stumps neatly chopped onto his dining table. Two of the man's fingers.

"That, Monty, is what I do to my friends. I'll give you two days to find the missing package. And, shall we say, two thousand pounds for medical bills? Your NHS has gone to the dogs, Monty! Plus, five thousand pounds for my personal time?"

54

He had barely slept, but decided an early morning walk would be the best thing to clear his head. Dawn had just come up. The streets were empty. It would be nice and peaceful, and for once, he might be the first to arrive at the transport café for breakfast. It was a pleasant walk there through a park, and if he was too early, he could always pause to read the plaques on the benches.

He spotted the shape instantly in the murky light. He moved closer to investigate. Sir Cecil, swinging gently on a rope from a tree in Lily's garden.

He felt sick, retreating inside and closing his door, mumbling to himself. For a while, he just stood there, uncertainly, before walking to his kitchen, and fetching a sharp knife and a cardboard box. She must not see it. She must think Sir Cecil just went off wandering, and was staying in someone else's home, perhaps, just a few streets away.

Cutting down the body, he put it in the box, walking briskly down the street. A few moments later, he returned to fetch a spade from the shed. There was a nice patch of soft earth he recalled in one of the places close to the river, a little away from the walking path and overhung by trees. It was a good place for cats to hide, watching the birds, perching on branches.

His mind felt numb as he dug. Occasionally, he had to pause, breathless, and wait for some strength to return to his arms. Half a dozen times, he had to stop, too, to wipe his eyes on his coat sleeve. The feeling was odd, entirely new. He was just relieved that no one was here to see him in this state. Above all, he wished he was at home, far from all the misery to be found in the mortal world.

55

It was frustrating that, once again, Hermes was not answering his phone. Zeus kept trying. Finally, he sent a text.

This time it is urgent. Life or death urgent.

In the middle of the night he heard a stone tinkle against his window. It was Hermes.

It took some time for Hermes to get the gist of the garbled story. All sorts of thoughts raced round his head as he listened. This gang, who, according to Ermias, were, *probably*, Albanian, might solve everyone's problems, with the possible exception of Zeus. If they finished off Mudge, while Zeus was in his body, the chances were that Zeus would never get back to Olympus. Even though he did not as yet know the identity of the host body, Zeus would be recognised on his arrival in the Underworld, immediately, just as soon as he attempted to burst out. Hades had prepared for that eventuality.

Hermes would be seen to have played his part in the whole operation, and would duly be liberated from his onerous role. All he had to do was to look the other way while events played out.

"Are you listening, Hermes? I want something done about these people. That Marku fellow, and the keres."

Zeus was tugging his sleeve. Hermes grimaced.

"You do realise that if you alert any non-mortals to anything that you could be in extreme peril. You have no idea how incendiary things are in Olympus right now. You may recall that Atlas has been let loose. If you pinpoint where you are, he – come to think of it, any of your enemies – could come for you. And take my word for it, you have plenty."

"I don't care!" shouted Zeus.

Hermes ignored this.

"Alternatively, if other gang members take vengeance, imagine Mudge's soul, finally, appearing in Hades with a tale to tell. Or one of these people you want me to obliterate. They don't sound like the sort to be transported to the Elysian Fields as a reward for being wonderful."

"I still don't care."

"Then again, if you put yourself in danger, what happens to the people you are protecting. These children – they are just mortals. Nothing to you."

"If it avoids risks, you don't to have to kill anyone," said Zeus, finally. "Just break bones. Lots of them. Maybe, pull out the tongue from the keres, so he can't make those threats again. And that Marku, the one who carries out the acts. I want his hands removed."

JOINING THE PANTHEON OF GODS: A BEGINNER'S GUIDE

1. Gods love to make wagers; you need to be seen to gamble even if it does not really float your Argo.

2. When placing bets, there are some strict rules that require adherence. If, for example, you are placing a bet that a certain god will indulge in lagneia with a certain goddess at a forthcoming symposium, it is bad form to be seen to be attempting to influence the matter, for instance, by surreptitiously attempting to engineer a tryst. Even the subtlest of hints, such as telling God X that Goddess Y has the hots for him, is likely to be viewed in a dim light. Anything beyond that would be viewed as unacceptable, and might have severe social consequences, including some degree of temporary ostracisation, not to mention rendering your bet void.

3. To collect your winnings in the event of a successful prediction, there needs to be firm evidence of the outcome. Witnesses are of variable value, but any god or goddess who is

connected to the Ethics Committee would be ideal.

4. The rules are altogether less stringent when it comes to making bets about outcomes of events involving mortals. In such cases, you are allowed to interfere, freely, though it would be sensible to check that your actions do not risk incurring the rage of Zeus or Hera.

5. For a less established deity it is advisable to tread with care in the early phases. For instance, if you have predicted imminent war between the Athenians and Spartans, it may be seen as a trifle presumptuous to go down to Athens, abduct a princess, and dump her in Sparta. That kind of intervention would be deemed more suitable for a well-established deity. However, it would be quite acceptable to send Hermes, in disguise, with a letter addressed to the King of Sparta, apparently signed by his Athenian counterpart, referring to him as a bolbiton-faced orrhos.

56

So febrile was the atmosphere in Tyche's palace that the most ridiculous bets were being placed. The odds had veered, markedly. As things stood, and they were shifting every few hours, they were now heavily against a favourable outcome for the KoG. They were:

Victory of Conspirators – 5 to one on
Assassination of Zeus – 3 to one on
Hades to become ruler of Olympus – Evens
Ares to become ruler – 3 to one
Atlas to take over – 5 to one
Hades and Hera to become joint rulers – 7 to one
Poseidon to take over – 9 to one
Apollo to take over – 12 to one
Victory of Kronos – 16 to one
Return of Zeus – 33 to one

It was interesting that Kronos had halved his odds without so much as raising a finger, and still more so, that Zeus was now a rank outsider. Due to all the volatility, with the possibility of the world ending at any time, some punters were putting down all their lifelong savings on the outcome. What did it matter if they lost if everything was to slip into an impenetrable void? Indeed, on this very subject, further odds of fifteen to one were being given for Hephaestus' Acrow Props to fail.

Hera was rather satisfied by her own odds, sending in a bet on herself in a false name. It was helpful that Hades remained the front runner, and no one else was taking up the two hundred to one odds on herself. Such was the figure that she put down, it was going to knock a big dent in Tyche's profits if, by some fluke, it came off.

57

These were not the policeman and policemaness with whom he was acquainted. The two people at his door this time said they were detectives. They just had a few questions, they assured him, which should not take up too much time. He invited them in, offering them Ribena. He was not sure they warranted hot chocolate.

"We found a certain Albanian, gentleman, Mr Mudge. Two gentlemen, to be exact. They did not appear in the most healthy of conditions."

Was that news a surprise to him?

Zeus hesitated.

There were probably lots of gentlemen to be found at any time in not too healthy conditions. The chances are that some of them might be from Albania.

The detectives seemed to concede the point. However, the thing about these two gentlemen was that there had been some sort of incident involving his good self. Indeed, one of the gentleman managed to tell them – and it was quite difficult for him to communicate, as Mr Mudge would appreciate, with tubes coming out of his mouth. Not to mention that, at some point during the fracas, the unfortunate gentleman appeared to have bitten right through his own tongue. Part of it was missing! And one way or another, his accomplice seems to have mislaid his hands. They were not to be found anywhere. Anyway, the one with the damaged tongue had suggested that there had been some sort of altercation, and while it may seem far-fetched, he alleged that Mr Mudge had threatened them.

Zeus shrugged, pointing out that he had never actually been to Albania. Strictly speaking, this was not true, as he had travelled extensively at various times through Illyria and Epirus, but he was pretty sure that Mudge had never been to the region. At most, it was a small fib.

"Apparently, you told these gentlemen that you had 'friends'."

Zeus treated them to the blankest look he could muster.

"*Do* you have friends, Mr Mudge?"

Zeus shook his head. Of course, he informed them about Bill and Lily, but they weren't really *friends*.

"Another funny thing, Mr Mudge, and most unusual, the two gentlemen had been smashed around by a heavy object. A round object. Might that mean anything to you?"

Once again, Zeus shook his head.

"And there were words on it, Mr Mudge: *Compliments of Newton Abbot Bowling Club!*"

We did make a few enquiries there, but nobody seemed able to shed any light on it. We wondered whether you might be able to help.

Zeus held out his hands. Life was a mystery. He hoped the unfortunate gentlemen had some form of medical insurance. One never knew with the NHS. Only the other day, someone was telling him that it had gone to the dogs.

58

Ares was not the most convivial company at the best of times. Nevertheless, it seemed to Hermes that he was preferable when being his usual dour self than when he was acting all hearty, as he was right now.

"After all, we're brothers. And brothers stick together."

"Half-brothers," Hermes reminded him.

"The thing is I know what you want. My mother let slip what she had promised you, although, of course, everyone knows you can't trust her."

Hermes' mind raced around the possibilities. Was Ares acting independently? Or was he just pretending to distance himself from Hera? Were the two of them conspiring to get information out of him?

"Quite rightly," drawled Ares, "you are fed up with all the demeaning work. Here are the rest of us, having a ball, while you're having to rush about like a blue-arsed Cretan bull! Or worse! Seriously, Hermes, Silenus' donkey has a better lifestyle than you. But the point is I can help you to change things."

Hermes waited to hear the price. Ares was not renowned for generosity. He would expect something in return.

"All I am asking for is a location. Where did he go, Hermes? Where did you take him?"

Hermes sighed. Had he not explained this already to Hera and the others involved in the... project? He had followed orders. Zeus had been told that he was on his way to the great city of Argos. Of course, there was going to be an error in the body he ended up inhabiting, but that was all Hermes had been told. At the last minute, Hera must have decided that Argos was not a suitable destination, as she did not want a place where she was honoured to be desecrated.

Something had gone very weird with the co-ordinates. Zeus and Hermes had got separated. Hermes had got a glimpse of the body Zeus had slipped into, and then he had gone. It was a feeble, elderly mortal – that was all he knew.

He did his utmost now to ignore the sceptical expression on the face of Ares. Had he not been doing all possible to find Zeus, as requested? That's when he wasn't being sent on wild goose chases to deliver Get Well cards! The fact was that it was like looking for a needle in a haystack.

"So what did the scenery look like? You must have seen something? You're going to have to give me more, Hermes."

"There was a river. Definitely a river. The old man lived in a house very close to it. And I got the impression that the country was part of an island. A large one, with lots of people. Definitely part of the same continent as Hellas. I'm looking, Ares. Gradually, narrowing it down."

Ares patted his shoulder.

"Well, you keep on trying, little bro. Incidentally, I've got a *Good Luck* card for you to deliver to Cadmus. I've always had a soft spot for him, and he's entering some competition. Collecting teeth from some of the dragons who dwell in one of those godforsaken places where they sometimes hang out. Cadmus is planning to make jewellery out of them. He's so creative! Well, he's out training right now with the Hydra of Lerna. It's all marshy swamps, so I'd advise rubber boots of some kind. Enjoy! Xaipe!"

59

No sooner had Hermes departed than Ares himself received a message, on this occasion, not delivered by Hermes.

Darling, just received some interesting information, and I know how keen you are to be the one to sort it all out. That device we hid in his chariot – do you remember, the Cyclopes' Eye ◉? Well, it's picked up something. He has this sort of monitor where he keys in his destination, and we have the first three letters. N-E-W... I'm afraid the rest is illegible. But we have the co-ordinates of the island. And there is definitely more than one word in the name of the place.

I didn't like to step on your toes, and I haven't mentioned it to Hades yet.

By the way, remember to run it past the Ethics Committee. I don't expect a problem. I spoke to Arete recently and she's still not forgiven your father for his – well, she called it, patriarchal hegemony, phallocentric use of dehumanising discourse, inappropriate and offensive language and general misogyny. I think those were the words she used.

Kisses and Hugs 💋 💚 🌺
Mummy

60

Frida was in trouble. She had hit a boy in the playground. He had been teasing Antonio for some time, and finally, it seemed, she had just walked up to him and punched him in the mouth.

Her mother was livid.

"What would happen if you got expelled?"

"That's never going to happen," replied Frida, archly. "I'm top of my class. They want me for their precious league tables."

"And when you move on to your next school? What then? Your brother still in the same place, and nobody to protect him. Do you think that boy will just forgive him?"

Frida said nothing. She had not thought of that.

"Anyway, punching someone in the mouth is not the way to resolve issues, as your Uncle Monty will tell you. Maybe, you'll listen to *him*."

"Your mother is quite right, Frida. You could hurt your knuckles on his teeth. Better to kick him in the orjiks. Or knee him, like this."

Zeus raised his knee in the air, thrusting it forwards and tumbling onto the settee. Frida and Antonio burst into laughter. Antonio now copied Zeus' motion, raising his knee high in the air, before jumping onto the settee next to him, wriggling around.

"Orjiks!" he shouted, delighted by the new word. "Knee him in the orjiks!"

"Really, Uncle Monty, you're an awful role model."

Turning abruptly, Ember managed to make it into the kitchen before anyone could notice her creasing up.

Later she tried to explain her underlying concerns to her uncle, all about her ongoing battle with the school. How they kept telling her that it wasn't the right place for a boy like Antonio, with his dyslexia and autism. How there was a specialist academy for children like him nearby. How she had told the school that Antonio wanted to be with his sister and they could not force him out. To which the response had been that nobody was seeking to force him out; they were, merely, seeking solutions in his own best interests. It was pointed out that they also had to consider the interests of other children. And in fact, if she checked, she would find that, legally, a child could be removed if its presence was detrimental to others. Not that anyone wanted it to come to that.

Zeus struggled to comprehend. What did such labels even mean? Autistic? Dyslexic? What were they and why did they matter? He was just Antonio. And what were SATs and SEN and EHCs? Avoiding eye contact; being silent; repeating words and movements over and over again: why was all that so important? Hard evidence of being *on the spectrum* – what did that even mean? And what were the teacher and this deputy head person talking about him never smiling? Just what had he been doing a few moments ago when they were on the settee?

Ignoring these questions, Ember now came on to how the school had implied that it was *her* fault if her son was bullied.

"Children have difficulties with difference," his teacher told me, "and you've got to admit that even his name marks him out as different. It's *they* who can't cope with difference. The bloody *school!*"

She looked so sad that Zeus felt he had to comfort her. He tried patting her knee, which he hoped was consoling.

"They say he's not making progress in any of his subjects."

"He's very good on gods and heroes. He remembers everything I tell him."

"How is that going to help him get a job in the future? Who will be there for him? You'll be gone. I'll be old. Frida will have her own family. He'll be all alone."

Zeus tried to explain all this to Hermes on his next visit, becoming confused in the process.

"It seems that the school is not even run by the teacher or this deputy. Not even by the person above the deputy."

He gave an outline to Hermes. The school was part of something called a 'mat', and the person in charge

226

never even came in. This was someone called a 'Sea Eyo'; presumably, because that individual lived on an island and crossed an ocean to get there. If so, Poseidon could surely locate and dispose of him or her, leaving his great-nephew in peace.

Hermes looked bewildered; most of all, he was bemused that this should even matter to Zeus.

61

All that could be heard was a ticking in the background and the occasional shuffling of papers. Otherwise, just an austere silence, an almost suffocating sense of decorum.

Arete cleared her throat.

"I think we can agree that there has been due diligence. Ares is very specific about the possible sites for the... intervention."

There were nods around the table, as they studied the charts.

"The paperwork shows extensive calculations with regard to velocity, likely scale of impact, number of potential casualties. I think that's all in order. It shows that Ares has thought this through with care. He even provides additional documentation to demonstrate how the intervention can be made to look as if it was all due to natural catastrophe."

There were some murmurs of agreement. They agreed with Arete that the circumstances were most unusual, and the rather negative outcomes for a few mortals needed to be balanced against the danger posed by the continued presence of a certain entity in the vicinity.

It was unfortunate that a few individuals were likely to be adversely affected, in some cases, even – *rendered absent* was the term they settled for in the eventual paperwork – but after all, wasn't that what mortals did? They were just getting rendered absent a little earlier than anticipated.

One by one, Horkos, Pistis and Dike added their signatures on the approval document beneath that of Arete, even though the last of the above-named did so with a low sigh of resignation.

SURVIVING THE 21ST CENTURY: A HANDBOOK FOR PENSIONERS

ENTRY 6

A FEW MORE TIPS:

1. GET A CAT. THEY ARE WONDERFUL CREATURES, PERCEPTIVE, INTUITIVE, COMPANIONS WHO MAKE VERY FEW DEMANDS.

2. TREAT THEM WITH TENDERNESS. THEY ARE JUST SKELETONS WRAPPED IN A BIT OF FLUFF, BRITTLE LIKE EVERYTHING ELSE HERE. DESPITE WHAT PEOPLE BELIEVE, THEY HAVE JUST THE ONE LIFE. YOU MIGHT WAIT FOR THEM TO COME BACK, BUT THEY DON'T.

3. THE FACT IS THAT YOU ARE TRAPPED IN A PATHETIC, USELESS BODY. IT IS VERY TEMPTING TO FEEL SORRY FOR YOURSELF AND JUST WAIT FOR THE KERES OR CHARON TO COLLECT YOU.

4. IF THE LATTER COMES, DO NOT GET INTO HIS BOAT.

5. DO GO ON AS MANY WATER SLIDES AS YOU CAN LOCATE. THE WATER SLIDE IS QUITE POSSIBLY THE GREATEST INVENTION THERE HAS EVER BEEN, AND IS ONE OF THE VERY FEW PLEASURES LEFT FOR PENSIONERS TO ENJOY.

6. YOU CAN SOMETIMES GET TO THE FRONT OF THE QUEUE BY PRETENDING THAT YOU HAVE A TERMINAL DISEASE.

7. ANOTHER PLEASURE IS BOWLING. IT IS A DECEPTIVELY SUBTLE GAME, WHICH PROBABLY EXPLAINS WHY YOU HAVE TO BE A CERTAIN AGE BEFORE YOU CAN MASTER IT.

8. THOSE WHO ARE YOUNG ARE LIKELY TO BE IMPETUOUS, WITHOUT THE MATURITY TO GRASP ALL THE NUANCES, SUCH AS THE FACT THAT, SOMETIMES, IT CAN BE A GOOD STRATEGY TO CONCEDE A SHOT. THIS MIGHT SEEM ILLOGICAL, BUT THE POSSIBLE REWARD CAN EXCEED THE RISK. ALWAYS PLAY THE PERCENTAGES!

9. YOUR PSYCHOLOGICAL STATE IS IMPORTANT IN BOWLING, ESPECIALLY, IF YOUR OPPONENT IS MORE MUSCULAR OR SUPPLE. IT IS NOT CHEATING TO PSYCHE OUT YOUR OPPONENT. AFTER ALL, YOU ARE THE ONE WHO HAS BEEN CHEATED BY HAVING BEEN PROVIDED WITH WEAK KNEES AND CREAKY JOINTS. WEARING BRIGHT COLOURS AND GETTING IN THE LINE OF VISION OF AN OPPONENT IS A GOOD IDEA. SNIFFING IN SNOT OR EMITTING SOME NOISE FROM ANY OTHER ORIFICE AT THE MOMENT

SOMEONE ELSE IS ABOUT TO BOWL CAN ALSO BE
AN EXCELLENT RUSE.

10. THE ARGUMENT ABOUT WHETHER DADDIES
OR HP SAUCE IS SUPERIOR WILL PROBABLY GO
ON TILL THE END OF ETERNITY. SOME DAYS IT
SEEMS THAT DADDIES BOASTS GREATER
PIQUANCY, AND OTHERS, THAT HP IS MORE
BEGUILING. I WOULD RECOMMEND KEEPING
BOTH IN STOCK.

11. DON'T EVER GET A CAT. THE LOSS OF IT IS TOO
PAINFUL TO BEAR.

62

That Newcastle upon Tyne, Newcastle-under-Lyme and New Brighton, Merseyside should all be hit by earthquakes and floods on the same day seemed unusual in the extreme. That smaller places, such as Newbiggin-by-the-Sea, Newby Wiske, Newington Bagpath and Newland Bottom endured the identical calamity made the coincidence still stranger. Those living closest to water were, in each case, the worst affected.

By some oversight, Newton Abbot had not been listed among the targets. It all further illustrated the pattern of life as a lottery, all creatures amounting to a series of tiny black and red dots on a wildly gyrating roulette wheel.

63

It was a throwaway comment from Bill that gave Zeus the idea to go for an accumulator bet. Apart from *Lucky Star*, who was down at four to one, the other horses on the ticket were rank outsiders. It was, thought Bill, more of a joke than anything else, and something of a waste of money. He had refused to put in more than three pounds, and was horrified when Zeus then placed a bet of one hundred and three pounds on no-hopers. However, by the time *Plodding Bob* came in first at 66 to one, Bill was utterly convinced that this was a dream from which he would awaken at any moment. He kept shaking his head, rubbing his eyes in disbelief.

"By Gum!" he muttered after each horse came in.

Zeus felt more alive than at any time he could remember, a rush of adrenaline that equalled anything on Olympus since the great battles. For his part, Hermes had not really thought about it when Zeus had texted, asking him for tips about which horse would win the selected races. Hermes' mind at the time was on other – and what he considered, rather more important, things.

It was most unfortunate that the incredible string of victories was reported on the local news. Hermes just hoped that nobody else had noticed it on Olympus. As if Zeus was not in sufficient danger, already, without attracting further attention to himself!

Hermes quickly calculated the percentages: risk versus reward. It was no good. Another visit had to be made.

Once again, he was followed, and once again, he had to carry out all sorts of manoeuvres to give his pursuer the slip. The vehicle behind seemed still faster than it had on the previous occasion. Whatever was going through Hephaestus' stubborn head!

This time, he parked at a distance, by the coast in the nearby seaside town of Dawlish, rendering himself invisible, and catching a train to Newton Abbot. Out of habitual honesty, he purchased a ticket from the machine, somewhat carelessly, alighting the cursor on the wrong place at the first attempt, and booking an unnecessarily expensive return trip to the recently flooded Newcastle upon Tyne.

He enjoyed the journey, admiring the moonlight on the sea as the train headed through Teignmouth and along the estuary. It was strange, he thought, how the beauty of Olympus surpassed this by so much, and yet, right now, this seemed still more exquisite for being set amidst ugliness and pollution. Something about juxtapositions, he suspected; perhaps, diamonds on a dung-heap shine brighter.

Zeus did not seem grateful to see him. He was about to eat, he said, and had not been expecting company. Hermes would have to make himself something if he was hungry; or maybe, get a takeaway.

Watching him, greedily, clear his plate, Hermes drip-fed him with news from Olympus. It was a difficult balancing act between alerting Zeus to the danger he was in while not sending him into a fury by revealing certain details about the identities of his betrayers.

"You're looking haggard," remarked Zeus.

"Well, my job does make certain demands. If we were to..."

"Not that again!"

"Yes, that again!"

Zeus sniggered.

"You do look funny when you're indignant. Pull that face once more."

Hermes just grimaced.

"How many times do I need to tell you what a huge privilege it is to have your job."

"Privilege! Do you know where Ares sent me the other day? To the swamps of Lerna to deliver a good luck card! I'm glad you think it's so funny."

It did take a while for Zeus to contain his mirth, and even then, he kept spluttering with laughter every few minutes.

"You know," he managed to say, finally, "the mortals down here view people like you as great heroes. They deliver nice things like cards, and sometimes gifts, along with a few not so nice things, bills and bank statements. But you don't need to open them. They wear shorts even when it's cold. They must contain something in the lining, some kind of special protection from the elements. They drive red chariots. We could make yours red. It's a strong colour. And you could wear shorts. They're very fetching. And you've always had good legs. If you've got it, flaunt it; that's what they say down here."

Zeus was never more infuriating than when he was being playful.

"Children here make up hymns to sing their praises. There could be one to you. *Postman Hermes, Postman Hermes, Postman Hermes and his black and white... spermes...*"

It occurred to Zeus that other deities had far better names for rhymes. Apollo, for instance, or Athena. Pan would have been really easy, too. You could get some great limericks out of that.

He fell silent.

"I miss Sir Cecil. He was a nice cat."

Neither said anything for a while. Hermes averted his eyes. Was Zeus crying? About a mortal creature?

"I want to go home."

Zeus tried to say it firmly, authoritatively, but it came out like a querulous whine.

Hermes pursed his lips.

"It's not so simple. What... as I was about to tell you... with Atlas on the loose, and... well, if you'd seen the state of Gyges. Dashed to pieces."

Zeus looked shocked. Why had Hermes not mentioned this at the outset, rather than jabbering away with news about the antics of the likes of Calypso, Dysnomia and winged donkeys?

"Who freed him?"

"Who knows?"

Hermes felt the scorching intensity of Zeus' gaze even through the bleary eyes of Mudge.

"Maybe, your brother, Hades, was involved."

"I need to get back to protect Hera. I need to be there NOW!"

This was not what Hermes had intended. Perhaps, this visit had not been a good idea. He stuttered something about Hera being able to look after herself. Her children were all around, and Ares had been visiting her quite a lot, recently. Hermes tried to play for time.

"You're in no state right now to do anything. Besides, I told you about the factory – you know, the one run by the Cyclopes Brothers. Well, it's, secretly, being rebuilt. They'd actually stashed away a reserve supply. But you need far more thunderbolts. The Cyclopes hate Atlas, but they are not miracle workers. It will take time. But if I can persuade Hephaestus to help..."

"Of course, he'll help. He's my son."

Probably, decided Hermes, it would be sensible not to follow that line of discussion at this particular moment. He had a sudden idea.

"Do you remember the prophecy last time? If a great hero, a mortal, fights on your side..."

"Of course," interrupted Zeus. "Heracles. Where is he now?"

"Erm... well, he was last spotted at..."

Hermes took out his phone, scrolling through his pictures. He held it out to show Zeus.

"What's that great pudding got to do with anything?"

"Look closely at the face."

Zeus gasped.

"What the bineo!"

Hermes nodded.

"It took me a while to recognise him, too. It seems that he's been on a katasuboteo regimen."

Zeus looked blank.

"You know – *ka-ta-su-bot-eo*; it means fatten like a pig. And my understanding is that it was a deliberate ploy to get him out of the picture. The fact is we need a new hero. It will take years to get him into shape. But I've had this idea. We find a strong young man, a fine specimen, fit and healthy but on the point of some premature death. *You* make the jump. Mudge exits. You inhabit this new body. *He* becomes the hero. Upon his death, he goes

239

straight to the Elysian Fields. Where he is granted immortality. You get liberated from that body, and return as yourself. Only now it's like there are two of you, because he has become, like an avatar. You and the hero fight alongside one another, toppling your enemies. Just like in the old days."

Hermes watched as Zeus took this in.

"I'll find you someone."

Hermes rose to leave.

"In the meantime, just keep out of trouble, and stay away from that stupid racecourse. No more crazy betting. Oh – and pay off those parking fines."

Zeus avoided Hermes' eyes.

"You know about that?"

"Of course, I do. Who do you think sorts out all those bills you mentioned?"

Zeus stared at some crumbs on the carpet, moodily, giving an insolently large one a kick in the direction of a less obvious spot by a table leg.

"If you must know, there's no longer an issue about demands for payments for – I don't know, electricity, water, road tax, all that stuff."

"Really?"

"Yes. I sent them a message to say that Mudge had gone away, and I was just a tenant in his body."

"You said that!"

Zeus savoured the look of horror on Hermes' face. He paused before correcting himself.

"I mean in his *house*."

"So who do they think was driving your vehicle?"

"That's where I was smart, you see. I informed the police that the chariot kept getting stolen."

"Then returned each time by the thief! That's considerate."

"I told the police I had spotted the Albanians driving it away. Using it for whatever it is they do. They were here in no time. Swarming all over it. Looking for something they call fingerprints. What did you do with that Marku fellow's hands? If you've still got them, you could go round dabbing them all over the place."

Ignoring the thunderous expression on Hermes' face, Zeus dug his heels in.

"Whatever, I'm not paying those fines as a matter of principle. You should be able to park your chariot wherever there is a space. These orrhos-brained mortals! They fine you for that but not for the chemicals your vehicle is pumping out. That's one of the reasons the air is so clogged up down here, you know. No! I'm not paying the malakas a penny, and that's my final decision."

Hermes sighed.

"I'll see if I can pick up a hand."

Zeus grunted, moodily, glaring at his visitor, who was, already, half way through the front door.

"Thank you, Hermes," said Hermes, with rather rueful sarcasm.

"It's a pleasure," replied Zeus, distractedly.

The bangs on the outside of the window a few moments later made him jump.

"Low profile!" mouthed Hermes.

64

It was a busy day. The crowds were gathered. The two of
them would barely be noticed. Here he was, with Bill in
tow, putting down bets, even though Hermes was
ignoring his calls. Nevertheless, Zeus was feeling lucky.

"Give me the names of those horses again."

Bill reeled them off.

"*Smokey, California Kid, Pride of Tipperary,
Invisible Helm...*'

"*Invisible Helm!* Go and place a bet on *Invisible
Helm*. Meanwhile, I'll go and take another look at the
ones coming into the paddock. Hurry up!"

Bill shuffled off, obediently.

When he returned, he was wearing an anxious
look.

"I had the impression I was being watched."

"Really?"

Zeus nodded without listening as Bill burbled on.
It was so tempting to go for another accumulator bet, but
maybe wise not to alert Hermes.

Neither of them noticed the security team closing
in around. Before they knew it, they were being bundled
away into an office by four burly officers. Giving up his
protests about the rough way he was being manhandled,
Zeus attempted, rather ineffectually, to bite one of the
men on the arm.

It was not easy to keep up with the questions being fired at them. Who was fixing the races? It could not be these two old buffoons. Was there a gang? Insiders or people unknown in the racing world? From the UK or overseas? How had they managed it? How had so many races been rigged? Were jockeys being bribed? Or were the horses being given some supplements? They must be new on the market as nothing was detected through the usual blood tests.

Bill could hardly speak, staring around the room like a timid child accused of setting his school alight. As for Zeus, he simply protested that he had no idea what they were talking about.

They demanded to see his phone. Apparently, cameras had caught him making calls before the bets had been placed. When he resisted they grappled it from him. Him! Zeus! Once, he could have swatted each aside like flies; had he wished, he could have turned each of them into a neat pile of ash, simply by raising his little finger.

They were looking through the names on his phone.

"Who is H?" snapped a voice.

Zeus shrugged. He'd never heard of H.

"Yet you called him several times on the day you won all that money. One of the calls came just fifteen minutes before a bet was placed. You've been calling him today."

One of the security men dialled the number now. They all listened to it ringing. It went to answer-phone.

Hi. This is Hermes. I'm busy at the moment but will return the call as soon as possible. Please, leave a message.

"Hermes," repeated the security man. "Does your contact work for the delivery people?"

"I thought they had changed names," commented one of his companions. "Is it *Evri* now? Or maybe, *Parcel2Go*, or *Parcel Monkey*."

Zeus and Bill were now informed that this person from *Parcel Monkey*, obviously, a go-between, would soon be identified through his number and traced. As for themselves, they could expect to be prosecuted by the police.

"*If* we leave it to the police," one of the men added in a sinister voice. It was the one that Zeus had attempted to bite.

"In the meantime, keep away from here or any other race courses."

They were now booted out of the office. As they left, Zeus spotted results coming up on a large screen behind them. With rather mixed feelings, he noted that *Invisible Helm* had come in last.

65

Wallowing in the spa in Tyche's Palace, the mighty heroes, Heracles and Perseus, had no idea about the consternation caused by their absence. So busy had they been enjoying the good life that neither had thought to requisition Hermes to send even a postcard. Not that they would have been encouraged to do so by their host. The large payment to Tyche had come with strict conditions to keep their presence strictly under wraps. Indeed, it had been purely by chance that Hermes had discovered them. He had been delivering a message to one of the small team caring for them, the sous chef, when he had spotted the pair stuffing their faces in one of the restaurants.

In any event, having spent such a long period in this paradise of sensual delights, Heracles and Perseus had all but forgotten their old homes on the lower slopes of Mount Olympus, the suburb where the D-Gs, or demi-gods, lived, forbidden as they were from owning properties higher up. Indeed, given a wall-to-wall existence of sumptuous feasts and banquets, massages, aromatherapy, manicures, pedicures and other beauty treatments, followed by wassailing and carousing on the grandest scale, any previous life seemed like the dregs of some bygone dream. Within this huge bubble, all petty gripes had evanesced. If only their former neighbours could have achieved such contentment.

For other D-Gs, despite the luxury and beauty of their own surroundings, there were constant reminders of their second-class status. All the restrictions! For instance, they were not permitted to be members of the same clubs as proper gods; no temples or shrines were to be commissioned for them by the mortals below, and if that did occur, they were to disassociate themselves from such edifices, completely. Even the erection of statues and monuments in their honour was viewed with disapproval. Hera was especially firm on such matters.

Herk and Perk, as they were known in the neighbourhood, were not the only ones to have felt aggrieved by this. Others, such as the already-mentioned Narcie, were perpetually peeved. How was survival possible without adoration from the masses of mortals? How could they subsist in the absence of offerings?

Many of the D-Gs suffered from depression or other mental health issues. There were self-help groups, and scores of publications with titles such as 'A Hundred Ways to Love Yourself More'. Advice included such tips as the following:

Realign yourself to your mission of self love;

Dedicate as much time as possible to connecting to yourself;

Stand in front of a mirror each morning, reminding yourself how good-looking you are;

Smile at yourself, and say three new nice things about
yourself every day;

Do things that make you happy;

Only socialise with those who are also happy;

Think only positive thoughts;

Change any negative narratives, forgiving your
mistakes;

Reward yourself for being so fantastic;

Before you go to sleep, remember to pay yourself a
compliment.

Despite such sage advice, a large number of D-Gs remained in therapy. Underneath the sense of low self-esteem due to being demeaned, many suffered from pre-existing conditions. Actaeon had a morbid fear of dogs, and was also edgy in the presence of deer, of which there were many on the slopes of Olympus. Deucalion was terrified by the prospect of erectile dysfunction, despite the lack of evidence for it. Even with all the support for his condition, Dionysus remained depressed about his alcoholism, consoling himself in booze whenever those feelings became overwhelming. Hippolyta constantly worried about her size, going on eating binges when she was similarly inundated with anxiety. Augeas suffered from some kind phobia about horses, and also had a cleanliness thing. Telegonus seemed terrified about stingrays, despite any obvious presence of them on Olympus. He also had a rather creepy thing about his friends' mothers. Talking of which, Achilles suffered rages about *his* mother, Thetis, particularly with regard to her stupidity. His therapists disagreed about whether it was healthy to tolerate his insistence on wearing thick socks beneath his sandals. Even though he knew this made him look ridiculous, Achilles could not desist from putting them on – which only made him more depressed.

Come to think of it, there was probably not a single D-G without one issue or another. Despite the never-ending boom in business, the therapists were, themselves, depressed, each visiting their own therapists. All in all, the D-G suburb was a tinderbox that could ignite at any moment.

66

It was a shock for Bill when he called round next to find his friend in such perky mood. Going back to the racecourse! Was Monty out of his mind?

"But they know who we are. They will have circulated photographs. They will have shared information about us with other courses."

Zeus looked sceptical. Had photographs even been taken? What *information*? It's not as if they had seen anyone with a pen or notebook.

"On their computer."

Zeus now recalled that someone in the office had, indeed, been using a laptop, but no problem: there was a way around that.

Despite his protests, Bill did as he was ordered – as he had done throughout his life – appearing on the day of the next race meeting, head hung low, like a forlorn dog. He looked still more abject when instructed to put on the disguise Zeus had acquired.

"By gum! It's a... I mean you don't really..."

Clearly, he needed help fitting it, putting it on askew before Zeus' assistance.

"You look good with hair," grinned Zeus. "I bet all the girls were after you once."

Bill shook his head. The idea of anyone pursuing him would have been terrifying. His friend's cheeriness only made him feel still more disconsolate.

"Well, never mind, you draw them in, and I'll sweep them off their feet. By the way, don't forget the beard. It matches your lush curls."

Zeus was staring at him with apparent satisfaction at having been the genius behind such a transformation.

"Now, then, what size tights do you wear?"

Bill looked appalled.

"It was a joke. I was watching an old *Batman* film last night. I couldn't stop imagining you as my *Boy Wonder*."

An hour or so later they were loitering at a short distance away from the offices of the racecourse. Nobody had challenged them on the way in. There had been barely any odd glances. After all, there were so many *characters* at the races!

Bill almost collapsed at the sight of the security officers emerging.

"Here's our chance," snapped Zeus. "You keep a look-out."

He slipped into the office, re-emerging within seconds to Bill's relief, and heading towards the exit. Bill followed, mutely, only remembering to breathe again when they passed out through the gates. Zeus slapped him on the back.

"You really don't need to look so scared. Sometimes you remind me of someone I once knew. However fierce he tried to look, he was terrified of everything. I shall call you Phobos in the future."

Twenty minutes later they were at a lonely spot beside the river. Zeus grinned.

"This is the moment you say 'Holy Macaroni!' or something like that."

Drawing out the laptop, he flung it into the water.

"We can dispose of our wigs and beards somewhere else. And right now, Robin, back to the Bat Cave! Or better still, let's stop off for an all-day breakfast. As I bought our disguises, it's only fair if you pay."

67

"You did what!"

Hermes was gawping at him. Zeus smirked. He could not have looked more pleased with himself.

"I outwitted them, Hermes. Gotham City can sleep at ease again, knowing that all its citizens can enjoy the races."

"You stole a laptop? Do you think you're not still out there? Your names will be in the Cloud."

Zeus looked upwards.

"I think you'll find mortals can't see that far."

"Just do as I say: do NOT return there."

At the next event, however, Zeus was back. With Bill in tow. They placed a string of bets, losing most. However, on the final race, Zeus put down a large sum on a long-shot. His horse came in first. He could do it – without the help of Hermes!

Zeus was walking, jauntily, down a stairway, out along a narrow path between two gates towards the exit, grinning from ear to ear. From Bill's face, it did not look as if he had taken in their success.

Which was when Porus struck.

PART 4 - ANAGNORISIS

JOINING THE PANTHEON OF GODS: A BEGINNER'S GUIDE

1. In recent years, along with temples and shrines,
    there has been a vogue for impressive
    monuments. It is advisable to exercise some
    caution in this matter. The aspiring god or
    goddess should be aware of the sheer number of
    applications that are currently in place in
    planning offices. It is not for the authors of this
    text to be too critical, or even to pass an opinion
    about the gods who have lodged such paperwork,
    but it might be sobering to reflect that, at time of
    publication of the current edition of this guide,
    there are more than six hundred known
    applications for a 'colossus'. Unless your
    resources can stretch to the most colossal of
    colossuses, you may wish to think along the lines
    of some alternative, a less quotidian token of
    prestige.

2. The very topic of tokens of prestige is
    contentious, and has divided those dwelling on
    Mount Olympus into two mutually antagonistic
    camps. It is useful to consider the matter with
    care, and wherever possible, to seek professional
    advice.

3. There is a purist position taken in some, highly respected, circles that such displays are 'tacky' and 'naff', undermining the dignity of the deified.

4. The venerable individuals in this camp point to those who are not actual deities who have been trailblazers in this trend. Examples include the following: a fashion company, named Versace, persuaded by the gorgon, Medusa, to turn her face into a logo; a jewellery brand, celebrating Pandora; a floor cleaner named after the warrior, Ajax. Even the horse, Pegasus, has got aboard the gravy train, with his image on an oil company, Mobil, and has even diversified with a computer company, Asus.

5. It might also be noted that a god who indulges in such opportunities risks association with entire groups that are far from suitable. The warlike group of females from Africa has sold its name to a company that appears to specialise in everything. The Trojans have done likewise with a product that mortals call 'condoms', which appear to be some kind of phallos accoutrement.

6. While it is true that most of the august, older, deities have eschewed this fad, some of the younger gods have embraced it. Nike, goddess of victory, has given her name to a sports brand; Apollo has sponsored a space programme. Hermes has been particularly active, with his name on a fashion house in Paris, not to mention a company delivering everything from parcels to flowers. He even managed to get his logo on a multi-national tire company, *Goodyear*.

7. The goddess, Aphrodite, has steered a middle course, allowing her most famous symbol, the dove, to appear on a range of soap and beauty products.

8. Seemingly, part of a campaign to revamp his image, even the discredited and dispersed god, Kronos, has managed to establish some kind of consultancy and software company. One might have supposed that association with a deity of no fixed abode might constitute an act with, potentially, negative consequences.

9. For the aspiring god or goddess, all this is liable to cause a great deal of confusion. The Guide's advice would be to steer clear of such

opportunities, reconsidering the matter only after election to the Pantheon.

68

"Definitely dead. Totally obliterated. It's over."

It was difficult to believe that the deed was done. The group in the cave gaped in wonderment as Porus boasted about how he had managed to locate Zeus.

"You wouldn't have recognised him. Shifty looking. Tottering around like a befuddled, old tortoise. Maybe, a relative of the one dropped by that eagle onto the head of Aeschylus. But the same old Zeus. As soon as he saw me, he tried to toddle away. But I got him. Good and proper! And the mortals around didn't even know it was me."

He jumped up, pumping a fist into the air.

"Porus 1 – Zeus Nil!"

It took a time for him to come down from high. Finally, he sat down again.

"You can call your empusa back, Hades. Don't pretend you didn't send one. Not that she achieved anything. But when Porus is sent on a job, Porus gets it done."

"Sent?" said Ares, sharply.

Hera gave Porus a cool glance.

"You were not *sent*, Porus, you requisitioned yourself. And nobody said *kill* him. You can check the minutes of our meeting."

"Minutes?"

"We always take minutes, Porus."

Hera looked for confirmation to Themis, who, slowly, leafed through some papers.

"Killing? No, I see nothing about that here."

"But what about... about Project Z-R?" stammered Porus.

"The minutes of our meetings referred to Zeus *Reformation*, maybe, *Removal*, if absolutely, essential. There was never any mention of actual bloodshed."

There was always something quietly authoritative about Themis' manner.

Ares' face was thunderous.

"It was *my* destiny to obliterate him, not *yours*."

He took a step towards Porus, the look on his face suggesting that Porus was about to be ripped into tiny pieces. Immediately, Hera stepped between them.

"Ares! Our oath! Everybody in this place is safe."

Following Hera's lead, a few others now joined Hera, shielding Porus.

"Safe whilst in this place," snarled Ares.

With that, he stormed out.

It took a while to restore order. When they were all seated again, Themis reminded them that proper procedure was required. The Ethics Committee would need to meet, to determine whether Porus might be given post project approval. If this was not deemed to be appropriate, then Themis' own committee would convene to decide whether formal charges against Porus should be made. In the meantime, he must remain in the confines of his own dwellings on Mount Olympus, where he would be provided with guards. With Ares in his current mood, Porus may need protection.

Hera was adamant. While her son may be impetuous, prone to violent rages, he would not be so foolish as to jeopardise his claim of succession.

It was all so difficult for Porus to take in. He had expected to be received as a hero.

When the others had left, and she and Hades were alone, Hera poured a celebratory drink. It would be gratifying, she noted, to get final confirmation, and possibly, illuminating to find out what her husband had got up to during his time as a mortal. Surely, the soul of Zeus' host would be passing through Hades' kingdom at any time.

Hades sighed. He was reminded how the pampered residents of Olympus had absolutely no notion of the difficulties of running the Underworld. How exactly did Hera think that the individual would be picked out? Did she know how many floated in every day?

"We can't keep up; by the time we get planning permission through for all the additional terminals, we discover that we need to put in for still more. There are camps with souls who have been waiting for an age for the paperwork to be processed. Poor Charon is worked to the bone!"

Hera would just have to make do with the knowledge that she was now a widow with the freedom to do whatever she liked. It's not as if anybody needed to know what Zeus had consumed for his last supper!

69

Such was the excitement in Tyche's palace that those in
the main hall were jostling in the queues to lay their bets.
The wondrous creatures along the myriad of passageways
were virtually unvisited.

For the record, the odds were as follows.

Ares to take over from Zeus – 2 to one on

Atlas to lead a revolt – 3 to one

Hades to become ruler – 4 to one

Kronos to return – 5 to one

Poseidon to take over on a temporary (caretaker) basis – 9
to one

Apollo to take over on a temporary (caretaker) basis – 11
to one

Hades and Hera to become joint rulers – 12 to one

Porus to take over – 33 to one

Return of Zeus – 1,000 to one.

70

When a man has no wife or children, only distant relatives, few friends, no connection to a workplace or any specific religious institution, it can be a wonder that a funeral can even get organised. In this instance, the local council did not need to step in. The Reverend Simon Buckland volunteered his services, not on account of any past connection or knowledge of the recently departed individual, but because he happened to be a decent man who believed that even a sheep belonging to no flock at all warranted rescue, however far it may have wandered astray. And surely, anyone departing the stage, even an auxiliary scene shifter, deserved some kind of send-off.

Not only did Simon Buckland offer to arrange a service, but he went to great lengths to discover the whereabouts and identities of the acquaintances of the deceased.

71

"*My* destiny. Not some nobody's. To destroy him muchly and bigly!"

However accustomed she was to Ares' strops, this was becoming tiresome. Hera had been planning a bit of a clear out, something she did regularly. A tidy home reflected order and harmony.

Finally, she managed to get a word in.

"Darling, these processes are slow. You know what committees are like, and just think how it is when there are several involved. I know how much you wanted to kill your father. It's the most natural instinct in the world. But you can rest assured that Porus will get a stern rebuke."

Although her voice was soothing, the words somehow only seemed to inflame Ares more.

"A rebuke!"

"Well, he is the son of a nymph... remind me, dear, what was the tart's name? Yes, that's the one, Metis. And there *was* that prophecy."

"What prophecy?"

Hera put her hand to her mouth, as if she had already said too much.

"What prophecy?"

"I shouldn't have mentioned it. Now you must promise not to get angry. Oh, must you, Ares?"

Inadvertently, he had picked up an abstract piece of sculpture, a solid-looking, metal object, which might have suggested a figure crouching, and he had squeezed it into a shapeless ball.

"What prophecy?"

"We don't believe in that sort of nonsense in this day and age. It's just a silly, old augury, dear. You remember, about Metis having a son who would become more powerful than Zeus and destroy him. Of course, everyone assumed that it would be the child she had with Zeus, who turned out to be Athena, but now that Porus has murdered Zeus, some of the deities around here – dafter ones, of course, and very minor – well, they are saying that Porus is the *one*. And he is destined to become our next ruler. You know how rumours spread. I hear that, according to the current odds, he is close to overtaking you as the favourite. All so ridiculous!"

Ares was already marching towards the door.

"Now, don't do anything rash, dear!"

72

Reverend Widdecome had exhausted the anecdotes he had heard about the deceased. In truth, there had not been many. The late individual appeared to have been the most ordinary of men. Almost as if he had not existed! Yet after all, was it not the meek who would inherit?

He now scanned the pews. There were only a few rows that were filled at the front, not that those there actually knew the recently departed. They were there because their pastor had managed to persuade them to attend the service as an act of charity. A dozen or so members of his congregation, the ones he could always rely on.

While he may not have been noted for his gifts of eloquence – indeed, his sermons were famously uninspiring – what Simon Buckland did possess was this Lord Kitchener on a poster gift: he was able to stare into a group as if fixing his attention upon each individual. Only whereas Kitchener's gaze was stern, his was benevolent. Saint Francis of Assisi could not have looked more compassionate or gentle. Such was the aura of kindness emanating from him that it felt almost possible to hear a collective, if inaudible, purring from the pews.

His eyes now alighted on one of the deceased's acquaintances he had managed to track down. The man was sitting alone at the end of the third row. He looked a little nervous, as if this was all a bit overwhelming.

Fixing him with his most benign gaze, Reverend Buckland beckoned him forward. At this point, he announced, he would like to invite a friend to come and share a few memories.

The man shuffled forward, a little reluctantly, avoiding the glances from those who were present. He looked as if he might tumble over onto his face upon receiving an encouraging pat on the shoulder from the pastor.

He cleared his throat.

"You will all be thinking that this was not a very interesting person... and you would be right: he was not at all interesting. Not very bright. Come to think of it, he was stupid..."

Zeus gulped. Perhaps, he should say something kinder.

"He was quite a nice person – not offensive. Just a bit wimpy. Everyone used to call him 'Phobos'. And although he was really stupid, and irritating – and sometimes, I hid when I heard his knock on the door – he tried to be helpful. He was someone who came round and brought me a newspaper and some bars of chocolate. They weren't my favourites.

I mean, a fudge bar! It's not that it tastes bad. It's just so unsatisfying. Like it's over before you begin. There was this nymph I knew once. I forget her name. And she used to say: *We could take our time. How about some foreplay?* Foreplay! What's the point in that? It's not something Hera ever went on about.

It's like... I don't know... going into a shop to buy a pair of trousers and spending an age just stroking them first. Why would anyone do that?

This nymph, whatever her name was, just lounging around, looking ridiculous. A bit like Bill. When I saw him just lying there, I thought: *By Gum! Bill's holding his breath for a long time!* And then I realised that – by gum, he wasn't breathing! It was surprising... unnerving to see him like that. He was so still.

I felt a kind of... sadness, because, although he was not a very interesting man, he was... Bill. Not deep sadness, of course, like you feel when you lose a cat – but still... regret. I will think about him when I buy a newspaper, not the one he got, or when I purchase chocolate... although not fudge bars, of course."

It was an interesting speech, Reverend Buckland assured him after the service, if a little unusual.

73

Psecas was flicking through a glossy brochure showing hairstyles, commenting on which were *hot* right now and which were unfashionable. Iasion, a youthful and rather striking, demi-god sat on the stool in front of her. He pointed.

"Maybe that one."

"Great choice," gushed Psecas. "The Porus look is so *now*. It sort of channels the inner femininity. We must do a dozen of them every day. When he takes over, he's bound to appreciate those who showed support by choosing his look."

"When?"

"Of course, I'm far more interested in aesthetics than politics, but one of the regulars was saying only this morning that he is now two to one on."

"What about Ares?"

Psecas pulled a face.

"What about him?"

"Well, won't he have a say about that? After all, there's big money on him."

It occurred to Iasion that the smart thing to do might be to hedge his bets: have one side of his head 'Ares', and the other, 'Porus'. Was there some style, perhaps, that combined Porus' sensitive, slightly effeminate, look with Ares' more manly cut?

Psecas was half way through what would have been her fifth Porus cut of the day when they heard the commotion outside. Someone opened the door, yelling, excitedly.

Had they heard about Porus?

Staff and customers listened, feigning shock while, secretly, delighting in the drama of the situation. However had someone managed to get past the security team? They were trained Cyclopes! Or was it possible that the security team had been complicit? Surely, the rumours that the assailant had been Ares were unfounded! He could not be so reckless as to take the law into his own hands, committing such a violent crime against a fellow immortal.

Did they say that Porus had been found impaled on a spear halfway up a wall? And hanging upside down! How dreadful! Yet also thrilling!

And that, subsequently, Ares had been discovered by the security guards, calmly sitting in the kitchen midway through consumption of Porus' tongue, eyes, nose and ears?

And that he had explained the action as being just in case some bright spark had the notion of reviving Porus!

And that he had commented, casually, that the nose was moist and surprisingly tasty!

What kind of monster was he?

It took a while to take it all in, before the stylists felt able to resume work.

"Maybe, a different look," suggested Iasion. "I don't know, perhaps, a bit more manly... like... maybe, Ares?"

"Anyone can do that themselves," said Psecas, tautly, "with a pair of garden shears and wearing a blindfold!"

SURVIVING THE 21ST CENTURY: A HANDBOOK FOR
PENSIONERS

ENTRY 7

BEING A PENSIONER IS A LITTLE LESS
PRESTIGIOUS THAN I WAS INITIALLY LED TO BELIEVE.
FOR MANY OF YOU, IT IS A BIT LIKE GRADUALLY
FADING FROM A PHOTOGRAPH, OR STANDING ON A
MUDSLIP THAT IS GIVING WAY. YOU SHOULD RESIST
THE TEMPTATION TO SLIDE INTO IRRELEVANCE.
MAKE AS MUCH NOISE AND FUSS AS YOU CAN. BE
FORTHRIGHT! BE RUDE! BE PRESENT!

UNFORTUNATELY, THROUGH A DESIGN
DEFECT, MORTALS WILL REACH A POINT WHERE THEY
CEASE TO EXIST. FOR SOME REASON – ABOUT WHICH I
STILL REMAIN, AT THIS STAGE, A LITTLE UNCLEAR,
PENSIONERS ARE AT PARTICULAR RISK.

IT IS INTERESTING TO SPECULATE ABOUT WHAT
HAPPENS TO THEM, AFTERWARDS. TO BE FRANK, I
HAVE NEVER REALLY INQUIRED ABOUT WHAT GOES
ON IN HADES' KINGDOM. FROM WHAT I HEAR, IT'S
ALL A BIT ON THE DULL SIDE. YOU MIGHT HAVE
THOUGHT, GIVEN YOUR PROPENSITY FOR DEATH, YOU
MORTALS MIGHT HAVE RAISED YOUR OWN QUERIES
ON THE MATTER, BUT THOSE I SPEAK TO SEEM
RATHER VAGUE. IS THERE AN OPTION? WELL, I AM
NOT ALTOGETHER CERTAIN HOW THEY MANAGED IT,
BUT A FEW INDIVIDUALS APPEAR TO HAVE ELUDED
HADES' CLUTCHES ALTOGETHER AT THE MOMENT OF

DEFUNCTION THROUGH THE ACT OF TRANSMOGRIFICATION INTO PARK BENCHES. HOWEVER, THE PLAQUES ON THOSE BENCHES MERELY TELL YOU THAT THOSE INVOLVED ARE NOW THERE, WITHOUT PROVIDING ANY CLUES AS TO HOW THIS WAS ACHIEVED.

FOR THE REMAINDER, IT IS TO BE HOPED THAT THEY ARE NOT AWARE OF WHAT IS HAPPENING. RECENTLY, I DISCOVERED ON A NATURE PROGRAMME THAT A MAYFLY ONLY HAS ONE DAY OF LIFE. DOES IT THINK: 'WHAT THE BINEO! I'M A MAYFLY. I'M ONLY HERE FOR TWENTY-FOUR HOURS. NOT EVEN TIME FOR MY MANDIBLES TO DEVELOP! NO OPPORTUNITY FOR EVEN A SINGLE GOOD SNACK! IF I'M LUCKY I'LL GET MY END AWAY IN JUST THE ONE QUICK LAGNEIA, THEN I'M OFF! TA VERY MUCH! XAIPE!'

I DON'T THINK SO. AND I DON'T EXPECT MOST MORTALS NOTICE EITHER. I NEVER HEARD BILL SAY: 'BY GUM! I CAN'T RUN AS FAST AS I DID IN MY YOUTH, EVERYTHING ACHES, AND WHAT'S MORE, MY NOSE AND EARS ARE SPROUTING HAIRS. I WONDER WHERE _THAT'S_ HEADING!'

YES −THERE MAY BE ONE OR TWO OF YOU WHO HAVE A SLIGHT INKLING, AND ARE MINDED TO START POINTING FINGERS. IT'S SO EASY TO ACCUSE OTHERS. WELL, I CAN TELL YOU ONE THING: IT WAS NEVER REALLY ABOUT THE THEFT OF FIRE.

NATURALLY, YOU WILL RECALL HOW IT STARTED: PROMETHEUS ROLLING CLAY AND ATHENA BREATHING LIFE INTO YOU. THEN THAT SNEAK HANDING YOU A GIFT NOT INTENDED FOR YOU.

AND WHO WAS TO KNOW THAT EPIMETHEUS, WITH ALL HIS PROMISE, WOULD TURN OUT TO BE AN ORRHOS-BRAINED SHIT-WIT? INSTEAD OF ENDOWING YOU WITH ALL THE WONDERFUL QUALITIES THAT HAD BEEN PLANNED, HE PRODUCED HUMANS LIKE... WELL, BILL. IMAGINE SENDING _HIM_ ON A MISSION TO BRING BACK THE GOLDEN APPLES. HE'D HAVE RETURNED WITH A FUDGE BAR AND THE _DAILY EXPRESS_!

SO, IF YOU REALLY WANT TO BLAME SOMEONE, YOU MIGHT START WITH THAT STUBBORN MULE, PROMETHEUS. A NAME! THAT WAS ALL HE WAS ASKED FOR! WHY WOULD HE NOT REVEAL THE IDENTITY OF THE CHILD WHO WOULD OVERTHROW ZEUS? HE WAS LIKE A BROTHER TO THE KING OF THE GODS. ALL THAT NASTINESS BECAUSE OF A NAME. THERE WOULD HAVE BEEN NO PANDORA, NO SICKNESS, NO PESTILENCE, NO GETTING OLD. ALL FOR AN AKOS-PEOS NAME!

WHERE WAS I? OH YES, MORTALITY. WELL, I SUSPECT THAT PHYSICAL DETERIORATION IS SOMEHOW CONNECTED TO TIME, WHICH SEEMS TO OPERATE IN A PECULIARLY LINEAR WAY DOWN HERE. ORDINARILY, IT SHOULD BE QUITE LOGICAL TO SAY – DO YOU REMEMBER WHEN WE GO TO? – OR –

275

WHEN WE WILL GO TO SUCH AND SUCH A PLACE?
EXISTENCE DOWN HERE APPEARS TO BE NEATLY
ORDERED, SEQUENCED AND PACKAGED, IN A WAY
THAT MAKES THIS IMPOSSIBLE.

THIS UNORTHODOX WAY OF ORGANISING
TIME LEAVES PENSIONERS IN A PARTICULARLY
VULNERABLE SITUATION. IF I CAN DISCOVER WAYS
IN WHICH YOU, MORE DECAYING, MORTALS CAN
PROTECT YOURSELVES, I WILL ADD SOMETHING IN A
FUTURE JOURNAL ENTRY.

IN THE MEANTIME, MY ADVICE WOULD BE TO SEEK
DISTRACTIONS, AVOIDING ATTENDANCE AT
FUNERALS, WHICH ARE, QUITE FRANKLY, ON THE
DEPRESSING SIDE. IF SOMEONE INVITES YOU TO A
FUNERAL, JUST SAY YOU HAVE A HORSE RACE TO
ATTEND, OR STILL BETTER, A GAME OF BOWLS TO
PLAY.

CHOCOLATE HELPS. BARS LIKE SNICKERS ARE MORE
SUBSTANTIAL THAN FUDGES. THEY CAN BE BOUGHT IN
MINI-PACKETS FROM LIDL – THOUGH YOU NEED TO
EAT AT LEAST THREE AT A TIME FOR THE EFFECTS TO
KICK IN. THE COMBINATION OF SOFT NOUGAT,
PEANUTS, CHOCOLATE AND CARAMEL IS ONE OF
YOUR GREAT ACHIEVEMENTS, AND SHOWS THAT
MORTALS CAN SOMETIMES COME UP WITH IDEAS
THAT HAVE NOT EVEN BEEN CONSIDERED ON
OLYMPUS. IT MAY NOT BE COMPLETE CONSOLATION
FOR YOUR SEEMINGLY INEVITABLE FUTURE,

PACKAGED INSIDE A WOODEN BOX, BUT IT IS
SOMETHING, AT LEAST.

74

Hermes was usually careful to ensure that his visits to the town of Newton Abbot occurred at a time when he could count on Zeus being alone. On this occasion, he had not checked to ensure that no other visitors would be around. He now found a fierce-looking mortal girl blocking his entry and asking whether he was here to try and rip off her great-uncle by telling him that he needed loft insulation or insurance or something like that.

She seemed reluctant to allow him inside even when Zeus assured her that this was a friend. A friend! He looked as if he could only have been in his early twenties. What sort of young man hung out with a *friend* of Uncle Monty's age?

She did not want to allow him in, even if he happened to be by far the most attractive young man she had ever seen, albeit a little too clean-cut for her own inchoate tastes. She was attracted to more rebellious looking types, and although she was not entirely sure, at this time, she thought that she might be finding girls more interesting.

"Are you a Jehovah's Witness? Or a Mormon?"

Before Hermes could reply, Zeus intervened.

"I told you, it's my friend, Her..."

"Herman," said Hermes, quickly.

It was the closest mortal name he could access.

Hermes now noticed the girl's brother, who had been standing, quietly, at the edge of the room.

"And you two must be Frida and Antonio. Your Uncle Monty has told me all about you."

"Herman!"

Antonio could not contain it any longer. He began to splutter. His body was rocking. Now Zeus joined in. Hermes noticed that the girl mortal had just covered her mouth to suppress the grin.

"Yes, Herman. Is there something amusing about that?"

There was something irritating in the extreme about the way in which the boy mortal shook his head while his body convulsed more rapidly. Fortunately, the girl mortal took pity on him. Did he want a drink? She led the immature brother into the kitchen. With his acute hearing, Hermes heard her admonishing the boy in a whisper, telling him to be polite. Then he heard them both sniggering.

Zeus' expression was particularly irritating.

"Gelos, Hermes! Can't you take a joke?"

Hermes scowled, before passing on his news, quickly and selectively. He had decided not to mention the Ares matter, though he did mention that Porus, who had been harbouring a burning grudge, had somehow discovered Zeus' whereabouts, and attempted an assassination. What good fortune that he had mistaken another pensioner for Zeus!

Reminding Zeus, that even someone like Porus would pose a major threat, given Zeus' current condition, Hermes added that extreme vigilance needed to be maintained. Zeus should inform Hermes if there was anything suspicious, in which case he could be moved somewhere else.

Meanwhile, Zeus could rest assured that Porus had been... *neutralised*. However, Atlas was still going berserk, and needed to be apprehended. And Zeus should not forget that, somewhere or other, hopefully in the other Argos, not the one here, there was an empusa searching for him.

He continued giving advice on how it would be unwise to stand out, and began to list some of the public places Zeus should avoid at all costs. How lucky he had been that nobody on Olympus, other than Porus, had come upon the local media news story about a pensioner's astounding luck on the horses!

Hermes fell silent on the children's return. The moronic boy appeared to have regained his composure. Hermes gave an account of how he had met their Uncle Monty at a game of bowls, and how impressed he had been by the skills of a senior player. Finishing his drink, he got up to depart.

For some reason, Zeus decided that a formal handshake was appropriate.

"Thank you for visiting... Herman."

The boy snorted. Herman glared at him.

"Gelos!" exclaimed the boy.

I'll give you *gelos*, you little orjik-sack!

Hermes only just held back from uttering it aloud. He smiled, thinly, letting himself out. On the way down the street he glanced through the window. Both Zeus and the boy mortal were lying on the carpet, wriggling with mirth.

"Herman!" they chanted, kicking their legs into the air. Catching sight of him through the window, Zeus was pointing.

"Herman!"

They both rolled over, clutching their sides. As he walked off, Hermes pondered about the mental degradation of the KoG while in the body of the Mudge. Clearly, the sooner he got him out of there, the better. Then again, he wondered why he even cared.

75

By some form of serendipity, Narcie had found his way to Psecas. Or perhaps, she had found him, spotting potential that nobody else recognised. Almost certainly, he would not have been offered employment anywhere else: he could not concentrate on a task for more than the briefest of periods; he had an infuriating way of mocking everyone else's work, while acting as if his own was superior. Even Psecas, herself, was an amateur compared to him.

However, if Psecas was nothing else, she was a shrewd businesswoman. Narcie's rather beautiful, androgynous looks, alone, brought in additional business; customers would stare at him in wonderment, the very sight of him a visual feast surpassing any other. Instead of sexual thoughts, involving touch or taste, their impulses were about aesthetics; they merely wanted to stare at this work of art, this embodiment of perfection.

Besides, there was something about Narcie that she liked, some combination of determination and vulnerability that reminded her of herself. He, too, had risen from nowhere; he was only trying to make something of himself.

And the fact was that, when he was able to focus on the job in hand, Narcie did have an eye for style. Psecas guessed, correctly, that customers would not mind him holding a large mirror, and then angling it so as to see himself. It meant that they could study two of him, one in the flesh and one in a reflective lens, whereby all could marvel at the grace, the lack of a single blemish.

Nor did they mind that his conversation was neither original nor penetrating. Indeed, even for a hairdressing salon, it reached hitherto uncharted levels of banality – and this despite the fact that Narcie described himself as a thinker who combined Aristotelian with Socratic ideas. If you don't get it, he liked to drawl, it was because of the challenge of keeping up with dialectic thinking merged with pluralistic contingency. When asked what this meant, he would just wave a hand, idly, ordering them to look it up. As Psecas had anticipated, this was all viewed as endearing, a charming quirk of this *marvellous boy* make-up.

Narcie also took indiscretion into virgin territory, unexplored by the even most intrepid of hairdressers. Right now he was talking about Porus and Ares, declaring, loudly, that Ares was, obviously, in league with Hades. Psecas looked round, nervously. Here in the Underworld, Hades' spies were everywhere. Nobody had dared mention Ares since his detention.

Narcie did not appear to notice the uneasy looks. He also forgot his train of thought about the link between Ares and Hades. Instead, he just laughed, loudly.

"They say he has fetishes! You know, Hades, in the bedchamber – some truly bizarre stuff. Man, does he love it kinky!"

There was some tittering, along with more uneasy looks.

"I heard from a reliable source that he's into rafanidosis."

"What a radish root up the..."

"Yes, right up the orrhos."

"Is he the rafanidosisist or the rafanidosisee?"

"Well, according to my very reliable source, a bit from Corinthian Column A and a bit from Corinthian Column B. And I've heard that he's also into..."

He was cut short by a nudge from Psecas.

His voice dropped to a stage whisper, during which he gave further details about Hades' sexual proclivities.

"He also likes doing it this way."

There was laughter as he contorted his body into an unusual position.

"Well, who doesn't?" retorted one of the more playful customers.

Narcie looked surprised.

"Well, dur, hello..o..o! Hera, for one."

"Oh – well, that might be a problem."

Narcie missed the tone of feigned surprise.

"Quite right it is. When it's shag-a-clock, Hera only likes the one position, darling."

"Are they, officially, an ... item?"

This was getting out of hand. Everyone knew that Hades and Hera were now an 'item', but as yet, nobody publicly referred to the fact. Least of all, down here in a salon so close to Hades' palace!

A hush fell over the place as a new client stepped up to take a place in one of the styling chairs.

Charon!

Had they not noticed him enter? He was good at that. For how long had he been sitting there, listening?

Charon!

If he came in more than twice in a millennium, it was a surprise. Psecas, herself, stepped up to the chair.

"The usual?"

"I think... something different. A makeover for Friend Charon."

He paused for a while, craning his neck and glancing around, as if registering the identity of each and every individual sitting there.

"Something with a look of bizarre fetishes."

A mirthless grin.

Shudders all around the room.

So acute was his hearing that Charon could hear the slightest intake of breath.

"Friend Charon hears that the Kronos look might be back in. Or, maybe, just something playful, if you prefer."

Psecas grimaced. She tried to concentrate on the task. What did *graveyard* playful look like?

"Don't let Friend Charon interrupt such interesting conversations."

Silence had fallen like a shroud, smothering the place. Just a snip-snip-snip sound of scissors. Until the departure of the frisky ghoul.

"What in the name of...?"

Even Narcie fell silent.

76

Newton Abbot had a cinema, an old-fashioned edifice called the *Alexandra*, all faded pomp and tatty grandeur. Zeus loved the place. He could sit here alone and watch films. He felt anonymous, safe, invisible. For an hour or so, he could feel that he was not Mudge; he was no one.

Just before the lights went down, he happened to glance round. She was there? Had she noticed him? Turning quickly to conceal his face, he sank a little deeper in his seat.

His heart started beating fast. He concentrated on being not Zeus inside Reginald Montgomery Mudge, but Reginald Montgomery Mudge inside Reginald Montgomery Mudge. Only, the more he thought about it, the more he felt like Zeus.

A cold sweat. Had she been following him? Was she the empusa Hermes had warned him about? Just biding her time – another small torment?

And then everything went dark.

77

A visit to the Underworld is pretty much on everyone's bucket-list, whether they know it or not. It is recommended that you push it as far down your list as possible, because there really is not an awful lot to do there. Indeed, for amenities, it must be one of the least well-provisioned destinations you can select. The accommodation is, frankly, shabby, and the choice of eating-places hopelessly limited. There is a theme park, which some company began to build and then gave up half way through. The spas are a bit of a joke, with something of the Siberian Soviet camp feel about them. Only less luxurious!

The only grand building is Hades' Palace – which to be honest, could do with some renovation. Visitors should take note of the sign outside: *NO ENTRY EXCEPT ON PUBLIC HOLIDAYS*. Only, there are no public holidays in the Underworld.

The other buildings worth seeing are the hairdressing salons. All very well if you go on holiday with the intention of getting your hair styled every day. Why Psecas should have set up so many in that part of the world is something of a mystery.

As for the transport system, it is an absolute shambles. The best way to travel is along the rivers, but try finding a boat! The ones that do not leak are taken.

The main river, the Styx, is eerily still, the sole sound the splashing of phantom oars from some boat that is never seen. The air is thick with stale, half-forgotten oaths made by the gods. As there is no wind, you cannot sail along it, so you are forced to row. It feels as if you are barely moving, however expert you may be, causing an incredible weariness. Nevertheless, it remains the best river to travel along.

The detour across swampland to the Asphodel Meadows do not warrant the effort; nor is it wise to make the side-trip to the Elysian Fields. The paperwork makes it impossible to get in.

Unless you enjoy rowing through flames, the River Phlegethon is best avoided. Should you be so foolhardy as to ignore this advice, it is to be hoped that you are overwhelmed by the sulphurous fumes before you and your boat catch alight.

The Cocytus, river of murderers, is also best avoided, if possible. It merely moves round in a circle, a whole host of malicious spirits dwelling on the banks and beneath the surface.

Still, it is less depressing than the ill-named River Acheron, the wideness of which makes it more like a lake. Utterly drab, with no landmarks and swampy sections where you are liable to get stuck, its single redeeming feature is that it is generally shrouded in mist. The low moaning in the air, described as 'charming' in some guidebooks, soon becomes monotonous, while a constant stench is of appeal only to a minority.

Your best bet may be the Lethe, clogged by rotting boats carrying travellers who have lost all sense of time, place or self. For a while, before you, yourself, are overcome, it can be diverting to stare into the faces of those doomed to choose this route, their empty eyeballs staring through you into eternal nothingness.

The actual *must-see* locations in the Underworld are somewhat overrated. The famous Elm of False Dreams has a rather shrivelled appearance. The Vale of Mourning is nowhere near as lively as its name suggests, its nightlife a particular disappointment. The vibe at the Rock of Unburied Souls is no better. The Grove of Persephone takes an age to reach, and when you get there, you find that access is completely restricted unless your name is... Persephone – and you happen to be a goddess. Even then, you don't get in unless you can demonstrate through official documentation that you are married to Hades.

More adventurous visitors are inclined to head straight for Tartarus, due to its reputation for dramatic sights. This may go against conventional thinking, but someone really needs to get this out there: Tartarus is so...oooo overrated. If you choose to drive, be aware that the roads are, at best, ill maintained, and more often, atrocious. If you are using a sat-nav, it tends to bring you back to the same places over and over again.

There is no central Tourist Information Office, just a squalid backroom in an abandoned station on a railroad that never got built. Scattered around, you may pick up a few leaflets, but bear in mind, the information is not always accurate. For instance, on one map it lists the places where bits of Kronos were supposedly strewn, but there is no veracity to them whatsoever. Even the supposedly reliable *Lonely Cosmos* guides to Tartarus have been taken in by this false information. Some sad joker had simply gone around listing anything shaped like bits of body! Be warned, too, that these supposedly unmissable sights entail trips that cover a vast distance.

Given the scorching temperatures and the exorbitant cost of sun-lotion, the rest of the Underworld – in the opinion of informed correspondents – is preferable.

For some, nevertheless, those of a certain disposition, Tartarus remains enticing on account of the entertainment. There are always a few tourists watching, in hysterics, as Tantalus stands beneath a fruit tree, not quite able to reach the fruit. Several will indulge in calling out comments, as encouraged by attendants. "Get a ladder, tosspot!" is a particularly popular shout.

It might be noted that the cafeteria at this location sells one of the best selections of sandwiches to be found in Tartarus, despite an unnecessary tendency (in the opinion of this guide's contributors) to add cucumber to each one.

Visiting Ixion on his fiery spinning-wheel is an attraction which some visitors rave about. Similarly, you can watch Sisyphus, pushing his boulder up the hill. Once again, you are encouraged by staff to join in, with louds cries of 'ooo' and 'almost there' and 'oopsy'.

Close by, you will find Salmoneus, undergoing his own torment. He has been placed as close as possible to his mutually-loathed brother, Sisyphus, for companionship. Paying little attention to his brother, Salmoneus prefers to interact with bystanders, telling anyone who will listen that he was not impersonating Zeus; it was just a bit of fun at a fancy-dress party.

Be warned: at this location, there is only a small booth selling refreshments, and it frequently runs out of supplies

At another popular tourist spot, it is recommended that you take a packed lunch while watching the giant, Tityos, having his liver gouged out by vultures. There is not even a sandwich bar, let alone a hotdog stall there.

78

The aroma of food brought him round. He was in his house. She was cooking something. Feeding him before she murdered him?

How long would it take for Hermes to arrive? He had no idea, having never bothered to ask Hermes about his journey in the past. If only he had been a little less self-absorbed. He groped in his pocket for his phone. It wasn't there.

He wondered now how he could have been so stupid as not to have noticed. She had been there when he had first arrived, probably after a tip-off. Having insinuated her way into his life, for some reason, she wanted to drag things out. They were like that, he now recollected, dimly; an empusa was reputed to enjoy the foreplay even more than the act. Like a cat with a trapped animal.

And, of course, she had owned a cat.

He could not deny that her cooking was good, the possibility that it could be poisoned only occurring to him midway through. Perhaps, he could drag things out with small talk, in case Hermes passed by.

"My niece was due to be calling in. She could pop by at any moment. She's been concerned about me."

The empusa smiled, watching with satisfaction as he took another mouthful.

"She's in a new relationship. With... another female, not a male mortal."

The empusa smiled again, commenting that it was hardly a surprise if his niece was with another woman. It was pretty obvious, after all. Surely, he had noticed. How long had he known his niece?

"About eleven or twelve occasions," he said. "Oh, and the times I met her at her house."

Years? How many years, she persisted. How would he know how many years he had known Ember? She was family. Presumably, all his life.

"Seventy-four years," he said.

"Reginald Montgomery Mudge!"

The sound of the name made him sit up. It brought doubt. Had she been in hiding here for so long that she had forgotten who or what he was? Might she be a very dim empusa? Or maybe, not an empusa at all? Might she be... just Lily Tucker?

"Sometimes, I think you are trying a little too hard to be funny. At others, like right now, I worry about dementia. There are exercises you can do to keep your mind in shape."

It didn't sound like an empusa. His mind slipped to the story of Odysseus' father, Laertes. Would he end up like him: sleeping rough in the goat shed, wrapped in rags, in ashes by the fire, no longer recognising old friends or family members?

"You were delirious after you fainted. We were going to take you to A&E, and you kept going on about wanting to go home. You told us to phone Hermes. Are you expecting a delivery? You were ever so confused. You seemed to think one of their drivers would bring you home. Did you mix them up with taxis?"

Zeus mumbled something unintelligible.

"Eat your apple and bilberry crumble."

He took a small bite.

"Are you absolutely sure you're not an empusa?"

"A what?"

Zeus took another tentative bite, and muttered something about shape-shifters, things that drained you of blood and feasted on flesh.

"What were you doing in the cinema?"

She was taken aback.

"I went to watch a film. Same as you."

He was still suspicious.

"You don't see many single women there. Especially not old crones."

"How do you know? Do you go looking for them?"

He didn't answer.

"If you must know, I go regularly. Since Sir Cecil vanished, the house feels empty. Besides, Joe loved films."

"Joe?"

"My husband. Don't pretend you don't remember him. You used to complain that he parked his car in front of your house."

If he could have been bothered, Zeus would have flicked through the Mudge Files.

Lily sighed.

"Funny, really. There's me, catching all sorts of ailments, and him never getting ill, not even missing a day from work. Then he's one of the first to catch Covid. And he's gone. They didn't allow me to be there... at the end. No goodbyes."

He looked away. It was really not considerate of her to make him feel awkward. What did all this have to do with him, exactly?

"It makes me feel close to him – going to the cinema."

There didn't seem any point in saying anything, so Zeus just cut himself another piece of crumble.

She sniffed, then smiled.

"You must be feeling better."

He informed her that he was not, actually, all that hungry.

"I'm only forcing it down to make *you* feel better."

79

How does a movement begin?

Not necessarily, in dusty committee rooms. Nor in ill-lit corners of hotel lounges. It can all begin anywhere. It might start with some idle comments in a hairdressing salon; some passing reflections from those who happen to be there ... a few comments on social media...

Before long, everyone is speaking of the same things – and there it is: something from nothing.

The beginnings of this particular movement are modest. *Hairdressers for Ares* has quite narrow aspirations: a call for a review of the case. Innocent until proven guilty. Bail. Internment only after a conviction.

For the sake of brevity, the name gets shortened to letters: H4A. This can stand for almost anything. Before long, others have picked up on it. New branches spring up.

They share symbols. They make badges. Posters.
FREE ARES!
ARES GETS THINGS DONE!
There is one from, possibly, Eros or an associate:
MAKE LOVE AND WAR!
Graffiti appears on walls, sometimes, just the abbreviation: H4A; sometimes in the form of slogans; other times as pictures: Porus hanging upside down, a

spear through him. Badges get made with this logo on them.

One morning you find that symbols are everywhere. The movement has moved into the light.

There are marches. Chants.

LET'S HAVE FUN: GET IT DONE!

A wave builds. Some individuals begin to get nervous. Perhaps, they have underestimated the power of social media.

80

"I want them identified and punished."

Hades' face was dark with rage. Hera massaged his shoulders, soothingly.

"Especially, that Narcie fellow. Did you hear what he was overheard saying? *Ares is a magnet; Hades a repellent.* And now people are wearing badges saying it! Openly! He will pay. Psecas will pay for employing him. They'll both be chained up in Tartarus with their hairdressing paraphernalia. And Ares will be tried and punished."

Hera returned to the matter of his shoulders, which were all tense and knotty. Neither of these things was going to happen, she continued in a quiet but firm voice. Instead, they would show that they were the ones pushing for clemency. They would send an appeal to the court, demanding that Ares should be granted liberty immediately. The request would be backdated. That way, she explained, the committees would be blamed for the delays. Members such as Themis, Astraea, Dike, Arete, Pistis and Horkos would take the flack.

Afterwards, when it had all calmed down, a more permanent solution could be found for Ares. Something fatal, with them far away when it happened.

A few days later, Hera made sure that she was present when Ares was released, having ensured that it had come to public attention that her own intervention, along with that of Ares' uncle, Hades, had been ignored by the committee, either deliberately or due to bureaucratic ineptitude.

Hera was even there beside him when Ares climbed onto the podium before an ecstatic crowd.

"They said I was gone. Finished. Fake news, my friends. All fake. Believe me, they were mistaken. Bigly mistaken. Ares is back!"

There was loud cheering. Ares waited for it to subside.

"Ares is a winner. And you know how you can tell: because he gets the cutest ass. Eos. Enyo. Aphrodite. All cute. Not to mention Harmione, Sterope and all the other nymphs. If only there was more of Ares to go round."

More cheering. Some hoots.

Scanning the rows assembled, it struck Ares that they included an unlikely alliance of disaffected youth, sybarites and hairdressers – but why should that bother him? They were his supporters, a swelling army, who would be rewarded when he took up his rightful position as king of the gods.

Ares surveyed them. He nodded. He gesticulated, wildly. His facial expression shifted from angry sneer to happy smile, before settling on determination. Now he wagged his finger, sternly.

"Those who tried to take me down – take *us* down – losers! Each and every one of them. We will meet them with fire and fury. Ares is back!"

More cheers. Louder still. A chant swept through the crowd:

"Ares is back!"

Indeed, Ares was back. There was a strong sense in the betting community that the over-cautious Hades had missed the boat. While Ares 'got things done', Hades requisitioned others to do his dirty work, or more usually, requisitioned others to get others to do his dirty work. By comparison, it all seemed painfully laboured when compared to Ares' approach. And those who had put down bets on Ares with the odds offered while he had been interned now stood to make the biggest killing of all.

Assuming, that was, that the schemes of his mother didn't come to fruition. At that moment, it looked that they were unravelling at pace. Even thinking about it left Hades despondent.

"All our careful plans. Atlas still on the loose, and now Ares at liberty. Of course, he'll insist on being there when we sort out Atlas, and he'll probably take the credit. At least, Zeus has been eliminated. One part of the ruddy operation that went to plan!"

Hera thought about soothing him, but then decided he had had quite enough massages over the preceding days. Surely, it was her turn for some TLC.

"And another thing: Charon has vanished."

Hera struggled to take in this news. She frowned. Hera liked order.

"Who is ferrying in the souls of the dead?"

Hades shrugged.

"They can bloody swim for all I care! Least of our problems! Anyway, I'm told these days there is a move to encourage customers to do things for themselves. Hermes told me about this contraption – called them pedalos or something. We can commission Hephaestus to make some. About time one of your sons did something useful."

81

Since his small boat had finally surrendered to the ravages of time, George Williams had given up his trips to the coast. Instead, his preference was to find lonely spots on one of the reservoirs where he could fish in peace.

At Kennick Reservoir there were rainbow trout, and also larger brown trout, up to eight pounds, though you had to throw them back if you caught them. At nearby Trenchford you could catch pike. At Tottiford there was carp. Whilst they were around a dozen miles away from his home near Widdecombe, and there were nearer places, George preferred to go to the reservoirs. He felt more anonymous there.

It was difficult to dismiss the sense of guilt, having been doing the same job day after day, seven days a week, but the truth was that his three sons preferred him to be away from the farm. The business had been struggling for some years, even before the difficulties caused by Brexit and then the pandemic. The boys had been going on about diversifying for as long as he could remember, but what did he know other than farming? The prospect of changing beds and making small talk was horribly daunting.

Although he had joined the Kennick Angling Club, George did not mix. He was not at ease in social situations. A brawny, ponderous man, his conversation was dull, delivered with drawn-out pauses, such was his fear of making a linguistic or grammatical error, or just saying the wrong thing. In his local pub, he tended to drink alone. Recently, however, he had made a friend.

It had been by pure chance that they had first got into conversation. A stranger had, inadvertently, picked up an item he had paid for at the bar. As it had not been some lairy youngster, George decided it was just a mistake.

"If you don't mind, those are my nuts you're holding," said George.

There had been a few chuckles. The stranger had looked surprised, though not all that apologetic. Somehow or other, they had fallen into conversation. By the end of the evening, George had told this man, Monty Mudge, all about himself: how farming was becoming too expensive to sustain a livelihood; how his wife had run off with a neighbouring farmer, and was now living on the other side of the world in New South Wales; how his sons had encouraged him to take days off, as there really wasn't all that much to do around the farm; how discombobulating this felt; how he had mooched around for weeks, watching old films on daytime television; how he had found some solace in rediscovering his childhood hobby of fishing, which felt as if it removed him from his own existence for a while; how his sons were trying to squeeze him out of his own business.

"It's what sons do," mused his new acquaintance. "It's only natural for them to seek to overthrow their fathers. The secret is to look like you are two steps behind them, but, actually, keep one step ahead."

George chewed this over for a while. How do you keep one step ahead when you are not a strategist? Perhaps, this newcomer might help. He reminded George a bit of an outsider from a Spaghetti Western, an unknown figure turning up in some remote spot for no obvious reason and without any warning.

"They want me to pass on their inheritance now. They say it's in all our interests."

The expression on the mysterious stranger's face suggested scepticism.

Before George knew it, his acquaintance had become his friend, something he had not had since leaving school as a sixteen-year-old. Indeed, derided for his slowness, there had not been many friends at school. In his gratitude, he insisted on paying for each round of drinks. After all, it only seemed fair: this new friend was the one making the effort to drive up onto the moor to meet up.

One day George summoned up the courage to invite him fishing.

82

A flashback. Wedged between two rocks, peering down from the heights at the goings-on far below. Two young immortals – not that you can tell age for sure with Titans or gods. Watching the schemes and antics of the mortals, they place wagers, making a pact not to intervene.

It is funny just observing, without interfering, not like with him and Hera, each having their favourites, doing their utmost to ensure that their champion comes out on top, and taking every opportunity to sabotage the progress of the one favoured by the other.

They are not, in human terms, watching *live* events. Olympflix beams things up, usually, not so much as chunks of real time but as stories, far preferable in the context of audience ratings.

Three flimsy-looking boats, bobbing across an ocean. Poseidon appears not to have noticed them. Or, maybe, he has, but is ignoring them. Great bounty will be scattered across his seabed as a result of this voyage, and if Poseidon loves anything, it is coloured gold and silver or in the shape of glittering jewels. Sometimes, in his impatience, he even takes the form of a great sea dragon to hasten the destruction of the vessels carrying such precious hoard.

Some clouds drifting across. It takes a while for Zeus to clear them away. An intermission, after which they pick up the story again. More ships, slightly larger, packed with soldiers and primitive versions of those pointy things that Zeus will notice one day in a picture on Mudge's wall, which he will assume to be for jabbing people. As in the future, he does not recognise them as weapons.

The two immortals now glance over to the distant destination to which the boats are heading. A multitude of warriors, no armour, but fierce-looking, carrying spears. Immediately, he puts down a wager on this lot to come out on top, not noticing the glint of satisfaction in the eye of his companion, who likes an underdog. Besides, he has examined the weaponry closely, and also scrutinised the leader of the marauders. Unlike Zeus, he recognises a trickster as soon as he sees one. He has registered, too, what has happened with the first three boats, when some of the inhabitants have mistaken the visitors for gods.

Stretching over the edge, precariously, to get a better view, Zeus finds himself hurtling downwards, an arm grabs his heels, swinging him back up.

They both lie on the grass, rocking with mirth. Not that a fall could have been fatal, even over such a distance, but it might have hurt. Zeus might have sprained an ankle, or incurred still greater damage.

They return hand in hand, still giggling, swinging their arms high in the air. They take turns leaping into the air, like salmon, over the precipice, allowing the other to catch hold of them. At one point, the two of them almost topple over, such is the force with which Zeus has flung himself.

The others are amused, though Zeus notices that, for some reason or other, Hephaestus seems to be scowling at the bit about him being gripped by the legs before he fell too far. Perhaps, he has gobbled down his food too quickly; even gods get indigestion! Whatever, his mind returns to the day with his companion.

Zeus and Prometheus – not just cousins, but friends, almost blood brothers. During the Titanomachy, while his own brothers had fought alongside Kronos, Prometheus had sided with Zeus. For a while, they were... are... will be inseparable.

And then the betrayal.

Only, it isn't ever really about the theft of fire, and it then being handed over to mortals – however much he likes to pretend that is the case. Not even the fact that Prometheus is casting lascivious glances at Zeus' favourite daughter, Athena.

No, it is because of what Prometheus knows, always knew: how Zeus' reign might not be for all eternity; how there will come one who might be destined to overthrow him. And yet this silence. What bond could be greater than that between blood brothers? A name. Some hint. Is it that so much to ask for?

Such is the jumbled nature of time on Olympus it can become difficult to recollect the precise sequence of events. Perhaps, if it was recorded as Prometheus being in Caucasus, chained to a rock, coming first, it reduces the sense of unease. An eagle with an insatiable appetite for a single dish, foie de titan, clawing into his entrails each day. All preceding the battles between the gods, the theft of fire, the innocent wagers, cause, effect, effect, cause – who knows what comes first?

Yet still, this yearning to un-happen events, to restore lost innocence.

83

It was an epic day spent carp fishing, with George enthusing that Monty was clearly blessed with the luck of some god. Zeus wondered whether Glaucus or Achelous might be involved. The former was, of course, a deity for fishermen, but as he recollected, usually remained around seas. The latter was a river deity, but did that include reservoirs?

Then again, the Potamoi, the river gods, numbered so many – well into the thousands. And after that, there were their children, the Naiads. Renowned for their beauty, they were often seeking to seduce those who might grant favours. He himself had had liaisons with several. He tried to recall their names. Thebe and Plataea were two for starters. Then, of course, there was Aegina. He had transformed himself into an eagle to carry her off; he could almost recall the feel of her in his talons. Her father, Aposos, had come pursuing them, but a few thunderbolts had seen him off. Zeus now smiled at the memory. Afterwards, had he and Aegina had a child together? A boy, he seemed to recall, who became king of somewhere or other. Perhaps, some local Naiad had spotted some inner regality in the figure of Monty Mudge and was sending fish in his direction.

Given the subtleties and elusive movements of the carp, it had required a good deal of patience to catch one.

And one over sixty-five pounds, the largest ever caught in the county! And on his first outing!

It had been a reward for hours of patience, with many cans of beer consumed. Afterwards, George had insisted on displaying the giant fish at their local pub. There had been a great deal of backslapping. George could not stop beaming, declaring it to be the greatest day in his life, even though, strictly-speaking, it had been his friend who had snared the monster. Photographs had been taken, a reporter from the local paper having rushed out on hearing the news.

It had been an error, after so much celebration, to insist that he was in a fit state to drive himself home. In his blurred excitement, he took a turn-off to Hound Tor, a quiet side road, where his car veered off into a ditch. He was lucky to emerge unscathed, and still luckier that another car passed by soon afterwards, giving him a lift back to Newton Abbot.

Despite that last hiccough, he tumbled into bed fully clothed, still delirious with joy.

JOINING THE PANTHEON OF GODS: A BEGINNER'S GUIDE

Matters pertaining to comportment:

1. For those wishing to become a god, a useful first step is to practise behaving like one. One of the purposes of this guide is to help you develop a regimen of exercises that will be of assistance.

2. One of the first questions that we invariably get asked by our eager neophytes is whether gods snore. The expectation is that they do not. Or that if they do, it sounds like a pastoral symphony. This is nonsense. As with all other bodily activities, most gods do this with uninhibited grandiloquence.

3. It is highly recommended that you spend time on developing your nasal muscles prior to your application to join the Pantheon. At least three times a day, you should lie on a comfy couch, close your eyes, squeeze tight on the bridge of your nose, and inhale. Do not take in air through the mouth. Ensure that the tissues in your throat are relaxed in order that your airway is partially blocked, enabling your tissues to vibrate. This

needs to be developed, gradually, many young hopefuls having suffered injury – in one or two cases, of a more or less fatal nature – through efforts to achieve the desired outcome too quickly. This is similar to the dangers when practising the art of thunderous farting, which is considered in a later section.

4. There are many misconceptions about eating food. How should one sit? How should food be transported from table to mouth in the most delicate way?

5. The most important principle is to eat with gusto. Unless you want to be a ponsy Persian deity – in which case, you should not even have purchased this guide – you should not be seated. You should be sprawled on a kline, the more elaborate the couch, the better, when possible, leaning on your left elbow. A jug of wine should be by your side, ideally, served to you by a youthful slave. If you do not possess such an item, you will need to procure the services of a helpful family member.

6. At actual feasts, you will be required to multitask, consuming food and drink while reciting poetry, telling lewd jokes and having sex.

It is advisable to allocate time each day to practise all these activities. Try doing so in front of a large mirror, one at a time to begin with. If all goes well, and you are accepted into the Pantheon, there will be occasions when you are acting as host, and you will be expected to provide entertainment in the form of performers, such as musicians and acrobats. A particularly gifted deity may be skilled in such areas him or herself, but when practising, it is not advisable, as already noted, at least in the early stages, to attempt all of the above at the same time.

7. Learn the rules of drinking games such as kottabos. Several aspirants have been caught out when quizzed about such games during the theory test. As you will be aware by now, if you have read the relevant section, kottabos can follow different rules. It may entail swirling dregs of wine in a cup, then pouring out the contents to form the letters of someone's name. In other versions, you might fling the wine at saucers or at a disk on a pole in order to knock it off. These can all be surprisingly difficult when you are as pissed as a Dionysian mule.

84

Hermes was waving a newspaper in front of him.

"Read the headline. Just read it."

Zeus stared at it, blearily.

Local man makes giant catch on very first fishing trip!

Hermes flung the newspaper across the room.

"Still worse in this other paper! Luckiest man on the planet, it calls you. Biggest orrhos-wit, more like!"

Winner of horse race accumulator bet now goes one better!

Zeus just grinned, unable to contain his euphoria – not that he wished to. Even in the dark dungeon of Mudge's body, his radiance burst through.

"How exactly is that keeping a low profile?"

Zeus ignored the question.

"I'll need my chariot back."

"It's already been found. And you've been photographed in a pub, drinking and looking merry. You are likely to be banned from driving your vehicle after this."

The prospect was unendurable. To be confined here without even the joy of fishing! Zeus' mood veered like one of his storms. Turning on his son, he demanded to know whose fault it was that he was stuck here in the first place. Hermes would have to sort this. He would need to demonstrate that Montgomery Mudge had not been driving at the time. A taxi had taken him to the moor. His chariot had been stolen again. By Albanians! Yes, Albanians. Who had, quite coincidentally, also been visiting a pub on the moor that evening. And, if he didn't still have that Marku's hand in his possession, Hermes would just need to go to Albania to acquire someone else's, some criminal with a record. Hermes would then be able to splatter Mudge's chariot with those incriminating things the police went on about. Fingerprints! It was the very least he owed Zeus given the fact that he had created this mess.

Rolling his eyes, Hermes walked out, without even closing the front door behind him.

85

It was just over a week later, the same two detectives who had quizzed him about the incident with the bowling ball. Whatever else Zeus said about Hermes, it could not be denied that he had acted efficiently. He had even acquired taxi receipts for the return journey.

The police had found a match for the prints in the car, a drug dealer, people trafficker and notorious gang leader – quite high profile, as it turned out.

"He claims to be descended from an ex-ruler, King Zog. Calls himself Zog the Second."

Zeus gave the detectives the blankest, old-man look he could muster.

"Now why do you think King Zog the Second would steal your old motor, Mr Mudge? Does he travel over here for joy rides on Dartmoor?"

Zeus shrugged.

"Life's full of mysteries."

"It certainly is, Mr Mudge, and you appear to be at the heart of so many of them."

SURVIVING THE 21ST CENTURY: A HANDBOOK FOR PENSIONERS

ENTRY 8

LIFE IS FULL OF MYSTERIES. THE BRAIN OF A CARP IS FILLED WITH MYSTERY. A CINEMA IS A JUMBLE OF MYSTERY, THE SCENES ON THE FILM-SCREEN AND THE INTERFACE BETWEEN THOSE IMAGES AND EPISODES AND THE DIVERSE EXPERIENCES AND MEMORIES OF EACH INDIVIDUAL IN THE AUDIENCE BEING IMPOSSIBLE TO PREDICT.

FOR INSTANCE, IT TURNS OUT THAT ALMOST ALL THE FILMS THAT I LIKE ARE DISLIKED BY LILY TUCKER, WHILE NEARLY ALL THE FILMS SHE LIKES HAVE LITTLE APPEAL FOR ME.

THIS SHOULD MAKE US INCOMPATIBLE, AND IT IS TRUE THAT SHE IS DREADFUL COMPANY, AND ONE WOULD RATHER SPEND AN EVENING WITH A GORGON. AND YET, SHE HAS A SAVING GRACE. SHE IS REMARKABLY GOOD AT BAKING, FAR BETTER THAN MR KIPLING. INDEED, ALL HER COOKING IS RATHER GOOD, SO ALTHOUGH SHE HAS VERY POOR TASTE, LILY TUCKER CATERS VERY WELL FOR THE TASTES OF OTHERS.

SPEAKING OF CONSUMPTION, NEITHER THE HEAD OR STOMACH OF A PENSIONER ARE DESIGNED TO INGEST MORE THAN FIVE PINTS OF ALE AT A

SINGLE SITTING. SADLY, YOUR CONSTITUTION IS NOT
UP TO IT.

86

It had been impossible for Hades to refuse Ares a place on the lead ship, even though he had had no part in the planning of the action. While Hades was nominal leader of the mission, it was exceedingly difficult to look the part, especially, when each time he gave an order, there was a pause before Ares repeated it, and only then was it carried out.

"Move in closer," called Hades.

"Move in clos-ER," echoed Ares, with a subtly different intonation.

As the designer of the weapon, Hephaestus was on board, along with many other notables. Hera, of course, was not there, warfare being of no real interest to her.

There were also a number of observation vessels, monitoring the drama below, including, rather irritatingly, in the view of Hades, one which included members of the Ethics Committee, there to ensure that no unnecessary suffering was inflicted on the army of Titans, ogres and giants assembled by Atlas.

The view below was dramatic, with Atlas and his allies having torn out huge chunks of cliff-side and rocks, which they were hurling up in their direction. The vessels had to dart from side to side, one taking a direct hit. Hades and those around watched as it hurtled downwards and crashed below. There was nothing to be done, with the hordes of Atlas converging on it, bashing and stamping it down till it was completely flat.

"Prepare the weapon," ordered Hades, grimly.

"Prepare the wea-PON," reiterated Ares, changing the emphasis on the consonants, slightly, which appeared to give the command a completely different meaning, sending minions scuttling into action.

Hephaestus craned forward. Far below, Atlas was holding above his head a great, missile-proof shield. Would it really protect him from a thunderbolt, and one tipped with explosives that he, himself, had prepared? Inevitably, there had been limited time to construct the shield, which, as the one commissioned to make it, Hephaestus knew all too well. He felt a churning guilt in his guts, as if he had pitted two of his own children against one another. Alongside a curiosity to discover which of his creations would come out on top.

There was a whirring sound as the machinery lowered the encased thunderbolt into position beneath their vessel. The tension was overwhelming. There was just the one thunderbolt, the anniversary present that Zeus had given Hera. It could not be allowed to miss its target.

There seemed to be a small difference of opinion between Hades and Ares with respect to the precise trajectory. Now someone was rushing onto the bridge, waving bits of paper in front of Ares that were covered in scrawled measurements. It was Linus, who had volunteered to come on the mission so as to compose an epic song about it. As the son of Urania, the muse of Astronomy, Linus reminded Ares that he knew all about geometry, and while Hades' calculation may have been a tad out, that of Ares was miles off the mark.

Glaring at him, Ares strode towards the poet cum geometrist, hoisting him high into the air and flinging him down from their vessel to the earth below, whereupon he was, enthusiastically, trampled by giants. While attention was on the stomping of large feet below, Ares, discreetly, adjusted the trajectory calculations, in line with those suggested by the recently departed Linus. Ares now ordered the firing of the weapon. It was already on its way by the time Hades repeated the order.

From a distance, they could make out the huge grin on the face of Atlas, who, casually, held his giant shield above his head. There was no time to spot the look of surprise as it shot straight through the *fontanelle* in the structure, a tiny, weak spot where metal had been welded together. The thunderbolt went straight through, passing through Atlas' skull, pinioning him to the ground. Then came the explosion from the modifications that had been added, a pillar of fire rising into the sky.

It took a while for the smoke to clear. When it did, they could see the remnants of Atlas' army scattering in all directions. There was something else, too, something uncovered by the blast and left behind, a gigantic figure of some kind. Whatever it was, it needed to be investigated. They landed their vessel and stepped out.

It was, indeed, colossal, a sort of unfinished statue. There was something vaguely familiar about it, despite the missing bits. It had one arm, and legs without feet. Other than a mouth, there were no features on the top bit, a head with no eyes, nose or ears.

It was laid out flat, ropes around it in position to haul it up.

A grand monument to forthcoming victory? If so, how arrogantly premature!

In case it was attached to explosives, as their own deadly projectile had been, Hades and Ares stood back to allow some of the minor deities to carry out an inspection. They were all rather geeky types brought along to check and calibrate the instruments. So intent were they on the task, that none of them noticed the single arm reaching down, grabbing them, conveying them to the mouth, snapping off their heads with a single bite, before swallowing the torsos. They had gone before anyone could react.

Not necessarily with any malice. After all, it was just instinct – what Kronos did. How had nobody noticed it was parts of him, not just any old stone monument? Beating a hasty retreat to their vessel, they agreed to send a dismantling team under instruction from Hephaestus.

A joyous crowd was waiting to greet the returning heroes. There were cheers when Hades raised his arm in triumph, rising to a crescendo when Ares stepped forward. Indeed, it was more than a little galling that almost the entire credit went to Ares. Just as well he got rid of that interfering ninny, Linus, before the mission had got wrecked, and how brilliant to make the precise estimate in terms of direction and timing!

The mission had been accomplished with only eight fatalities: Linus, of whom no remains could be found; three swallowed by Kronos, again, no trace of them, along with four others, whose vessel was blown out of the sky at the outset of battle. Of course, strictly-speaking, as an immortal, you could never be a 'fatality', but this did not mean that an eternity might not be spent as a pulped, flattened piece of flesh now ground up with sand and rock. Nonetheless, as Hades observed, it was the way that members of the Ethics Committee would have wished to go.

87

Banned by a series of English monarchs, lawn bowling was seen as a distraction from acquiring the skills of warfare, and in particular, that of archery. Henry VIII forbade the sport to all of 'common birth', except on Christmas Day. In 1555 his daughter, Queen Mary, signed off a statute curtailing even that privilege. The game, she proclaimed, was a front for 'unlawful assemblies, conventiclers, seditions, and conspiracies'.

Although not fully cognisant of ensuing history, Zeus and his companions from the Newton Abbot bowling team were eternally grateful to Queen Victoria for rescinding that law three-hundred years later, to the Scots who rediscovered the sport, and, perhaps, above all, to Edwin Beard Budding for his invention of the lawnmower in 1830.

Science, mathematics and even ethics govern the sport of lawn bowling. For those who are not versed in its intricacies, it might be noted that a small white jack is rolled first. The bowls are biased, not quite round, allowing them to follow a curved path.

As this happened to be a tournament, Zeus, as the best player on his team was involved in everything: singles, pairs, triples and fours, and here they were competing against the fearsome Kings Bowling Club of

Torquay, packed with internationals and multiple winners at national level.

It was the final event. The teams were neck and neck. Everything depended on the last bowl from Zeus, which looked nigh on impossible. There was a narrow, impermeable barrier. The opposition had been bowling just a little short, creating two blocking layers. All routes to the jack seemed blocked, especially those available to right-hand bowlers. All the Newton Abbot team were right-handers.

To the surprise of his teammates, Zeus picked up the bowl with his left hand. It looked like he was going for a backhand, rather than forehand draw, a left hand thumb peg rather than the finger peg delivery a right-hander would use.

So wide did the course of the bowl begin that it looked certain that Zeus had lost his line. And then it began to spin. They held their breath.

A fluke?

Both his own team and opposition players agreed that, if not the greatest ever, it had to be the finest bowl since David Bryant's in 1979, which also took a wide path before curling its way around everything to nestle against the far side of the jack.

But, of course, it had to be a fluke!

88

Reports of the demise of Atlas came as a shock to those who had wagered hefty sums on his victory. Cannier punters had hedged their bets, with many still having the name of 'Ares' or 'Hades' on other betting slips.

Nevertheless, visits to the Underworld were massively up, though the Tourist Board there were disappointed by the low spending of this latest influx. Without even stopping for a snack, many visitors were going straight to the rivers to fling themselves into the Acheron, the 'River of Woe' being a particular favourite for the leap into oblivion. The authorities were quick to set up tollbooths at favourite jumping points, ensuring some profit at least. Large nets were put in place to dredge up immortals who found wetness rather than death in the dark waters.

Nobody was more disappointed by the outcome than Charon. So convinced had he become about the imminence of Atlas' victory that he had already begun spending his retirement pay-out. The sole consolation was that Hades' own absence from the Underworld had, at least, given him time to construct a story.

"Friend Charon has been ill. Self-isolating. He would have sent a message but Hermes has been elusive lately."

One of Hades' talents was to drain all expression from his face, remaining completely inert in a most unnerving manner.

"There's this virus – came in on one of the souls of the mortals, don't ask me how. Seems to survive the demise of the body. Can be deadly even to immortals."

Was that a slightly raised eyebrow? Quizzical?

"It could have been fatal. The team has been working around the clock for an antidote. You know, before an epidemic across the Underworld."

Not so foolish as to turn up without evidence, Charon now produced pictures of a score of very minor deities and demigods with apparent inhalation difficulties. Hades barely glanced at them.

"As for Friend Charon, he's tip-top now. Can't wait to get back to work."

A nod? Relaxation of posture? Wishful thinking. Hades remained as he had been, completely still, no expression on his face or in his voice. When he did speak, it was in an undertone.

"Just as well. You should see the backlog."

An awkward silence.

"If I'm not mistaken, the ailment appears to have affected your hairstyle."

"Oh that! Got it done a couple of days before falling ill."

Charon ran his bony fingers through his hair.

"Lucky, really. Psecas is very strict about payment for late cancellations. Forty-eight hours is the minimum notice. What with work demands and all, I'd already had to re-schedule twice."

He remained rooted to the spot, hoping to be dismissed.

"How opportune! What a lucky chap you are!"

Hades gave a particularly sinister smile.

"One in a million," croaked Charon.

He remained waiting for a while.

"Well, I suppose I shouldn't hold you up. So much catching up. I guess you'll need to be doing nightshifts after all that missed time. Unpaid, too, as a medical note was never received. Rules are rules, after all."

89

On his doorstep there was a parcel. A gift! That was nice.
He wondered who might have sent it. Hopefully, his
niece, as it was likely to contain a new game, if so. Or
perhaps, something from his friend, George. One of those
portable hand-held fish finders that he had been talking
about. Apparently, you could get sonar sensors that
indicated location and water-depth. Not that Monty
needed one, George had pointed out, in case his friend
was insulted. After all, they were really more for
beginners. An expert, such as Monty, could achieve far
more through instinct and intuition.

The contents inside the package were neither.
Inside, rather disappointingly, there was a box with a
carved figure. It seemed to come from Africa. There was
no accompanying note or letter. Perhaps, it was wrongly
addressed, and had been intended for a different
Montgomery Mudge.

Only a week later did it become clear, when he
bumped into his neighbour, Ermias, who asked him
whether he had liked the gift. Which gift? It took a few
moments before Zeus remembered the wooden animal he
had slung onto a chair.

Zeus only just stopped himself from calling him
'Pygmie' when he replied.

Ermias seemed to be keen to converse. He had wanted to apologise for causing trouble for his neighbour. His housemates had pressurised him about finding a safe place to hide the drugs they dealt in. He had not been the one to suggest Monty Mudge. He was frightened because they knew he was living there as an alien, under an assumed name, of a young man from a country that was not even his own. The gift, he added, quickly, was made in his real country of birth.

He was trapped, he added, because the men he shared a house with could expose him at any time to the authorities.

Zeus stared at him, dully. What exactly was *he* expected to do?

"They think you have contacts. People who can help," added Ermias. "After all, you sorted out that gang. They are all a bit wary of you."

"I had a friend who helped. He's sort of dropped off the scene."

It sounded a little lame. The great Zeus, slayer of Typhon, the most fearsome monster ever – *I had a friend*. He thought about it. In subsequent times, there had been no need to keep demonstrating his authority through his actions. His reputation alone sufficed.

"Perhaps, I can do something," he said.

Afterwards, it struck him how needy these mortals were. It really was time to wrap things up here and get back home, even if this would entail an interlude, as Hermes suggested, with another mortal lifetime as a hero. He must call Hermes to hurry things along.

90

As he was the official messenger, it seemed rather peculiar to be summoned to deliver a message addressed to himself. It was an invitation from Charon to a meeting.

In a remote cave! What was this sudden thing about caves?

It took a full three days to reach there. Far quicker, and presumably easier, to have set up something in the Underworld. Or did Charon not wish to risk being seen there in Hermes' company?

It was an arduous journey for both of them. Presumably, the matter was of such urgency and secrecy that it had to be arranged in a place visited by nothing except a few reclusive lizards and the odd, ravenous carrion bird.

Hermes arrived first, squatting down on a rock and having a bite of lunch. Spotting Charon as he approached, Hermes noticed that he was wearing new, expensive-looking sunglasses, possibly, *Ray-Ban Wayfarers* or *Sungod Classics*, it was hard to tell which at this distance. He was absolutely oozing sun cream, that was for sure. The stuff glistened on his neck, belly and legs.

Perching next to him on the rock, Charon did not waste time with chitchat. Despite the fact that no living thing could be seen for miles, he covered his mouth as he spoke.

"Not over yet. Far from it?"

"What's not over?" asked Hermes.

"The rebellion. Friend Charon has information."

He tapped his nose.

It seemed that Charon was unwilling to tell him more without an agreement like the previous one.

"Secret for secret?"

Hermes assented. Once again the scales appeared. Charon now gave him small bits of intelligence, allowing it to trickle out in dribs and drabs. The army that Atlas had gathered was slowly reassembling. With nothing to lose if final victory went to Ares and Hades, they were continuing with the original plan. Some spy had revealed the location of the mountain under which the unfinished statue of Kronos had been hidden. A race was on: Hephaestus had been commissioned to build weapons to blow up the statue into pieces. Friend Charon knew something of which Hades wasn't cognisant: Hephaestus had been working for each side, designing both the missile launcher to destroy Atlas and the shield to defend him. In the meantime, other parts of Kronos were being unearthed: soon he would be whole again.

A spy had burrowed into the mountain. It would have aroused Hades' suspicions had Friend Charon gone missing again, so he had sent an associate, who had succeeded in establishing communication. Kronos had responded. As soon as he was restored, he would arise, break out from beneath the mountain and lead an assault on Olympus.

It was Hermes' turn. He stammered out some information that might be of value without being critical. Again, he was pushed to disclose information about Zeus. Where had he been at the time of the assassination? What information had he given mortals? Where was his body interred? Charon told him that this last issue was important as Zeus' soul had not yet turned up in the Underworld. Of course, there was a backlog, so it could have got snagged up there.

Hermes racked his brain, trying to think of something he could say that would make the scales move a little.

"Very unhealthy eating habits."

An almost imperceptible flutter.

"Also, he went a bit, you know, soft in the head."

Nothing. No movement at all.

"Simple. Starting to behave like an idiot. Laughing at stupid things. Like names."

He was disappointed, and surprised, that there was still barely any impact.

"There was a little friend. A boy. A moron. Name of... Tony. Maybe, Anthony."

A slight quiver. A minute shift in his favour. Yet nowhere near enough. It was a surprise and relief that Charon seemed content to leave it there. Instead, he seemed excitable, on edge, keen to pass on further information of his own. Charon, himself, had acquired the secret to re-animate Kronos, even minus one or two minor parts. Those amygdales things, the tonsils. Did Hermes know that you did not even need them? Charon did not wait for a reply. Hermes was now told that, after his victory, Kronos was not interested in the Underworld. It could be left to rot, which meant that Charon would be liberated from his interminable role on that dead river.

Was Hermes with them?

Even if unwilling to help by delivering communications, all that was required would be for him to keep quiet. And not to assist Kronos' enemies by servicing their channels of intelligence, given that the speed of communication was so critical for those in the midst of battle. In return, Hermes, too, would be released from an existence of endless tasks.

There was something else that Hermes needed to see, stowed away at the back of the cave. Charon pointed to an object rolled up in a bundle.

As Hermes stepped towards it, he did not notice Charon backing outside into the light; nor did he hear him utter the spell that Hecate had shared with him. By the time he leapt back, the entrance had snapped shut. He was sealed in.

He put his ear to the rock. More words. An incantation. A kind of double fetter. Hermes was trapped.

As he had already slunk away, Charon missed the information Hermes was relaying: the precise details about the amount of chezo that was going to be poured down the opening after the ferryman's head had been removed; the plans for the removal of his akos-peos; and the extremely remote, future domicile of his orjiks.

Finally, Hermes slumped to the ground, trying to slow down his breathing and ruminate in the darkness. How careless of him! His suspicions should have been aroused when Charon made so little effort to even up the scales. It had just been a ruse to trap him. His concerns branched outwards, turning to other matters: Zeus, alone, who would assume himself to have been forsaken. One way or another, he would have to fend for himself.

91

Another flashback.

It was sparked off by the noise of a baby crying as he was walking home from the shops. The sound of wailing. Another infant, abandoned by its mother, in a dark, enclosed place. A cave.

Who was it?

Someone – maybe, some *thing*, was hunting it.

Shadows from flames, rearing up the walls. An odour of burning logs and animal sweat. The slightly caramel smell of warm goats' milk. The wild, sweet scent of nymphs. The sound of a goat, bleating. And cries of a baby. Drowned out by jangling bells and spears banged on drums. Distracting attention away from the crying.

More shapes. Shaggy-looking figures, silhouettes dancing close to the entranceway. Kouretes, mountain spirits. Sometimes, they would wheel away, with much noise, zigzagging, crazily, down the slopes, away from the cave.

Zeus narrowed his eyes in concentration.

He recalled who the hunter was, and why the Kouretes had been trying to distract that monster.

Outside his house, a cat was watching, back arched, as if to rush inside.

"Get lost!" he hissed. "This is not a sanctuary."

He put his key in the lock and sighed. He remembered who the infant was now: himself.

Another whiff: the nourishing milk of the goat, Amaltheia.

The forgotten sounds: a cacophony of bangs and jangles. The nymphs and Kouretes: risking their own lives to protect him from his deranged father. In all the time afterwards, had he uttered a single word of thanks?

92

Hermes had managed to regulate his breathing. As methodically as he could, he began to work through the possibilities.

Charon may have been working with Kronos, as he had implied. If so, why seek to trap Hermes? Kronos could have no particular grudge against him that he was aware of – other than being a son of Zeus, and how many countless others could share that claim?

Was it not more likely that Charon was still working for Hades? Perhaps, it was not enough that Hermes had enticed Zeus into a helpless, mortal body. Hades might not have forgiven him for, subsequently, protecting Zeus by not giving away his precise location. And Hades was famous for holding onto grudges.

A slight variant on this hypothesis was that Charon was acting under orders from both Hades and Hera. True, this did not change things much, but surely, there was less malice in her. He might be freed after being left there for a while to stew, repenting for his disloyalty after his oath. Not likely, perhaps, but any straw was worth clutching.

Another possibility was that Charon was colluding with Hecate. Only *she* could have given him such a spell to seal up a cave in such a way. This one was complicated. However much Hermes may have tried to obliterate it from his memory, the fact was that he and Hecate had had a relationship, albeit a fleeting one. Indeed, and rather embarrassingly, mortals continued to celebrate that union by leaving offerings at crossroads, a constant reminder of a brief fling. How exactly did a one-night stand become the perpetual transcendence of liminal space? Well, maybe, a few nights; it was difficult to be certain, given Hecate's command of darkness. But who knew? It may have meant more to her: she may not have forgiven him for, subsequently, choosing another as a consort. It was impossible to guess, as she was such an enigma.

Rising to his feet, he felt his way round the sides of the cave, feeling for any fissures or weak spots. There were none, other than the tiniest of cracks. Feeling a large web between his fingers, he had an idea. A slim hope, but something.

Long ago, there had been a mortal so skilled in her weaving that foolishly, she had declared herself to be still more gifted than the goddess, Athena. The young woman, Arachne, went so far as to issue a challenge to the goddess. Such impertinence could not go unpunished, with Arachne finding herself transformed into a spider.

Hermes had observed the whole thing, summoned as he was, to bear testimony to this warning about the punishment likely to be inflicted on mortals for hubris. He had taken pity on Arachne, who had scuttled outside, almost straight into the jaws of a hungry lizard. Hermes had shooed away the predator. Picking up Arachne, he had moved her to a safe place. Would she even remember the small act of kindness?

He now whispered something to the unseen spider in this web. He could feel the web vibrating, though it was impossible to tell what this meant.

He sat down again, and waited.

93

Zeus had been snoozing. For how long? An hour, perhaps.
He was awoken by the sound of knocking on his door.
Lily Tucker.

"Did you not hear it, Monty. Outside your door.
The poor thing is lame. Hurt its paw. Wouldn't come
into my house. Waiting, patiently, outside yours."

She was holding it in in her hands, setting it
down, gently, on a cushion.

"Stroke it, Monty. It wants you."

She moved it onto his lap. The animal began to
purr.

"See! You have a way with cats. Now you give it
some loving and I'll rustle up something to eat. You need
to look after yourself better."

She bustled into the kitchen, humming. He could
hear the running of a tap, and the clattering of pots and
dishes. He sighed. She was a good cook. It wasn't that big
a price to pay.

He was feeling drowsy. The memory of the cave
weighed, heavily. The nymphs, the Kouretes, even the
goat. Willing to be torn apart to save him.

He closed his eyes, overwhelmed by fatigue. The
cat felt strangely heavy on his lap. The weight of one of its
legs, draped over him, was painful. Its body seemed
longer. Plumper. Its paws felt more like... hands.

With a great effort, he opened his eyes. Was he hallucinating? The leg weighing him down was made of bronze. The paws *were* hands. The shape was still transforming between one incarnation and something else.

Fascinating! It was shifting position. Its head was now facing him, monstrous, but definitely, a woman. It opened its mouth wide. Four needle-sharp fangs and the pinkest tongue he had ever seen.

And then, behind the creature, holding a large pan, Lily. She hit it round one side of the head. Again on the other. The creature turned with a hiss and leapt at her. Lily fell beneath it. It struck her with its fingered paw. Why did it not bite her? It had been about to bite *him*. Perhaps, it was saving its venom for him

His mind began to clear. He remembered the word. Empusa. Hermes had warned him that one was there.

There was a phone in his pocket. Hermes had not been answering his calls for a few weeks. He tried another number.

"Hello."

It was Ember's voice.

"Help!" he managed to gasp before the phone was knocked out of his hand.

The creature's face was close to him. Not a cat. Now it was something in between states. And then it shifted again, back towards its true form.

The creature was smiling at him. Zeus tried to think, clearly. All he could do was play for time. Play for time, and hope.

"How long have you known?"

"Known what?"

Her voice belonged to another place. A dark forest somewhere. The sound brought to mind dead leaves swept up in a gust of wind.

"Known who I was. Why did you not attack me earlier?"

"I had to be sure. Besides, I was enjoying myself here."

Perhaps, he could make a deal. He proposed it. Again, she laughed. She already had a deal.

He tried to think who would have made such a contract with her. She enjoyed watching him try to work it out.

"With your brother. Hades. He took time out from his visits to your wife in order to commission my services."

She was delighted by the mingling of confusion and pain in his eyes. It was fun toying with him.

"I can better it. What are the terms?"

"You know I cannot tell you that. We have rules. Our own code. Hecate would not allow it."

"I can offer you more. What do you want?"

There was no reply.

"You were attracted to me. Even in this form. I could make you a consort. A wife."

"A wife! Pah! What does that mean to *you*? What about number one wife? I couldn't settle for less. Would you get rid of Hera?"

His hesitation was fatal.

"Tell me," she rasped in her strange voice: "do you prefer to die quickly or slowly?"

"Slowly," he said, although part of him just wanted it over.

"Good, because that is how I prefer to kill."

Sliding down the chair, she sunk her fangs into his leg, just above the ankle. He could feel the injection of poison, numbing. Perhaps not enough to finish him off yet. It would work its way up slowly through his system towards his heart.

Her head rose back up, blood all around the edges of her mouth. She stared at his face, a feigned look of concern, suffused with pleasure.

"You do know my sons will take revenge."

"Your sons? Which ones, exactly?"

"Ares."

The name might frighten her.

She just smirked.

"He hates you. He was in on the plot with Hades from the start."

It was satisfying for her to detect a further torment in his eyes. She watched for a while.

"All those you thought loved you have betrayed you."

She scrutinised his face, before turning her attention to his body. Where should she make the next incision? Where would cause him the most suffering? Which vein would prolong it the most? Allowing her to watch the life drain from him.

As she was ducking her head to strike, she was caught by surprise when the door burst open, turning too slowly to avoid being hit round the head with a cricket bat. And then a spade. Antonio and Frida were raising their weapons to strike again.

With another hiss, she turned and leapt at Frida. At that point, Ember plunged a kitchen knife through her back.

There was a screech. Not human. Not like any creature from the world of mortals. A rush of wind. A low moaning. And then she just disappeared.

94

There was no wind here, not the slightest exhalation. An airless void containing a primordial creature without form.

Hollow footsteps the only sound. He stops and stares down. Nothing. His own thoughts shrieking through the silence. Asking the same question over and over: how to broker a deal with a thing that does not talk back. All he has is Hecate's advice on spells, those spoken aloud and those simply thought.

The same Hecate who had always been in cahoots with Hades. Hecate of the forked crossroad, sometimes pointing toward a good place, more often towards doom. Only a desperate spirit would trust Hecate.

She had told him that she, too, was dissatisfied. With what? Tiredness with her role? Or maybe, jealousy? Hades' recent closeness to Hera had left her just a little outside the magic circle.

One more time Charon went through things in his mind. His fallback position, if Hades discovered the act. Why, had not Hades himself suggested that it would be a good idea to get Erebus on their side before Ares swayed him? And had not Hades reminded Charon that, after all, the old ferryman was the progeny of Erebus and Nyx? Surely, he had some influence with his father!

Charon had swallowed his thoughts at the time of the conversation. It had not exactly been the sort of family where they went on holidays together or played boardgames when Daddy got home from work! He reminded himself now that, while it may look as if he acted without direct orders, he could argue that he was, in fact, responding to a previous suggestion.

He began with an invocation, ending with the words: "Your liberator is..."

Even now, he could have said 'Hades'.

"Kronos. With the aid of your son, Charon. To Kronos you are sworn."

The dye was cast. He mouthed the rest of the spell. Thought the thoughts. Waited. Here he was, a creature of few words speaking to one with none. And yet somehow, it felt as if they had managed to come to an agreement.

At least, Charon thought so. And there was a feeling, something in that dank, motionless air was awakening, freed from its invisible shackles by a silent incantation. There was a swishing sound, a single breath emitted that swept upwards from the void, on across parched land until it met the first construction in its path, a mouldering tower on the outer edges of the Underworld. As if made of paper, it came crashing to the ground.

95

It was of some concern to Ember that both her children seemed to be trying to bury the memory of the events in their great-uncle's home, and yet it was also a relief. Neither of them seemed keen to talk about it. Perhaps, it was best to leave them time to process the images, which now felt like something of a blur. As a consequence of not discussing the event, the confusion around it never came to light, for the fact was that each person had seen something entirely different.

This had been an aspect not picked up by the police, who had been called on Frida's phone, as Ember had driven over to her uncle's in a panic. Having assumed the intruder to be human, the police had asked few questions, and those they had asked had been directed at Ember. Was there anything distinctive about the assailant? Ember had just told them that she had not got a close look. Either a slightly-built male or a female. She had been keen to put on record that she had told the children to wait in the car, while she investigated.

No questions were directed at Antonio, who was pretty sure that what he had hit with his cricket bat had been a large cat, a puma or lynx, or something like that. He had heard that such animals had been spotted in England. He thought that, in all the confusion, it must have escaped out of the door, which was good, as he would not have wished to kill anything.

Nor were many questions directed at Frida, who gained the impression that what she had hit had been a rather peculiar-looking snake, which must have slithered away. This turned out to be consistent with the unusual bite marks found on Monty Mudge's leg, and the traces of poison detected in his system, subsequently, as reported by hospital staff.

The police report, however, noted that the presence of a venomous snake at the scene could not be confirmed by the victim's niece. Presumably, it had escaped through the open door during the struggle. The assumption in that report was that this was an assault, probably, organised by members of the Albanian gang already known to the victim. A snake had been brought to the crime scene to intimidate him, implying that, in one way or another, Mr Mudge was still involved in criminal activities, and that he remained a person of interest. The recommendation was for renewed surveillance of his movements and activity around his home, even though the initial phase of tracking and video recordings, as authorised by RIPA, the Regulation of Investigatory Powers Act, had produced no evidence that might give grounds for prosecution.

The detectives who questioned her were a little disappointed that Ember had been unable to identify pictures of known gang members, including Zog the Second.

For some reason, she chose not to reveal that, for a brief second, she had seen the creature's face. It was a relief to discover that neither of the children appeared to have glimpsed that face. And if her uncle had recognised his attacker, he made no mention of it. He had only met her the once, after all, and in frightening circumstance, how easy it must be for an elderly person to be left disoriented!

Despite everything, she did not wish anyone else to know the identity of the assailant. She, however, was quite certain. Besides, if proof were needed, the fact was that Mo had vanished. Almost as if she had never been part of Ember's life.

Ember tried hard not to analyse the reasons for the attack. Surely, it could not have been due to her uncle's foolish behaviour during the meal at her house. And if there had ever been anything more than the attempt to fondle her bottom, Mo had given no sign. Perhaps, Mo had not been of sound mind.

It was worrying that Ember had allowed someone so dangerous to insinuate her way into her own world and that of her children. Right now, however, she thought it best to focus not on her own misjudgement of character, nor on the aching sense of loss, but on the needs of the neighbour who had, somehow or other, got caught up in the melee, and had, subsequently, got knocked to the ground and suffered a stroke.

It seemed that, if able to remember anything, the poor woman was unable to articulate any memory of the event. Not only was she unable to speak, but she was paralysed down one side.

Ember visited her uncle two or three times a day during his recuperation. Subsequently, she encouraged him to visit the woman in hospital. Even if he was, himself, in a state of shock, it struck her as insensitive in the extreme that it seemed not to have occurred to him. He had managed to get out to places like the shops, after all – even his ruddy bowling club!

96

Strange events! And not only in the kingdoms where the immortals dwelled. Across all worlds, for three minutes, mobile phones stopped working. Admittedly, this caused less panic in the Underworld, where reception was often hit and miss.

There was a swirling darkness, visible even in the murk of the Underworld. On Olympus, itself, the Palace of Pasithea just vanished. If one had expected the goddess of relaxation and meditation to take this with equanimity, one would have been mistaken. Pasithea was positively fizzing with fury.

Down on Earth, too, weird stuff was going on. An elderly lady from Wimborne, Dorset, waking up in a hut on the South Sandwich Islands. Fortunately, a Chilean scientific team happened to be there at the time, carrying out environmental research.

Still weirder stuff: a twelfth century Mongolian warlord seen riding his horse through an Abu Dhabi shopping mall. A former US president awaking to find that he had reverted to a foetal state.

Such things were not normal.

In the Vatican, the incumbent pope was surprised to bump into one of his medieval predecessors emerging from his personal bathroom. A toad was discovered running the Kremlin and a hen found itself to be CEO of

Kentucky Fried Chicken. Three yetis were spotted in a McDonalds in Toronto. They looked disappointed.

Some particularly peculiar events were recorded in the country where the former king of the gods happened to be residing. A statue of Lord Cardigan disappeared from its usual spot in Maidstone to be found outside the Crimean city of Balaclava, ironically, close to the very spot where the disastrous Charge of the Light Brigade had taken place.

For some obscure reason, a high proportion of incidents seemed to be concentrated in the North-East of England. Part of the Great Wall of China was found in the town of Bishop Auckland. A monkey, which spoke fluent, if outmoded, French was discovered in Hartlepool. Rather sheepishly, residents elected it onto the town council.

Still on the theme of animals, a gigantic crocodile was found in a shopping centre in Sunderland. Choosing to purchase nothing, the creature managed to swallow two unsuspecting customers and remove the leg from a third before it could be restrained.

In a parallel exchange, perhaps, a Somerset politician found himself transposed from his club in Westminster to an African swamp. He was greeted with rather mingled emotions upon his safe return to his constituency.

PART 5 — PERIPETEIA

97

Like two cats with intersecting territories, tiptoeing around one another, Hera and Tyche were being assiduously polite. Over-assiduously, if truth be told! The only common ground was in the desire for stability: one for family, the other for business reasons. Each was wary, waiting for the other to make some kind of offer before responding. As a consequence, it took a great deal of time to engage, let alone arrive at some sort of conclusion.

Tyche had not always been the buxom, imperious persona facing Hera right now. Indeed, Hera's first recollection was of a slender figure who wore barely any make-up, certainly, none of the jewellery she had acquired in recent centuries, a rather diffident being. Hera found it impossible to imagine that previous incarnation of Tyche daring to display such contempt for males, which many, incidentally, mistook for flirtation.

Even now, Hera assumed that it was an act; that Tyche could not really hold male deities in such low esteem. It was also difficult to contain her irritation. Was that a pitying look? The effrontery! If the Queen of the Gods had chosen to indulge her husband's indiscretions for so long, that was *her* business.

And yet, this ambivalence. Rather grudgingly, she admired Tyche for her independence, her aptitude to inhabit the universe on her own terms.

"You never considered marriage."

The words came out abruptly, and Tyche was not quite sure whether it was a question or a statement.

"You'll have to forgive me, Sweetie, if I do not enjoy being rolled onto my back or just pawed by drunks."

They considered one another.

"You really are quite strange."

"We can't all be passive and demure, Hun."

"It is our role... our burden."

"To be raped?"

Hera could not deny that there was barely a goddess who had not had that experience. Was it so awful? Unpleasant at the time, but something you got over. What was the point in making a fuss?

"This endless cycle. Our own part in it. The way we tolerate all that savagery. Sons growing up to murder their fathers, then to behave in precisely the same ways."

"You have no sons."

Tyche said nothing. She knew all about Hera's deep attachment to her own brute of a boy.

"Such ferocity," she sighed.

"It's what keeps everyone in their place," replied Hera. "My family and I," she added, slowly, "we respect tradition."

"You mean like sons cutting off their father's balls? Husbands cheating on wives."

Hera's face showed no expression. She would not be goaded. She had calculated everything with great care: the risks in the dethronement of Zeus; the possible responses of all the influential figures on Olympus; the beginning and possible end points of her alliance with Hades; the timing of her son's succession, and the things she would need to do before that to make Ares more malleable. It was not as if she had embarked on this course on a whim. Zeus had been pushing her further and further back into the shadows. How soon would it have been before she had been replaced by one of his concubines? Everyone knowing about his liaisons – even the mortals! How hysterically funny the residents on Olympus must have found it – all her endeavours to appear respectable! Indeed, she had sensed the laughter as soon as she left a room.

Ultimately, whether her son or lover came out on top, she would be better off. She knew all too well the fate of goddesses after the overthrow of their husbands. How many social events had been inaugurated by Gaia after the mutilation of Uranus? Was anyone interested in Rhea's opinion after the demise of Kronos? How long had it been since any deity had chosen the Rhea hairstyle or fashion look? Hera, herself, would never have dreamed of scheming against her husband had he not begun acting in such erratic ways. Besides, there was insurance: she had kept closer to Ares than Rhea had to Zeus. With the proviso, of course, that he did not overstep the mark. For by now, even she had been forced to recognise the liability Ares posed.

"You might suppose," smiled Tyche, "that all the uncertainty that has been stirred up is good for my business. A rush of blood and all kinds of mad wagers get placed. The house plays it so as to win either way. It's what pays for all this."

She gestured round the room.

"But right now our masters are making a mess of things. They can't help it; it's how they are designed. All phallos and ego."

Tyche allowed a silence to fall. Given Hera's conservatism, not to mention her devotion to her son, she would need time for thought. An idea would need to be implanted in her mind, not one that would grow quickly and straight, like a poplar. More like an olive, slow, crooked. Others might come along, chop down her idea, but like the olive, it would regrow, at a slightly different angle, perhaps.

Hera gave the smallest nod of acknowledgement. It could not be denied: the current state of flux was not good for family or business. In particular, the presence of Erebus was disastrous for both.

By the time they parted company, it was with a mutual understanding. The matter of Erebus needed resolving before anything else. Despite the confidence of deities, this would require the intervention of heroes. It had been an egregious miscalculation to allow Heracles and Perseus to turn into such... puddings. It was imperative to get both of them onto an immediate training regimen and back in shape. Given the vanity of male deities, it might be provident to keep this course of action between the two of them.

There were just a few minor details to iron out. Given that Hera had been the one to requisition Tyche's services, getting the heroes into this state so as to prevent them from undertaking a mission to rescue Zeus, it was only fair that Hera should cover the main costs – and in particular, the extortionate charges of the self-styled 'Monster-slayer Psychotherapist' who had been commissioned. Brazenly declaring that 'you get what you pay for', he had insisted that to achieve legendary physical feats, your mind needed to be in the right, *legendary*, place.

To the bemusement of the two goddesses, he had tapped his head when he said this. Surely, he meant...

Tyche had tapped her heart.

The psychologist shook his head. Then he tapped it again.

But had not Aristotle taught that you thought with your heart? That thing in your head, the 'brain', was just a radiator and cooling device, a system to keep the heart from overheating.

Aristotle was a goose, the psychotherapist informed them. All polymaths were geese, knowing a little bit about everything and stepping on the toes of genuine experts.

He seemed very sure of himself, and as his CV mentioned numerous awards and citations, Hera decided it was worth paying for. She wondered what Hades was getting up to. She pictured him alone in his palace, brooding.

98

Hades was not alone. He was with Hecate, though it was difficult to recognise either of them in the outfits they had ordered from the *Auxo Theros* catalogue! Strewn around the bedchamber were some of the more bizarre accessories from the *Satyr Satisfaction* section.

Hades and Hecate went back a long way. There were rumours that they were embroiled with one another long before the whole thing with his niece, Persephone. If such had been the case, Hecate never let on. She had been Persephone's closest friend, among the first to make the perilous journey into the, as then, barely charted Underworld. It had been she, who, along with Hermes, had brokered a deal permitting Persephone to return to the world above for half the year.

Surely, the whispers that Hecate had enticed her friend to the place where she was seized were untrue. And if she knew that Persephone was merely a trophy bride for Hades, a means of showing his brothers that he could possess the most beautiful of flowers from above, Hecate gave nothing away.

"Only you truly understand me," whispered Hades.

His words were a little muffled, speaking, as he happened to be, from the other end of the bed with her big toe in his mouth.

"Really? What about Hera? You spend an awful lot of time with her. Does *she* not understand you?"

Hades grinned. How he loved that husky voice, the wicked, lascivious glint in her eye! He squirmed up the bed, kissing different parts of her body on the way, before re-emerging beside her, a little red in the face.

"Hera is a prude. She is not exciting in the way that you are. She would never squeeze into a hydra outfit and dig in her talons like you do. There is no mystery. No playfulness."

Hecate did not seem quite satisfied by the answer. Too wily to be content with compliments, she wanted something more. She now bit his ear. Her arm stretched under the covers. Grabbing hold of a clump of hair, she pulled hard, twisting her wrist to increase the pain.

"You win," he gasped. "Once, my legitimacy is secured, I will dispense with her. You have my word."

Sleep did not come easily, exhausted, as he was, after her departure. So many things to do, and whatever was going on with his trusty servants?

99

The Lethe, river of forgetfulness, has its source in a spot that is neither light nor dark. Shrouded in perpetual mist, a hidden grotto provides a home of sorts. Poppies grow all around the entrance, and the interior is festooned with sleep-inducing flora: lavender, lily, valerian, snake plants.

No sounds reach this place. Nothing moves. On an ebony bed, a figure lies, listless, eyes half-closed: Hypnos, Lord of Sleep. Long before a shadow appears in the entrance, he has detected Hades' approach. His brother, Thanatos, further back in the grotto, shrouded in murk still darker than his surroundings, is also aware of the visitor who is drawing near.

Hades surveys them. He does not expect hospitality; nor is he offered it.

"I have a job for you. Warders. Custodians, if you prefer."

He knows they will demand a high price upon learning the identity of their ward, but is, nonetheless, taken aback. A large portion of land in the kingdom of mortals, where the old borderlands could be collapsed, and in which the two of them would be left free to bend natural laws.

"Where corpses sniff and taste through cavities that once housed organs. Where they can breathe, eat, walk around, make love."

The words sounded odd coming from the mouth of Thanatos.

"Where the inhabitants can wander freely, seeing in their sleep, unable to distinguish between dream and reality."

"You already have such things here," Hades reminded them.

"We want it on Earth, so that they can build great temples to honour us."

Some of the others may not like it, but it struck Hades as a fair bargain. If he could buy time, it was a price worth paying.

100

Far away, in less smothering darkness, a little boy lay in his bed. He thought about what he would really like, wondering once again whether there was some deal to be made with a powerful deity.

He was not entirely certain who that deity was. Not so long ago he had believed in some intangible, though definitely bearded, entity called 'God', who was very wise and knew exactly what you were thinking. The boy never mentioned this to his mother or sister, as he knew they thought it a bit silly.

Recently, he had come to believe in someone a little younger, very big and strong, who could throw thunderbolts very hard when he was angry. Or maybe, he merged that idea in his mind with that of 'God'.

Whichever was in charge, there seemed no harm in proposing a deal. The worst that could happen is that his words would drift off somewhere into the ether, gradually, reducing in resonance to the point where they lost all meaning. At best, his wishes – some, at least – might be granted. So the boy promised now to be good, really, really good, and unwavering in his dedication, so long as his deity would make good things happen in his life.

He turned on his bedside lamp. Very carefully, so as not to make a noise, he shuffled onto his belly, hanging over the edge of his bed, till he felt the hard edge of his drawing pad.

There were already lots of pictures in the book. Now he drew another, a boy and an elderly man in a rubber dinghy, laughing as they came down a water chute. He tried to make the man look a little straighter and stronger than he was. If the god thought he was younger, he may allow the man to live longer, so that he would still be able to share adventures when the boy was grown up.

It took a while to get it right, and there were quite a few rubbings out of pencil marks before he was satisfied. Finally, he closed the book, putting it back beneath the bed.

Of course, the god was likely to know, anyway, what it was the boy wanted, but there was no harm in providing illustrations, just in case there was a need for a reminder. After all, there might be loads of other little boys making their own deals.

101

It was almost too good an opportunity to be missed: Hermes' chariot dumped in a side alley here in the Underworld! It seemed destined to fit in with their plans. Neither Hypnos nor Thanatos had been able to think of anything else since Hades' visit.

It was surprisingly easy to operate. You could even look up co-ordinates for recent journeys: the thing could drive itself! And why not Argos? It seemed as good a city as any? They could choose somewhere discreet, well away from the great edifices built to honour Hera.

So excited were the pair that they did not even notice the startled expression of an elderly local, who scuttled back into his own vehicle upon sighting them. The man's mind was racing. Why had Hermes not warned him that these two would come looking for him? Farts of Boreas! Only by pure fluke had he spotted them first.

It had taken a long while for it to sink in that Bill's untimely demise meant that he would no longer be fetching a newspaper. It was more than inconsiderate, but there was some compensation for the inconvenience in the proximity of the Sainsbury' supermarket at which he had first arrived to the industrial estate where his transport café was situated. He could pick up a paper on his way, and read it over a cooked breakfast.

Overcoming the impulse to flee, he sank in his seat, watching them. They seemed disoriented, heads down, keying things in on the dashboard of a vehicle Zeus had recognized immediately: even when camouflaged, it was, quite obviously, Hermes' chariot. Zeus wondered what on earth these two were doing driving it.

They began moving. He followed. They were heading to his industrial estate. Not only had they been tracking him now, he must have been under surveillance beforehand. For how long?

Yet, for some reason, they went straight past his café, heading, instead, towards a large building. Their briefcases made them look particularly incongruous. After a few moments, Zeus followed them, pausing as they entered the building. They headed for an office signed *Planning Applications*.

The office looked half-empty. Perhaps, most employees had not yet arrived. Or maybe, they all worked from home. Zeus watched through a window, as they went to a booth. Hypnos was taking out a sheaf of papers from one of the cases. Zeus could just make out drawings, with what looked like arrows and measurements.

The official speaking to them was shaking his head. Now Thanatos was opening his briefcase, drawing out a bulging envelope. The man glanced round before pocketing it. There were smiles. Zeus only just ducked down in time behind a pillar as the twins emerged, heading towards the exit.

Instead of following them, he now went inside, picking up an envelope and some bits of paper from an empty desk. Retreating again, he tore the paper into small pieces, stuffing them into the envelope. Only then did he return advancing, confidently, to the man's desk.

Could he tell him what the two gentlemen had been doing there? The official apologised; it was not protocol to reveal confidential information about planning applications. Zeus opened his coat, just wide enough to reveal the envelope. There was a look of surprise, then brief hesitation. As the proposal was at such a preliminary stage, he supposed he could disclose the general nature of the proposal. The discussion had been about possible sites for a new place of worship, as he recalled, a Hypnothan temple. No, he had never heard of such a sect either, but apparently, it was a fast-growing religion, and this was going to be the very first of its kind in the country. Quite a coup for Newton Abbot, and one that might attract welcome tourism and revenue!

Zeus thanked him, putting the envelope down on the desk, before hurrying away as quickly as he could. Once outside, he breathed a deep sigh. Was it possible that the arrival of this odd pair was pure coincidence? It seemed unlikely, but far preferable to his initial assumption.

102

In another office, far away from the realms of mortals, the working day is dragging towards its end. Despite all the pride in its heritage, CLA, or Clotho, Lachesis and Atropos, to give the firm its full name, stands as a monument both to egregious pride and bumbling incompetence. To be fair, this is not entirely the fault of the partners, Clotho, Lachesis and Atropos.

That it operates from two buildings, each bearing the name *Moirai House* above the entrance, one on Olympus, the other in the Underworld, is obviously a complete nonsense, and arises from a dispute between Zeus and Hades that has been ongoing for as long as anyone can recall. The consensus is that this has been of benefit to no one except lawyers. Neither of the litigants is willing to back down, each putting in appeals whenever a court finds in favour of the other.

Zeus and Hades alike have preferred to view it more as a metaphysical than a legal issue, despite the evidence of the astronomical charges – the bills sent in by metaphysicians being far more modest than those of their counterparts from the legal profession. As Zeus sees it, fate concerns a person's living condition, whereas his brother, Hades, insists it is a matter that pertains to death. The different courts appear to have found it impossible to establish clarity on the matter. Hence there are two branches of CLA, far removed from one another, relying on a system of communication that is, at best, intermittent.

Each branch has been designed along similar lines, with three separate areas. The first of these, for weaving, overseen by Clotho, is filled with cumbersome looms. The second is laid out for cutting, with pieces of thread littering the floor, not to mention all the pairs of scissors and shears, no two lives being identical in texture. This section is run by Atropos, and those who are assigned to this part of the operation live in constant dread of displeasing her. The final area, the domain of Lachesis, consists of vaults, constructed for the purpose of record keeping, with desks, ladders and shelving reaching to the lofty ceilings. Neatly laid out on each desk are pens, notebooks, rubbers, rulers and tape measures.

Herein lies another flaw. Anxious to seem more *state-of-the art* than his brothers, Hades has instructed all workplaces in the Underworld to move to a computerised system – with only partial success, it might be noted, given the atrocious connectivity across the Underworld. Meanwhile, CLA on Mount Olympus continues to use the traditional system of manila files, paperclips, index cards, even microfiche being viewed as a *new-fangled* fad. Lachesis, in particular, takes immense pride in the rows and rows of vintage, wooden drawers, dignified by smart, metal ornaments.

It is by pure chance that one of the clerks has spotted the most recent screw-up: two cards for a single subject. Right now, he is holding them out to a colleague. Someone is going to have to inform Lachesis, who, it so happens, is in the Olympus branch today. They seem reluctant to be the one, with Lachesis being in a particularly grouchy mood.

"*You* tell her."

"Why me? You found it."

There follows an awkward moment, until one of them remembers the new intern. An opportunity, perhaps, for him to gain useful experience. A bell is rung. The intern appears.

Do they want coffee?

They shake their heads.

A few minutes later, a timid knock on an office door. Lachesis stares at the information on the two cards, her thin lips tight.

Mudge, Reginald Montgomery...

The intern hopes Lachesis will be impressed by his eye for detail.

"Each card shows the same address, birth details, medical records, inoculations, dental appointments, and then this slight... divergence."

"Divergence?"

"We seem to have lost track of one of them."

"One of them?"

"Perhaps, they are twins."

"With the identical name?"

"Some parents are not very imaginative."

Lachesis gives the intern a withering look. He gulps. It is hard to believe that she is considered to be the most genial of the three partners.

"There seems to be some confusion about his... their... fates. One of them has been dispensed; the other..."

The first two clerks are waiting round the corner of the corridor when the intern re-emerges. They have to sit him down, bring him a coffee, with plenty of sugar.

"Well? What did she say?"

It takes a while for the intern to get it out. One of the accounts for this Mudge needed to be lost. And very quickly. Before the next audit.

103

It was close to midday when Narcie sauntered in. Although time was not measured, specifically, it could be estimated by the number of customers whose hair had already been styled. As ever there was an audible sigh, a wave of never to be requited desire, as he strolled in, eyes following him as he moved, gracefully, towards the changing room.

Psecas intercepted him, handing him an envelope. Surely, not his notice! That would be unbearable. There was a collective intake of breath.

The eyes of staff and waiting customers searched, anxiously, for a clue. It was something of a relief that Narcie was opening the envelope so nonchalantly, that he was reading it with surprise rather than dismay.

Why had Hermes not delivered this invitation, he wanted to know. Because, explained Psecas, as everyone else appeared to have noted, Hermes had not be seen for a long while. Perhaps, he had been sent to Boreas again. Narcie still looked bewildered. Of course, as Psecas observed, it was a great honour. Not as if everyone got invited to the palace. It was just that Hades was not renowned for entertaining. He rarely invited guests to dinner parties. As far as anyone could recall, the word 'rarely' might be substituted by 'never'.

And this very evening! He would need to leave, immediately, to select the appropriate items of dress. Was there a code for such occasions? Psecas shrugged.

A small bluebottle – a very pretty one, it should be added – could not have rung the bell at the home of a giant spider with greater trepidation. Narcie had the impression of being inspected, before the automatic gates swung open. Before him there was a courtyard, vast, empty, weeds growing between the cracks in the paving stones. There was not a soul there, just some sculpted figures dotted about. Narcie had the impression that they were staring at him, mockingly, as he crossing towards what looked like a grand doorway. As he neared it, he saw that it was not so grand, tilted a little, hanging off ancient hinges.

There was another bell. He rang this one, too. The sound echoed down corridors and hallways within. Once again, there was a sensation of being watched. And then the door creaked open.

He made his way down the passageways, up and down a series of steps, passing nobody. Who exactly ran this palace? Who swept the steps, cleaned the carpets, polished the old silver? Not that it felt like a palace; much too austere. Narcie was still grappling with these thoughts when he reached a large banquet room with a long table in the centre. There was a hearth with a fire burning away, the first warmth he had felt since entering this draughty place. Still no homely touches, but warmth, at least. The candelabra on the table were also lit. There were plentiful bowls of food across it, yet only two dining places set, one at each end of the table.

Perhaps, he was meant to wait here. He perched uneasily at the edge of a couch, close to the fire. He waited.

And waited.

Twisting round when he heard a cough. Another couch. In the shadows. A figure, sitting utterly still. Had it been there the whole time?

It rose, headed towards him, arms open in welcome, an affable wraith. Hades was slapping him on the shoulder, as if, thought Narcie, they were a pair of old buddies, who had not seen one another for ages.

"Shall we eat?"

Narcie glanced over his shoulder, uneasily. Was it just the two of them? Really? All that food?

Hades was already, seated, piling up his plate. It should have felt safe, sitting at such a distance at the other end of the table, when, actually, it felt to Narcie as if his head was in the jaws of a monster.

He felt a mad urge to rush into the fire, crackling and spitting on the other side of the room. The agony could not have been more acute.

"I hear you are achieving wonderful things. Your work at the salon."

Even the most inane comments seemed somehow alarming.

"Oh, did Charon tell you?"

Something spat out of the fire, making him jump.

"I guess it was Charon only because he came in not long ago."

"So he did," recalled Hades. "I hear he had to re-schedule twice."

"I don't think so," said Narcie. "Psecas keeps a book of cancellations. She's so..ooo anal! Three times and you're out. I'm sure I'd know."

"Perhaps, I'm mistaken."

Was that a smirk? Perhaps, a trick of the light.

"And did you attend to Charon's hair yourself?"

"Oh no, darling! Psecas did that."

He gulped. Did one use such a term of endearment for Hades? Too late now.

The same smirk – or trick of the light.

"Of course, it's not exactly the easiest hair to style. More like bits of sticky string. Not like your lovely locks."

Perhaps, Hades was quite nice, after all. Narcie breathed more freely.

"Yes, mine does have a beautiful sheen. All natural, too. But there aren't many like that. Not any, come to think of it."

"Quite," agreed Hades.

"It sort of goes with the rest of me."

"So it does," agreed Hades. "You are the very portrait of perfect harmony."

He grinned, broadly. It was a little scary to behold, as if an actor had not had quite enough rehearsal time.

It was turning out to be rather an enjoyable encounter. Why had he been so worried? Hades was, after all, a very nice fellow, with good taste.

The conversation continued in this pleasant manner, moving swiftly from hair products, to clothing colours suitable for particular complexions, to idle gossip about which deity was dating which, a topic about which Hades seemed surprisingly well informed. By the time they moved on from the main courses to some sweet delicacies, they were laughing about who was hot and who definitely was not! They even began scoring and placing others in league tables.

Hades seized a chance when the name of Ares came up.

"I hate to discuss business at the table but I have a task for you; more of a small favour, really. I would like you to spend some time with Ares."

Narcie's initial alarm sparked by the term 'task' was replaced by relief. This was not so arduous. Narcie admired Ares. He was one of the few immortals with style, an image.

"It's a small gift from myself and his mother. We want to show our gratitude, and Ares must not know that we have arranged it. He must feel that you have selected him out of all those who have been pursuing you. And there are very many if I am not mistaken."

Narcie nodded.

"I have lost count."

"And you don't need to be any more intimate than you wish. A tiny piece of yourself will suffice, I am sure. You just need to scintillate in your usual way. It will not need to be anything long-term."

Hades knew full well that there could never be space for a third person in Narcie's relationships! Not for anything longer than the briefest of periods.

"Oh, one more thing: I would like you to keep this, hidden. It's a device patented by Echo. You can either keep it in a pocket or strap it on like this, under your clothes."

104

Echo!

The whole of Mount Olympus was an echo chamber. Rumour and tittle-tattle. Across the vineyards and groves, around the valleys and lakes, inside the deepest recesses of the palaces, the whole place was riddled with the stuff. If you stood in a garden, you could feel it rising up from the flowerbeds around your ankles. The ground dished up dirt, which blew upwards, babbled into streams, dripping down into other worlds. It was in the air, the water, the flames in the hearth, indestructible.

Quite how Tyche had managed to keep her own past secret was unfathomable. Nobody guessed that the redoubtable hostess of the casino, who sensed the movement of a spider across its web in the furthest turret, whose employees would rush about at the snap of a finger, suffered from pangs of sadness at the memory of a doomed relationship.

She liked to pretend that it had been laid to rest, faintly remembered like something implanted by Morpheus, not quite deep enough to take root. And then the ruined seeds uncovered through a single comment!

It had been a customer, ordinary enough, but increasingly, loud and coarse. Having taken a break from his card game, he was having a drink with a fellow player,

taking no notice of those around him and making no
effort to limit the volume of his voice.

Was it different shagging different types of
nymphs? He had tried them all: Oreads, mountain
nymphs; Dryads, oak nymphs; Meliae, ash nymphs;
Nereids, sea nymphs; Naiads, freshwater nymphs – you
name it, he'd sampled it.

And how was it different?

How? Well, for starters, the nymphs of the trees
were more... sylvan. They found more shady, secluded
spaces, where you could lie for hours with no one
noticing. Some of these nymphs were quite shy, and there
was nothing better than breaking in those who were
particularly reticent. There had been this one – he now
named her.

Tyche's heart skipped a beat. Him! He who had
stolen and defiled *her* nymph, a translucent being of the
woods, diaphanous, a skipping flurry of joy.

Not that the oaf would have had the wit to
recognise such delicacy. He was only interested in
possessing her for the briefest of times because he *could*.
Just another quickie for his phallos in a hole it had not
visited before! And what did *he* care when she protested
that she had promised herself to another?

When forced to divulge a name, she had kept
Tyche out of it. It was a mortal, a huntsman, who lived
close by, entering the forest in pursuit of prey. As she lay

on the ground, whimpering, her clothing ripped, he exacted his own retribution. Then, declaring that it made him want to vomit, the knowledge that he could have been induced to stick a part of his divine body in a place defiled by a human, he had her dragged before a council, demanding that both the mortal and the nymph should be punished in the traditional way for the offence against nature. For surely, this was far worse than adultery.

Tyche had never forgiven herself for hiding away, as her nymph and the supposed lover were subjected to public humiliation, the excruciating, burning pain of repeated figging, skinned ginger root being forced into their orifices. Meanwhile, Tyche's name was never brought into it.

She watched him now, the kopros-faced choiros, throwing his head back and roaring with laughter, lunging, lewdly, at a cocktail waitress. Beckoning to one of the card-dealers, she whispered something to him. He, simply, nodded, it not being his job to query the orders of the mistress of the house. It was her business if she wanted a player at her tables to win small, then lose big. And if an unusual request was made to slip something into a drink, then leave the imbiber naked in the company of one of the more priapic inhabitants of the lower corridors, then that, too, was her prerogative. And finally, if an audience was requested to watch him waddle out, euryproktos, one would be assembled.

"That part-donkey creature," she suggested, "you know, the one that is permanently on heat."

"You mean Shaggakles?"

He shifted, a little awkwardly.

"It's our pet-name for him."

"Is it?"

"There's a lot of betting on how many times he's going to get it up each day."

"Is there?"

Such juvenile pranks, even here, in her house! It struck her again, the fragility of everything. Only her fabulous wealth protected her.

105

There was a sound in the distance. It was difficult to be sure. He was lying still, trying to conserve energy. The fact that he could not, actually, perish from hunger and thirst did not mean that he did not feel the effects.

He felt woozy, drifting in and out of sleep. The noises may have been part of a dream. And then there was an explosion. The walls around him were caving in.

Someone was stepping through the wall.

Hephaestus!

Surely a vision in his mind! What would *he* be doing here?

He had imagined his mother, Maia, cradling him, or better still, Aphrodite, not this burly, rough-handed fellow who glowered at him. In his state, half-famished, mind in a fuzz, it was difficult to imagine how one small spider had made its way to Arachne, who had then decided that, as none of the sorcerers or sorceresses could be trusted, Hephaestus was the next best individual to approach. Why use spells on an enchanted doorway if you could enter from the other side, blowing up any rock in your way?

Nor could Hermes have had any idea how Arachne might have persuaded Hephaestus to rescue him. How could he have known that, like himself, Hephaestus had also shown compassion towards her when she had first found herself transformed, trapped in dark world of cobwebs. It's not as if anyone knew what went on in the smoky, metallic depths of the creature's mind.

Hephaestus was now opening up the knapsack he carried on his back, flinging a small bag onto the floor beside him.

"You'll probably need something to eat and drink before setting off. It's a long journey."

There was a flask inside.

Hephaestus was already walking away through the hole in the wall.

"Thank you, brother."

"Half-brother," Hephaestus reminded him, without turning.

Hermes grinned. Inside the bag, there were pieces of pitta bread with nourishing food inside. Only Hephaestus could have prepared it in such a ham-fisted, careless fashion.

106

One of the most irritating things for those who worked within the industry was the way that the complexity of the job was barely noticed. The assumption amongst the more plebeian masses, the uninformed *idiotikon*, was that a customer went in and some half-trained oaf would just go snip-snip before the customer emerged with hair shorn.

Apart from everything else, there were the products to prepare to give fragrance, aromatic essences utilising flowers, spices and oils. It was not simple to create the various blends using rose extracts such as vine leaves, lemon juice olive oil, vinegar, not to mention frankincense and myrrh.

Pots were mixed up with hair softeners, combinations involving items such as beeswax. There were also dishes for hair tones, using soda and soaps and alkaline lyes from Phoenicia. Items such as pollen and flower needed to be prepared for those who preferred to be blonde. Saffron, indigo and alfalfa were all sorted in their separate dishes. The roots of rubia tinctorum plants needed to be chopped, crushed and mashed for those who favoured red hair.

And now with so many regulars switching to the Medusa look, with all the preparation entailed, Psecas' staff, the *psecades*, were having to come in extra early each day.

One of the busiest branches was the one close to Hades' palace. Which was where they found Narcie, slumped in the doorway. It took a while to identify him. At first, they thought it was a dead animal dumped there in a sack. He was badly battered, with more bones broken than unbroken.

When they got him inside, Echo's device was discovered. Miraculously, it had survived the assault intact. When it was played back, they heard shouting and threats, in what was, recognisably, the voice of Ares. Although it was widely known that Ares couldn't be with anyone for more than a short time without some outburst, the assumption was that these were rarely acted on. Of course, it was also well known that, despite his excellent looks, Narcie could be irritating. But never so much as to warrant an attack such as this.

It was touching that Hades, himself, was one of the first visitors. The words he uttered, quietly, were picked up, and soon being repeated by almost everybody: if Ares could do such a thing to dear, sweet Narcie, then nobody was safe.

Observers noted, from a respectful distance, how gentle the King of the Underworld was with Narcie. They had not known about this soft, sensitive side.

Comments were made, too, about the way he was holding Narcie's hand.

Indeed, Hades was now stroking Narcie's forearm. He bent his head low, asking, sorrowfully, whatever could have sparked off Ares? Narcie was unable to raise his voice above a murmur. Hoarsely, and with obvious pain, he managed to convey the fact that it had been dark and he did not get a close look at his assailants.

"Assailant," Hades corrected him.

"I'm sure there was more than one," croaked Narcie.

Hades patted his shoulder. Narcie groaned with the pain.

"Oops! Sorry!"

"Two or three of them," whispered Narcie.

Hades clicked his tongue, shaking his head in sympathy.

"It feels like that, so I'm told, when Ares beats people up. Great guy and all that, but a proper brute!"

When the recording on Echo's device was made public, it was fuzzy in parts, but the cursing and shouted threats were clearly audible. Despite his protests of innocence, it seemed incriminating – especially after the Pores incident. What's more, Narcie was highly popular, far more so than Pores. Something of a mascot! A source of pride who embellished their own sense of perfection. Deities minor and major shared a sense of outrage. It was admirable that Hades, and also, Hera sought to defend his good name, but Ares' own popularity ratings plunged.

Just a passing thing, Ares' supporters reassured him. Pales into insignificance next to your heroism in the battle with Atlas.

"But I didn't do anything. I didn't touch Narcie," protested Ares.

It was difficult to soothe him.

107

It had not been his idea. Ember had persuaded him that it was the right thing to do. The *right thing!* What did that even mean? Surely, the right thing was what you *wanted* to do. And he did not want to push Lily past ducks in the park.

It was most infuriating, and right now, he disliked Ember even more than Lily. Perhaps, he had been wrong: she was not feisty, like a number of his own daughters, she was a... a... drip! He groped around in his memory for who it was she reminded him of, and, after a while, it came to mind.

He had spotted her at a banquet, a rather winsome-looking thing, not the type he usually went for. She looked melancholy. Perhaps, he would cheer her up. He had made a move for her, and instead of being flattered, as she ought to have been, and hopped straight into bed with him, she had bored him flaccid by going on and on – and then still on some more, about having been hoping to meet him, so as to discuss the narrow notion of the gods about kindness, and the way they all appeared to view it as being about good fortune rather than compassion or empathy.

What was her name? Eleos, that was it, one of the daughters of Nyx and Erebus. Come to think of it, most of their children were on the dull side! He had humoured her for a while, before slipping away in search of someone more exciting. He seemed to recall mentioning it to Hermes, who had informed him that there was just a single temple dedicated to her in Athens. Typical of those malakas, he had thought. You would not have got the hardier souls of Sparta or Macedonia giving her the time of day.

"You remind me of Eleos," he had snapped at Ember.

"Who?"

"Exactly! Who! Nobody even knows of her, and a jolly good thing, too."

Nevertheless, he had felt cornered by his niece's nagging. He had chosen a time in the morning when he hoped few people were around, with children in school. He had forgotten about parents with children too young. And also about other pensioners, with nothing better to do than stare at those around them.

"Your wife's rug has slipped," said one busybody.

It was true. He had not noticed the edges of the rug on her lap dragging along the ground. But what business was it of this old codger?

"That's how she likes it, orrhos-malaka," he muttered. "Besides, she's *not* my wife."

A sound came out of Lily. A giggle? She was gesturing for something – a notepad and pen that she had insisted on bringing along. It took an age for her to compose the message, during which Zeus let out a series of sighs and yawns. It was a short message with a few misspellings crossed out.

Say nice things. ~~Endymonts.~~ ~~Endermunts.~~ Endearments.

He read it and shrugged. She gestured once again for the pad. He grimaced. What a drag!

~~Kul them...Luk them up in a buk...koob~~ ... look in book.

He nodded, fully intending to dispose of all her notes as soon as they got home. He continued pushing her. The wheelchair was heavy, especially, going up slopes. It had been Ember's instruction to remember the rug, but it was not exactly necessary. He did not feel at all cold, and the bloody thing kept sliding off her knees.

He remembered something else that Ember had told him.

"Do you want a cup of tea?" he now mumbled, grumpily.

Lily smiled, a slightly lopsided smile, giving him a small nod. He grimaced. It was not the right response. Otherwise, he could have pushed her straight home, shoved her into an armchair, then gone off for a game of bowls or even a fishing trip. Or maybe just back to his own house to play on his Xbox. Only he had given his word to Ember.

His favourite café was not far away. Instead of the café by the park with all the busybodies, he headed there. The all-day breakfast would compensate for this drudgery.

The waitress beamed at him.

"You've brought your wife, Mr Mudge. Out on a nice walk?"

"She's *not* my wife. Just a neighbour. Don't really know her very well. Usually a... dog-walking agency sends someone to take her out, but no one turned up today."

"Well, that's very sweet of you," said the waitress.

"Yes, it is," agreed Zeus.

Once back at home, he ran a nice, hot bath and climbed in. From out of the blue, a notion came to him about Lily. He did not wish to think about her while he was in the bath, but she just popped up. It struck him that she had risked her own wellbeing twice in order to protect him, once from the Albanians and later, from the empusa. Why was he feeling this way? He struggled to dismiss this tinge of guilt.

It was not as if he had *asked* Lily to get involved. She was old, anyway, probably with not all that much time left to live. What's more, he had done her favours in return. He had found her cat. He had buried it. He had eaten her cakes and told her they were nice. If anything, he had done *more* for her. She owed *him*.

What business did she have coming into his mind, anyway? It was not fair of Lily to make him feel this way. It was most sneaky of her!

108

The season had ended, the time of year for reflection, planning, and if possible, celebration. And this year, more than any other, the Newton Abbot Bowling Club had earned the right to celebrate. There was a great deal of laughter, backslapping, and at one point, a Mexican wave.

The old clubhouse, decked out in the white and blue team colours, was packed. The shields and photographs on the walls, dating back to the early 1900s, had been dusted down, with new ones now unveiled, celebrating the recent triumphs.

As this was his first year as a club member, Zeus had little idea what to expect. It came as a delightful surprise to be summoned to the front during the presentation of awards. There were raucous demands for him to give a speech. It was all a little overwhelming; as he had not prepared anything, he stumbled over his words.

"Everything is about ... you know, teamwork," he began, modestly.

There were cheers, lots of fist pumps and a couple of enthusiastic hoots.

"Only the other day, I heard someone say that there was no I in TEAM. And there isn't, if you check."

Never before had there been such a noise in the clubhouse. The place was rocking.

"Of course, every team needs at least one good player. I mean a really good player, who can carry the others. Especially those who are not very good."

After the briefest of pauses, more cheering. Apart from all his other qualities, Monty Mudge, as they were beginning to realise, had a droll sense of humour. And now they were being treated to a very literal account of the trajectory of his winning bowl, where it started, how it curved, what it passed during its passage, and where it ended. Just in case any detail had been missed, Zeus repeated the description.

Returning to his seat, he cradled his trophy, running his finger on the embossed, shiny letters: Reginald M. Mudge – Player of the Year.

Glasses were still being raised when Derek Doble, the club secretary, sidled over to him. Would Monty like to take over as club captain in the coming season? Naturally, it was all under wraps for the time being, but between the two of them, Derek could reveal that the current incumbent was due to have a hip replacement operation in the coming April and was unlikely to be available for the start of the season.

Zeus considered the suggestion. It was so out of the blue, an honour he had not anticipated. Was it the norm for the best player to be club captain? Obviously, it should be, even though their current captain was not even the third best player at the club. Why – his own average scores were far higher! And had the club secretary witnessed his winning bowl? Close-up?

Indeed he had, and it had quite defied Newtonian laws of physics.

It was not altogether clear to Zeus what this meant, and he doubted whether it was worth checking through the Mudge Files. Obviously, it must be a compliment!

He treated Derek Doble to his most fulsome smile. Reginald M. Mudge – Player of the Year, would be pleased to accept the invitation. He would drag the team up by the orjiks to the highest level. They would wipe the floor with the Kings Bowling Club of Torquay, cut them to pieces and scatter them all over the county.

Later the club president, Hazel Chubb, came to congratulate him on his new position. And yes, she, too, had enjoyed a close-up view of the triumphant bowl.

"Perfection. Something you only see once."

This was gratifying to hear.

"It defied Newtonian laws of physics."

"Quite so," concurred Hazel.

109

In the enclosed spaces in which he dwells, stiflingly hot, filled with dust, smoke and clanging echoes, thoughts are ponderous. The ground beneath feels solid, and yet always this feeling of falling. There is an urge to cling to something. Another trapdoor might open at any moment.

A memory etched deep in his mind, the only time when there had not been this sensation – when he actually *had* been falling. At first, a panic: the inner parts of the body feeling as if they were shooting up the windpipe and into the mouth. Twisting. Spinning.

Then settling into a fall. The whooshing of wind. Calmness. A sensation of floating on a springy cushion of air. A sense of time suspended, in a space without distance or proximity. Moving at a constant speed gives no sense of movement.

His mind clunks back into the nowness: day after day in this stifling place, a compulsive and meaningless repetition of the same acts. And yet, so preferable to an outer world of pointless social interaction. Here at least he has his *children*: things he has invented; things he has repaired. It does not really matter whether they are used to good or bad effect; he has fulfilled his role through their perfect design.

This new idea – where did it come from? The rescue of a fellow being, albeit one who meant nothing to him? A deity as busy as he, himself, only, in his case, running errands for others. Conveying messages! Of what value was that?

Nevertheless, in a peculiar way he feels grateful to his half-brother for, unintentionally, introducing this notion to his mind, an idea that subverts an implacably benign cycle, a tiny dot of purpose on a meaningless canvas.

So it is that he finds himself now in this empty, barren place, staring down into the void between mighty cliffs. It has been artfully designed. The cliff face is sheer and smooth, with barely any ledges for footholds, no roots or branches to grasp hold of. There is no way for the prisoner below to escape, even if he could break the chain that tethers him.

He lies down at the edge of the precipice, peering at the tiny figure far below. Fettered to a rock, he is exposed to merciless, boiling heat during the day and freezing temperatures after the setting of the sun. He has been placed in such a way that he can just stretch far enough to reach the food and water that is on the rock that holds him. How did that food get there? Some cruel magic devised to keep him alive and prolong his suffering?

The colour of the rock stands out, starkly, the only thing there not chalk-white, stained, as it is, by endless puddles of blood from livers, pecked out before regenerating. There is something fascinating about that rock; perhaps, a geologist would be able to calculate the number of days the unfortunate captive has been here by the depth to which the blood has seeped.

A movement above. He glances upwards. A tiny speck in the sky. Hovering. Waiting for nightfall.

Taking out some tools from his backpack, he hammers a spike into the rock-face. Leaning over the edge as far as he can, he notes how the cliff-face at this end of the ridge is shaped in such a way as to make descent impossible, even with a rope. The angle of the overhang would leave you dangling towards another valley entirely. There is no way of reaching the prisoner. However, it looks as if you might just be able to scramble upwards from an outcrop below if a long enough rope was hanging over the precipice.

He sits for a while in deep thought. With sudden decisiveness, he secures the rope, before scanning the landscape for items that might be useful. Just a few carcasses, mostly dry bones, but also, a few unfortunate animals that had wandered there to die more recently. He takes some things from his knapsack: a sharp knife, a ball of string, a needle, some thread.

He searches for somewhere hidden from the sight of the speck in the sky. It takes a while to fashion things from bone, skin and sinews, but he is nothing if not patient. Surveying the apparatus he has constructed, he cannot be sure it will work. He knows he cannot die, whatever height from which he falls, but that does not mean he can't be smashed up again. And, this time, with no Sintians to tend to his injuries.

Better not to ponder on it. Picking up his appliance, he rushes to the abyss, leaping headlong over. Not so far as his first fall, but far enough for the rush of a familiar feeling. One of *not* falling. Almost euphoria. Floating down to the ground. And then a ripping sound above his head, and he plummets earthwards.

Not far enough to break him, but enough to hurt. He groans, lying still for a long while. He stretches out, stifling a low cry.

He tries to stand, but his knees give. He begins to drag himself towards the blood-spattered rock. The dishevelled creature there pays no heed. As he gets close, it gapes through him. There is a look of pain at the sound of a voice, as if it is unbearably loud. He is not sure whether the creature comprehends what he is saying. He takes out a tool from his bag and begins to smash at the chain. It has not been designed to break easily. The valley is now shrouded in shadow. Already, the air has an icy chill. He can no longer see the speck in the sky but senses that it is closer.

A final effort. Then a snap. The creature is free, but it does not attempt to move.

"Do you remember anything?"

Again, an empty gaze.

"Your name is Prometheus."

Nothing. Just a fearful glance upwards.

"We need to find somewhere to hide for the night. In the morning we will climb."

Whatever it has become, it is no longer itself. He has to drag the creature away. It is broken, he thinks, though not in the way I am. This thing has been cracked apart from the inside.

"I will give you a new name. A disguise. In time you will learn to work with me, in secret. I am Hephaestus, the mender of things."

110

They clinked glasses, and before long, Hera and Hades were both quite merry. What a brainwave of Hera's to propose Ikhnaie, deity of finding lost things, for the job!

It was more than satisfactory. Ikhnaie turned out to be even better at the job than anticipated. Her website really failed to do her justice, enthused Hades. She should update it, giving examples of the commissions she had carried out – though not this last one, of course, which was, strictly, a private matter.

While Hera and Hades agreed that a discreet, celebratory banquet was appropriate, it was difficult to decide on the right people to invite, with Hades strongly opposed to the children of Zeus through other relationships. Much too obvious and bound to raise eyebrows, he argued, given Hera's well-known hostility towards them. There was need only for a select group, one that was obscure, with no obvious connection to either the Lord of the Underworld or the Queen of the Gods. Moreover, it needed to look as if the event might have been arranged in the natural course of things.

Members of the Ethics Committee were surprised but pleased by the idea of a small gathering to commemorate their recently lost colleagues. It was all very tasteful, subdued, a reception at which some delicacies would be provided, and intoxicants sufficient only to provide a warm glow. All to be followed by just a few words from Hera about the dignity of the Committee members, a toast from Hades, and then a brief response from Arete.

The fare was of high quality and not over-extravagant, even if some of the petit fours had a slightly unusual aftertaste. Hera and Hades looked on with satisfaction. The event had been well-received, winning the favour of an influential, highly-respected institution. Moreover, the more fanatical followers of Kronos were unlikely to search for the heart and feet of their hero in the stomachs of members of the Ethics Committee.

111

As it was difficult for her to get to the front door, Lily had provided Zeus with a key. He found her sitting by the fireplace, without the small electric heater turned on. The room was chilly. Having dressed her, hurriedly, the helper had forgotten to turn it on. A plate with a piece of toast and a half drunk cup of tea was on a small table beside her.

"I have a surprise for you," he said, fumbling beneath his coat and holding out something. It was a small kitten.

Lily's eyes lit up. She opened her mouth to say something but the words tippled out in a jumbled mess. She gestured for her pad, scrawling out what she wanted to say.

You found ~~sursurseal~~... ~~Ses~~ ... Sir Cecil. I... ~~nwek~~... knew you would.

She squeezed his hand.

Turning away a little awkwardly, Zeus went to the kitchen, poured some milk into a saucer, then made an apology about some jobs he had to do. Once outside, he breathed a sigh of relief. All debts were paid.

SURVIVING THE 21ST CENTURY: A HANDBOOK FOR PENSIONERS

ENTRY 9

CUPS, SHIELDS AND MEDALS ARE NICE THINGS TO HAVE. OTHERS COME INTO YOUR HOME AND ADMIRE THEM. PERHAPS, YOU HAVE NEVER WON ANYTHING IN YOUR LIFE. NOT EVERYONE CAN BE A WINNER. THAT DOES NOT NEED TO BE A PROBLEM. BUY YOURSELF SOMETHING THAT LOOKS NICE. THEN YOU CAN GO INTO AN ENGRAVER. EVEN SHOE SHOPS WILL DO IT!

I NOW HAVE LOTS OF TROPHIES AROUND THE HOUSE, EVEN THOUGH I DID NOT NEED TO GET THE EXTRA ONES, AS I AM ALREADY A CHAMPION.

THE NEXT POINT IS QUITE A DIFFICULT ONE, BUT REFERS TO A CHALLENGE YOU WILL ALMOST CERTAINLY CONFRONT. AS A PENSIONER YOU WILL, INEVITABLY, FACE UNANTICIPATED CHANGES OF CIRCUMSTANCE. ONE DAY EVERYTHING MAY BE FINE, ABSOLUTELY CALM. YOU MAY HAVE SOMEONE IN YOUR LIFE WHO IS USEFUL, A FRIEND, OR WIFE, OR JUST A NEIGHBOUR. THEN SOMETHING HAPPENS TO THEM. ALL OF A SUDDEN, THEY ARE A BURDEN.

YOU NEED TO DISTANCE SUCH PEOPLE FROM YOUR EXISTENCE. FIND A NEW HELPER. IT MAY SEEM DIFFICULT. THERE COULD BE UNPLEASANT SENTIMENTS, OR OTHERS AROUND YOU WHO TRY TO

PRESSURISE YOU, SUCH AS AN INTERFERING NIECE.
THEY MAY TRY TO IMBUE YOU WITH GUILT.

GET ROUND IT BY GIVING YOUR EX-HELPER A
SMALL GIFT, A TOKEN OF APPRECIATION FOR THEIR
EFFORTS IN THE PAST. THEN MOVE ON.

FINALLY, A QUICK NOTE ABOUT BATHING:
WHEN IN THE BATH, MAKE SURE YOUR MIND IS KEPT
QUITE CLEAR. JUST SOAK, CONCENTRATING ON THE
FEELING OF WARMTH. THERE HAS NEVER BEEN AN
INSTANCE OF ANYONE HAVING A GOOD IDEA WHILE
IN THE BATH.

AND IF ANYONE WHISPERS THE NAME,
ARCHIMEDES, I'LL THROW UP. WHAT THE BINEO! A
MAN GETS INTO A BATH AND NOTICES THAT THE
WATER LEVEL GOES UP. WELL DURR!

112

When a mob sets out, quite often, it is without any clear purpose. They were coming now, up the hill from the suburbs. Carrying placards. Some were tooled up for some kind of more forceful action, though at this stage, there was little clarity about what that might involve. At first, there was a lot of chanting: the gods needed to know how angry they were, and this act of a terror against one of their own was the final straw. As they marched, the chanting became more militant. There were a few random acts of vandalism on the way. Windows of palaces smashed.

Soon things were bubbling up into a full on riot. A surge of fury passed across the crowd as it reached the very first salon opened by Psecas. It may have been true that their very own Narcie had worked in one, but had they protected him? The one employee who was targeted by the rabid beast, the single victim, just happened to be a D-G.

Besides, the swell of support for the vile creature had begun in the salons. All that *Hairdressers For Ares* nonsense! It was only appropriate to vent their collective fury on this stinking den. By the time they had finished, the place was a wreck.

Thanks to social media, the news spread quickly, and members of H4A were soon making their own plans, determining where to gather. As it is well known, it is dangerous to mess with hairdressers. What's more, no group is so well connected to others.

It was not long before a second mob set off on a counter march, down the hill, into the D-G Favela neighbourhood, vandalising homes on the way. On their respective return journeys, the anger of each mob only partially sated, the two groups chanced to bump into one another. There was an almighty scrap, resulting in many injuries, the worst inflicted by some quite lethal hairdressing utensils.

In the posh parts of Olympus, higher up the mountain, the reverberations were felt for many days. Somebody needed to restore order. Who better than the mastermind behind the victory over Atlas? A hurried invitation was composed and sent out to Hades to act as an interim leader.

113

"I'm taking you out for lunch... petal."

"Petal!"

For some reason, he had looked up terms of endearment on his laptop, as Lily had proposed. From Ember's expression, it was clear that he should have followed his original impulse to ignore everything Lily scribbled in that malaka notebook.

"Sorry. I forgot your name for a moment. It's been happening more and more recently, ever since you made me spend time with that woman."

He gave his niece an accusing stare.

After the initial excitement, Ember had been low for some weeks. Despite her... *shortcomings*, Mo had not been uninteresting. For a brief time, she had lit up Ember's life. It was hardly surprising if she felt depressed now.

"And I'm going to buy you a big present," added Zeus.

Ember smiled.

"Thank you but we'll buy each other a gift and go dutch over lunch. Not that I don't appreciate your well-meaning offer of subordination and heteropatriarchal hegemony."

"I'm not sure I understand that," grinned Zeus, "but it's a deal. You can pay for lunch, and later, we'll exchange presents."

He had booked an expensive restaurant in Cathedral Square in Exeter, a place he had discovered recently. The meal was good, but overpriced. They chatted, small talk, at first. Towards the end of her second glass of wine, Ember's mood suddenly changed.

"That day of the... you know, in your house... I never asked you what you thought it was. That thing, the creature... its... well, it sounds ridiculous, but I thought I saw a face. A person's face."

She looked around to check that nobody was listening, before lowering her voice.

"Of course, it doesn't make any sense whatsoever, and I came up with a theory. I think when you are close to someone, you know, intensely close, you can develop a sort of telepathic bond. In a moment of crisis, something else was going on in my life. For whatever reason, and with no explanation, Mo had decided to walk out on me. Somewhere in my brain, I must have sensed that, and as that animal savaged you, I glimpsed her face. Does that sound crazy?"

Zeus shrugged.

"I believe in real stuff, not psycho-babble. Things that are evil, lurking in dark places; things that can shift shape."

It struck Ember that either she had never really known her uncle or he had turned very weird in recent months. Her mind slipped back to Mo.

"Funny how she appeared from nowhere, then disappeared from my life without trace. As if she had never been."

Better if she hadn't, thought Zeus, privately planning what he would do to the empusa, if he could find it, on his return.

"I guess I have a knack for making people disappear. Like the children's father."

Zeus had never really thought about Frida and Antonio's father before. Amongst those on Olympus it was quite normal to have consorts, then offspring with them, never really seeing them afterwards. He had lost count of the number of children he himself must have had. Perhaps, more than a hundred. Over half of them, he estimated, had mortal mothers. A few he could name, Heracles, of course, Perseus, Minos, Helen of Troy...; but in most cases, their names were forgotten. While some with mortal mothers had, eventually, made their way up to Olympus, he had no idea about the others. All in all, it seemed a bit weird, fathers hanging around long after there was any need of them.

Why would you even choose to stay with a particular female for any length of time? That would be ever so dull! For all Hera's complaining, she would never have wanted him about the place for more than brief periods. Did mortals clasp onto one another out of a fear of growing old and ending up alone? Like holding onto rotting logs in the water.

His reflections were interrupted by Ember's voice.

"Apart from the children, you're probably the most stable element in my life right now. No offence but that's depressing."

She changed subject.

"Do you know, Antonio got into trouble at school? Maybe, it's because he gets embarrassed about his slow reading. I had to make him write an apology. A supply teacher came in to their class, and got them to take turns reading aloud. The children overheard another member of staff calling her 'Helen'. Antonio said something about her running off to Paris, and being desperate for a shag."

She shot him a suspicious look, which Zeus ignored.

"Makes you wonder where he might have picked up such language."

Zeus shrugged.

"I seem to recollect *you* using the word."

"I probably picked it up from Ant, and he had probably heard it from another boy in his class."

He topped up their glasses.

"He also keeps coming up with weird expressions, such as 'farts of Boreas'. Naturally, Frida and I are delighted that he is beginning to speak out, but when it comes to calling the principal a pile of 'bolbiton', I am not so sure. I have no idea what that means, but it does not sound polite. Sometimes, I think you are a terrible influence on him and feel I should ban you from seeing him. But then..."

She appeared to hesitate, considering whether she should inform him of another incident.

"They read a poem about friendship in class, and afterwards, they were invited to write a poem about their best friend. He wrote about you."

"Really?"

Zeus looked pleased, but then noticed a tear rolling down her cheek.

"He should have friends his own age. I worry so much about him."

She composed herself, and to Zeus' relief, the conversation returned to mundane things. When they had finished, and she had sorted the bill, they went and sat outside on a bench, each alone with their thoughts as they watched the world go by.

For some time, Zeus stared at the building that dominated the square. The cathedral intrigued him. Clearly, it was a sort of temple, but one without flowers or food or sunshine. Not a place to celebrate living gods. It would make a suitable shrine in the Underworld. Perhaps, he should mention it to Hades.

Which made him think. What had he done to make his brother hate him so much?

The thought was interrupted by Ember.

"Do you want to go inside?"

"Do *you*?"

Ember grinned. It suited her, thought Zeus. Her whole face lit up. It occurred to him that she did not smile anything like enough.

"I tend to steer clear of all religious buildings. Places where people go to gibber nonsense-words, as if their gods care!"

Zeus turned pink, opening his mouth as if to make some indignant response, before changing his mind.

"At the same time, if you really want to look inside, I'll go with you."

Only, when he got to the door and peeped in, for some reason, he was frightened to cross the threshold.

Instead, they went into the shops. After all, they had promised to exchange gifts. While Ember chose a book from *Waterstones*, Zeus opted for a rather pricey games bundle for his Xbox.

"It's been a great day! We must do it again," enthused Zeus on the way home.

"Umm."

If Ember's enthusiasm was muted, it may have been because, all in all, their shared day had left her around two hundred and fifty pounds out of pocket.

114

Hades, back in the Underworld, alone, brooding, plotting. Erebus, in some deeper chasm still further beneath the worlds of mortals and immortals, swirling in murk, indefinable, yet now conscious.

As was his wont, Hades was playing out all the possible outcomes in his mind. He was one of the few gods who did not enjoy gambling – unless, that is, the outcome was already fixed. And no one fixed odds better than Hades. A master of introspection, he was convinced that in every setback, there was an opportunity to be found. You just had to search long enough.

He considered the matter again. Containing Erebus was proving more of a challenge than his advisers had assured him. Destruction in the realms of mortals was one thing, but it was quite another matter when seas rose up high enough to inundate palaces on Olympus; when the sun was blotted out for days on end, leaving immortals blundering around; when they listened, fearfully, to the gurgling of sludge far below. The gods themselves trembled.

Hypnos and Thanatos were proving a disappointment. Hades had the impression that their main skill was in delegation. Had he known about their penchant for subcontracting work, he would never have taken them on. And the quality of those they had employed was debatable. Something more powerful was required to hold down Erebus in the bowels of the Earth.

However, Hecate's counter-spells were not working either. She was working round the clock – though, strictly speaking, there were no clocks in the realms of the gods. Her charms were failing to put the primordial thing to sleep. It was taking all her minions to use soothing spells to contain it for even short periods. Meanwhile, the cost of a perpetual choir of Sirens was draining the resources of even Hades.

More help was needed. The situation called for desperate measures, a frantic training regime in the hidden vaults of Tyche's palace. It was axiomatic among the gods, learned from countless epic battles, that a champion from the ranks of mortals was required to achieve victory.

There was great rejoicing when Heracles and Perseus, still formidable, if a little podgier than recalled, entered the fray. It was difficult, perhaps impossible, to fight something without form, but they were, after all, heroes, and the impossible is what heroes did.

The reputations of each were hugely embellished through their great deeds in the struggle against Erebus. That each perished in the labour provided an additional bonus: much of the credit for the restoration of order went to Hades, strengthening his position as regent and enabling him to pass some draconian laws, and more crucially, to raise taxes so as to cover some of the extensive costs.

115

"I thought you might be pleased to see me."

Zeus shrugged. After such a lengthy period of abandonment, he was not prepared to let Hermes off the hook so easily. Nor did he seem satisfied by the excuse. How had he allowed himself to get trapped in a cave so easily? What was he doing at a rendezvous with Charon, of all people? What was Charon even doing out of the Underworld, and how had Hermes got involved in a relationship with such a dubious character?

Hermes squirmed, uneasily, in the armchair in Zeus' front room, wishing he had never mentioned Charon in his account. He attempted to bring the conversation round to present needs. It was imperative that Zeus should begin the journey back as soon as possible. As the transition into Mudge had somehow or other got embroiled with provisos and stipulations that were binding, and which prevented a direct return, it meant the need for an intermediate switch to a superior body, one that was capable of progression to the status of future immortality.

Hermes glossed over the question as to exactly how the *provisos* and *stipulations* had crept in. However it had occurred, as already mentioned, it could now be converted into advantage, a double incarnation as king of the gods and as a superhero.

On another positive note, all was prepared for the youth identified as Zeus' next host body. Although he lived in Hellas, Hermes had put it into his mind to book a holiday in Albion. He had even arranged for it so that he thought it had been a burning obsession since early childhood to visit the South-West of that country. It would mean that there would be no inconvenience to Zeus. He just had to be close by when the young man attempted suicide. In case, the youth had any last-minute doubts, Hermes would slip him a potion to give him courage.

"You've thought of everything."

If Hermes was taken aback by the tone of the comment, he hid his feelings, reminding Zeus, instead, of the need to act speedily. The situation was quite chaotic back home on Olympus. Hades was getting well above himself, passing all sorts of acts. The D-Gs were rioting, and there were problems with the hairdressers.

"Hairdressers!"

Zeus sat up in his seat. Had he heard that correctly?

Hermes went over the background once again, the plot to oust Zeus, the rivalry between Hades and Ares, and then the unfortunate injuries inflicted upon Narcie.

"Narcie?"

Zeus could not even recall who he was, and Hermes had to remind him. Even then, Zeus seemed unable to take it in.

"So all this is going on because of Narcie!"

"Well, Narcie, and also Atlas, and Kronos, and Erebus."

It was a terrible mess, sighed Hermes, and Zeus was needed back as soon as possible to sort it all out. The entire universe was at stake, not just Olympus. Zeus just peered out of the window, grumpily. He would need to check his diary before confirming his availability.

116

Hera was far from convinced by Hades' explanation that it was simply all the endless, low-grade, bureaucratic matters that accounted for the recent periods of absence. Surely, Hera would not wish him to trouble her with such trivialities when she had their wedding to prepare!

On the contrary, his machinations struck Hera as transparent, and when she ran them past her new ally, Tyche, her suspicions seemed to be confirmed.

"He's positioning himself, Sweetie."

Hera grimaced. Apart from anything else, she disliked being referred to in such a way, but as terms of endearment, such as *Honey, Ducky* and *Sweetie.* seemed to be part of Tyche's style, she tolerated it – for the moment, at least. Right now her shrewdness was useful.

"As regent, even only on a temporary basis, he feels more confident. But you do realise, don't you, Honeybun, that underneath he's a writhing maggot-bucket of insecurity."

Hera considered this. If she had made errors in the past, it was, perhaps, at least partly, due to taking males at face value. If Hades was not really all that confident, was the same not true of his brothers? All that wealth that Poseidon had gathered, stored, initially, in huge underwater caverns, or just left littered across the seabed, the shiny crown and trident, the bling, the showy displays. More latterly, the list of offshore accounts, the rumours about an invisible presence in innumerable investment trusts. It was really about impressing his brothers, showing how much better he was doing than them. And what about Zeus? It now struck her that an awful lot of his behaviour had been down to bluster and bravado.

"You do see, Ducky, that he's cutting you out. The narrative right now is all about Hades."

Tyche, who seemed very well informed despite the fact that she hardly ever left her palace, now recounted how Hades had insisted on the display of giant pictures of Zeus in all public buildings.

"Why ever would he do that?"

"Because, Sweetie, he, also, features in them. Always standing close to Zeus. Wearing that sinister smile, the one where his facial muscles remain tight. Like they were best buddies. Or with a serious, penetrating look, the confidant, the consigliere. It all makes him look like the anointed one, chosen by the KoG as his successor."

Hera considered this. She had never been good at projecting different aspects of self. It was how Zeus had invariably outflanked her, making her look like the petty one for her acts of revenge against his mistresses.

"And where it begins to affect you, Honey, is how he is now getting his accomplices to spread whispers.

How your ex had been such a great ruler. How he was a martyr, betrayed by a mysterious group, parties close to him. It may not have struck you at the time, but with your Z-R group, he was always careful to lurk in the shadows. It's not *his* name on any of the documents."

Hera now recalled how Hades had convinced her that it would be liable to be an off-put in some quarters if he was seen to be central to the plot, with so many of the other deities viewing him as untrustworthy. If he had ever been named, it was invariably in some coded way. And he was never there in meetings as a protagonist, but as a kind of guest. He could not really be implicated in any of it. How could she have been so naïve?

Running over Tyche's words, she recalled, too, that Hades had asked her some time ago if she had pictures of the family, borrowing ones which included images of the two brothers, wholesome, partying – not that anyone could recollect ever seeing them out together. Not that anyone could even imagine Hades partying!

Of course, the pictures now being put up in offices would be cropped. Others cut out, so that it looked like just the two of them – Zeus and Hades; Hades and Zeus.

There was further information that Tyche had acquired. Hades was planning an election, something that would legitimise a more permanent kind of regency. Such was his current popularity that victory was all but assured.

"Don't get me wrong, Hun, but I'm not seeing that you are actually needed any longer in his schemes."

117

The expression on Antonio's face was one of disbelief. How could anyone conceal that sort of fact for so many years?

"Never learned?"

Zeus shook his head.

"Not in school?"

"Nope."

"Not parents. A big sister or brother? Not a friend."

Zeus just smiled.

It wasn't exactly a lie. Not as if the Kouretes would have been interested in that kind of thing. If Zeus knew how to do it, it was because he could just access certain knowledge, automatically. He had never formally learned, in the same way that he could had never learned to drive his chariot, and would need to engage with new information apps if the vehicle had a clutch and gears.

"That's why I need you to teach me now. Our secret."

They fell into a certain pattern. Once a week, after collecting the children from school, Zeus would settle down at the table with the boy, while Frida went upstairs to do homework or just read. They would take out a picture book, with Antonio going through the letters, very slowly, and Zeus imitating him. It was gratifying for the boy to see Zeus picking it up; he barely noticed his own progress.

"You're a very good teacher, Ant," enthused Zeus.

"Really?"

Afterwards they would play a quick game of *Fenyx Rising*, then go for a meal. Zeus would insist on covering both their plates with brown sauce, and Antonio would pretend that he liked it.

There were also occasional half days spent with Frida, such as when Ember took Antonio to get new clothes. It was incredible how quickly the boy seemed to grow out of things. One Saturday, while Ember and Antonio were on one such shopping trip, Zeus asked Frida whether she would like to go anywhere. He regretted having given her an option as soon as she expressed a preference. Why would anyone choose to go to a museum?

They settled on a compromise. Zeus liked seaside towns, and Teignmouth had a small museum. If he got bored, he could go and sit on a bench overlooking the sea and wait for her.

Frida agreed, quickly. Whilst there, they could check out the address where the poet, John Keats, had once lived, when nursing his brother who was dying of tuberculosis.

Zeus zoned out as she prattled on about poetry, which did not sound all that interesting. For some reason, the girl had chosen to memorise some lines.

"I don't always understand it at first, but then I wait for the patterns to settle into meaningful shapes."

Zeus made a noise that made it sound as if he was listening. Given the time, he said, they could grab some lunch before finding the museum. He parked close to a second-hand bookshop, heading into it on a whim and re-emerging quickly. He handed her a poetry book. A book of famous poetry, with a couple of poems by Keats, himself, in it. Perhaps, she might forget the museum.

"Uncle Monty – that is so sweet of you!"

"Not really."

He winked.

"It's not as if it cost anything. I took it when no one was looking."

Frida looked shocked, insisting that they returned inside to pay.

"But they still have plenty of other books."

The girl was implacable. They either paid or put it back. Rather grudgingly, he followed her back inside.

"My great-uncle was so distracted that he had a... senior moment," she was explaining to the assistant.

"My great-niece had a... junior moment, and was very silly about it," Zeus corrected her. "It's not as if anyone minded."

The assistant looked confused as Zeus, after a nudge from Frida, now took out his wallet, removed his payment card, completing the transaction with obvious reluctance.

Frida opened the book over lunch.

"Ode on a Grecian Urn," she began.

"Grecian?"

"Yes. What do you think they used urns for in those days? Ashes?"

"More likely, wine," he corrected her.

He watched her mind vanishing elsewhere as she began to read aloud. The first few lines went straight over his head, but his attention was caught by the next ones:

> *What men or gods are these? What maidens loth?*
> *What mad pursuit? What struggle to escape?*
> *What pipes and timbrels? What wild ecstasy?*

For some reason he could not explain, he, suddenly, felt a wave of homesickness, only returning to the moment as she came to the final lines:

> *Beauty is truth, truth beauty – that is all*
> *Ye know on earth and all ye need to know.*

Zeus considered this, idly, while Frida, too, reflected on it. She picked at her lunch, distractedly, while he tucked in. She still looked perturbed, when they walked outside.

"I am waiting for the meaning to become clear in my head, but I can't help thinking that it kind of assumes that everyone understands truth and beauty in the same way. Take truth. If that is beauty, then telling lies must be ugliness. But, then, what about a fib – and what when that fib is told to protect someone's feelings? Besides, in an argument both sides may believe they speak the truth. So it's never really fixed."

Zeus did his best to concentrate. The King of Gods should really be able to keep up with a ten-year-old girl, even if his own mind was more focused on whether or not he should buy an ice-cream now or wait. It really was annoying to become a bloated belch-machine after even small intakes of food. How nice it was going to be to get his own stomach back!

"Aphrodite, Artemis and Apollo all thought the Greeks were to blame for the Trojan War. Privately, I agreed with them. But Hera was convinced that it was all the fault of the Trojans. Maybe, real beauty is sticking to your beliefs when everyone else is against you."

"And how do we measure 'beauty'?" continued Frida, ignoring the interruption. "Why should it be truthful? A sea-horse is beautiful; a slug is not. But are they not both equally true?"

Zeus grinned.

"I bet your friends hate getting into arguments with you."

"They probably would, if I had any."

The remark was not self-pitying, just stated as fact. Nevertheless, Zeus felt an overpowering urge to put an arm around her shoulder. He hesitated. She seemed to inhabit a perfectly harmonious space on her own. He did not wish to infiltrate it.

Instead, he bent forward and picked the prettiest flower from a soilbed close by.

"It's all right," he murmured; "there are plenty more left there."

With a very small smile, she accepted the gift.

"Ice-cream?" he suggested, having reached the conclusion that the pleasure it brought would more than compensate for the subsequent discomfort.

The great thing about an Xbox is that it enables you to block out everything else for hours on end. Or days, if you prefer. His niece had been warning him about it over the past months.

"It messes with your cognitive processes. I read that it can take only ten or fifteen minutes playing violent games to affect your brain. Those areas associated with anxiety, anger, arousal – that sort of thing – get over-stimulated. At the same time, activity is reduced in the frontal lobes, where the emotional regulation and executive control should be going on."

"The frontal lobes are overrated," he retorted, not that he had a clue what she was going on about.

He did his best to zone out while Ember went on about evidence from neuroimaging research. Over recent days, he had been playing his game, repeatedly. And when he got that out of his system, he would go for a food binge at the transport café. And then he would go fishing, maybe. Anything to put off all the farewells.

It was impressive just how many street artists there were when you asked around. And how, after you had found one, so many imitators sprung up, like colourful weeds through cracks you had not even noticed. Best of all, they could be commissioned for practically no more than the fun of it. They were not even all that interested in the motives of their patron.

Just a few words on walls, at first, then graffiti all around Olympus. After that, bits of artwork – pictures of their current regent, the aspiring king of the gods, in lewd and compromising positions, wearing the strangest outfits. In general, the denizens of Olympus were pretty easy-going about odd, sexual fetishes, but these seemed beyond abnormal. Some of the pictures had captions, ridiculing him, along the lines of: *Hades likes it like this –* or *Getting it on in the Underworld.*

Nowhere was the gossip more fervid than in the salons. In the waiting areas, at the hairdressing chairs, in doorways and on the stairs, all you could hear were customers and staff exchanging jokes about it. Soon – and no one seemed to know who was producing them – Hades dolls were appearing. Dressed in his outfits, many came with words stitched on. *Have a Hades night in –* was particularly popular.

Then came the calendars, with each month of the year showing Hades in different outfits and in unusual sexual positions, some beyond the physical possibilities of even a god.

It was all a bit of a laugh, but Hades, himself, had no doubt that it was damaging his credibility. While there may have been some headshaking about offences such as rape or incest, it was far worse for a god to be seen taking a submissive, female role. Whatever creature he was dressed up as!

Other words and pictures found their ways onto walls. There was a popular one of Hades in one of his *costumes*, with the name *Lady Hady* on it. Next to it was the title – *Re-Gent*. In the background, there was a picture of Hera, in male clothing, with the label *She-Gent*.

Hades' heavy-handed search for the culprits only alienated him further in some quarters. With uncharacteristic rashness, he struck out at those he suspected without any evidence. Yet despite all the arrests and incarcerations, it kept spreading. It was as if the adversary stalking him was wearing his own helm of darkness.

With the election date looming, there could not be a worse time for his popularity to be waning. However, if his enemies believed that he had no more cards to play, they were mistaken. There was support to be found elsewhere.

Here he was, hanging around the Favela, mingling with the very D-Gs he had recently suppressed. There were meetings, marches, rallies, during which he shared the platform with prominent activists from the community.

Was it fair that only the gods should have a vote? Had not other immortals earned the same right? Although he was no natural orator, his awkwardness seemed to convey sincerity. Besides, he was improving. He began to affect a slight stutter in the style of Demosthenes. Like Demosthenes, he started to alternate emphatic and unemphatic words. He threw in oaths. He made sudden and dramatic sweeps of his arm. He let the occasional silence fall. He used hypophora, asyndeton, paraleipsis and metaphor. He fired questions into the crowd.

How much further could the D-Gs be degraded, ignored, pushed into the margins? Had they not been humiliated enough? Was not poor Narcie the symbol of that suffering? But he, Hades, had sworn to make him whole again. He, personally, would pay for all the medical work it would take to make Narcie as immaculate as his former self.

He made sure that he was seen on the streets with Narcie. In the bars. Wherever there was a crowd. Had he not been Narcie's protector against the savagery of Ares?

Although he never mentioned it, he ensured that his minions made it public that he was setting up a shrine in honour of Narcie in a village somewhere remote in Hellas, one with no temples to other gods or immortals.

The preposterous notion that D-Gs should be allowed to vote, quickly, built momentum, until it was an unstoppable force.

Sometime afterwards – and nobody could, actually, recollect who came up with it – with suffrage extended, a still wilder idea began to form: if D-Gs could vote, why should there be an impediment to one of them standing for actual office?

120

He needed to get his farewells in. He would begin with neighbours. He rang the bell on the front door of Ermias' home. It did not work. He knocked. After a while, he went to the window and banged his fist on that.

Eventually, the straggly Circe female who visited the house opened the front door, just wide enough to peep out. Without invitation, Zeus pushed it open and strolled in, finding one of the scurvy-looking housemates sprawled across a settee. The man sat up, quickly, looking terrified by the sight of Zeus. He blinked at him, staring like a timid, pasty-looking rodent caught doing something wrong.

"You should get out more, baubon-face," remarked Zeus. "Not healthy spending all of your life indoors."

"I will," promised the man.

They stood, staring at one another.

"Is the Pyg... is Ermias in?" asked Zeus.

"Ermias," the man called, hoarsely.

Ermias now appeared.

"Let's take a walk," Zeus drawled, slowly. "I have a job for you. I may be away for a while, and I will need you to keep an eye on things here."

All the time he spoke, and while Ermias slipped on his jacket, Zeus kept his eyes fixed on the rodent-like housemate.

In the pub he seemed not to notice Ermias' unease. Nor did it bother him that Ermias was still sipping his tomato juice while he had downed two pints of stout. While Ermias sat, timidly, Zeus worked through two bags of nuts and a large packet of salt and vinegar crisps. Despite that, he also managed to do all the talking.

Ermias seemed taken aback to hear that Zeus was leaving. His eyes opened wide when Zeus added that he could get his neighbour some paperwork through his connections. Ermias would be able to get out; go wherever he liked.

The cost? There was no cost. Zeus was dispensing a favour. It was what he did.

Ermias seemed too overwhelmed to articulate his gratitude, but two days later a package was delivered to Zeus' address. Three creatures, a lion, elephant and deer, all exquisitely carved. Zeus pulled a face. Whatever was he supposed to do with the ruddy things? Ember, however, was delighted when Zeus later presented them to her as an early birthday present.

"Well, you don't seem to take it all that well when such gifts get forgotten," he added, somewhat unnecessarily.

A few days later, there was another gift: a large manila envelope on his doormat with handwritten poems inside. Down the margins, there were pictures of animals, drawn with careful attention to detail. Zeus was about to shove it in a drawer when he had another brainwave.

Zeus watched Frida turn away, a tear in her eye, as she read through the poems a few days later. Were they that awful? Zeus was about to explain the identity of the poet, when she added in a quiet voice that they were beautiful. She had no idea that her great uncle wrote and drew with such sensitivity.

His expression became suitably modest. He only dabbled, and they had not taken up much of his time.

121

His farewell gift to Lily was a lunch. A Chinese takeaway.

Apart from finding it difficult to co-ordinate movement, it was a challenge for her to enunciate words with any clarity. She signalled for the pad, and wrote down a thank you.

"It's not as if you had anything interesting to say, anyway."

The edges of her lips drooped, in what might have been a smile.

"It wasn't a joke," he said.

She added another note. Would he mind a walk in the park? She had not had any fresh air for a few days.

It was a bit of a struggle getting her out and pushing her wheelchair, especially up inclines.

"You're heavier than you look," he panted. "Scoffing too many of your own jam tarts."

A sound came out of her. He thought it might be a giggle. He gathered his breath. He was Zeus, king of the gods! He could push a malaka wheelchair!"

Despite everything, it was pleasant being outdoors. They listened to the squeals of children in the playground before arriving at a small lake. Lily opened her bag, scattering bread for the birds, at first pigeons, then a few ducks, and then some huge ones rushing over, honking, loudly. He thought about Penelope's geese, and also the goose that Aphrodite liked to ride. Once again, he was struck by a wave of homesickness.

What in the name of... well, *himself*, was he still doing here? It really was time to start the journey back, even if this did need to entail an interim period in another body.

He pushed Lily back in silence, helping her into her house. They settled down with a hot drink, watching an episode of *Repair Shop* together. How Hephaestus would have enjoyed the programme! He must tell him all about it when he got home.

For some reason, and uncharacteristically, Zeus waited, until a helper arrived to feed Lily and put her to bed. She was one of the earlier calls organised by the agency, so she was tucked up by six-thirty, well before sunset.

"Thank you," Lily seemed to be trying to mouth as Zeus departed, only the shapes formed by her mouth did not look quite right. She grabbed his hand, giving it a squeeze. He felt awkward, uncomfortable with all these recent emotions that perhaps signalled the onset of some illness. Once more, he reminded himself that it was hardly *his* fault that the woman had flung herself in front of the empusa. No one had asked her to do it.

He hovered for a few moments. Then, very awkwardly, he bent low and kissed her on the forehead.

"That was nice," she murmured, clear enough to be understood.

"Nicer for you than for me," came the retort.

Having made his farewell, he stumbled outside into the light.

122

It took quite a time to alight on an appropriate gift for George Williams. George had plenty of fishing equipment, so that seemed unnecessary. Then a flash of inspiration: there was a shop he had gone into many times, specialising in medals and trophies.

It was difficult to alight on the best words. He thought of *Fishing Champion*, but to his knowledge, George had never actually won anything. Finally, he settled on a trophy with the words *Good Fisherman* engraved on it. He also bought a medal with the same wording. For good measure, he went into a newsagent and bought a card with *Best Friend* on the front. As an afterthought, he threw in a fishing simulator game he had bought for his Xbox, not that he knew George actually had an Xbox.

It was difficult to determine whether it would be better to hand over these gifts during their final fishing trip together or in their pub on the moor. He decided on the latter. It would reflect well on George that he was receiving largesse from such a renowned angler.

It was rather awkward when Zeus told him that he would be leaving the area, permanently. Tears began to well up in George's eyes. Zeus looked away, pretending to be engrossed by a dartboard that no one was using. He wished he had sent it through the post, as Ermias had done.

Worse still, George had grabbed him by the wrist. Why was he leaving? Was it something George had said?

Zeus did his best to assure George that it was not about him. There were things he had to do. Far away from here.

It was a relief to get away. What was it about mortals, he wondered? They could be so cloying, so needy.

123

As there had never been an election on Olympus, it was hardly surprising that some errors were made. From the outset, *Team Hades*, the few trusted aides from the Underworld who were organising the campaign, found themselves at a disadvantage. Quite simply, the older, more established, gods were not so expert with social media. Those around Narcie were far more savvy.

It cannot be denied that there was also an element of complacency. Surely, thought those in *Team Hades*, once the senior Olympians were seen to be supporting their candidate, it would be a formality. It was a coup to have the impressively gaudy figure of Poseidon on board. Here he was, making an appearance, united with his brother in indignation about the effrontery of the D-Gs. Looking resplendent, his arm draped around his brother's shoulder, he declared that *Little Hay* had always been his fave bro. It was, perhaps, just a little unfortunate that nobody had thought to remind Hades not to slouch, grimace or twitch. Perhaps, just one small smile would have made all the difference.

While *Team Hades* spent a great deal of time enumerating the achievements of their candidate, their counterparts made no effort to boast about Narcie's exploits. They were aided by the fact that Narcie did not need to say anything to look good on a podium, and

Hades now regretted that those who had beaten up his rival had not done so in a way that made the damage permanent.

Nor did it help that canvassers for *Team Hades* took to arranging meetings, furtively, in backrooms, scheming about ways to undermine Narcie, whose own team were on constant parades. Wherever you looked, they were in your face: Dionysus and the younger gods singing, dancing, pogo-ing through the streets – like a carnival with fabulously decorated floats. Hades' campaign remained flat, by comparison, without any vibe. Hades and those around him watched, suspiciously, as Narcie's election drive went on and on, one long party.

Surely, they agreed, voters would not be taken in by such superficiality, pointing out that their own slogan, *Vote Hades*, was both pertinent and dignified, unlike that of the opposition: *Getting Arsie; We're with Narcie* – which, as they said, didn't actually make much sense.

"The problem with Hades' campaign team," explained Tyche to Hera, "is that they don't feel the zeitgeist."

"The *what?*"

"The point is, Ducky, they have missed their moment."

Naturally, she agreed with Hera that there was no substance to Narcie's campaign; that his team consisted

448

entirely of dilettante hedonists; and that, of course, there was no sense to anything they said.

"The thing is, Honeybun, when you have been around for as long as I have, you should have learned that you either surf on the big waves or get rolled under."

Hera looked pained. In the first place, it was irritating to be lectured in such a way by someone younger than herself. Family relationships could be a bit confusing among gods and Titans, but she was pretty sure that Tyche was either a niece or a cousin at least once removed. The nerve! More annoyingly still, it now occurred to her that Tyche was hinting at something she, herself, may have missed: Hera's own role in this. She had done her utmost to prevent Hades' rise to power, only to assist this ludicrous rabble to get in, instead! And there was something extremely condescending in the way that Tyche was now giving her a reassuring pat on the shoulder.

"Of course, with no experience of office in any post, the chances are that Narcie won't last long. Between you and me, our punters are already placing bets on it."

Hera thought about this. Swallowing her sense of indignation, she asked how long Tyche thought he would last. Hera did not share her other thoughts, even though she suspected that her new ally had already guessed them. She was wondering whether that would give Ares enough time to manage to restore his reputation. Of course, he

449

would need to master the art of demonstrating contrition while not appearing weak. And he would need to appreciate the importance of keeping his mother close by. In the meantime, if Narcie could be induced to make enough mistakes, there might come a moment of advantage for her son; when there would seem a certain prescience in being identified as the one who had beaten him up.

All that was required was to get close enough to Narcie to encourage his excesses. That should not be too difficult; the approval of the queen of the gods was not a thing of small value.

"Would you like me to invite Narcie to a small party, Sweetie?" asked Tyche, who had, indeed, read her thoughts.

124

Far below Olympus, in rather less sumptuous surroundings than Tyche's palace, Charon's mind was also whirring round. Sitting in the shadowed lodgings on the banks of the Styx, he contemplated the possibilities. Frankly, they looked bleak. If his situation had seemed irksome before recent events, it had become far worse since his flirtation with the idea of a new patron, one who might free him from his interminable role.

Kronos had not manifested himself as the powerful benefactor he had been anticipating. Indeed, Charon felt most let down, as if he had been drawn in, deliberately, seduced by the old deity's fearsome reputation. When push came to shove, Kronos turned out to be toothless. Come to think of it, bodiless! Nothing of him was traceable.

It left Charon stuck with his old mentor, in a worse position than ever. Of course, Hades was too wily to expose his malice. He had simply smiled at Charon as if nothing had occurred, re-installing him in his old role. Rowing spirits across a lifeless river for the measly fee of a single, lousy, old coin, which he, himself, had to extract from the mouths of the deceased! Currency that was not even accepted any longer in the updated system now used in the Underworld!

Aeons ago Hades had changed his job title from 'Ferryman' to 'Executive Psychopomp', and for a brief time, before he realised that there were no actual contractual changes or fringe benefits, he had actually been flattered!

It all felt intolerable, as he was now not only stuck with that job, but he was also being given general dogsbody roles. Knowing Hades as he did, Charon realised that the vindictiveness might stretch out, interminably. Retirement? Fat chance!

In desperate times...

Charon gathered himself. He would need to be as sly as his master; perhaps, still more devious. There could be no sense that he was doing any other than, casually, calling in. If Hades caught wind of it, it needed to look as if it could have been reconnaissance on his behalf.

As ever, a hush fell over the place as he strolled in. Just a slight amendment of style, he suggested, a little closer to his previous appearance. Perhaps, the leap into something more daring had been a little too sudden.

While Psecas was snipping away, he asked her questions, cagily. She replied, still more cagily. They talked about the recent swings of weather, following a circuitous route to more immediate matters.

"So, about Narcie – what do you reckon as to his chances?"

Psecas did her best to dismiss the question, but he persisted.

"I mean if he..."

Relishing a new sense of power, Psecas did not help him by filling in missing words. Charon twisted his body, as if in great pain.

"If he wins – not that it's going to... happen, of course."

"Of course," she agreed.

"But if he did, in some..."

It was a struggle to come out with so many words at once, but Charon ploughed on.

"Some alternate reality. What do you think his... policies...?"

Psecas waited, politely. Charon gulped.

"What they might be: his policies?"

Psecas shrugged.

"As you say, it's not going to happen."

"And what do you think his...?"

There was a longer pause.

"His attitude to – I don't know – say, my sort of role, what might that be?"

"I shouldn't worry. You'll still be needed."

"Unionised?"

"I doubt it. He's not the kind of person to be interested in details. More the type to leave things as they are. All hypothetical, of course."

"Of course," he agreed.

She held up a mirror for him to inspect his hair.

"By the way, Hermes came by the other day, asking if I'd seen you. I think he's looking for you.

125

"It's a birthday treat. A surprise night-time trip."

Ember was eyeing him, suspiciously.

"Where to?"

"Well, it wouldn't be a surprise, if I told you."

Ember looked dubious.

"It's nothing stupid, is it? You've already been in trouble with the police."

Zeus gave her his most solemn, adult look. Of course, he wasn't going to tell her that he had managed to acquire a large rocket, some way beyond the maximum legally permitted size for public sale. He had discovered some time ago that, despite her appearance, Ember could be strangely cautious and conservative in her actions.

"It will be fine. It's not as if I'm taking them to the bottom of Mount Etna to visit Typhon! We're only going up the road. Besides, Frida will be with us to keep everything in order – won't you, Frida?"

The girl nodded.

He could sense Ember's resistance weakening.

"But no drugs, alcohol, or other illicit activities. Nothing dangerous. Above all, no police! And home by eleven."

"I'd have liked to visit Mount Etna," remarked Antonio, as they exited a roundabout and drove up towards the surrounding hills.

Zeus grinned.

"Perhaps, another birthday. When you are a little bigger and have acquired the powers to resist dragon-headed demons."

After a while, they turned off the dual carriageway onto narrow side roads. Although the sky was clear, the moon was the thinnest of slivers, with overhanging trees cutting out what light there was.

A triangular, white tower loomed up in the distance. Zeus parked on some rough ground beneath it.

"It's as close as we can get."

The hill up was steeper than he had anticipated, the rucksack on his back feeling heavier with each step, and soon his breathing was laboured. They paused for a while. A little further on, Zeus stopped again, struggling for breath.

"I'll tell you what to do. You two go on, I'll watch from here."

"It's all of us or none of us."

There was a snarl across Frida's lips. He loved her fierceness. It was so much stronger than her mother's. With Ember, it was all on the outside, hiding her inner vulnerability. She was like the rose in *The Little Prince*, he thought. Whereas with Frida, the core of iron ran straight through. There was not just a fiery exterior; there was an inner volcano, always about to erupt.

She took the rucksack, and they helped him up, one on each side. It had seemed impossible at first but one way or the other, they reached the white tower. With its Gothic windows and circular turret, it looked like something ripped out of the page of a fairy tale, miraculously transformed into something real. A wide patch of grass spread out next to it.

Zeus gave himself a few minutes to recover his breath. He had come prepared, soon setting to work, banging a stake into the ground, taping the launch tube to it, and inserting the rocket

"Wow!"

Antonio's eyes were shining.

"Is it big enough? I got my friend, the Pygmie, to acquire it. He knows people who can get things you can't get in shops. I've forgotten the name – *Hell's Firebolt*, or something like that."

"The Pygmie?"

Frida looked perplexed.

"Never mind. He's an acquaintance."

Antonio walked round it a few times, with admiration.

"Is it dangerous, Uncle Monty?"

"I hope so," grinned Zeus.

He had taken out some matches from his coat pocket.

"Do you want to light it?"

He noticed the look of horror on Frida's face.

"Aren't you supposed to have a special safety lighter, keeping your distance?"

"Maybe, *I'd* better do it."

Zeus flapped his arms, indignantly. He was the adult. He was the one who had got hold of *Hell's Firebolt*. He would do it.

Frida pulled Ant back as Zeus fumbled with his matches. A few spilled out onto the grass. By some good luck, and with much cursing, he managed to light the blue touch paper at the third attempt.

They watched the rocket rise in the sky with a loud whistling. There were a series of flashes.

They remained, staring up at the sky for quite a while, as if expecting it to return. Ant shivered.

Opening his rucksack, Zeus now removed some more contents. A Bluetooth speaker, some packets of hula-hoops, a giant bar of fruit and nut, a flask...

"I made some mulled wine."

Frida shot him a look.

"You can't stay in lane when driving before a drink."

Zeus gave her a reassuring pat on the shoulder.

"I'm better afterwards. More relaxed. Just a small cup each. To warm up."

"So why did you need to bring two flasks?"

"In case, any other people were around, just by chance," replied Zeus, quickly. "You wouldn't want me to be impolite."

They had two cups each, before Frida confiscated the second flask. Zeus shrugged.

He was trying to decide on the best kind of farewell, but the right words were not coming to mind. All he could think of was to tell them how handy they were, respectively, with a bat and spade. Emotions never felt previously were impeding him. If only Hermes were around; he would know the right kind of thing to say.

"Let's dance," he said, rather abruptly. They waited, undecidedly, as he put on some music.

"One of my favourites: Zorba's Dance from *Zorba the Greek*. It's a kind of sirtaki, with slow bits of hasapiko and fast bits of hasaposerviko."

The music began, very slow at first. Zeus had moved away, giving himself space. He spread out his arms, taking a step to the side.

"Come on!"

Frida held back but Antonio joined him. Putting an arm round the boy's shoulder, Zeus stepped forward, tapping his right foot against his left heel. Antonio copied the movement. Zeus kicked into the air; Antonio kicked into the air. They stepped inwards then outwards again, repeating the motions. The music started to speed up.

Zeus stretched out a hand to Frida. After a slightly awkward hesitation, she joined them, linking arms with her brother on the other side. Zeus stretched his free arm to the left; Frida stretched out her free arm to the right,

"Kick ...step ...kick...step... kick... step," shouted Zeus.

They moved clockwise, then anticlockwise.

The bouzouki music was playing faster. Zeus was getting short of breath. He had a stitch down one side. He didn't care. If all Time could become congealed within a single moment, this was the moment he would choose.

Now they were all interlinked in a circle.

They were laughing as they weaved around, stepping out, kicking, stepping back.

Rather abruptly, Zeus lost his footing. He went crashing backwards, bringing the other two down with him.

"Are you all right, Uncle Monty?"

"The bineo I am!"

"That was a great song," enthused Frida.

Zeus was pouring a sneaky cup for each of them from the second flask. "Just a small one. To help us get our breath back."

For a while they lay still, gazing at the stars. Antonio fell into a light slumber. Frida cleared her throat, hesitating before taking the plunge.

"As a poet, yourself, you will know how hard it is to show people what you write."

Zeus nodded. It did not feel the right moment for a confession.

"I just wondered what you thought of something. It's not very good. My teacher thought it was terrible. We were asked to write a nature poem. Then they made us come to the front and read them aloud. They just laughed at mine."

There was a silence, during which they both continued to peer at the sky.

"It's called 'The Last Survivor'. I don't know why I'm even telling you. It's really no good. My teacher said it had no real meaning. And no rhyme. Not really a poem at all. They all just think I'm weird."

There was a rather awkward pause. Frida cleared her throat.

Alone in a wood.

An old aluminium bar.

Made to let cars pass in and out – when there were such things as cars.

Those who created it have long gone.

One long arm rising

As if in salute,

Still performing its duty;

Alerted at intervals by some vibration,

A gust of wind, a rumble in the air.

For no living creatures come here now;

No movement at all.

Just this one-armed salute,

Greeting some imaginary passer-by.

Any onlooker might wonder,

Concluding that its inventors must have been

... courteous.

Frida remained with her head turned away, awaiting a response. The silence widened. If only Ermias were here, thought Zeus. He would be able to say something wise. Better still, his son, Apollo, who could have suggested a word here or there to elevate the poem. He really should have spent more time with Apollo. And then there were the Muses. Were there three of them for poetry – epic, lyric and drama? He had never been particularly interested. If it were left to him, he might have kept the epic form, but replaced the others with one for getting off your head *methusko* at a drinking party, and one celebrating the might of the phallos.

Thoughts which did not seem particularly appropriate to express right now. He concentrated hard in search of some more suitable response.

"You're not weird. *They* are. Frightened of anything they don't understand. And when you think about that poor creature in the wood! It sounded so lonely. But steadfast."

She nuzzled against his shoulder.

"I knew you'd get it. When we have destroyed everything else through our greed and stupidity. Just this old car park barrier. Somehow still operating in an overgrown wood."

So that's what it meant! Just as well he had said nothing. He had been thinking along altogether different lines. Thank goodness he had not raised the question as to whether the hero had had his arm lopped off in battle.

Crooking his own arm, the one Frida was not leaning on, he stroked her hair. Diffidently, careful to make only the faintest of contact, in case she recoiled, like a cat that did not welcome touch. She deserved so much better. People should be fighting for her friendship. He wondered whether he should say it out loud. Or would words just spoil the moment? Perhaps, it was enough for a child to just sense that you cared.

She saved him from having to make the decision.

"I guess we should get back home."

They were on the way back, driving down a hill on the dual carriageway, all rather subdued – not at all the right mood for those about to head off in separate directions, thought Zeus. He grinned.

"We can put it on again. That music. It's on a playlist Hermes put together for me."

"You mean Herman? The one we met?"

"Yes, that's right: him."

Frida reflected on this. There seemed to be a great many things she did not know about her great-uncle.

The music began again.

Zeus extended his arms as if about to dance.

"Uncle Monty! The wheel!" shrieked Frida.

He put his hands back on the wheel.

"You're quite right, Frida."

The tempo of the music increased. Zeus tapped his foot on the accelerator in rhythm.

"Uncle Monty – do you think you're going over the speed limit?"

Frida was looking more than a little concerned.

Then they heard the siren and saw the flashing lights behind. When it became obvious that his old chariot was not going to outpace them, Zeus slowed to a halt.

"There may be a big fine, even a ban," mumbled Frida.

"It was worth it."

Zeus looked defiant.

"Besides, I know how to handle policemen and policemenesses."

126

"One hundred and three miles an hour! And ignoring the police vehicle behind you."

His niece was standing close. She looked as if she was about to push him over.

"Not to mention under the influence of alcohol!"

"Nonsense! I just had the one small cup – one and a bit. Not enough for them to charge me. And I was not ignoring the police; just looking for a safe place to stop."

"You'll probably get banned from the road. What then? It means a walk every time you want to go out to the shops. Or bowling. And how will you collect Antonio and Frida? You like doing that."

"There is something called a 'taxi'. I will come in that."

"Do you know how much that will cost you?"

"Lily has a saying about that: you can't take it with you. Besides, I have a plan. Hermes will have a plan..."

"Hermes?"

"A friend. He will know how to make police records go away."

Ember studied him. Was he serious? Had he gone mad?

"Or better still, do you know it turned out that Bill had his own vehicle? An old one that he kept in a rented garage, though he never drove it anywhere, as I recall. Well, down here, they rely on something called registration plates to identify you. We could put Bill's old plates onto the images of my vehicle. Hermes is very clever at that sort of thing. And then, it won't even be my problem. Imagine his surprise when a letter is delivered to poor old Bill in the Stygian Marsh or the Halls of Night, or wherever he hangs out down these days, summoning him to court for all his speeding and parking offences! He'll find it hilarious."

He may not have been legally 'drunk', but, quite obviously, he was delirious. Ember said that she would call for one of these new inventions, the *miraculous* taxis he spoke of.

His head drooped, giving the appearance of a chastened child. He tried to cut out her voice, preferring to hold onto the earlier emotions of the night.

"Antonio wants you to go up and tell him a story."

It took a while for it to sink in. He trotted up the stairs, obediently. It was as if the air had been deflated from him. Slumped on the beanbag in his great nephew's bedroom, he struggled to think of a story worth recounting. The only thing that came to mind was one about how he had chopped his father into little pieces and strewn the bits all over the place. It did not seem all that appropriate.

What about other tales of his exploits? Most entailed shagging or thunderbolts; sometimes both! Maybe, the Sisyphus tale, in which Zeus and his brother, Hades, had colluded to come up with a suitable punishment for a mortal who had tried to cheat death. Pushing an immense boulder up a hill, making him watch it roll down, then having to follow it back down and fetch it. Endlessly. But that, too, hardly felt the most upbeat note on which to end an evening. Besides, he did not want to think about his treacherous brother. He would deal with all that when he resumed his rightful place.

Salvation came in the form of Frida, who came in, picked up a storybook from a shelf and began to read it. Her brother's thumb popped into its place in his mouth. Zeus felt the boy's head, nestling into his shoulder as he listened. Now there was a hand, clutching his own. The sense of the smallness of the child's fingers in his palm was overwhelming. So soft! In six or seven decades, a mere blink for him, this same hand would feel gnarled and rough. His eyes filled with tears, not just for those who grew old and faded away but for those forced to witness suffering, those left behind to bear testimony.

He recalled again how little time he had spent with his own children. Not that they had had long childhoods, which now struck him as rather incongruous, given the eternity stretching out ahead of them. His daughter, Athena, had, of course, been fully formed on

467

coming into the world. His son, Apollo, a relatively slow bloomer, had taken four days to assume his adult form, hidden away by his mother, Leto, out of sight of the vengeful Hera, on the desolate island of Delos. Apollo's sister, Artemis, was born mature enough to assist her mother with her twin's delivery, but, subsequently, she had chosen to linger for a while in childhood. If only he had realised how precious that time was.

He was not accustomed to such feelings. When he returned downstairs, he looked drained.

"Well, I just hope you have learned a lesson..." began Ember, before noticing the expression on his face. Putting down the hot drinks she had made, she held him, while he rocked like an anxious infant.

Why was it so hard to be a human being?

"It's all right," she soothed. "You may not get a long ban from the road."

It took a while to gather himself. Hermes had been wrong about all these farewells. How much easier it would have been to have slipped away without a fuss!

127

"We are ushering in the Happy Epoch," declared the new KoG.

Whether the *ushering in* had begun yet was uncertain, the residents of Olympus having lost count of the number of times that the coronation date had been pushed back. Just when everything seemed prepared, Narcie would keep coming up with some new spectacle that just had to be added to the programme. In each case, additional performers needed to be requisitioned, new sets constructed.

It had caused some distress that a huge triumphal arch, commissioned to show the families of gods with Narcie at the apex, had included, in a prominent position, his parents, Cephissus and Liriope. It was a major project, rising five hundred metres upwards and spanning four hundred and fifty metres. Umpteen sculptors were involved in the carving.

Unfortunately, nobody had thought to inform those working on the project that Narcie had now changed his position on certain aspects of his backstory. The new narrative went as follows. Upon the hour of his birth there had been portents of something momentous, causing alarm among enemies and sparking off a hunt for the infant. An obscure river god and nonentity nymph had been deliberately selected as his guardians to keep him safe. Indeed, he had needed to be moved at one stage to the foster care of the lunar goddess, Selene, and her mortal lover, Endymion, such was the peril he faced. So important were his actual parents that, even now, it remained secret, challenging, as it did, the fake mythology around the entire pantheon of gods.

Hints began to be made on social media. There had been another child of Kronos and Rhea, before the prophecy about a son overthrowing the father. Nevertheless, as a precaution, and foreseeing the coming madness of Kronos, Rhea had spirited the infant away, and when interrogated about it, maintained that it was a girl. Consequently, the child had eluded his pursuers and been spared from being consumed by the tyrant.

Narcie had been grateful to Hera for putting such an idea in his head. Making him the equal of Zeus, a lost brother, such an idea would once have been a heresy, carrying the penalty of punishment in Tartarus. At the current time, however, everyone seemed happy to humour him; if Narcie said it, why not? All it meant right now was that the sculptors working on the arch had to amend the whole thing.

There were other stories about him that Narcie now declared to be fake. In particular, his treatment of the nymph, Echo, his rejection of her advances appearing to place him in a rather poor light. Indeed, so callous did he seem with regard to her obsessive love, that it made it look as if he had deliberately driven her into madness. Similarly, presenting his admirer, Ameinius, with a sword looked calculating, as if he had somehow predicted that the infatuated young man would disembowel himself on Narcie's own doorstep!

Such tales were now discouraged. Yes, there had been admirers – thousands of them – but Narcie had been saving himself; no single person should have his love when he was destined to belong to, not to say, be adored by, everyone.

Criticism of this new narrative was muted. Naturally, there were a few raised eyebrows, some scepticism here and there, but not all that much in the way of open condemnation. Hera promised to have a word about comments made by her daughter, self-appointed goddess of truth, Eileithyia, although she was not quite so protective of another daughter of her husband's, Dike. Along with other members of the Ethics Committee, Dike was threatened, then roughed up a bit when she continued to declare that the recent stories about Narcie were utter nonsense.

Worse still befell Pistis, whose home was vandalised. Stripped naked, she was made to parade around the streets, with objects hurled at her. There were shouts of 'Pig-Pistis', as a rumour about her parentage had been circulated. Had no one noticed her snub-nose? If they wanted a reason, they need only ask her father about the sty where he had located Pistis' mother.

There were similar stories about another troublemaker, Horkos. His shaggy white hair should have been a giveaway! Not to mention his incessant, self-righteous bleating! To find out more on that one, you would have to ask his mother, Eris, goddess of discord. It seems that she had taken a fancy to Horkos' father, a ram called Rastus, who just happened to live in a field next to the very sty inhabited by Penelope Pig, Pistis' mother. Or, maybe, Eris just thought it would be funny to try it on with such a funny-looking, woolly creature. Anyway, it explained why the two committee members, Horkos and Pig-Pistis, were so close.

Accosted on the street, Horkos reminded the mob facing him about the need for law, order and decorum. His words were greeted by laughter. Had he not heard that the Rule of Anarchy had been announced?

A dim view was taken about his pedantry in pointing out that this was a contradiction of terms, paradoxical, antithetical, not to say oxymoronic. Who was moronic now, he was asked after receiving a good kicking.

"A-Narcie rules," came the chant, as the throng trotted off in search of the next target on their list.

While Narcie himself stated that he did not approve of violence, no efforts were made to apprehend the perpetrators. The Happy Era was going to be one long, riotous laugh!

PART 6 – CATHARSIS

JOINING THE PANTHEON OF GODS: A BEGINNER'S GUIDE

Congratulations! You are almost there. Let's not stumble at the final hurdle. Below is an overview of the final procedure:

1. Ensure that the potion is prepared with great care by a fully-trained expert. Remember that there have been more aborted attempts than successful metamorphoses.

2. Arrange for the placement of the body on a pyre that has been constructed on a high mountain within sight of Olympus. Do not make the error of being so presumptuous as to choose Olympus itself.

3. Remember to have ensured that evidence of hero status has been posted and acknowledged before terminating your mortal existence.

4. Remain calm while the flames are lit and your mortal part is consumed by fire.

5. Do not wriggle as your divine part ascends towards Olympus.

128

Hermes went over the plan once again. They would need to be very slick between the termination of Mudge and the leap into the new body. The lad was a fine specimen, of excellent physique, built like a young Heracles. As he was someone destined, anyway, to terminate his own life, there could be no dilemmas that might have concerned the fuddy-duddies on the Ethics Committee.

Hermes would remain invisible, close enough to ensure that the whole operation ran, smoothly. And after a very different life, heroic, action-packed and fun-filled, Zeus would return in triumph to Olympus. Winning it back was going to be an absolute cinch! Things could not have fallen into place better. Atlas and Kronos both eliminated. Hades back in his place; Ares under lock and key. About the worst that could happen to the returning Zeus was getting hit by a couple of flying handbags.

"They're very popular these days. Everyone carries them around."

Hermes was surprised by the glum look he got in reply.

"Sounds like Level One in *Fenyx Rising!* Hardly much glory in that!"

Zeus sighed. At least, it would mean he would get to see Hera again. She must have been at her wits' end worrying about him.

It was, thought Hermes, as if his father wore magic armour, protecting him from negative thoughts about his wife. However much Hermes had hinted at Hera's treachery, nothing seemed to have sunk in. Nor did it seem the best moment to be more explicit about her scheming, given the odd mood Zeus appeared to be in.

How much better, suspected Hermes, if Zeus had shown the same sort of devotion to one of his other consorts! His own mother, Maia, for instance, loving and caring, who had risked the malice of Hera by protecting not only a biological child but that of another nymph.

The other nymph's name, as he recalled, was Callisto, and she had also had an affair with Zeus, after he had spotted her in the woods in the company of his daughter, Artemis, and taken a passing fancy to her. Zeus had stuck around just long enough to produce a son, Arcas, who would grow up to live in the forest, and teach others skills, such as weaving and baking bread. Unlike his father, Hermes had an aptitude for finding out such things. Anyway, Hera had turned Callisto into a bear for the impertinence of allowing herself to be seduced by her husband. As if she had a choice!

Afterwards, it had been *his* mother, Maia, who had looked after the abandoned infant, Arcas. How frustrating that Zeus did not value such things! Perhaps, Hera had cast some spell on him.

However desperately Hermes may have wished to share such thoughts, now really was not the time to do so. Instead, he informed Zeus how he had arranged for the young man to be in the area at the start of the coming week, explaining that he had put it into the youth's mind to embark on a late afternoon walk between two villages, Beer and Branscombe. He would pass high cliffs from which desperate mortals occasionally leapt into the seething waters or fell onto the jagged rocks below. Hermes and Zeus would arrive there before him.

"You've got it all planned," muttered Zeus.

His face clouded over. Hermes studied him. Was there some flaw in the details, something that could go wrong?

"Lily needs me. George Williams needs me."

Hermes just stared at him. Was his mind disintegrating?

"The bowling club need me. They're a pile of bolbiton without me. Frida and Ant need me. I think even Ember needs me, although she may not realise it."

Hermes stared at him. Was he serious?

"I don't want to miss them growing up, Frida and Antonio."

This was a problem that could never have been anticipated.

"My own children. You, Hermes. Your childhood over in a flash, and I wasn't around. There had seemed so many more important and exciting things to do. And another thing..."

There was a frantic look in his eyes and he was pawing at his son's sleeve. Hermes wondered whether he was being kept awake at nights with these mad thoughts zipping through his brain.

"It was never Atlas holding the sky up; it was mortals – through countless, everyday acts of kindness."

The only explanation Hermes could think of was that Zeus had been left in this miserable excuse for embodiment for too long. This was something to remember in the future; a risk the Ethics Committee should be made aware of.

Reiterating what he had already said, ignoring the irrational guff he had just heard, he went over the plan, patiently. The youth was strong, eminently, suitable. Hermes had calculated time and co-ordinates. Zeus could make the leap, living a full and exciting life as this new person. Carrying out great deeds, he could become a hero, returning to Olympus as himself when he was ready.

"I can't tell you how needed you are. It's as if their minds have been transformed to mush. And you would not believe the packages I have to deliver. The things people waste money on these days! The cosmos needs Zeus."

"What if I don't want to be Zeus anymore?"

Hermes looked shocked. It occurred to him that, previously, Zeus had thought through his phallos, but now – who knew – maybe, through Mudge's orrhos! Clearly, it was an outcome of having spent too long in Mudge's body. What had Zeus called those traces of memory: the Mudge Files? They must have leaked out into him.

"Those files have corrupted your own thinking," he now explained. "You need a complete reboot. The sooner you are out of there, the better. Then a new life, filled with adventure. You will be able to satisfy each desire, every hunger. You might grant the person you inhabit immortality on account of his exploits. You could even return incognito if you like."

Zeus sighed. It felt to Hermes as if he was not listening. What was the point in repeating himself?

"Do you know the risks I have taken?"

"You are a good son, Hermes."

It felt more like a smack in the face than a compliment. In all the endless years had Zeus ever said such a thing? Was this even Zeus talking?

Hermes took some long breaths. No point trying to argue with someone in a half-baked state. His father was obviously so entrenched in the mind of Mudge right now that he was not himself. Best to say nothing and procure something that would restore Zeus to his proper senses a day or so before the event. Or just dull his mind sufficiently to put to rest these ludicrous doubts. Was he not expert in such potions?

Who had saved Odysseus' companions when their minds had been wiped of all traces of home, any sense of self, obliterated? If not for him, they would have spent their remaining days there, trapped in a pig pen by the sorceress, Circe. Only a daughter of Hecate could have laced a harmless cheese and barley gruel with such an artfully poisonous blend of honey, Pramnian wine, and the most sinister of drugs, such as jimson weed. Had he not managed to analyse each ingredient and come up with an antidote from the snowdrop? Nobody knew the hidden secrets of plants and herbs better than himself.

It would not be difficult to concoct something for Zeus. It was for his own good.

129

Never has Olympus staged such an event. Never such pomp and ostentation. This is pageantry on the grandest scale. A huge procession. Marching bands. Spectacular sound and light shows. Homage from creatures believed to be mythical.

And then a swirl of activity, a fluttering in the wind, bells chiming, a golden carriage descending from the sky, drawn by winged horses, Pegasus himself leading them. Its registration plate bears the number: N1 KOG.

A charmingly playful touch: attendants rushing to open the carriage door, all dressed up as two-legged versions of the horses, with their own wings, manes and tails.

A drumroll. Pause. A collective sigh of anticipation. And finally, Narcie stepping out, surrounded by a host of heroes, a golden crown placed on his head by the queen of gods, Hera.

A mighty figure strolls forward, Poseidon, bowing, then raising his trident toward the sky, as if summoning a blessing.

Loud cheering as he is handed a mirror. Narcie inspects himself. Unique! Immaculate in form! The quintessence of male, female, or any other gender between or beyond! If the king attains perfection, then each of his subjects gets a little closer, too.

Only one onlooker turns away, having seen enough. Barely noticed, wandering back to a smoky forge. Not missed.

The party going on and on, day after day, year after year. Plays, epic poetry, statues, monuments, musical compositions, all commissioned to herald in a glorious new era. In countless ways, the commemoration of the story of an ordinary boy made good: the *adopted* son of a minor deity and a common nymph; with only his extraordinary looks and self-belief to propel him on the road to fortune; overcoming all disadvantages and obstacles to reach the highest office of all.

Which turns out to have been his rightful destiny all along.

An age will pass before anyone attends to the business of government. Finally, Narcie appoints ministers, which, he explains, is the 'modern' way to do things, leaving him free to shower everybody and everything with his radiance. Several of his ministers come from the hairdressing fraternity, but there are also leading roles for many of the younger, friskier gods. His *brother*, Poseidon, gets the position of Chancellor, responsible for commissioning work and organising funding for state projects.

Poseidon gets busy with contracts, immediately.

"If you're lucky," he whispers to Hephaestus, during a business visit, "there will be a lot more coming your way. In some cases, you won't have to lift a finger. All we'll need is the paperwork."

He winks.

Narcie's first act is to order the construction of fifty temples in his honour, and in line with a suggestion made, privately, by Hera, he adds that no other god shall be permitted to run more than five temples. It may not suffice to dent his popularity, instantly, but it is a start, something that might fester in time.

Narcie's former rival, Hades is offered a minor role, Minister of Sport. Politely, he declines the opportunity, preferring to resume his work in the Underworld. It is probably just as well. He would not really have fitted in with all the bright, fun-loving, young things around him.

Another rival, Ares, placed in a luxurious prison under the previous administration, is now re-tried, in absentia, on the more serious offence of attempted murder of the King of Gods. It is pointed out to Narcie that *Inmate P*, previously, the sole internee at a detention centre in Tartarus, has, mysteriously, vanished. An eagle, stationed there as warder and carer, with an insatiable taste for liver, remains on the payroll, its contract indefinite. It would be a most dishonourable breach not to identify a new inmate for such a loyal employee.

Narcie informs the court that they, not he, must select the most appropriate candidate for the vacant position. Through distancing himself in this manner, he cannot be held accountable by others in the future. As a ruler renowned for magnanimity, he is incapable of the slightest whiff of spite. All he does suggest is that the eagle might be weaned onto a new diet. He has heard that having a liver pecked out each evening is excruciatingly painful, even if it does re-grow during the night. He understands that having one's testicles munched off is altogether less painful, though it should be shared on social media. It is a wily suggestion; one who has been viewed in such a compromising way can hardly be considered appropriate for a prominent role on Olympus in the future.

When Hera gets wind of the plan, she has to be restrained by her friend, Tyche. It is not the moment to oppose a new ruler. Besides, while it may be a tad uncomfortable, Ares will recuperate each night. Hera is only partially pacified.

"Everything I have done has been for family, and especially, for him. Not now, maybe, but one day."

Tyche studies Hera's face. Perhaps, she really believes it. And anyone who would fling an infant off the top of a mountain for the good of *family* was not to be taken lightly.

She deems it circumspect to reassure her friend. Perhaps, a period of time in exile will give Ares the

opportunity to grow up. A gap-epoch is often the making
of young lads.

She adds that it might be provident not to be
around when sentence is passed, so that Hera cannot be
implicated in the future. There is a forthcoming
conference being organised in distant Amazonia.

"I think the theme is 'The Role of the Goddess in
a post-Zeus Universe'. I understand that your daughter,
Hebe, is giving a keynote talk on – I think the title is:
Nutritious Eating and the De-masculinising of Food."

Hera pulls a face.

Tyche is making her own calculations. Narcie
could remain in power for millennia. It is conceivable
that, one day, Ares might return. By that time, Hera may
be in a more powerful position – who knows, there could
be something chic by then in the notion of a Queen,
instead of a King. Whatever the outcome, the House
must win.

It is an age of slogans: 'Beauty is Glory'; 'Style
Conquers All'. Hedonists and Epicureans are IN! Stoics
need to find other ways of seeing out the epoch, but they
are nothing if not good at that! There are wonderful
opportunities for clothing designers, beauticians and
personal trainers. Fortuitous, too, for the Cyclopes
Brothers, being in a rebuilding phase. With war out of
fashion, they dabble with firework displays, but finding
them too seasonal, they set up a subsidiary business

producing exclusive handbags. Of course, it leaves them with some redundant stock, but they come up with an offer: Buy from our *CB Prestige Range* and get a free thunderbolt. Designed only for use in the field by Zeus himself – who has not put in an order for an age – these giveaways soon become trendy sculptures in gardens.

Narcie has been shocked by the sloppiness he has discovered. How could gods expect to be worshipped when they are so uncaring about their personal appearance?

Each morning the tinkling of bells, reverberating louder down corridors. The sound of feet, hurrying, all in the same direction: the hair stylist, the couturier, the trouser valet, the footwear selector. Each item of clothing involves a different expert.

The routine does not vary. Narcie will bathe. His teeth will be attended to by two valets, one a brusher, the other a flosser. If the likes of Jason and Cadmus could be celebrated for their exploits with the teeth of dragons, Narcie will be acclaimed simply on account of his teeth being in his mouth. Rows of shining pearls! And while the dragons' teeth of Cadmus might be sown and metamorphosed into warriors, those of Narcie, were they to be implanted in the ground, would be transformed into angels, encircling the world in a broad smile of sweetness.

Only after all this will he make his way to a dressing room each day, a huge hall overlooked by a gallery, a fortunate few from the excited throng outside, being admitted within to watch. There will be 'ooos' and cries of 'OMG: it's him!' when he appears. Many of those who have been disappointed will return each of the following mornings in the hope of being one of the blessed.

130

No point leaving such a small amount in the bottle.
Ember poured out the last dregs. There was a crash as she
knocked over a lamp. She lurched over the edge of the
settee to pick it up.

She was not aware of Frida till she saw her
daughter close up, peering at her, anxiously.

"I heard a bang so I came down."

The girl tidied a few things before squatting on the
floor alongside her mother, their backs against the settee.

"It's natural to miss her."

It took a few moments to take in the words.
Ember was just relieved that Frida had not seen the
creature's face.

"Do *you* miss her?"

Frida paused before answering. She did not want
her mother to feel less secure about her choices, but she
could not bring herself to lie.

"I never really liked her. Something about her that
was a bit different each time. As if she had not really
settled on who she was."

Ember grappled with the notion. It had never
occurred to her. How had she missed that? How could her
daughter be so much perceptive than she was?

"Perhaps, that's what I found so attractive."

They remained silent for a while. Frida leant across and stroked her mother's hair. She might have been soothing a child.

"Don't worry. You'll meet someone better. You just need to be patient. Do you know in Spanish it's the same word for 'wait' as it is for 'hope' – esperar?"

"Did they teach you that at school?"

Frida shook her head, vehemently, as if the idea was farcical.

"I read it somewhere. Talking of school, I suppose I should go and get some sleep. Can you get yourself to bed?"

Ember watched her daughter head out of the room and up the stairs. On the way, she had quietly removed her mother's wine glass, leaving it in the kitchen. Not just more perceptive; also wiser. It was as if she had been born fully formed.

131

Hera was beginning to regret having accepted Tyche's invitation to celebrate. Who could have guessed that the capricious goddess could put back so much booze without so much as a hint of drunkenness? Her own head was a bleary fuzz.

Not so much as to miss that Tyche's conversation was not just risqué, but funny. She literally seemed to know everything about everyone else's liaisons. Not for nothing was there the saying that if something was going on that Tyche did not know about, then it wasn't going on.

She did not so much as blush when she spoke of things that were taboo. Contrary to her normal comportment, Hera found herself joining in.

"Clitoris! When I asked Zeus if he knew what it was, he looked puzzled and wondered whether it might be the name of the wife of one of the Hecatoncheires. You remember, those giants with a hundred hands."

"If only," giggled Tyche.

They both burst out laughing. While Hera was aware that she was talking too loudly and slurring her words, for once, it really didn't matter. She wanted someone to know what she had put up with over all the years.

"And the babies he gave me! You do know that none of his favourites are his legitimate children. It's as if he deliberately saved his best seed for his sluts! And I've tried so hard, Tyche, to make them better than they are. Especially, Ares. Endless hours. Sometimes, I think that Hephaestus was the best of the bunch, and look at *him*!"

The maudlin moment passed. Hera noticed the bracelet that Tyche was wearing.

"I haven't seen one like that in a while."

"I acquired it only recently, and as we were just speaking of Hephaestus, coincidentally, it was made in one of his workshops. Not by him, but an apprentice."

Hera looked surprised.

"Doesn't sound like him to take on young trainees."

"As it happens, this trainee is far from young. I understand that he is a doddery, old guy. I heard that from a D-G delivery driver, who happened to spot him shuffling around in the grounds, gripping onto Hephaestus' sleeve. He kept peering up, anxiously, as if something was about to swoop down and carry him off. Apparently, Hephaestus was ever so gentle with him.

Hera was about to make a sardonic comment before dismissing it. It seemed strange. Why would someone so gruff and awkward suddenly seek a helpmate? And one so ancient and useless!

492

"I was thinking," continued Tyche, "and I'm sure, it's totally unrelated, but when a certain prisoner went missing recently, there was something left behind in the valley where he was chained, an ingenious device, I'm told, enabling someone to float down slowly from a great height. Whoever could have constructed such a thing?"

The conversation moved on to others, until it felt as if they had covered everyone they had ever known! The hours had flown by. Hera tried to get to her feet. It was no good. Despite being desperate for her own bed, she would have to stay with Tyche and spend the night in her palace. She really wished she had suggested a meeting-place nearer her own home.

And the indignity of being put to bed like an infant! Though she couldn't deny that Tyche had soft, velvety hands, and undressed her with wonderful tenderness!

She watched Tyche through half-closed eyes as the other goddess went to a nearby chamber and bathed. Was this Tyche's personal room? Surely not! She gasped as Tyche turned. Without make-up, she looked entirely different. Younger, far softer. An almost doe-like innocence. And the scent of her! Like wild flowers.

For some reason, she said nothing when Tyche climbed into bed alongside her. There were strict codes about this sort of thing. Of course, the male gods had their dalliances. Which was fine so long as they were in the dominant role. Hence, many of these adventures were with lesser deities or mortals. Zeus had had Ganymede, of course; Hera was pretty sure that something had been going on between Boreas and Hyacinth; that Dionysus had a long-term relationship with Ampelos, as well as something briefer, and extremely odd, with some young shepherd called Prosymnus; while the likes of Apollo and Hermes had had a string of relationships with other males. Then there were Achilles, Heracles and that lot, of course, with their *gentlemen's* club, which propagated all sorts of nonsense, such as the idea that pure, virtuous, truly *noble* love was only possible between males.

It was all far rarer amongst the goddesses, barely heard of. There was Aphrodite, of course, who was a bit of a law unto herself, and there were one or two tales about Athena and some of her daintier nymphs, not to mention a mortal maiden, a trinket called Myrmex, which had not turned out well, the girl in question being metamorphosed into an ant. Even Athena couldn't have carried off a relationship with someone in that condition! In general, however, outside of the small island of Lesbos, such activities were not viewed with approval.

Yet here she was being caressed, and it was... nice.

More than nice. She shuddered with pleasure. Tingles all over. Tyche knew where to touch her, and how. And there was... such tenderness, and playfulness. Nothing like she had ever experienced.

How different from being with Zeus, with his rush and clumsiness, or Hades and his... weirdness.

Their mouths met in a kiss. Fierce, then drifting apart. Something needed to be said.

"Of course," sighed Hera, "while you are... extremely attractive, I am not inclined to take this any further, even, that is, if I did have yearnings of such a kind, which, incidentally, I don't."

"Quite," agreed Tyche. "Do you think we should try one more kiss, just to prove how neither of us could be inclined in such a way?"

It seemed a sensible proposition in the circumstances.

132

During the morning he tidied the house. How delighted his oldest sister, Hestia, would have been to witness such a sight! Zeus imagined Hera's face, too: how shocked would *she* have been?

Hermes had already selected the clothing. Having checked the weather forecast, and bearing in mind the terrain, he had selected the sturdy shoes that Zeus wore on fishing trips, and a warm coat with a hood.

It was a relief for Hermes to watch Zeus behaving like an obedient child. Leaving nothing to chance, he had been with him for the last forty-eight hours, preparing all his meals, adding small drops of liquid from a phial he had hidden in the kitchen, which induced a sense of wellbeing and passivity. His potion bore a slight similarity to Circe's, even sharing some of the same ingredients, only it was far less sinister. Its effects were to bring similar forgetfulness, without impeding the person using it.

Zeus pottered about, his mind fuzzy, doing exactly as he was told. When asked if he wanted to write any messages for anyone, he furrowed his brows in concentration, before deciding that he could not think of anyone. All the people he had met during his residence here felt like figures from a dream. It was gratifying for Hermes to note that he was not pained by the exercise.

Zeus would not have been able to explain why, after spotting a photograph on a shelf in the bedroom, he slipped it into his pocket. He had no idea who the individuals were in the picture: a small boy, thumb in mouth, slightly askew on a beanbag, leaning into the shoulder of an elderly man.

Around mid-afternoon, they set off towards East Devon. Zeus settled into the passenger seat, an amiable look on his face. They drove past Haldon Hill, spotting a white tower in the distance. Hermes asked whether Zeus had ever been here before. Zeus shook his head. He did not think so.

As they came over the brow of a hill, they glimpsed a city below. Zeus pointed towards the cathedral. That looked like an interesting building.

As they were early, they could stop at a pub, have a cream tea. Zeus gazed around as if he had never been in such an establishment, enthusing about the cosy interior. He would like to come to one of these places again. Hermes slipped drops from another phial into his drink. While they could not restore youth, they would provide sufficient vigour for the short but arduous walk ahead.

The sun was beginning to drop in the sky when they parked in the village of Branscombe. Hermes had planned the route up, twisting along the uneven path of the Hooken undercliff: a mess of thick, unruly vegetation, speared through by soaring pinnacles, as if some tetchy deity had rained them down from above.

It was an ideal landscape, one that would give time for him to move to the second phase. All traces of Reginald Montgomery Mudge may have been erased, but now Zeus needed to be reminded of who he was, and how he would return to incarnation of self.

Deep shadows engulfed them as the path descended into woods. Zeus followed the unearthly glow emitted by Hermes, his mind strangely clear, taking in only the soggy air and the fusty reek of damp earth. He tried to make sense of the landslip through the spreading murk, porous chalk and greenside beds higher up and clay marls beneath. Unable to hold back the rainwater, with no grip on the upper chalk, rocks had slid down into the thick greenery below.

Padding behind Hermes, it felt that there was something familiar about this place, although he was certain he had never been here before.

"Where were you born?"

"Here?"

Hermes shook his head. They stopped and Hermes poured a drink from the flask. Sweet caramel through the smoke; shapes on a wall, clambering over one another; bleating and jangling sounds; dancing figures against the firelight.

"Who was your father?"

"One of them, the spirits of the mountain?"

"Think harder."

His voice was even, patient, as if dealing with a very slow child.

Zeus's gaze was drawn to a large black hole, gaping up the cliff side. Not the place he was groping for in his memory, but like it. He imagined wild figures careering down the cliff towards them. Everything was jumbled, the pieces of a jigsaw forced together in the wrong places.

"Do you remember your father?"

Zeus pondered the question. A thing filled with spite. Its identity eluded him. Some sort of clue might help.

"Your last view of him was in small pieces."

A memory rose up: a vile creature. He was gripping its head while hacking, wildly. It was slobbering curses into the earth, which sizzled with each drop of spittle.

Might one small bit of him have been sliced away and dropped here? That dark hole in the cliff, like an empty eye socket. Some sort of cave, perhaps. He imagined a creature crawling out.

He caught sight of something moving, slowly, a figure ahead on the track, ascending steps towards the summit.

"Is that my father?"

Hermes considered the matter. It might be useful.

"Yes, that's him. Your father, Kronos, arisen. He's trying to escape. What you see is a stolen body."

The thing, Kronos, had to be caught and destroyed before it returned to its true form. Had Hermes said it or had the idea grown in his own mind? When they caught up, he must put his hand on its back. Push through it. Inhabit that body before it became Kronos, permanently.

Again, he was not sure whether Hermes actually spoke the words.

The climb was becoming steep, but the potion seemed to be working. He could only just make things out now, but they were slowly gaining on the figure, which was standing at a gate at the top of the path, uncertain about which way to turn.

They paused, too, resting on a bench overlooking the precipice. Hermes took out his flask, pouring out a final drink. Zeus sipped it down, and Hermes rose again. There was a cold gust of wind. Zeus shivered, instinctively, slipping his hands into his pockets. He felt the corners of a photograph. He took it out and inspected it. An old man and a boy: who *were* they? He returned it to his pocket, getting to his feet and following his guide upwards.

They came on it suddenly at the summit. The figure they had been pursuing had walked on and was standing close to the edge. It seemed too absorbed to notice them.

A hole appeared in his clouded mind. It was not his father, just a strapping youth. He remembered now: their plan, a brief life within that body. He noted with satisfaction its health and virility, imagining what it would feel like to become this youth: strong arms, muscular torso and firm phallos; powerful lungs; pumping heart; red blood pounding. Everything lacking in Reginald Montgomery Mudge's shambolic old body. Like transforming from the shrivelled satyr, Geras, into Heracles. All he had to do was to predict the moment and time his leap.

"Now," urged Hermes.

Whatever was wrong? Zeus was holding back.

"It must be you," hissed Hermes. "You must be touching him."

Zeus stretched out an arm. But instead of shoving the man over the edge, he was grasping his shoulder. He could feel the uncertainty in the body of the other. For a few moments the two of them were frozen in mid action, caught between tumbling downwards and stepping back from the brink.

Do you want Kronos back?

Were they *his* thoughts or implanted in his mind.

He's only a mortal.

Only a mortal! What was that: a brief flickering. If you were lucky, perhaps, two and a half million heartbeats.

He's not Kronos.

He tried to say it, but no words came out.

Just a young lad, and he should have his whole life in front of him.

How could Hermes have anticipated this? Some vestige of the new Zeus still left there, and maybe, a hint of *Mudgeness*. Surely not: he had given Zeus enough potion to remove a thousand Mudges!

Yet here was Zeus, dragging the young man back from the edge.

The youth stared at Zeus with incomprehension. And then, with a look of fear, he trotted away, onwards towards the village ahead, towards life, like a dog summoned by a whistle.

Zeus stared after him. There was no hurry. Perhaps, someone else would come along; someone who truly wanted an end of things. Or perhaps, not. In which case, he would wait for whatever might come. After all, he had no concept of death; it would be a new experience.

133

The gods will be watching. Checking on their own shrines and temples; casting envious glances at those around them.

Any time now Helios will be expecting the erection of a colossus. It will need to be at least seventy cubits, that is to say, about one hundred and five feet high, and should stand on a white marble pedestal. The cast iron and bronze plates will need to be reinforced at the joints.

Its magnificence will almost certainly infuriate jealous deities, who are liable to attempt to remove it, such as Zeus, or maybe, Narcie.

Sometimes it can be difficult to remember which will come first.

And now for today's weather forecast:

Erebus – unsettled; Tartarus – hot and humid during the day, with temperatures falling below freezing at night; Stygian Marsh – dank and misty; Acheron Delta – overcast; Thalassa – calm, moderate visibility, with chances of some gales building later in the day; Phlegethon – dense smog, with air quality poor: those suffering from asthma are advised to remain indoors; Asphodel Fields – chilly, with fuzzy light; Mount Olympus – sunny...

134

Zeus squats down on the grass. He feels such lightness that he might almost float away. Hermes, by contrast, is assailed by an unbearable weight, pushing him down into the earth. He slumps. It is difficult for him to gather himself, his thoughts having spilled over the precipice.

"For the sake of... a mortal?"

It is impossible for him to comprehend.

"Yes, and other things. Above all, I will see them grow up, Antonio and Frida, take their first real steps, and know that their lives have taken a slightly different course because of me."

"But you'll get even older, feebler, and then..."

Zeus reflects on the matter.

"You know, if you never change, it does not truly feel you are alive."

He puts his arm around his son's shoulder, watching the sun setting in the west. Hermes stares in the opposite direction, back to the east, where Helios will re-emerge on his golden throne. How *he* would have laughed had he been watching right now! The destroyer of his Colossus, reduced to such a state!

Hermes feels an overwhelming urge to confess.

"I betrayed you."

"You remained by my side, like a proper son."

For a long while, the two of them sit in silence on the cliff top, staring at the chalk limestone haemorrhaging away into distant red sandstone.

135

A relaxing sound: snip... snip... snip. Listen carefully, and you may pick up the whispers in between.

"Have you not heard?"

Snip. Whisper. Snip.

"They're doing it quite openly. They have been seen. In her garden. They were swimming. Laughing. Ready poetry to one another. And kissing!"

"And... without their...?"

"Oh, yes! Naked as Erotes at a rave."

"Surely, not! Not Hera! You must have misheard."

The whispers slink out through the doors of the salon, across fields, hills, even up into the clouds. An eagle picks them up on its way to its favourite valley. It conveys them to the sole inhabitant there.

Peck. Whisper. Peck.

The prisoner is appalled. He slobbers out his spleen on learning of his mother's behaviour; tells the eagle how unnatural it is; and what he will do when he gets out of here.

"Incidentally," he adds, "I am going to have *you* barbecued. Skewers right through you. I will piss all over you before throwing you into the rubbish pile, to be devoured by my lowliest subjects."

The eagle glances around. Not a *subject* to be seen. It continues with its meal. Not quite as satisfying, perhaps, and more fiddly than he has been accustomed to, but he understood that delicate and lighter fare was part of nouvelle cuisine, and he couldn't fault the presentation.

The prisoner veers between threats and entreaties. In passing, he mentions something he has heard from his sister, Hebe.

"It's not healthy, you know, this unbalanced diet of yours. Far too rich. And all that Vitamin... is it C? Not to mention the zinc, magnesium, potassium. And... and all that lactic acid."

The eagle pauses. It does not appear to be able to recall which vitamins or minerals are contained in different parts of the body.

"And you know, they're quite fatty. Filled with fructose. All sugary. Mine are particularly sugary? If you're not careful, it could turn you... diab... diabollock?"

The eagle has not heard about this. It cogitates for a while. Oh well, you have to pop your clogs one way or another, and right now this is a pretty good gig. Guaranteed meals; no long searches for your grub; no buffeting from gusts of high wind, while straining your eyes checking for the slightest movement; compliant, if rather talkative, prey. All in all, this is easy street.

Peck. Whisper. Peck.

SURVIVING THE 21ST CENTURY: A HANDBOOK FOR PENSIONERS

ENTRY 10

A PENSIONER'S ORJIKS ARE A COMPLETE WASTE OF SPACE. THEY ARE NEVER LIKELY TO GET USED, SO THE BEST THING YOU CAN DO IS TO FORGET ABOUT THEM!

UNABLE TO DRINK FROM THE VESSELS OF SUBLIME PLEASURE, THE PENSIONER IS FORCED TO SEEK OTHER TYPES OF RELATIONSHIPS. THESE ARE LIKELY TO ENTAIL GIVING WITHOUT EXPECTING ANYTHING BACK IN RETURN; GETTING CLOSE TO ANOTHER BEING, WITHOUT REALLY TOUCHING.

IN ALMOST EVERY WAY, IT IS TOO LATE TO CHANGE YOUR OWN LIFE; BUT THAT DOES NOT MEAN THAT YOU CAN'T SHIFT THE DIRECTION OF THE LIVES OF OTHERS.

YOU MIGHT START BY FINDING A YOUNG PERSON WHO NEEDS GUIDANCE. GET THEM TO SHOW YOU HOW TO DO SOMETHING THAT THEY ARE NOT VERY GOOD AT. THE FEELING YOU ARE LEFT WITH IS SWEET AND WARM AS HOT CHOCOLATE, AND WHEN YOU WATCH THEM COMING ON, IT'S LIKE FLOATING IN A SEA OF MARSHMALLOWS.

IT IS IMPORTANT TO REMEMBER THAT MORTALS REACH THEIR PEAK AT AROUND THE AGE

OF TEN. AFTER THAT, THEY MOVE INTO A STATE OF GRADUAL DECLINE.

LIFE IS BOTH UNJUST AND SAD. THERE IS NOTHING TO BE GAINED ON DWELLING ON THAT. IT IS ALSO RATHER WONDERFUL.

PENSIONERS GET GIVEN LOADS OF RUBBISH GIFTS THEY DON'T NEED. A GOOD IDEA IS TO RE-GIFT THEM TO OTHERS. IT DOES AWAY WITH CLUTTER AND AVOIDS TIME WASTED LOOKING AROUND IN SHOPS WHEN YOU HAVE NO IDEA WHAT A PERSON WANTS.

ONE FINAL THING: DO NOT WAIT FOR FRIENDS AND FAMILY TO DIE. START MISSING PEOPLE WHEN THEY ARE STILL AROUND.

Some time later in a place where there is no later

It takes a while for your eyes to get accustomed to the viscous pea-souper that envelopes the scene, making it difficult to define the identity of shapes that loom out of nowhere as you get close. For the newcomer, it is all too easy to bump into things before seeing them.

If the light is Stygian, it may be because you are not far from the Styx. Helios never visits this place, nor indeed any other part of the Underworld. A vaporous miasma drapes itself around everything, permanently. No wind ventures to these parts; the row of black poplars nearby, neither living nor dead, remain utterly still.

Most graciously, Persephone has granted permission for a new salon, close to her grove. Although far off the beaten track, so remote that only a fool or a genius would consider opening a business there, it is flourishing. A few other shops have sprung up at a discreet distance away. Beyond that, unobtrusive, out of Persephone's sight, a small shanty town is developing. Customers hike from there to the salon or shops.

There is one small store that is becoming quite popular. It sells newspapers, sweets, chocolate powder for drinks, along with other bits and bobs. One day a soul happens to walk in, who is recognised by the owner. They get talking, and before you know it, unknown to the likes of Tyche, the proprietor begins operating, illicitly, as a bookie.

Another day another soul turns up, and next thing you know – and don't ask how – but the store is also running a sideline in fishing. Soon anglers are appearing, having heard that you can buy rods and bait and all sorts here. Trips are organised to nearby Oceanus, where you can sign up for sea fishing outings. For those who prefer freshwater fishing, a partner runs a shuttle to the distant rivers. Of course, unless you prefer your fish of the non-swimming variety, pre-cooked and very overdone, the fiery Phlegethon is a non-starter. However, and quite remarkably, the ecosystem around the Acheron has allowed for the development of quite a varied assortment of fish, especially, around the deeper lake area. Even the Styx has reported new life.

A cat slips in and out of the office. It has an aversion to trees and is wary of new male visitors. Mostly, it snoozes in a comfy chair, waiting for the arrival of its owner.

At certain times of the year, business is slow, but it's a living. Of a kind.

END

Some terms and swear words used in the novel

The use of terms below is sometimes rather loose, not based on accurate translation of Ancient Greek.

Akos-peos – 'lettuce-dick'
Baubon –dildo
Bdelyros – bastard
Bineo – fuck; to fuck
Bolbiton – cowshit
Chezo – to defecate
Choiros – literally, piglet, but became crude term for female genitalia, as in 'pussy'
Euryproktos – literally, with a wide anus, as a result of repeated sexual penetration, used quite commonly, as an insult in Attic comedy
Gelos – laughter; joke
Grason – stinker (like a goat)
Idiotikon – ignorant or uneducated person. In classical Greek, also connected to privacy. *Idios* was associated with someone with their own ideas, hence, 'idiosyncratic'.
Ithyphallos – erect penis
Kairos – the right, critical or opportune moment to strike
Kopros – shit
Lagneia – act of coitus; also lust
Malaka – effeminate man; wanker
Methusko – drunk
Orjiks – testicles
Orrhos – arse – can refer to buttocks, rectum or anus
Phallos – penis
Xaipe – salutation that can be used when meeting up or departing, meaning 'Rejoice'; 'Enjoy yourself'

List of Gods, demi-gods, Titans, monsters, nymphs, heroes, etc. referred to in the novel in alphabetical order

Achelous – *Son of Oceanus and Tethys. Father of the Sirens. Main river god. Wrestled Heracles.*

Achilles – *Warrior. Hero of Trojan war in the Iliad. Killed by arrow in the heel, his only point of weakness, where he had been held by his mother, Thetis, when dipped in the Styx.*

Actaeon – *A hero and hunter, transformed into a stag and hunted after offending Artemis.*

Ameinius – *Young man who fell in love with Narcissus. His advances were spurned.*

Ampelos – *A satyr. Personification of the grapevine and lover of Dionysus.*

Anteros – *One of the Erotes, the winged gods who were part of Aphrodites' retinue. As the god of requited love, he punished those who scorned the love of others.*

Aphrodite – *Goddess of beauty and love. In Homeric tradition, daughter of Zeus and Dione.*

Apollo – *Son of Zeus and Leto. One of the Twelve Olympians. God of numerous things – arts, pastoral, medical: knowledge, healing, art, music, archery, etc.*

Arachne – *So skilled in weaving that she had the temerity to challenge Athena. Shamed, she hanged herself and was transformed into a spider.*

Arcas – *Son of Zeus and Callisto. A hunter, who became king of Arcadia, teaching many skills to his subjects, such as farming, weaving and baking bread. Unaware that a bear he was hunting was his mother, transformed by Hera into a bear, Arcas was about to kill her, when Zeus intervened, turning him into a bear, too.*

Ares – *Son of Zeus and Hera. One of the Twelve Olympians. God of war, with a reputation for brutality, and viewed by mankind in an ambivalent light.*

Arete – *Goddess who personified virtue and excellence.*

Arges – *A cyclops. Son of Gaia and Uranus, one of the three Cyclopes.*

Artemis – *Daughter of Zeus and Leto. Goddess of the hunt, nature and wildlife.*

Astraea – *Virgin goddess of innocence and justice.*

Athena – *Daughter of Zeus and Metis. In some stories, Zeus swallowed Metis while she was still pregnant with Athena; in other versions, she was born through parthenogenesis from Zeus' head. Goddess of wisdom, war strategy and handicraft.*

Atlas – *A Titan who sided with Kronos in the Titanomachy. After their defeat, he was condemned to the punishment of standing at the western edge of the Earth and holding up the sky.*

Atropos – *One of the three Moirai, the Fates. The oldest of the sisters, and often depicted as an old woman. Deciding how mortals would die, she cut the thread.*

Augeas – *King who owned vast stables for cattle that had never been cleaned.*

Boreas – *God who personified the North Wind and Winter. One of the four Anemoi, along with Zephyrus (West), Eurus (East) and Notus (South).*

Brontes – *Son of Gaia and Uranus, one of the Cyclopes.*

Cadmus – *Hero, monster-slayer, and first king of Thebes. Born in Phoenicia. Introduced alphabet. Began his wanderings when going in search of his sister, Europa, abducted by Zeus in the form of a bull.*

Calypso – *Nymph who trapped Odysseus.*

Cephisus – *River god. Father of Narcissus.*

Charon – *Ferryman who transported the souls of the dead along the Acheron and the Styx in the Underworld. Son of Erebus and Nyx.*

Chimera – *Fire-breathing hybrid monster, part goat, part lion and part dragon. Spawn of Typhon and Echidna, and sibling of Cerebrus and Lernaean Hydra.*

Circe – *Enchantress renowned for her skills with herbs and potions and her ability to transform people into animals.*

Clotho – *One of the three Moirai, the Fates. The youngest of the sisters, who spins the thread of life.*

Cretan Bull – *The white bull that Pasiphae, queen of Crete, fell in love with. Their offspring was the minotaur. One of Heracles' tasks was to capture it.*

Cyclopes – *Giant, one-eyed creatures. According to Hesiod, the three brothers, Brontes, Steropes and Arges, skilled craftsmen, who made Zeus' thunderbolts.*

Danaides – *The fifty daughters of Danaus, all but one of whom murdered their husbands on their wedding night. They were condemned to spend eternity in Tartarus, carrying water in a sieve.*

Deucalion – *Son of Prometheus. Connected to Greek version of Flood Myth. Constructed an ark, landing on Mount Parnassus, and repopulating the world. Father of Hellen, the mythic founder of the Hellenic race.*

Dike – *Goddess of justice and moral order.*

Dionysus – *Son of Zeus. God of harvest, wine, fertility – also theatre, festivity, ecstasy and insanity. Although one of the Twelve Olympians, there is some debate about his origins, with some* sources suggesting that these were not Greek, with him entering the pantheon at a later date. More recent sources suggest he was one of the first gods.

Dysnomia – *Daemon (lesser deity) of lawlessness, daughter of Eris, goddess of strife.*

Echo – *An Oread nymph. When Hera came to Earth spying on Zeus, she tried to distract her with her chatter. Hera punished her by making her only able to repeat the last words spoken to her. In Ovid's Metamorphoses, she fell in love with Narcissus, but was unable to express that to him. She wasted away, only her voice remaining.*

Eileithyia – *Daughter of Zeus and Hera. Goddess of childbirth.*

Eleos – *Minor goddess of mercy and compassion.*

Empusa – *Shape-shifting, female spirit or phantom, in the service of Hecate. Described as having one leg and also a copper leg. Seduced young men and consumed their blood and flesh. Associated with Lamia, night-haunting daemon who preyed on children, and Mormo, a spirit from legend to frighten the young.*

Endymion – *According to one myth, a shepherd prince, loved by the moon spirit, Selene. He selected immortality and youth in eternal slumber, when offered it by Zeus. A second myth depicts him as an astronomer. In another story, he was a Greek king, given foreknowledge of his own death by Zeus. Setting up a race course, he ordered his sons to compete for his throne.*

Erebus – *Primordial deity of darkness. Son of Chaos and consort of Nyx.*

Eris – *Variously depicted as goddess, spirit or daemon of strife, discord, envy and rivalry, delighting in bloodshed and war. As such, she is a close ally of Ares. Described by Hesiod as a daughter of Nyx. She has a link to the Sleeping Beauty tale. Uninvited to the wedding of Peleus and Thetis, she turned up with malevolent curses, flinging a golden apple into the crowd, inscribed to the fairest. The action was said to have instigated the Trojan war.*

Eros – *God of love and sexual passion. Viewed by Hesiod as a primordial god, but subsequently, as either a child of Nyx or of Ares and Aphrodite.*

Erotes – *Winged gods of love. Part of Aphrodites' retinue.*

Eulabeia – *Goddess who embodied piety, duty and discretion.*

Eurystheus – *Grandson of Perseus. King of Argos. He was the favourite of Hera, a challenger to Zeus' champion, Heracles.*

Gaia – *Primordial deity. Personification of the Earth. Mother and consort of Uranus.*

Ganymede – *Beautiful mortal youth abducted by Zeus to serve as his cup-bearer. On Olympus, Ganymede was granted immortality.*

Glaucus – *A fisherman who became immortal and developed gifts of prophecy.. After finding a magical herb that brought fish back to life, he tried it himself, growing fins and a tail. In an alternative version, Zeus caused him to throw himself into the sea whilst in a state of 'divine madness'. Became a god of the sea, rescuing sailors and fishermen.*

Gorgons – *Female monsters, three sisters, with hair made of live snakes, the sight of whom could turn mortals to stone. Medusa was one of the sisters.*

Gyges - *One of the three Hecatoncheires, sons of Gaia and Uranus, the hundred-handed giants who sided with Zeus during the Titanomachy, the battles between the Titans and their Olympian children.*

Hades – *King of the Underworld and god of the dead. Eldest son of Kronos and Rhea, the last to be regurgitated by his father. Abducted his wife, Persephone, with the connivance of his brother, Zeus.*

Hebe – *Daughter of Zeus and Hera. Goddess of youth and cupbearer of the gods, who served nectar and ambrosia at feasts. Wife of Heracles.*

Hecate – *Goddess associated with sorcery, witchcraft, necromancy, night, poisonous plants and herbs, crossroads, entranceways, etc.*

Hedone – *Goddess who personified pleasure.*

Hephaestus – *Son of Zeus and Hera. God of smiths and those working in crafts.*

Hera – *Wife of Zeus. Sister of Demeter, Hestia, Poseidon, Hades and Zeus. Daughter of Rhea and Kronos. Goddess of marriage and the family.*

Heracles – *Reputedly, greatest of Greek hero, famed for his Twelve Labours. Son of Zeus and Alcmene, half-brother of Perseus. A cult grew around him, and he was worshipped as a god.*

Hermaphroditos – *Child of Hermes and Aphrodite. One of the Erotes, the winged gods associated with love and intercourse. According to Ovid, a naiad, Salmacis, fell in love with him when he was still a teenager. She appealed to the gods to join them for ever, their bodies becoming fused.*

Hermes – *Herald of the gods, moving between human and divine worlds. Son of Zeus and Maia.*

Hestia – *Virgin goddess of the hearth. One of the twelve Olympians, a sister of Zeus.*

Hippolyta – *Daughter of Ares, Queen of the Amazons.*

Horkos – *God who avenged acts of perjury. Companion of Dike (Justice).*

Hyacinth – *Spartan prince and a lover of Apollo, who held him in his arms as he died, before creating a flower from his spilled blood.*

Hydra – *Offspring of Typhon and Echidna, a multi-headed, snake-like monster that lived in water.*

Hypnos – *Embodiment of sleep. Son of Nyx and Erebus, though, according to Hesiod, he had no father. Twin brother of Thanatos (associated with death).*

Iasion – *Cretan youth and favourite of Demeter. In Ovid's Metamorphoses Demeter struggles as she watches him age.*

Ikhnaie – *Titan. Goddess of finding lost things, tracking and tracing.*

Ixion – *King of the Lapiths. Murdered his father-in-law by pushing him into burning coals and logs. Subsequently, when brought to Olympus, attempted to seduce Hera. Punished in Tartarus by being attached to a fiery wheel.*

Jason – *Hero. Leader of the Argonauts, leading the quest for the Golden Fleece.*

Keres – *Female death spirits, drawn to the battlefield.*

Kharites – *In Homeric tradition, the retinue of Aphrodite, with a role to attend the god during feasts and dances. Sometimes three were named, elsewhere more. Also depicted as the Graces. There was an ancient cult around them, with shrines dedicated in their honour.*

Koalemos – *The god of stupidity (sometimes depicted as a very minor deity).*

Kouretes – *Wild mountain gods, skilled in rustic arts and warfare.*

Kronos – *Leader of first generation of Titans. Son of Uranus and Gaia, father of Zeus. Usurped and castrated his own father, and was, in turn, overthrown by Zeus.*

Lachesis – *One of the three Moirai, the Fates. The middle sister, who measured the thread of life.*

Laertes – *Father of Odysseus.*

Linus – *Linus of Thrace, a son of Apollo in some traditions, or of Urania, according to others. Founder of lyric song.*

Liriope – *Naiad nymph, mother of Narcissus.*

Lyssa – *Spirit of crazed frenzy, madness and rabies. One tradition identified her as a daughter of Nyx, sprung from the blood of Uranus after his castration by Kronos. Hera commissioned her to turn Heracles insane, resulting in his murdering his wife and children.*

Maia – *A nymph. Mother of Hermes. Daughter of Atlas and Pleione, an Oceanid.*

Maniae – *Spirits personifying insanity, fury and rage.*

Metis – *An Oceanid nymph, associated with wisdom and cunning. Helped Zeus to free his siblings. Their daughter was Athena. According to a prophecy, Metis was also going to have a son mightier than*

Zeus, who would overthrow him. Zeus swallowed her, Athena being born, subsequently, emerging fully-formed from his head.

Morpheus – *One of the Oneiroi, the daemons or spirits of dreams. Variously, described as a child of Nyx, or of Nyx and Erebus, or the son of Hypnos and Pasithea.*

Myrmex – *A maiden from Attica, loved by Athena. When the girl boasted that she, not Athena, had invented the plough, she was transformed into an ant.*

Naiads – *Female spirits, nymphs associated with fresh water.*

Narcissus (Narcie) – *A hunter, famed for his beauty, who rejected all advances, eventually, falling in love with his own reflection in a pool of water.*

Nike – *Goddess who personified victory.*

Nyx – *Primordial goddess of night. Daughter of Chaos and sister of Erebus. Even Zeus was reputed to fear her.*

Odysseus – *Legendary Greek king of Ithaca, hero of Homer's epic poem. Famed for his cunning.*

Otus and Ephialtes – *Aloadae giants. Attempted to storm Mount Olympus and punished in Tartarus.*

Pan – *God of shepherds and flocks, from the mountain area of Arcadia, connected to the spring and fertility. In common with the faun or satyr, has the legs and horns of a goat.*

Pandora – *Supposedly, the first woman, a creation of Hephaestus under the instructions of Zeus, an act of revenge after Prometheus' theft of fire. Hesiod, subsequently, added details to the myths: Athena taught her needlework, Aphrodite gave her grace and charm, while Hermes imbued her with the power of speech, putting in 'lies and crafty words', along with 'a shameless mind and deceitful nature.' All the evils of the world were introduced when she opened her jar or box.*

Persephone – *Daughter of Zeus and Demeter. Queen of the Underworld, where she was taken after abduction by her uncle, Hades. Permitted to return each spring in her function as earth and nature goddess, enabling re-growth.*

Perseus – *Son of Zeus and the mortal, Danae. Great hero and slayer of monsters. Defeated Medusa and saved Andromeda from the sea monster, Cetus.*

Phanes – *Primeval deity of procreation. According to the Orphic tradition, he is depicted as emerging from a cosmic egg entwined with a serpent.*

Phobos – *God and personification of fear and panic. Son of Ares and Aphrodite. Portrayed as causing disorder in battle.*

Pistis – *Personification of trust, good faith, reliability and honesty. Possibly, a daughter of Zeus. Was supposed to have been one of* the good spirits to escape from Pandora's box, before abandoning mankind and fleeing back to Olympus.

Plataea – *Naiad nymph, abducted by Zeus.*

Polyphemus – *One of the Cyclopes and savage giant in Homer's Odyssey, one-eyed son of Poseidon.*

Porus – *Son of Metis and half-brother of Athena.*

Poseidon – *One of the Twelve Olympians, brother of Zeus, king of the sea.*

Potamoi – *Ancient river gods.*

Prometheus – *Titan god of fire. Often depicted as a trickster. Said to have created mankind with clay, then stolen fire from the gods for him, bringing the possibility of civilisation. Despite having sided with the Olympians during the wars with the primordial gods, he was punished with imprisonment and torture in Tartarus.*

Prosymnus – *A young shepherd, whose story is recounted in the Dionysian Mysteries. Having guided Dionysus to the entrance to the Underworld, he requested, as a reward, to become his lover. On his return, finding that Prosymnus was dead, Dionysus opened his tomb, placing a carved, fig wood phallus in his anus.*

Psecas – *Nymph who attended Artemis, combing her hair.*

Rhea – *Mother goddess, daughter of Rhea and Uranus, wife of Kronos, and mother of Demeter, Hestia, Hera, Hades, Poseidon and Zeus.*

Salmoneus – *Evil king, brother of Sisyphus, whom he loathed. Ordered his subjects to worship him as Zeus and was struck down by Zeus, and condemned to be punished in Tartarus.*

Selene – *Titan goddess of the moon.*

Silenus – *Companion and tutor to Dionysus. Often portrayed drunk, being transported by a donkey.*

Sintians – *Pirates and raiders, according to Greek tales, from the island of Lemnos, who tended Hephaestus after his fall from Olympus. Subsequently, they worshipped Hephaestus.*

Sirens – *Creatures that appeared in Homer's Odyssey, luring sailors to their deaths through their singing. Subsequently, often depicted as birds with women's faces.*

Sisyphus – *King punished for attempting to cheat death. Forced to roll a boulder up a hill for all eternity. Just before he reached the top, it would roll back down again.*

Sphinx – *Mythical creature, part woman, lion and bird, who murders those who cannot answer her riddle.*

Steropes – *Son of Gaia and Uranus, one of the Cyclopes.*

Stymphalian birds – *Man-eating birds living in a swamp. Defeated by Heracles in one of his Labours.*

Telegonus – *Son of Odysseus. Accidentally, killed his father with a lance tipped with stingray venom.*

Thanatos – *Personification of death, twin of Hypnos.*

Thebe – *Naiad nymph, courted by both Zeus and Poseidon.*

Themis – *One of the Titan children of Uranus and Gaia. Goddess and personification of justice, order and law.*

Thetis – *A Nereid, sea nymph. Mother of Achilles. A prophecy had suggested that she would have a son more powerful than Zeus. She played a role in saving Zeus from a plot to oust him, engineered by Hera, Poseidon and Athena. She also looked after Hephaestus for a while after his fall to the volcanic island of Lemnos. Dionysus, also, took refuge with her in a bed of seaweed while on the run.*

Titans – *The children of Uranus and Gaia. There were twelve of them, six males: Oceanus, Kronos, Hyperion, Iapetus, Coeus and Crius; and six females: Theia, Rhea, Themis, Tethys, Phoebe and Mnemosyne. They were the first gods, preceding the Olympians. Prometheus, Helios and Leto were among the titans from the next generation.*

Tityos – *A giant, and son of Zeus, who attempted to rape Leto, killed by her children, Artemis and Apollo, and punished in Tartarus.*

Tyche – *Goddess of Fortune.*

Typhon –*Monstrous, snake-headed giant. Fought Zeus. He and his mate, Echidna, spawned many monsters.*

Urania – *Muse of Astronomy. Daughter of Zeus and Mnemosyne.*

Uranus – *Primordial deity. Personification of the sky. Son and consort of Gaia. Overthrown by his son, Kronos.*

Zeus – *King of the gods. Sky and Thunder deity. According to Hesiod, he had seven wives. The first was Metis, whom he swallowed to avert the prophecy of his own downfall. The second was his aunt, Themis, who provided counsel. That union produced the Horae (Seasons) and Moirai (Fates). The third was Eurynome, the Oceanid, who bore the three Charities (Graces). His fourth wife was his sister, Demeter, Persephone being their daughter. The fifth was an aunt, Mnemosyne. That marriage produced the Nine Muses. The sixth was the Titan, Leto, and their children were Apollo and Artemis. Hera was his seventh wife. There were also innumerable affairs.*

Acknowledgements

In appreciation of Cath, Jess, Nadia and Miri for shared hours of happiness.

Also my mother, who has soldiered on in great discomfort while still bringing the gift of laughter; Ruby, who shows that you can face loss with grace; and my wider family for all the love and affection.

With particular gratitude to Avril, for the kindness of her spirit and her unwavering support across the decades.

And to Sam, for his IT skills, his patience and invariable courtesy.

To people such as Ian, Andy, Rachel and Judy for their enthusiasm, past and present, with regard to my writing. Blame yourselves if more follows!

Many thanks to Sally Porch, in appreciation of her artwork for front and back covers, which so perfectly conveys the playfulness of this story.

Finally, celebrating the memory of Steve Arnett, among the first to die during the Covid pandemic, who, cocooned in his music-filled hinterland, faced adversity over many decades with incisive humour and barely a word of complaint.

Printed in Great Britain
by Amazon

38404389R00300